sister mysteries

OTHER BOOKS BY CLAUDIA RICCI

Dreaming Maples

Seeing Red

sister mysteries

August 2018
To Eleanor, with
all good wishes!
Thanks for all
your advice

Claudia

a novel by

C L A U D I A   R I C C I

Sister Mysteries is a work of fiction.

Names, characters, places and incidents are the products of the author's imagination or are used fictitiously. Any resemblance to actual events, locales, or persons, living or dead, is entirely coincidental.

COVER PAINTING BY Claudia Ricci
PHOTOGRAPHED BY Stephen Donaldson
BOOK DESIGN BY The Troy Book Makers
"THE OTHER" POEM BY Judith Ortiz Cofer

Printed in the United States of America

Star Root Press • Great Barrington, MA

To order additional copies of this title, contact your favorite local bookstore or visit www.shoptbmbooks.com

ISBN: 978-1-61468-448-0

For my husband,
Richard Kirsch,
a fountain of love
and support

"THE OTHER"

By Judith Ortiz Cofer

A sloe-eyed dark woman shadows me.
In the mornings she sings
Spanish love songs in a high
falsetto filling my shower stall
with echoes.
She is by my side
in front of the mirror as I slip
into my tailored skirt and she
into her red cotton dress.
She shakes out her black mane as I
run a comb through my close-cropped cap.
Her mouth is like a red bull's eye
daring me.
Everywhere I go I must
make room for her: she crowds me
in elevators where others wonder
at all the space I need.
At night her weight tips my bed, and
it is her wild dreams that run rampant
through my head exhausting me. Her heartbeats,
like dozens of spiders carrying the poison
of her restlessness over the small
distance that separates us,
drag their countless legs
over my bare flesh.

*Many thanks to the literary estate of Judith Ortiz Cofer
for granting permission to use this marvelous poem.*

AUTHOR'S NOTE

I've told this story before, how *Sister Mysteries* came to be, how Renata first came to me.

It was January, 1995. A snowy day. I was lying on the floor doing morning leg lifts, the radio playing.

Suddenly, I was enveloped in beautiful flamenco music. As I explained in my second novel, *Seeing Red*, "the deeply passionate music set my heart beating faster. The music bypassed my brain and felt like it could melt the ice on the windows; something inexplicable caught fire in my soul and wouldn't let go."

In short order I had the first vision: Sister Renata painstakingly disrobing in front of a small oak mirror; Sister Renata donning a flame red dress with billowing ruffles. Lipstick. Cleated shoes. Renata climbing on a table and dancing for her lecherous cousin, Antonie, who played guitar.

Shortly afterward, Sister Renata brought forth the first entry of her diary: the nun accusing her cousin of making it all up, him telling the first of many incriminating stories that paint her as a seductress given to dancing flamenco.

Little did I know what an astonishing and often torturous journey this story had in store for me. Little did I know that it would come to live with me, almost as a family member. I would write thousands of pages trying to figure out where the book was going. I would consult a hypnotist, various therapists and other healers in an effort to find my way.

Little did I know that I would go to endless lengths to try to deny the truth: that I had a past life as a nun in California in 1883.

Meanwhile, I am reminded of something that I tell fiction-writing students. Novels, I say, can be a sneaky, insidious kind of creature. Embark on a short story, and even if it ends up 30 or more pages, you can be pretty sure that you will keep your arms firmly around the fiction, retaining a fair share of control over the characters.

But a novel? In my experience, a novel puts its arms around you, the writer, and invades your heart and mind and soul, and in a real way, takes over, turning you inside out, remaking your own inner story as a writer and human being. So powerful this invasion can be, that when the story is finally "complete" (and in this case more than two decades later) you wonder what exactly happened.

There have been more moments that I can count when I wished to be done with *Sister Mysteries*, when the book would have been better entitled *Sister Miseries*. My dear friend Peg Woods—a wonderful writer who has read countless versions of the book—laughed every time I told her that I was back at work on the novel once again. I am deeply grateful for all her help and feedback through the years.

Peg predicted that I would keep writing *Sister Mysteries* forever.

There were plenty of times that I too never thought I would finish. But in the end, something magical brought me back to the nun's story one more time, and finally, I can now say three delightful words, here it is.

North Egremont, Massachusetts
January 26, 2018

1

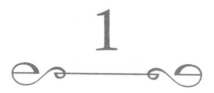

ANTONIE

"Renata Dancing"

At this moment, Sister Renata isn't doing what she should be. Instead of attending to the steaming and starching of altar cloths in the convent laundry, instead of standing at the kitchen sink washing spinach or shaving carrots for Father Crucifer's soup, she is instead standing before the familiar oak chest of drawers undressing, catching an eyeful of herself in the small wooden mirror propped on top.

The nun's childlike fingers move in the normal manner, even if they aren't attending to prayer, even if they aren't locked around the black onyx rosary beads, even if they aren't fingering the carved silver surface of the crucifix. Instead, her damp fingers are trembling slightly as they unfasten the three black buttons at the side of her wool skirt and the row of buttons at each of her wrists.

For the long line of buttons at the back of her shirt, she reaches awkwardly behind, elbows askew. If she were at the convent, as well she should be, husky Sister Teresa would be standing behind, whispering warm air into her neck, laughing, assisting her, all the while persisting with one of her ribald jokes about the older, crippled priest, Father Ruby.

But Sister Renata isn't there, she is here unfastening the long string of rosary beads from the hook at her waist, and then collecting them into a rattling handful that spills over her fist, onto the oak dresser next to the mirror. She lets the skirt and shirt drop limp to the floor, and momentarily she stares at the heap of black wool lying in disarray at her feet, noting with some horror that the habit looks like the discarded garb of a storybook witch. The thought shudders her, but not for long.

She steps out of the habit. Bending low, she unties the knotted laces of her blocky black oxfords and she pulls them off one at a time. There she is, she the youthful nun in her soft white underclothes and short black veil, standing in the flow of desert sun streaming through the window, staring at one pale coin of herself reflected in the small round mirror.

Slowly she peels off her heavy black stockings and the white cotton underclothes and finally, she unpins the short black veil and lifts off the starched white headpiece that binds her forehead.

The skin beneath the white headpiece is moist. She rubs the creased line above her eyebrows and shakes her hair loose, gathering it through her fingers. The thick waves fall away from her forehead reflecting almost blue in the light. The hair grazes her naked back and clings in bold shiny curves to her shoulders. She is fully disrobed now, completely herself, absent of all habit, and she is sliding open the oak drawer, meeting with some resistance, and the perfume of dry sage rises up, and she is taking from the drawer the satin bag that Antonie sent, and she is unzipping the bag, removing the red dancer's dress, shaking out the beloved ruffles, each ruffle edged in black lace and ribbon.

Soon the dress pools on the cool tile floor by her ankles. A pert smile flirts across her lips.

When the shoes are in place, and the red satin bows are tied, she attends quickly to her face in the mirror, adding two ovals of rouge to her cheeks, and two dark horizons to each eyelid. Finally, with some purpose, and with evidence of some practice, she smears the tube of red lipstick from the top drawer full across her lips accentuating the natural deep pout. Just below the corner of her mouth is a mole, too large to ignore.

The handle of the door rattles behind her. Glancing into the mirror, Renata sees reflected the doorknob, its silver surface engraved in the same style as the crucifix of her rosary. The handle moves frantically against its lock.

"Ready?" The voice hovers low at the crack of the door.

Renata inhales, her flat bosom rising. The top ruffles of the snug dress resist, move only slightly.

"Soon," she calls back. "Yes…" she glances at herself in the mirror.

Yes, she thinks, Renata is ready for the dance, only—only she is never quite ready for the dance partner and with this thought of Antonie waiting outside the door, one muscular arm leaning into the frame of the door, the palm of the hand flat against the narrow band of wood, Renata's eyes close and she smiles slightly and suddenly her hand drops to her right hip. The other arm rises into the air, and she throws her flood of hair back.

Her head twisted to the right, her neck high, her eyes the cocked slits of a cat, her bottom lip curled, she turns from the mirror and bends her knees. Soon comes the clatter of her heels on the worn pine floor. Slowly she turns, dropping her arms to one side, then gathers up ruffles in either hand.

Elbows bent, arms taut, her hands begin pumping in rhythm with her feet, her circles gather, her heels rattle faster and faster, she dips left with one shoulder, she twists right with the other, her head drops back, her torso arcs to a perfect C, and soon she is spinning, swaying, feet drumming, now one hand raised, the wrist twisted, the fingers splayed, as if she were grasping a wide fan, her fingers branched out toward the sky. Her body moves effortlessly through the routine, her arms and legs assuming their positions automatically, much the way her mouth moves mindlessly through her prayers the rest of the week.

"RENATA!" The voice cuts sharply through the door. A fist pounding now joins the metallic sound of the door handle. "NOW!"

She stops, her eyes open slowly, giving her a sudden glimpse of her slightly parted red lips in the tiny mirror. She is breathing hard. Instantly, she begins giggling, covering her mouth with both hands. And then, striking the pose again, head up, chest thrust out, she walks majestically toward the door, unlocks it and opens it slowly.

"Your games..." Antonie says, head shaking side to side beneath the wide-brimmed hat, dark eyes dropping, then bouncing back up, as if eyesight were a rubber ball, rebounding from the floor. "Your games...I am...honestly, I am tired of them."

Renata smiles, lifts her chin, passes beneath Antonie's raised arm planted on the door frame. Antonie wears the wide-brimmed felt hat, the black velvet jacket, the tight-fitting black pants that accentuate his narrow hips, pants threaded on the outside edge in a line of clear red and emerald beads and a purple and turquoise braid.

"My games," Renata says, quietly, setting one hand on her swaying hip as she stares out beneath the velvet arm that forms an arch, not unlike the small arch to one side of the main chapel, "my games are exactly what I am here for. No?" She gazes over her bare shoulder. "Tell me, Antonie, without the games, what precisely would there be?" She pivots and gives him the look, and he moves swiftly from the door after her, as if riveted to the sharp metallic rattle of her shoes on the cool adobe tiles of the hall.

As they reach the halfway point in the long hallway, Renata stops, turns again, and grazing Antonie's smooth face with her fingertips, she brings the outside of each delicate hand to rest on the black velvet shoulders. For a moment, Renata seems poised, the couple looks ready to dance. But instead they embrace, Renata reaching up, Antonie down, the two pressing their open mouths together. Renata pulls away.

"That," she says, pivoting on the point of her toe, proceeding down the white stucco hallway of the elegant Spanish hacienda, "that is to show you I do sometimes need you in the way you think you need me." Antonie lurches out, tries to grab her, to catch her slight waist but Renata slips away and laughs.

She picks up her ruffles and her pace, so that she is practically running through the hall, so that her cleats make a ragged clatter of metal against the floor as she hurries toward the dining room. There, the light is brighter. Hanging from the ceiling is an antique wagon wheel, into which are set thick candles. Today the candles are all lit. The ceiling is braced in dark beams, and the white walls are hung in turquoise and grey wool rugs and the thick trestle table runs almost the length of the immense room. The table is set for two, as it always is, with a wooden plate at each side, and heavy silverware resting on white cloth napkins. In the center of the table are two thick white candles, also lit, and a large shallow wooden bowl full of milky white gardenias. A painted clay plate to one side holds a variety of castanets, each set different, some pairs carved out of ivory, some of carved and painted wood.

Without waiting for a cue, Renata takes up the white ivory castanets, imbedded with abalone, and slips them on her fingers. As she does, she steps effortlessly from the floor to the leather saddle seat of a chair directly to the top of the trestle table, so that as Antonie arrives in the room, she is standing above, adorning the trestle, her muscular calves at work, both arms raised above her head, her feet pounding, already immersed in the rhythms of the dance. The sharp crackle of the castanets alternates with the pounding of her shoes on wood.

Antonie picks up the Spanish guitar leaning against the far wall, and raising one leg to the leather chair, rests the instrument there. Setting one hand to the strings, and the slender fingers of the other hand to the narrow neck of the guitar, he strums, softly at first, but gradually gaining momentum to fit Renata's pace. She sweeps a tight circle, her brow knotted, her mouth wide. One wrist raised and twisted, she crushes the red satin-edged ruffles of her dress in the other hand, exposing first one and then the other thigh.

Antonie eyes the naked leg, then looks down at the guitar, slipping the right fingers in a nimble rasgueado across the strings. Slowly, Renata makes her way the length of the table, working her heels, her hips, all the while her red lips are set firmly in a line. As she approaches the wooden bowl in the center it begins to rattle, to twist, the drumming of her feet setting the bowl, the fragrant gardenias, in a slow tipsy spin.

The flames of the candles thin and flicker as she steps delicately between them, and the bottom-most ruffle of her dress just grazes the lip of hot wax pouring over the top edge of the thick candle. The heavy silver candlesticks, engraved like the door knob and crucifix, canter slightly out toward the edge of the table. Still Renata moves on, slowly, methodically, approaching the end of the long thick table as Antonie brings louder and louder rounds of sound from the guitar.

Antonie too moves forward, approaching the table. As Renata reaches the end, Antonie lays the guitar aside and extends both arms and Renata steps down, knees bent, both legs tucked into the ruffles. Delicately, she collapses into the waiting velvet arms, pushing Antonie's hat to the floor. From beneath the hat cascades a flood of blue black hair, hair that takes the shape of a thick cloud, a mass of regular waves that form a cloak over the black velvet shoulders.

You could say this about the pair: they share a remarkable resemblance: the same color hair, the same exaggerated mouths, strongly curved lower lips, the same hue in their caramel skin. In a word, they are cousins, and they are sinking into more than one kind of sin there on the floor.

GINA

Dear Señora Ramos:

And now, this morning, I find you lying there in your bed, not speaking, staring wide-eyed into the ceiling.

The sun has not yet cracked over the horizon. As soon as I awoke, I crept into the convent kitchen and prepared your coffee. Walking very softly, I carried the cup up the stairs to your room. Your door is ajar and I knock softly and walk in. Your eyes are open and riveted on the ceiling, and so I know immediately that something is wrong. Your expression is fixed, your face a coffee-colored mask. I set the coffee down on the night table and place one hand on your forehead. Warm. I pick up your hand, which lies limp on the sheet. It too is warm. The skin of the back of your hand is soft but the palm has that dry papery feeling I know so well.

"Señora," I whisper, leaning over to put my lips close to your ear. "Can you hear me?" I am close-up to your long silver hair, lying in ripples on your shoulders.

Your lips are parted but frozen. You don't move a muscle. Only an occasional blink of your eyes and a faint breath when I put my finger beneath your nose tell me that you are still alive. I set my ear on your chest and there is a slow and steady beat. But what has happened to you? Is it a stroke? And if it is, what can I possibly do for you here? What can be done for a stroke victim in 1884?

I drop into the chair beside your bed. The other nuns will be up for morning prayers before long. What will they do? Bring the doctor I suppose. But for what purpose?

I sit here with tears gathering. I sit here thinking that you are nearing your end. We've had such a long history together. I don't want to let you go. And yet, I know better. I know that you came to me for one reason only, and that soon your mission will be accomplished. I just wish you could live forever.

But then I realize, you do live forever. Or at least, your spirit does. You exist beyond the confines of time and place. When you first came to me 18 years ago, I was living through hell. I had dropped so low that I saw no reason to get out of bed. I thought I would never emerge from that dark grey tunnel of despair. It was such a hellish time. I saw a series of doctors who didn't have much of a clue what to do. One or two of them wanted me to have electroshock treatment, or ECT. And I was petrified. I didn't want to have some machine sending shock waves through my brain, frying it from the inside out.

I remember two things about the morning you came: the snow outside the window was heaped in great mounds. We'd been having wicked winter weather that year, and it most certainly hadn't helped my mood. I remember, too, me lying in bed staring into the ceiling, much like you are now. And of all things, I was listening to the flies. Flies in the middle of winter, crazed and buzzing around the light fixtures and against the window glass. Maybe their last desperate gasping to escape.

I remember getting up to pee. And seeing a rather large fly in the window of the bathroom. Quite unexpectedly, I reached over and very gently wedged it against the glass. I set my finger and thumb on one of its wings. There I was, I was actually holding a fly.

I carried it that way to the door that leads out to the balcony of my third-floor bedroom. I opened the door and was greeted by a blast of cold air. And then I set the fly free. I watched as he (she?) zoomed off in a giant graceful arc. Something shifted in me. How very strange, but somehow that gesture—freeing the fly—gave me hope. Put a small smile on my face.

Soon that became my purpose. I would get out of bed at least four or five times a day—whenever I got up to pee or to eat something—and I would set free three or four flies. One thing that mystified me, where were these flies coming from at this frigid moment in winter?

But no matter where they came from, there they were. I got very good at catching them in my hands. Between my fingers. I was delicate but determined. I looked forward to catching them. I looked forward to liberating every fly that I heard buzzing in my bedroom.

When my husband happened to be in the room one morning, he asked me why I insisted on opening the door to release flies. Why, he wondered aloud, did I not just use the fly swatter? He was no lover of flies.

"Because I refuse to kill them," I said simply. But what I didn't say was, this act of freeing flies seemed to give my life some immediate purpose. It was, after all, a kind of existential grip that had taken hold of me, that is, life had lost its meaning. I no longer felt that I was steering my life course in a direction that mattered. But here was something that, if nothing else, was a satisfying distraction.

If I could do nothing else, I could release a few flies into the universe. Perhaps I couldn't relieve my own misery, but at least I could save these little black-winged creatures from suffering.

My husband watched cautiously as I released another fly. Then he came up to me and gently folded his arms around me. "Just hold me," he said, his voice low and trembling. I felt so bad. I had become such a burden to him. He was so desperately worried about me. But of course he was. For all intents and purposes, he had lost his wife.

I hadn't been out of a nightgown in weeks. I was surviving on a diet of soup and saltines, coffee and oatmeal and an occasional salad. Or an apple, sliced and smeared with peanut butter.

Worst of all, I had begun to say to my husband with some regularity, "I don't want to live another day."

I had also taken to praying to the Virgin Mary, asking for help from the divine feminine forces of the universe. Mary had never let me down before. When I suffered cancer, and I was in the thick of misery with the chemo, I would pray to Mary, and something would always happen to relieve my pain. At the worst moments, I would envision myself protected—tucked beneath her sky blue veil. That image comforted me so much. Now I needed comforting of a different kind. I needed her to help heal my troubled mind.

It wasn't long after I started catching and releasing the flies that you appeared, my dear Señora. I remember that morning so clearly. It was a Monday and the sky was the crisp blue color you only get in the winter. My husband had to fly to DC for a meeting - he had left just after eight a.m. He was nervous at the thought of leaving me alone. "You must promise me you won't do..." and then he'd shaken his head. He wouldn't finish the sentence.

"I'll be OK," I said, and then we kissed and he left, his forehead wrinkled in worry.

I had finished my morning coffee. I was waiting for my morning meds—the ativan, the mood stabilizers—to kick in. My neck and back felt really sore, and so I decided to pull myself out of bed to stretch my body a little. I lay on the braided rug on the bedroom floor, pulling one knee at a time up to my chest.

The rest of it is like a dream. An amazing and incredible dream. A dream that felt more real than real life. I lifted my leg a few inches and straightened it out and pointed my toe and suddenly there it was—a low but persistent sound. Music. It started to grow louder and clearer. I could hear someone strumming a guitar. I looked over to the radio on my husband's side of the bed. Had I left it on? I know I hadn't. I hated the morning program on the FM station so I would have kept the radio turned off.

But there it was—guitar music, and it was growing so loud I could feel it in my chest. I didn't know it at the time, because I knew virtually nothing about flamenco, but that was a soleares I was hearing. Soleares, a form considered the mother of all flamenco. The word solear derived from the Spanish word, "soledad" or sorrow.

I stopped exercising and sat up on the floor, cross-legged. I closed my eyes and just listened to the music for a minute or two. It was quite beautiful. It made my heart race.

That's the moment you chose to speak. "Por favor, ¿eres tú la Señora Rinaldi?" My eyes flew open and my heart started banging like some kind of drum. Behind me, in the rocking chair across the room in the corner, I heard the chair squeak as it rocked forward. Slowly, I swiveled around. You were sitting there, you with the peaceful face. You filled up the chair with your portly form. You were dressed in black, and strumming a guitar. My arms and legs started shaking and it's a good thing I wasn't standing because I'm sure I would have lost my urine.

I didn't say a word. I just stared at you, with a million things flying through my head. The first thing I thought: your clothes were the same color as the flies. You were completely in black, even your stockings, as if you were in mourning. The only color was the red and pink and yellow roses embroidered on your magnificent shawl.

I thought back to the question that the last doctor, the super expensive one in Manhattan, had recently asked me. "Do you ever see things?"

"See things?" I asked.

"Yes, do you have visions?"

I remember thinking at the time that at least I was that sane. At least I wasn't psychotic, having visions. But now, what was this?

I covered my eyes with my hands, and shook my head back and forth, hoping to make you go away. But you continued strumming. I looked up. You were waiting for me to answer. You smiled and introduced yourself. "Yo soy la Señora María Curocora Corazón de Ramos." You nodded your head once as if to give emphasis to the name.

I knew the word corazón meant heart in English. I wouldn't know until much later that ramos meant tree or branch.

"Wha...what do you want?" I croaked.

You switched into broken English. "I am here to have your help if you please." It's embarrassing to admit this, Señora, but at first I thought you were offering me help, as in house help. I was just about to answer that I already had a house cleaner, when I realized my mistake. You wanted *my* help.

"I ...I don't understand."

You nodded and stopped strumming. The guitar was a beauty. Blonde wood. Rosewood body. Just lovely. "Es importante," you began, but then you switched to English again. "Important, very important. You are a writer of stories, yes?"

I shrugged. By this point I was sitting up against the brass bed, my arms hugging my knees, as I was desperately trying to get my arms and legs to stop shaking. But I was still trembling and my mouth felt like it was stuffed with cotton. The truthful answer to your question was, "No, I am not writing stories anymore." I had stopped writing just about the time I had started getting depressed. The reason I stopped writing had something to do with the fact that my last novel had sold so few copies.

My husband had tried time and again to convince me that the key to turning my depression around lay in finding the courage to start writing again.

"No stories anymore," I whispered. I felt my throat grow thick. Tears were pooling at the rims of my eyes. All these months, all these doctors, all these meds, and yet I still refused to label myself "MENTALLY ILL." But now, here, with this portly Latina woman sitting in front of me, in my fucking bedroom in my fucking rocking chair, how could I possibly resist that label? I was fucking crazy.

"Es important story that I need for you to write." She reached under her shawl and took out an old journal with a chiseled leather cover.

She opened the journal and in it were a stack of blue pages folded in half and tucked into the front cover.

By now I was feeling like I might need to throw up. I was so desperate for you to disappear. I wanted no part of your story or anything else. "PLEASE," I said, breathlessly. "Please go away." I started to sob. "I have been very, very ill," I said, choking on my tears. "I have wanted to take my life. I cannot be cured. No one can help me. No one knows what to do for me and so...I really need you to...you must go."

But of course you didn't budge. You sat there and had such a calm look on your face. I found myself wanting to stare at your round face, at its coffee color, at its sculptured flesh, at its slight sheen, at the way it warmed the center of my chest.

You stood up from the chair and wobbling slightly, you walked over to me. You reached down and took my hand. Slowly you helped me up. I was shaking so badly that I had to let you put your arm around me. Your arm was strong and fleshy. Your breath reeked of garlic. I felt your bosom against my own skinny chest. I thought for a moment that you were going to put me back to bed. But instead, you helped me into the rocking chair. And then you made yourself comfortable, taking a seat on my unmade bed, facing me.

"Señora Rinaldi, you need something to help you, yes?"

I snorted, and suddenly my nose was flooding, and I was desperate for tissues. You reached over to the night table for my Kleenex and handed some to me. I sniffled an answer. "I need help, yes I most certainly do." I was about to say, but not from you. Only you continued talking.

"This story"—and here you held up the leather journal—"is for me, so so important. Life and death important."

I inhaled. I had absolutely no interest in your story. I had only one thought, that you should disappear, taking your guitar, your flowered shawl, your journal and all those blue pages too.

"I'm sorry, but...you really should go," I whispered. How I wished my husband hadn't had to go out of town.

"I will go I will. But may I tell you just why I am here? It will only be a moment of your time." I was about to say no but you plowed forward. "I am a poor old woman who made a big big mistake." You said the words "beeg" and "meestake." You stopped talking.

You reached over to the tissue box and took one for yourself and dabbed at your dark eyes. "I let a poor innocent woman die," you said, and now you were starting to cry. "You see, I could have stopped it. The hanging"—here your face crumpled—"would never be happening."

Hanging? What hanging? In spite of my impatience, and my desire to see you go, you now had snagged my attention. And something else: seeing a poor old woman sobbing into tissues on my bed had struck up a chord of compassion in me. I was distracted, at least for the moment, from my own worries.

I waited.

"After Renata got hanged," you continued, "I could not live. I could not sleep or eat. Nothing was inside me but worry and shame and regret. I prayed. I prayed in daytime, I prayed at night when I am sleeping. I asked the Virgin for help. I told her I would be happy to die myself if she would bring back my dearest Renata."

I blinked. Suddenly I was thinking not about how crazy all of this was, but how real you seemed to be. I couldn't explain it, but I just knew that you were not an illusion. You were a flesh and blood person. You were a poor old soul who needed help.

"Who...who is Renata?" I whispered in a raspy voice.

At that moment, Señora, your face collapsed onto your chest. You raised a hand to either side of your forehead. And then you just cried and sobbed and said nothing. You looked so pitiful that I found myself getting up out of the rocking chair. I came and sat there right beside you on the bed. I put my arm around your shoulders and squeezed you and tried to comfort you. It helped. You stopped crying and convulsing.

"I need you please so so much your help is what the Virgin said I must get."

"What?" I couldn't understand what you were saying, Señora, as you have never had a knack for English.

You sniffled and wiped your nose. "The Blessed Virgin. In the night she came to me. I was awake all night, not sleeping. And then she was there, glowing in golden light. She was so beautiful. I...I even touched her blue veil." Here you smiled and I saw your crooked teeth. Your face was glowing and I found myself drawn to it once again.

"I need you, to write the true story of Renata, and if you do, then the Virgin Mother promised it would all be mended and Renata would be free and not die like she did hanging from that horrible horca—you say, gallows. Will you will you please Señora Rinaldi, will you take this journal of Renata's and just write the story, so the whole world knows the truth, that she never killed Antonie?"

"Antonie? But who is *he*?" I was struggling now. I still wanted her to go, but I also wanted to know more, at least enough to satisfy my curiosity.

"Antonie is cousin to Renata," you said simply. "And he also jefe, hmmm..." here you were searching for the word. "The boss. I am keeper of his house."

I reached over to the night table for a drink of water. My head was dizzy. And I wanted something to eat. But curiously, this was the first morning in months that I actually felt like getting out of bed.

"Would you like some tea?" I said.

You shook your head. "Coffee for me."

And so I put on my blue bathrobe—I bought it because it's the same dreamy sky color as the Virgin Mary's veil—and you followed me down two flights of stairs to the kitchen, where I made you a cup of coffee and listened while you pieced together your story.

Such a long, long time ago all of this seems. How quickly the years that we've known each other have gone by. And now you lie there, Señora, and your time is up. And now I am reminded of something that you said so long ago, that very morning when we first sat together at the oak table in the kitchen.

You said "time is always there the same way and at the same time moments all on top of each other." I was completely puzzled. I thought I didn't understand you because of your broken English.

And then you said something else that intrigued me. "No one dies for good and doesn't come back another day." Of course I couldn't possibly understand what you were trying to say. It has taken me 139 years and an endless amount of writing and praying and therapy to figure it out, and to understand exactly why it was I had to write Renata's story.

2

SISTER RENATA'S DIARY

April 3, 1883

I write now because I must. I cannot trust memory anymore. I certainly cannot trust Antonie. When I close my eyes, I still see the wretched way he looked at me tonight. What is that horror that clouds his eyes? Hatred? Lechery? Lust? I know not what goes through that scheming mind of his, but I am afraid. So I write because I need a careful record. I need to see myself, to defend myself safely in the tabernacle of my own words. I need before me my own version of events: what I see, what I hear, all that I have seen and heard, for I fear that Antonie is orchestrating me in a distinctly murky light.

Ah but it frightens me to think how completely his disease has eroded his senses. What else could possibly explain his bizarre obsessions? When I sat beside his bed two nights ago, he took hold of my hand in his own sweaty claw, as pale and skinny a hand as I have seen, and he lapsed into babble anew, insisting that my dancing would surely do something for his spirit. By implication, he was saying that my dancing would help his cure. Me, dancing? What absurdity! My face went pink with shame as he gave details.

"I have the dress ready," he murmured. "The red dress with the ruffles. The one that exposes your sculptured shoulders and clings to your breasts, and becomes you so well. And oh, the heeled shoes, too. The ribboned shoes and the castanets await you in the other room."

I shuddered at the thought. He caught my wrists, and it took all of my strength to disengage.

And then, the story. "Renata Dancing." He left it under his pillow yesterday morning. His wobbling handwriting, black ink on thin blue paper. I know he left it for me; he knew I was coming to change his bedsheets while he sat downstairs, Señora fixing his breakfast.

I stood there reading, the soiled sheets in my arms, trying not to sob. The words he had written were too horrifying to absorb. His story had turned me into a seductive Spanish dancer in a flame-colored dress.

The man is sick and daft. I see now how his illness is ruining his mind, and I see now how he fully intends to ruin me.

After I got back to the convent, I sat down in the tiled courtyard, and with the birds chirping, and the sunlight warming the chilly air, I started writing in my diary. Soon it was time to go to chapel, and then, in the afternoon, Teresa and I stood side by side scrubbing altar cloths. I told her about Antonie's story.

She turned to me, told me to stop going to my cousin's bedside. I laughed. "Do you really think I have the power to decide?" I reminded her that Father Ruby has warned me over and over again. "I expect you to be a steady source of support to your poor cousin," he said.

Naturally he would say that, as he so values Antonie. My wealthy cousin is a steady financial "support" to the convent.

Teresa resumed scrubbing the altar cloth, but the stain of red wine was fixed forever in the linen. She stopped for a moment and gazed into the soapy grey water. She looked up, those blue eyes of hers wide with fear.

"Oh Renata." She shook her head. "This is far more serious than I suspected. Your cousin is bent on destroying you!"

"I know he is but what can I do?"

She bit her lip. "You must write it all down. Writing will protect you." And so now I am committed. I will write every chance I get.

Dear Lord, I cannot let his version of me prevail. I pray that You will keep me safe, deliver me of all his evil and any of my own. Also, I thank you for my dear Teresa.

This morning as we were walking to chapel she stopped. "Look, Renata, look out there, where God emerges anew in the sun on the golden field." She pointed beyond the garden wall, to a field of red and orange poppies. "Such a delight the flowers are." Thank you Lord, for keeping Teresa in my presence as I suffer over Antonie. Her love soldiers my soul and keeps it tender too.

I told her the other day that I must have known her in another life an eternity ago.

3

SISTER RENATA'S DIARY

April 4, 1883

It was after midnight. I woke in a black well of darkness and the familiar music rose up. I heard the guitar and immediately it drew me to the window. I crossed the wooden floor, barefoot, and I peered down into the dark soup of night. Señora Ramos was holding the candle. Only the top half of her brown face was clear in the scanty light. Her eyes were stark and sober. From her invisible mouth, there rose an urgent whisper.

"Por favor Señorita, please, you must come. He needs you now, Señor Antonie needs you right away tonight."

The candle shifted, throwing her face into angles of yellow light. My heart responded, pumping faster.

"But my dear lady, I cannot possibly leave the convent now. Certainly not at this unseemly hour."

"Oh but he is calling for you," she insisted, her speech falling completely into Spanish. She reached one hand up toward me. "I'm afraid his fever has soared, at least he sweats and sweats more profusely than ever. His face is slick, his color a sickly green, and his bed clothing drenched. When I left him, he was thrashing. He says you cannot keep him waiting any longer, that he is losing strength, but more important, he is losing his mind. He keeps wringing the sheets, and ripping and tearing and clawing at his own clothes, he cries out all kinds of foul and impossible things, and he makes dark and ghastly threats, even at me, at *me*, and you know I am practically his mother! I hear him and his threats and I cover my ears, I cry in fear to my Dear Lord and Blessed Mary because I know not from where it all comes, and why sometimes he can be normal and at other times, virtually a madman. What can I do? Only you can help him."

I leaned further over the sill. It was never easy to refuse Señora, and tonight was no exception. Still, my head was full of reasons that I shouldn't go. No one to escort me properly, and no one to make Father Ruby's early morning bowl of coffee. No one to shake Mother Yolla awake. I would be expected in the kitchen at five. And in chapel by six.

And yet, as I gazed down at Señora Ramos, I knew I couldn't refuse her. She was a mother to me in childhood. And here she was more distraught than I had ever seen her. I worried for the old woman's health.

"Señora, please come inside, will you?"

In the amount of time it takes to strike a match, she was beside me in my convent room. She settled onto my bed and I right beside her. She spoke in a fast rattle of Spanish.

"I will bring you there and have you back here before the morning sun cracks over the horizon. I will vouch for your whereabouts, too, I will tell Mother Yolla exactly what I asked of you tonight. Please do this thing for me, or if not for me, for him, or if not for him, then for your dear Uncle Rio, for his memory. Please Renata! Because I fear if I return to him tonight without you, he may take his life."

Reaching beneath her blue shawl, she took out a single rose. She held it out to me. The yellow flower looked as though it had been dipped in blood. At first I refused it.

"Ah, Señorita, ayudame, por favor," the old woman said. She kept the rose there, her eyes pleading. So finally, I took it.

"Ahora, ven conmigo," she whispered. "Rapidamente."

I dressed quickly. Just as I was reaching for my black traveling cloak, Señora grabbed my hand. She took the sky blue shawl from her own shoulders and dropped it to my own. I tried to protest, but Señora was already leading me by the hand out the door. As we crossed the courtyard behind the convent, I looked up. I saw the smallest sliver of moon, a silver curl in the black inky sky. Something in that peaceful curve, like an open teacup, reassured me, made my spirits rise. I hoisted myself up onto the grey wagon, and turned to help Señora.

She handed me the lantern and we set off. We rode silently together for the next hour in darkness, the sky a black platter for the sparkling stars.

We rode sitting close, my leg pinned into her fleshy hip. The draft horse moved slowly, his hooves clop clopping on the hard mud of the rutted road. Soon there came the first screech of the coyotes. I tensed, and Señora sensed my fear. "No tengas miedo," she whispered. She handed me the reins, and reached back into the wagon for the guitar.

As I guided the wagon, she strummed, and soon she was humming, and then wailing the way she sometimes does. As I heard the song rise up from childhood, and settle around my heart, I feared the music. This was always the music that accompanied me to my cousin Antonie's bedside. It was this same music that infused his mad visions, helping him to remake me into something I am not.

GINA

At first I thought that writing the story for Renata would be easy. Señora would point me in the right direction. She would help me if I got stuck. But months went by and I wrote the opening chapters and then something happened.

I would write every chance I got. I would get excited about what I was writing and then I would show it to my husband or to my writer friend Meg and both of them said the same thing: "It isn't working."

About nine months after Señora visited, I was ready to give up. I couldn't see any way forward. I couldn't write because my inspiration had dried up. I knew that if I pushed myself too hard, I would quicksand deeper into depression.

* * * *

One summer day at the end of July, I decide to take the afternoon off. It is sunny and warm outside without being humid.

I make myself a tuna sandwich and take it out to the back deck, where I sit down on a chaise lounge and prepare to read a magazine while I'm having lunch.

Suddenly I am there. Back there. I have no preparation. No warning. I look up and I am sitting in a dark damp jail cell, my ankles bound in a rusty chain. I try but I cannot stand up.

"Hello," I yell. Is there anyone here?" No answer. "Please, I am not supposed to be here." A gangly man, hunched over, shuffles toward me. Keys jangle at his waist.

"Yeah whaddisit now?"

"I…I am here by mistake. I…"

"Yeah, that's what they all say." He smiles and I am staring into a mouth without many teeth. A face grizzled in a white beard.

"No, please, tell me is there someone I can speak to? A lawyer perhaps? Somebody?"

He cackles as he shuffles away. "You got your day in court lady." He turns. "You know what they say, Sister, you made your bed, now sleep in it."

How could this be? Señora never told me it would happen like this. Where is Señora? Why isn't she here to help me?

I look around.

The jail cell is half the size of a horse stall. The walls are dark and slimy and smell like rotten eggs. The bench I'm sitting on is splintered and wobbly.

In the corner is a bowl of what looks like coagulated grey scum. I sit back. I am terrified. Where do I turn?

Suddenly she is there beside me. Renata. She too has her ankles chained and the rusty metal has made her skin bleed. Her bloody wounds have crusted over.

"Hello Gina," she says.

I am trembling. Dear God, how is this happening? When did my life turn upside down? Is this what insanity looks like? My voice cracks as I speak. "Wh..what exactly am I doing here? I agreed to write your story, to free you, but I didn't sign on for this."

She smiles. "I apologize. But it appeared that you were going to abandon the story. Señora thought we should meet in person to discuss it."

"DISCUSS IT? Oh no. There is no discussion. Uh huh. Not in this cell."

"Please, Gina. You and I must work together. As you see, we are in the same predicament. So now you know what it feels like."

"I do indeed. But I need to get out. Immediately! I am about to have a major anxiety attack and I have no ativan with me."

"If you'll excuse me, I am afraid that I have to…pee." She motions to the other side of the cell. "I will tell the jailer I need the f.p. (foul pail) and he will remove the ankle chain."

"How will you explain that there are two of us?"

Renata smiles. I see that she is a very pretty young woman.

"He will only see one of us," she says, but doesn't explain why.

And so she calls for the jailer and he shuffles back to the cell. He unlocks the door and her ankle chain.

He leaves and she lifts her habit and squats over the pail. I close my eyes while she wipes herself with a rag that hangs on the wall. I can smell the pail from here and it is clearly not something I intend to use.

She sits down again.

"Will you pray with me?

I am tempted to say no. But then I realize I have no other choice.

She takes out her rosary and begins saying Hail Marys and Our Fathers. I inhale and start praying with her.

At some point my eyes close. I lean back on this filthy wall and I feel myself falling asleep.

I'm not sure how it happens, but I wake up. It's not at all like any other nap I've ever had. I'm in the chaise lounge on the back deck. The tuna sandwich is on my lap.

It's as if I was dreaming, but it wasn't a dream. It was too real for that.

I hear Renata speaking to me. "I want you to try praying to the Virgin whenever you lose hope. Just ask for help. Ask for a miracle. I want you to know that I believe in you completely. In your power to set both of us free."

I respond out loud. "Me? I don't need freeing!"

She ignores me, saying that I have to find a way to write this story "in purity," as she puts it. In order to clear her name. In order to mend my soul.

"But what is 'purity?'" I ask. "And who is going to mend my soul?"

"Purity is the willingness, over and over again, to let go, to stay so focused on the present moment, on surrendering to the will of our Almighty Creator, that we become pure Being."

Since then, I have tried to keep an image of the nun in my mind's eye as I write. She is a wisp of a girl, and she has a shallow whistle when she breathes.

"I'm going to write now," I whisper. No answer.

I finish my lunch and sit down at the computer. I close my eyes and see Renata. Her black hair sticks up like ragged toothpicks. Her cheeks are sunken grey pods. But her dark eyes, how they sparkle. She lifts the chunky crucifix that dangles from the rosary at her waist. She touches it to her parched lips.

"Go with God," she whispers. "I know you will find your way."

4

ANTONIE

"Roseblade"

Renata rose early to go to him, and when she arrived, Antonie was waiting in the bedroom, as he always was, sitting before the silver mirror at the dressing table, idly gazing at a book. Always in the morning, she looked so fresh, she wore a full-length white apron over her trailing habit. It was the apron she wore for convent chores, an apron with blousy sleeves and long ties that she brought into a tight bow at the back of her waist. So that she arrived covered in many layers, white on top of black on top of white again, and she was veiled thoroughly head to foot, and the bottom edge of the apron was coated in fine red road dust, and her heavy black shoes were scuffed and coated too. Her forehead was bound tightly in its white linen wrap.

That she was covered so well, that he could see so little of her, just the shy half-moon of her clear face, was thrilling to him, maybe because she looked so clean, so crisp and efficient and orderly at this early hour of the day, so much the sweet-smelling, hardworking novitiate, a sister, a mother to all men, a woman in white who would be ever present to attend to daily care—his and that of others.

But perhaps too he was thrilled because of the promise of what was to come, the promise of how she would be transformed before the sun descended into its afternoon arc. He wanted what she would become as he wanted nothing else, but he wanted to wait for it, to hold it off as long as possible, to extend the inevitable as one might try to preserve the life of a flower. She was for him, in the peachy morning light, a rose anticipating full bloom. Indeed, each morning that he greeted her there in the bedroom, he held out to her a single rose, of an exceptional color. It was lined in yellow, but dipped deeply in red, so that the inside of the rose petals looked to be soaked in human blood.

What thrilled him about the rose, and about Renata herself, was the notion that he would watch them both unfold, that he would witness the opening of their soft petals, that he would be present at the moment when each of the flowers became full and whole. Antonie's greatest intoxication lay in inhaling the fragrance of the rose, and in thinking about what would happen to Renata under his influence, in comparing what she was when she arrived with what she would become through his coaxing, through the driving, unrelenting force of his emotions and his passion for her. Indeed, if the truth be known, he believed it was the very act of his gazing on her, his breathing on her, his being near and touching her, that opened her to the possibility of her transformation. For as long as possible, he put off her change, and was thoroughly aroused by its contemplation. Certainly he put it off for as long as it took her to shave his face with the straight blade, and for the time it took to apply cologne with her cool palms, which she pressed with gentle certainty against his face and neck.

Antonie smiled shyly when he heard Renata knocking softly at the ornate oak door. Like most everything at the hacienda, the door had its own elaborate story. Built and carved by her grandfather and his, Gabrielo Lopez Ruiz, the door had been chiseled from a prized stand of live oak. But before the old man could build the door, he had to hack down the monstrous oak tree himself. He did, but when he tied the felled oak to the back of his mule, the animal refused to budge, the tree being much too heavy. Gabrielo's strength was legendary and according to the story, he ended up dragging the oak to the hacienda with the tree balanced over his own shoulders. He built and carved the door in a fine manner with the same determination that had produced the magnificent Spanish house between 1838 and 1844.

"Please, come in," Antonie said, and Renata appeared in the open door, where she paused and gazed briefly at her cousin. For just that instant, she was double-framed, once by the heavy door, and a second time by the mirror into which Antonie caught her reflection. Almost instantly, she dropped her eyes demurely to the floor. Demurely, though, only from his point of view. Had she the freedom of description, surely she would have used another word, one that captured the modesty, the sincere reserve she felt as she averted her eyes. But then she wasn't free to choose the word, because she was, as we have said, framed entirely by his gaze. Thus, he would do with the language, and with her appearance in it, much as he pleased, and he would attempt the best interpretation he knew. But in the end, it was his word, imperfectly matched against her feeling, that held sway. Had she heard the word spoken aloud, she would have at the very least colored an embarrassed red. But she would have forgiven him just the same, of that he was sure. Because she would know that he was doing the best a man could do to describe the subtle interior hue of a woman.

"So you came. Sometimes I worry that…and especially after the other night, too, I wanted to…I must tell you, Renata, I must apologize for…for…" But she was shaking her head and holding her finger first to his lips and then to her own and then closing the door.

"No, no, don't, I don't want you to apologize. I won't in fact hear of it. I won't have you speak of…any of that. And if you insist, then I too will have to insist, that is, on leaving." And so they eyed each other across the space of the room, each gazing at the other in the silver mirror they now shared, the mirror with the hammered silver frame. The mirror in which they were reflected belonged to the grandmother they also shared, Gabrielo's wife, one Magdalena Sanchez y Quiero, a woman of blue eyes and black hair, a Castilian, who, despite her fair skin, was said to be part gypsy.

And so they began always in the same way, speaking to one another in hushed tones, in something of a ritual manner, dancing in words before they actually proceeded to dance with their feet.

In the next few minutes, Renata prepared to lather Antonie from the small silver bowl, a bowl she heated slightly with the light of a candle set underneath. All the while the candle glowed, Renata sought to distract Antonie, to call his attention away from herself. She spoke of Father Ruby or Mother Yolla or Sister Teresa, laughing when she mentioned the latter's name, because in the same breath she spoke of Teresa she had also to tell one of Teresa's jokes, because Teresa would do that too, making up some lewd tale about Father Ruby or even Mother Yolla. Teresa was known for the way she could spin a farfetched tale about any one of the nuns at the convent.

All the while Renata spoke, she continued with the elaborate preparations, readying Antonie for a shave he didn't need. Indeed, the truth be told, his face was as smooth and hairless as that of a young woman, save for the downy shadow of hair that grew above his fully-defined lips in the form of a vague mustache.

"Wash me," Antonie whispered, his eyes closed, and Renata laid a large towel on his chest and tucked it around his neck, and proceeded to dip a smaller hand towel—una toalleta—embroidered at both edges, into a bowl of warm water. Wringing the towel dry, she laid it on his face. She then ran the fingers of both her hands through his hair, gently lifting back into place a strand or two that had come loose from the leather tie at the nape of his neck. Then her fingers moved deftly across his forehead and temples and neck, massaging him lightly, left to right, her fingers fluttering like the legs of one of the colorful birds that Antonie kept in a large cage swinging from the center beam in the dining room. Had they been in that room now, the birds would be heard in a raucous outpouring, starting up as they always did when Renata visited, almost as if they were connected to Antonie's pulse, his very heart.

"Close your eyes," she whispered, and Antonie slumped slightly in the large chair, leaned his head back, closed his eyes, and inhaled her. Without a sound, she began to apply the lathered soap to his chin, dipping the brush repeatedly into the bowl. Soon the foaming soap covered all but his upper lip, masking cheekbones and jaw, grazing his earlobes and the Adam's apple protruding sharply from the front of his throat. She set the bowl down, and laid in the brush, and with one of her little fingers, she caught a long curl of hair at his temple and laid it behind his ear. In that moment, he reached out, caught her free hand, and kissed it, coating it with shaving soap. Swiftly she pulled back her hand.

"And how many times have I scolded you before, and how many times, my dear cousin, must I scold you again? I have told you time and time and time again that you must never distract a hand that holds a blade." She whispered thus into his ear, and the sound of the words, and the warm breath that brought the words forth sent chills clear through the center of his back. And when he opened his eyes, she had taken up the razor, and her eyes had the slightly dazed look they always got. That was the first signal, the clue that Antonie knew so well. He knew it wouldn't be long now, that she was beginning to undergo the metamorphosis inevitably imposed by the task.

So he relaxed, and let her drag the blade slowly and purposely across the front of his chin, and into his dimple that lay there, and onto his cheeks and the sharply curved edges of his jaw. The skin of his face tingled in the razor's wake, and he kept his eyes closed, imagining how her face looked above his, serious at her work, her dark eyebrows poised in a slightly knit brow. He imagined too the swift movement her hand would make as she snapped the excess soap from the blade into the ceramic bowl.

At one time, he had believed that magic lay in the way she moved the razor, the way she swept it over the contour of his face. But gradually he knew the magic was simply in the way she focused her concentration on a completely unessential task. Yes, the magic lay in the fact that she was caring so intently for him, for his face, erasing a mustache he barely showed, and a totally nonexistent beard. The thought of it never failed to thrill him, never failed to make him feel new and whole and reawakened to himself. It sent chills down his arms to know that at least for the moments Renata shaved him, there was someone who gave herself over to him, truly cared for him, someone who was present to a task that was completely an unnecessary whim.

By then she had finished skimming off the soap, and now she had indeed been transformed by her work. Moving silently, Renata unwrapped the towel from Antonie's neck, and loosened his collar, pulling the two sides of it apart so that a triangular area of his hairless chest was exposed, down to the center of his breastbone. A small circular depression, the size of a gold coin, lay at the center of his chest. Around that point his rib cage swelled, filled with air, fell, swelled again, over and over, with the regular insistence of an ocean wave, or the boat rocking on that wave.

Renata leaned across his heaving chest and reached for a crystal bottle from the dressing table. She shook a liquid balm, sweet with the fragrance of jasmine, into one cupped palm, and slowly she applied the tingling liquid against his face and neck, refreshing his heated body with her two open hands. The liquid evaporated as soon as it touched his skin. She moved progressively lower and lower, going in circles. Finally, she unbuttoned his shirt completely and pulled it apart, so that his shoulders lay exposed, and his head hung back, his eyes closed and his mouth limp and slightly open.

A third person watching in the mirror would see Renata's hands fluttering across Antonie's slightly protruding breasts, his hardened nipples, while Antonie's own hands were lifeless, his arms draped across the elaborately carved wooden arms of the chair. The third person might decide then to look away, or say a prayer, particularly if that person were a God-fearing Christian, because Renata at that point lifted Antonie's limp hand close to her lips, and folding his hand into a fist, she laid the fist to her mouth and kissed it, and then she unfolded the fist and kissed each finger in turn along its length, leaving no skin untouched.

By the time she finished with the hand, Antonie looked to be barely breathing. Moving swiftly, Renata tore the gold cuff link from Antonie's sleeve, and threw it aside. Pushing the sleeve of his shirt away, she kneeled on the floor, as if she too were going to pray. But instead, she set her delicate lips, and the tip of her tongue, gently, gently, gently, to the soft white skin that lay along the inside of his wrist.

5

SISTER RENATA'S DIARY

April 8, 1883

This time when I arrive at Antonie's, he is sitting up. His face has that ghastly purple hue, but it is one I am getting used to. He reaches out a bony hand. "I beg you, sweet cousin, to shave me." I recoil. I have never in all my life shaved a man and certainly not Antonie!

"I see no reason why I should do that," I say, moving out of the way of his grasp.

"Oh but my dear cousin, you know that Father Ruby would approve." He leers at me. "And so would my physician. If you shave my face, I am told by the good doctor, it will hurry my cure."

He closes his eyes but manages a sleepy smile.

"Surely you don't expect me to believe that," I say. "Your doctor is an intelligent man, and to my knowledge, he is well grounded in science. And I am an equally intelligent woman. Shaving your face will have no influence whatsoever on your syphil..."

"Will you please stop telling lies," he screams. "I may be ill but it isn't syphilis that ails me. It is you always pulling away!"

I feel my cousin's forehead. Damp, and feverish again. This much I know: when Antonie's temperature rises, his mind begins to spin the most perverse fantasies about me.

Still, I agree to shave him. Together with Señora, I heat the shaving cream in the metal bowl and we scrape his face clean.

And because it is so late when we finish, Señora prepares the guest room for me, and I sleep at the hacienda in the room adjacent to Señora's.

The next morning, before breakfast, I go to his room to check his temperature. His eyes open when I place my hand on his forehead. He asks me to change his sheet, so I pull back the blanket.

That's when I find it. I lift the mattress and I discover the pile of blue pages, all in Antonie's slanted handwriting. There, at the top of the pile is another story he wrote about me, the one called "Roseblade."

Once again he's made me into the seductress he wants me to be. When I threaten to burn the pages, he musters all his strength and sits up in bed and goes into a rage. His eyes are demonic as he demands that I hand back the pages.

Dear Mary in heaven, help me to know what to do!

Later in the afternoon, when I got back to the convent, Teresa and I escaped to the shade of the grape arbor. There, I told her about the most recent of Antonie's writings. It made me tremble to think back to those dark words accusing me of sin. What he had written was evil, but what was I to do about it?

Teresa's normally cheerful blue eyes were muddied and solemn. "Oh my poor Renata." She took my hand. "He…your cousin will destroy you for sure."

"Yes, I fear that he will. But what am I to do?"

She gazed out at the golden hillside, still holding my hand. Slowly she shook her head. "Other than stealing his vile stories and burning them, I'm not sure. But there is one thing you absolutely must do." The sky color sailed back into her eyes. "Remember I told you to write the story of how things were when the two of you were growing up?"

My stomach lurched. "Yes. Of course I remember. And I have considered it. But how is writing such a history going to help?"

"You will see for yourself, and show others too, how the past, your past with Antonie, has shaped things. You will see how things have come to be the way they are."

I considered her. Usually such a jolly soul, Teresa was wholly serious today.

"Yes, I suppose it can't hurt," I said. But I knew I couldn't write the whole story. There were things that even Teresa didn't know!

"And now Renata, I've got to get back to my chores. Mother Yolla instructed me at lunch to attend to the henhouse today and I dare not show up late to supper without having done it, or I will pay."

"Oh yes, of course, and I'll come, I'll help," I said, standing. But she stopped me.

"NO." She held up one hand. "You my dear sister, you are going to sit down and write."

"But it might wait, I could…"

"NO." Another hand up. "Go fetch the diary now. Go straight to a clean page. And begin. Write about your cousin and you. In the old days, when you first came. Maybe buried in your words you will see, if there were clues, already, back then."

I sighed. Without another word, I took my diary and a blanket up the golden hillside and went to my favorite live oak. And then I closed my eyes and tried to remember everything. Soon I was writing down all my early memories of my cousin.

6

SISTER RENATA'S DIARY

April 10, 1883

I will do now what my dear Teresa insists: write the story of my early years with Antonie.

To begin, I'm seeing my cousin through the grimy window of the stagecoach which brought me west to California so many years ago. I had been sleeping, mouth open, chin resting against the glass, but as soon as the driver shouted out to stop the horses, my eyes flew open. I couldn't see much at all, so I rolled the window down, and a cloud of red dust billowed up. I began coughing, and had to wipe my eyes. When I stopped, I realized that through the dust and haze there was a tall, lean boy standing below me. He had the most earnest brown eyes I had ever seen, as if they had been toasted in the sun for an eternity. His wavy hair lay in black rivers on his shoulders, too, which amazed me only because his hair so closely resembled my own both in length and color.

The boy, who looked to be about fifteen, gazed up at me and I returned the stare, and instantly something passed there, as if an ancient link was being rekindled. So many times I have contemplated this connection between me and Antonie, and I believe that there is only one satisfying explanation: that we knew each other in another time and place, under different names and circumstances and faces. Somewhere in the past, our souls were linked and we were kin of some sort to each other—long before our first meeting in 1872.

I wore a black veil that day I arrived on the stagecoach, because my mother had passed away just three months before. I let the veil down over my face, and stood up and grabbed my small traveling case. The driver opened the door, and still more dust rose up, so that I descended through a bluster of red powder. When it cleared, my cousin was standing beside his father, who was a big blocky fellow, with a thick handlebar mustache riding above his lip. Oddly, my uncle was not nearly as tall as his son.

"Finally, you are here my dear little girl." My uncle came forward and reaching out to me, he took my shoulders and pulled me powerfully to his chest. We stood there and he held me, refused to let go, and I could smell his soap, and his cherry tobacco. I could also hear him sobbing. My uncle, Roberto Guillermo Quiero, or Rio for short, had reason to be heartbroken: in the space of one year, he had lost not only his own wife, Mariana, but his younger sister as well. His younger sister being Regina, my mother.

That afternoon, I met Señora Ramos for the first time. After Uncle Rio's wife died, Señora's influence in the household grew steadily more important. I remember her so well from our first meeting. I was sitting between Antonie and Uncle Rio in the wagon bumping along the hacienda road, for what felt like an eternity. All I could see was the very tops of trees. Road dust forced me to cover my mouth so that I wouldn't keep choking.

And then, suddenly, the wagon turned, and tipped downward, and then the magnificent house came into view. There in the clearing between the two ancient live oak trees out in front of the hacienda stood Señora. Ah but she was so much younger—and thinner—in those days. She helped me down from the wagon, and all the while, she wouldn't stop smiling at me. "¿Tienes hambre, m'ija?" were the first three words she spoke. And of course, I was famished after my journey, as I had spent weeks in travel, not having proper meals and often not eating at all. She led me into the kitchen and warmed some corn tortillas, and spread them with beans and rice. And I sat with her at the table in the kitchen, and she spoke to me in Spanish, and when I finished the meal, I was so happy because we were already friends.

In the weeks that followed—I had arrived in the middle of the summer—I wasn't in school, and so I often found myself alone. Antonie studied me constantly. He would stare at me during meals until I started to squirm in my chair. And then there were those times he would appear in the doorway of my bedroom, and stand there until I looked up. His dark eyes were lively and fiery. But the eyes were brilliant gems caught in a dead and stony face. When I tried to speak to him, he just stared at me with his troubled expression, as if he might start to cry. Apparently, he had spoken to no one since his mother had died the year before.

Uncle Rio knew that I had some musical talent (I had spent several years studying piano in Madrid). And so he gladly provided me my first guitar. I would sit in my room, pressing my small fingers to the strings, trying to callous up my fingertips. I was slowly learning to make music out of the chords that he had sketched out on paper for me. It was a tedious endeavor, though. Weeks went by—most of July—and I didn't think I would ever get the hang of the stringed instrument.

At dinner one night, Uncle Rio asked me how my guitar was coming.

"I'm afraid it's not coming at all," I said. "I am ready to give it up." Secretly, I hoped to convince my wealthy uncle that he should buy me a piano. But I didn't know how to ask for such an indulgence.

"Be patient my dear. Wait a while before you let go of the guitar."

A few days later, I was in my bedroom, practicing my chords. Trying to switch between C and G and A minor. Back and forth I went, strumming each chord. And knowing how clumsy I was. How discordant I must sound. Suddenly I heard something. Or more correctly, I felt some warmth settle around me. When I looked up, Antonie was only inches away. He was so close that I could see the thick black brooms that were his sad eyelashes.

I blinked. He had his guitar. His eyes searched mine. Without a word, he sat down beside me on the bed. He bent over the guitar as if he was bowing before the priest at Sunday mass. As soon as his fingers hit the strings, they flew. Rivers of magical sound poured out of the long slender fingers of his perfectly curved hands. Streams of music more beautiful, more heart wrenching and soulful, than anything I had ever heard swelled up.

He stopped playing, and I touched the strings. And then he smiled at me for the very first time. His smoldering eyes softened and I knew, it didn't matter that I had no piano. I was already smitten, totally in love, with Antonie's guitar!

GINA

It was a beautiful November afternoon, not too cold and perfectly clear. The light was soft and lemon yellow—and the sun was low in the sky. It made the leaves on the red oak glow outside the window. Meg had driven all the way over from Massachusetts, where she teaches at the state university, just so we could write together. And now here she was sitting in the kitchen staring at me, and blinking in surprise. "I think you're kidding me but I'm not sure. You're kidding me right, Gina?"

Her voice was up in that higher register, the one she occupies when she's either delighted or dumbfounded or just confused.

"Yeah, you heard me right. I am... I am writing again. A story about a nun, accused of killing her cousin."

"Ok, fine, but what did you say? Who told you to write it?"

I poured hot water over the tea bags and carried the cups to the table. "I know it's crazy, I mean it sounds impossible, but there is this old woman, she speaks Spanish...Señora. She...visited me." I whispered the last two words; I was holding my breath. I wasn't sure what she would say next.

She shook her head. And the way she looked at me, I thought maybe she was wondering if my depression had advanced into... something more serious.

"This is all so...strange," she said.

"I know it is, but I promise, I'm really OK, totally fine." And then I told her a few more details of what transpired the day Señora appeared in my bedroom. I told her that my husband was skeptical, to say the least.

"Whether or not he believes me, or you believe me, doesn't even matter," I said finally. "Because I am finally writing again! And it's hard and I get stuck but there are these... characters cheering me on."

"Well I am glad for that. I'm glad you're back." Meg has always loved my writing, and she has been my biggest champion. After the last book nosedived, we stopped writing together because I grew more and more depressed that I couldn't find inspiration anywhere.

Now she sat holding her face in her two hands. She started to laugh.

"Gina, this is crazy." When Meg says that word "crazy," she always draws out the last syllable, making the last "zee" swing back and forth for about half a sentence. It's quite comical actually.

She didn't say anything for a minute or two. She just smiled. Finally, she got up from the table and went to her canvas bag near the door.

"Now this is really really odd," Meg said, pulling something bright turquoise out of her bag. "This has got to be one of the strangest coincidences." She chuckled. In her hand was a small square gift wrapped in turquoise paper.

"Gina, I really think you should open your birthday present right right now," Meg said, handing me the gift.

"For heaven's sake, what are you doing bringing me a birthday present, my birthday isn't for three weeks." She said nothing but watched me rip the tissue paper apart.

I gasped. My face turned warm and my hands went clammy. In my hand was a beautiful tile, painted with an image of the Virgin Mary.

"I love this tile, I love it," I said in a whisper. "But how did you know?"

"Know what?"

"That the old lady said that she prayed to the Virgin. That the Virgin promised her she would save Renata's life."

She shrugged. "I have no idea, all I know is that when I saw this tile in a little shop in Northampton the other day, I said, 'oops, gotta buy this for Gina.'"

OK, so some people will think all of this is absurd, but to me, this serendipitous event seemed like a sign, one that confirmed that I am supposed to be writing this book.

We sat drinking our tea in silence, and then we wrote. I started writing about the day that Antonie stole Renata from the convent kitchen. I wrote page after page in my notebook.

At one point I looked up and Meg was staring at me. "You go girl," she said.

Before I knew it, I had a full chapter written.

7

SISTER RENATA'S DIARY

July 21, 1883

Mother Yolla had chosen me for a whole week of lunch duty, because she said cooking "suited" me, so there I stood on Friday morning in the kitchen, patiently chopping a large onion, dropping the pure white slices into the hot sputtering oil.

I hummed to myself, and my thoughts turned to the falseta I had been strumming the night before on the guitar, and I had a flash out of nowhere of the altar, and the large silver cross that keeps watch over the chapel. And then once again I was back in the kitchen, mindlessly pushing the wooden spoon through the sizzling onions, mixing them together with the tiny slivers of garlic that had already turned golden and crisp at the bottom of the cast iron pan.

A cloud of onion fumes rose into my eyes (I write this here and can still feel the sting of the tears). I set three red peppers on the wooden cutting board, and as I prepared to slice them along their length, Teresa appeared, carrying a pile of plump green chilies in her garden basket. She added a couple green chilies to my pepper pile, turned and disappeared into the garden again.

A second cloud of onion rose up, and this one got my tears flooding, and at first I tried mopping them on the sleeve of my habit, but finally, as the tears wouldn't stop, I pulled my long white apron up to cover my face. Holding the cotton apron in two hands, I began laughing, thinking, here I am crying over one large onion in a frying pan.

But when I dropped the apron, my laughter vanished, because there filling the small window in the pantry behind the kitchen was Antonie's wilted face. As he was pressed up close against the wavy glass, his features were distorted. He looked more ghastly than I had ever seen him look before.

Where had this sad specter of a man come from? Certainly he wasn't supposed to be here, he was never ever supposed to appear at the convent, that much he knew as well as I did. Antonie himself had told me repeatedly that Father Ruby had clearly forbidden him entry. When I asked why, Antonie replied that at some time, he would explain "every last detail" of the arrangement that he had with Father Ruby regarding me; but indeed, I had been told this much: he was forbidden at the convent, which explained why I always went to visit him.

But here now was his face flushed and streaked and red, pasted against the crosspole of the window.

He looked all the more odd, divided as he was into four window panes. At first it looked to me as though he had been running, because his skin was shiny with sweat, and his long black hair was slicked to his head and his black hat dangled on his back by the leather strings tied at his chin. He was open-mouthed and breathing hard, and in his eyes was a tired, sallow look. He met me at the door.

"Why have you come?" My voice quivered. I had opened the door no more than a crack, and I was whispering and trembling. I was angry and afraid, and something else too, something I couldn't identify clearly, but it too was crawling all over me and made me feel soiled. Antonie took one step forward, and wobbled there, barely able to place the square toe of his boot against the door, and his face swerved forward to the opening, and I could see the remote look in his eyes.

Suddenly he lifted his hand and he bit hard, desperately, into his own knuckles. His eyes shone large and empty and glossy. He raised one hand up, and he braced his open palm against the doorframe, and he gasped for breath. Looming there, his arm arched over me, he scared me. He trembled, and those eyes of his bored into me.

"I want to ask…I must ask that you accompany me," he wheezed, and I was already shaking my head before he finished, in complete and utter amazement and disbelief, that he was here, that he was asking something that I clearly could never do. All the time I stared at him I was aware of those liquid black eyes on me, eyes that looked like they had been ladled out of death. His moist red face was inches from my own, and the smell of his breath was rotten.

"You…must be crazy, that's impossible," I said, and thought then in a great rush that he would indeed prove to be the death of me, or certainly the dishonor. "You know that I cannot think of such a thing, and that you could even imagine it, or propose it."

"Listen," he demanded, and despite his exhaustion, he maintained his imperious stare. His eyes opened wider still. "I will explain. I have Señora with me. I have also hired a coach and a driver, for your…for all of our comfort. I need you to come with me to see the specialist in San Francisco. We leave immediately."

He had spoken before of this doctor. We had discussed his worsening condition, how he would need to see someone with skills beyond those of the local physician.

"But I am in no position to go, not now, not ever, you must know that," I said, letting the door swing open a little wider, and with that, he stumbled forward and he grabbed onto me.

And the two of us back stepped inside. The frying pan sent up its woeful steam of onions, now turning black. The noon hour was quickly approaching and the nuns would be clamoring for lunch, or as Mother Yolla called it, "our midday repast." Meanwhile, here was Antonie straddling over me, barely able to stand up.

His heavy boots clattered on the kitchen floor. And he filled the room with his height, and with his foul smell. I caught another glance of those pained, brooding eyes.

"Please, Antonie, please, you must leave, you must go, now, you know that, please, before anyone discovers you, because if you are here, I don't who knows what could happen to me, I'm not sure what Mother Yolla will do, but the two of them, please..." I managed to push him away.

He swayed, and took hold of the wall. I raised my apron in both hands and twisted it. I thought of trying to hammer him with my fists, because I was so angry, but I was much more afraid to touch him, as he listed so weakly.

His mouth opened twice before he got the next words out. "My dear Renata, pl...ease pl...ease cousin." He whispered and leaned forward as he did, so that I could smell that fetid warm breath. Then he bent his head slightly to one side. "'Father Ruby...likes me," he said, a queer smile spreading across his lips. A glaze of sweat lay there too.

"And he is most urgently concerned about my...health. The good father... needs me, my..." Here he started coughing. His head came forward and when he raised his face again, I was horrified to see a paste of blood on his chin. He leaned forward again and forced his words out, between gasps.

"You see, he ...Father Ruby is most concerned that I continue making my donations." Here Antonie paused and his face was a leering grin. He lifted the back of his hand to the side of my face. I shuddered. And then he uttered five words that I wish I had never heard.

"He insists...that you go." And five more. "I've got to take you."

With this, Antonie swiveled and sank to the floor. Here was the man who had once commanded whatever he willed, who thrilled in his own power, who delighted in satisfying his every desire, who dictated even to the likes of our own priest and master.

I cried out to see him look so pathetic.

At that moment, Señora's face appeared at the pantry window, and seeing Antonie, she rushed in. Her face. Lined. And worn.

And behind her. Father Ruby. Giving me a look that I will never forget: something I can only call primitive, he motioned to the two of us to help him lift Antonie up. And as the onions turned to blackened wisps on the stove, and then to char, the three of us dragged Antonie to the grey wagon. And lifted him to a pile of blankets on the back.

As we set off, I turned to see Father Ruby pivot and retreat into the rectory. Rage flooded me and so too, did utter hatred, and then I reined in both emotions: this was no way to feel toward the priest. God was almost certain to punish me for my evil thoughts. But in my heart, I could see. He was simply a despicable old man.

My eyes filled and I closed my hands around my face. Señora murmured something to try to comfort me. But I would not be comforted. For there I was, still in my apron, and with the odor of the kitchen onions still clinging to my hair. I had not a stitch of extra clothing with me, not even a cape or my shawl, and I was off for who knew how long to God knew where.

But no sooner did I feel a chill than Señora patted my hand and I saw that she carried for me the blue satin shawl, all covered in red flowers, and dripping in long golden fringe.

"Un rebozo," she murmured wrapping my shoulders and that just made me cry harder.

She began to hum something. Ah. But it was the same lament that Antonie liked to strum on his guitar. That music just played more cruelly on my mind and I cried harder.

"No más," I said. And so she stopped. But the tune kept up for hours in my head as we drove over the bumpy roads. The music coiled and coiled there, reminding me of my poor mother, and her untimely death, and the childhood that I never had because of my cousin.

GINA

I could start anywhere, because it always trickles back to the same place. But today, I may as well start this way: I will tell you about the sky.

I am lying on a table in a small room with wood paneling. I can see through the top of the window. Right there, above the crackled frost on the glass, the sky is a kind of blue that is so tender and milky and beautiful that it makes me want to cry out. And the sun is bright enough to make the ice on the grey branches shimmer.

It is 1997 and I have been trying to write the nun story for two years. I write and write and then I rip half of it up and throw it away. I have come to see a woman who lives at the end of a long and very steep dirt road, a road that leads into the foothills of the Berkshires, not far from where I live. The woman runs a tiny clinic, or as she calls it, a holistic health network. Its name: The Garden of Light.

It is a stark November day. The air stings and smells of coming snow. I arrive about eleven a.m. after maneuvering the long drive up the deeply rutted road. The house is small, red clapboard and it is set back from the road and surrounded by gardens, now dry and brown, and a picket fence in serious need of white paint. When I knock on the door, Michaela answers. We shake hands and she tells me to make myself comfortable.

I take off my boots. And my socks. And soon I am lying.

No, no, no. I am not lying here at all. Finally I am telling the truth: I am lying here on this table so that Michaela can lay a hand on my forehead. In the other hand, she takes hold of my big toe, so she can give me: "zero energy balancing."

I do it because a friend of mine, a fellow writer who lives nearby, swears that she was helped by this woman. She promises it will help me with my writing.

I do it because I am desperate.

Michaela asks why I have come. So I tell her:

Because. Because I am IamsososodepressedIdon'tknowwhattod oIamsodepressed I am suffocating I hate it I hate this I am trying to write a book and I just don't know how. I don't know how to write the book andandand Idon'tevenknowwhy but I am suffocating and I hate it.

The room is quiet. Michaela nods. Her eyes are wide and blue green, the kind of eyes that shift from sky to ocean sky to ocean, depending on what she wears and what the light is like where she stands.

I could lose myself in those eyes and so I do, I go quiet as the room and then my own eyes fall shut and out of nothing I begin to see purple turtles upside down and strange lime green salamanders crawling up walls of darkness.

When I open my eyes, Michaela asks,

What kind of story is it?

I blink. I don't want to think about the story. I just want to sink into the colors that are lighting up there, behind my eyes.

But Michaela is waiting for an answer. Suddenly I have tears filling my eyes and spilling down both cheeks and I am so upset I feel like I am going to choke.

Michaela is very patient. She keeps waiting.

It's a story about a nun, she lived in 1883 and she is accused of murdering her lecherous cousin. But I keep seeing it all the time I am ... I am there with her I think I am, I'm not sure but sometimes I think...

In those days I couldn't bring myself to say what I was thinking. Michaela nods.

But now, now, I have stopped writing and I don't think I will ever be able to finish it.

Why not? Michaela asks.

I sniffle. I inhale. I am so scared, I say.

She says nothing.

And I say nothing, at first. But then I stare into her ocean eyes and words begin to flood out, in waves and waves and I tell her, I have to tell her, I have to tell somebody, in a rush and a whisper I babble about the blood how it wouldn't stop how it kept coming and coming how I kept screaming we've got to do something, I screamed and screamed but no matter I couldn't help him and neither could she…

She? Michaela asks.

Señora, I say. I turn away.

I don't want to think about it anymore.

Michaela says nothing. And when I finally turn back to look at her. Her look is completely blank.

The room is so, so quiet. I hear a dog barking outside. The sky has gone from azure to dark grey. The trees are whipping around in the wind.

Michaela gives me a second tissue. I blow my nose.

She places her hands on me again. My eyes fall shut and I begin seeing colors. This time, a yellow glow. Some kind of light slithering inside an animal. Eggs. An animal with two legs. Two bright green arms. Fingers and hands. But no face.

This time when I open my eyes, Michaela tells me. Simply.

Your body wants to write this book.

I nod, not really understanding. My *body* wants to write this book? I want to understand. I want to cooperate. But what is she saying? How could my body possibly write…?

I am having nightmares, I say. I keep seeing the man, Antonie, dying in a pool of his own blood.

Don't be alarmed, she responds. You will figure it out one day. Just ask the universe for help. Do you pray?

I nod my head. Sometimes.

Well, then, go ahead and pray. She smiles and looks at her watch. I think we are done now.

Slowly, I get off the table. I thank Michaela and I write her a check for fifty-five dollars.

I am heading toward the door when she says, "Oh. Just one more thing."

I turn.

"Yes?"

Michaela cocks her head slightly and says.

"You might want to consider past life regression therapy."

"What...what...I guess I could try that."

"If you want to, I can refer you to a couple of women I know near Northampton."

"Sure. I'll...I'll uh.... call you for the names."

I turn and hurry out the door.

It would take almost 20 years for me to find the courage even to think about making that call.

8

SISTER RENATA'S DIARY

July 21, 1883

It was our first night at camp en route to San Francisco. We had been traveling all day, all the way from the convent and I was exhausted. Shortly before dusk, when the sun's rays had fallen behind the horizon, and the sky was a milky blue, Señora Ramos pulled the wagon up to a stream where the horses proceeded to water.

After a simple dinner of cornmeal and beans, I withdrew from the fire. I was still trembling over the hellish way the day had started. I wanted nothing to do with Antonie. I hugged Señora's blue shawl closer around me. The shawl was satin, and hardly offered protection against the chilly night. A brisk wind came up. A tall line of trees made a ragged black silhouette against the sky and a couple of tiny stars looked like diamonds.

Antonie was making an odd collection of noises—coughing, wheezing, congestion and steady chattering—that rose from him as he lay on blankets on the ground. I covered my ears and began saying Hail Mary's so I could try to block him out entirely.

I was facing the steep ridge of the Santa Cruz mountains— mountains we would climb the following morning. I watched the last of the sun slip down the western sky. I wondered how the travel would go, with Antonie so ill.

Once the sun had disappeared, I walked back to the fire. There were more night noises now and I shivered thinking—mountain lions, bears and coyotes roamed the shadows beyond the campfire.

Señora hummed a low wordless melody, huddled over her open-toed sandals, her yellow skirt spread in the powdery red dust. I couldn't identify her tune and couldn't tell if I had heard it before. If only I had my guitar. I hadn't had time to pack even a single set of clothes. Hateful thoughts flooded me!

As if he were reading my mind at that moment, Antonie looked up from his makeshift bed, which Señora had prepared as soon as we had made camp. Antonie had instructed Señora to place his head close enough to the fire, so if he woke during the night he might have sufficient light to write "his pages." Señora defied him, however, saying in Spanish that she dare not place his blanket right next to the flames, lest stray sparks set fire to the bedroll or to "el pelo," the long black hair that covered Antonie's shoulders.

"I would like it so much if you would sing to me," he said now to me, lifting one limp hand in my direction. He spoke slowly but with deliberation. I saw that he was shivering, and that his face was wet beneath the brim of his hat. The flames of the fire licked a golden stripe in each of his eyes.

"You know I came on this trip only because you forced me to come. I have no intention of singing to you," I responded. I was going to add the word 'ever' but just then, the coffeepot toppled over and sent boiling liquid into the fire.

Señora rose abruptly, yelling "¡Dios mío!"

She grabbed at the fiery pot with the bottom of her cotton skirt, revealing her brown wiggling thighs. She missed the pot, which hit the ground, splashing sizzling liquid all around. Hot black coffee shot out at my feet and Antonie's head. He turned and I jumped away, so that the coffee all but missed me and his black hair. She crossed the distance to where I stood gazing at the coffee pot as it roasted in the flames.

She began a furious stream of Spanish.

"No, no, Señora, please, don't worry, I am fine," I said, touching the woman's thick graying hair. Señora looked up, and shook her head, her eyes large and round. There was contained in those eyes a pleading look that I had never seen before.

"You...we...Dios, I believe, He is telling us that we must be more kind to him," Señora whispered, at which I recoiled, mouth open. For the rest of the evening, until the sky went pitch dark, and the fire settled into glowing red and white coals, and the stars were dull sparks glittering above my head, I sat on the same warm rock where I had eaten dinner.

I listened to the coyotes call, and I prayed that we would see no mountain lions. And then I whispered a second prayer asking God that whatever He had in mind for us as we traveled to San Francisco the next day to see the doctor, that all would be well.

9

ANTONIE

"Seduction at Camp"

Only with great reluctance did Renata return to the campfire to lie in the bedroll that Señora had prepared for her.

Antonie was in a deep sleep when Renata woke him sometime during the night. The first thing to catch his eye as he came to consciousness was the moon, a glowing curl, visible just over Renata's shoulder.

Her hair was tied back and completely curtained by her dark veil. Her eyes shone, or at least the whites stood out, circling the irises. All but the stark white swath of linen binding her forehead was black.

For a moment, he imagined the linen to be some insurmountable white barrier, the fence he once faced, years before, back when he was a child struggling to master the forbidding Arabian steed that his father had called "Paolo." In an instant, Renata's face had displaced the frustrating memory of the horse. Her breath was shallow and insistent, and before he was altogether sure what was happening, she was drawing him in over the white wall. Her lips were moist and warm, and her mouth lingered tenderly on his for a long time.

In the morning, he knew for certain she would deny that she had ever left her bed. In the morning, she would deny she had ever approached his cot, or knelt beside him, or that she had kissed him repeatedly, cradling his head, or that she had laid her own head briefly on his chest before she got into his bed and proceeded with her seduction.

Nonetheless, he let her proceed. He kept his eyes closed and tried to breathe in calmly as she unbuttoned his shirt and slipped the belt out of the hammered silver buckle of his pants. Silently, she set to work with her fingers, letting them pass lightly across his raised nipples, dipping them gradually toward the ribs, letting them dance down his chest until he was heaving with impatient desire. Soon she traded lines for circles, the circles following the slight swell of flesh around his stomach. She enlarged the circles so slowly that he hardly noticed them widening, expanding, until, her hand just grazing the uppermost edge of his pubic hair, she proceeded to leave it there.

Her circling abruptly stopped, and her hand remained, poised, lightly running back and forth along the line at the top of the triangle of hair. He lay there, head flopping side to side, teeth digging into his bottom lip, not daring to moan because it might wake Señora, or the driver of the wagon, but praying all the while that Renata would keep on, dip further with her fingers, let them encompass the rest of him. His legs turned liquid, and limp. Tired of waiting, he groped impatiently for her hand. He allowed himself to groan, and to call out once, "please, Renata, now." And then, his own hand shaking, he pulled at her fingers, desperately pushing them downward, at which point she froze, and grabbed her hand away from his groin.

"No," she said abruptly, her voice stern. She rose and he lay there, his eyes wet, his chest heaving. For the first time he realized that he was almost completely exposed to the damp night air. He shuddered, but made no attempt to cover himself, there, where his desire welled.

"You...you are so cruel to me," he began, tears pooling. "You are..." but he couldn't finish, because his voice had risen to a high pitch, and he felt choked off and breathless. After a moment he was able to continue, but only in fits and starts. "I...I lie here...I ...I am...half-crazy with desire...I am in sheer agony when I'm near you...I am helpless around you, and you, you know that, you know that so well. Helpless. I am helpless to do anything about my...myself, the way I am...you know that too, you know me so well, so long. You know, and yet you...you just...you just keep teasing me."

The last words were barely audible. She stood over him, and he was horrified to see that she was smiling, she was delighting in his humiliation once again. Whenever this happened, whenever she led him to his breaking point, and left him there, abandoned him, unwilling to follow through, to show him she cared, he felt as though he had to start over, invent himself anew.

"It's too bad that you've developed such an…attachment to me," she murmured after a moment had passed. "You know," and here she sighed deeply, and he wondered if it was just for effect, "you know Antonie, or you should, that this is…this has been so…so hard for me, too, your illness especially, trying to coax you through, this has been more difficult than you can imagine."

He raised himself to both elbows and poised there, trembling. He turned away. If she could have seen his face then, she would have observed an unusual fury in his eyes, a brutal anger creasing his forehead and pulling back his lips and chin.

"Difficult? For you? Difficult for you?" His voice was coarse and throaty. "For you, no, this isn't hard. This isn't hard at all. And this isn't new either. This is, this is what you do best, best in all the world. You mock me, yes, you mock me, you scorn me, you always have, forever, ever since you were the horrifying child I grew up with." Exhausted, he dropped back off his elbows onto the make-shift bed, which wobbled with his every move.

She was silent again, and again, he couldn't imagine her face. Nor did he want to. He vowed not to think of her again, not to let her come near him, to tempt him, and then, let him down. But it was fruitless, and he knew that too. Within a few days, another episode, another encounter, another seduction by Renata would follow, because that is how it went, always.

Gazing at her now, he could barely make out the white linen fence.

"I suppose I could lie with you, lie next to you, that is, for a short time, if that would calm you." Her voice blended into the night wind.

He stared at the stars, pinpoints of light in the black sky.

He watched one of the points flicker and blink. "Am I awake or asleep?" he asked himself then.

It occurred to him that if he would just keep asking that same question over and over throughout the night, then it might not matter what Renata said, or did, because she would simply assume a place beside him, a place in one of his grand illusions. She might seem real, or she might not. But she would be fixed for certain in her uncertainty and she could not hurt him anymore. She would become, simply, a matter for discussion, observation, an unstable image or object evading direct perception, one of a myriad fluid aspects of reality. Simply, she would reside apart from him behind a curtain. He could live with that. At least he thought so, in that moment, lying there, staring at the winking stars.

But almost immediately, and maybe because of the way the stars flickered, he wasn't sure. After all, he knew so little about the boundaries of trickery and sorcery and witchcraft. And Renata, after all was said and done, was of that nether world.

"Yes, I would lie with you," she said in an enchanting whisper. And before he could answer, or refuse, she stretched herself along-side him on the cot. As he felt the rough black fabric of her habit against his bare skin, he thought of her soft white underclothes beneath, and beneath those clothes, her flesh, as soft as the under-belly of a new puppy. As she cupped her clothed body submissively around his, his mind circled around one fact: that black is black and white is white, and the world, understandably, wasn't ready to accept someone like himself, or Renata, either, people who so casually blurred the distinctions of propriety and good taste.

"But why," he asked himself, "should we be any different than we are? Why should we be shy about our desire?" That thought squared him, gave him assurance and peace, eased his mind, al-lowed him to let go of his anger and frustration. He folded her in his arms and stared into the dark sky and held her black and white layers to his yearning flesh, and he felt terror about what was to come, the grotesque treatments the doctor would soon prescribe. He feared dying, but even more, he dreaded living through the suffering that was in store.

But now he lay quietly beside Renata, happy to absorb himself in the stars, and in her, and in the curl of the moon slowly drop-ping toward the horizon. In his feverish state, her words echoed and reverberated in his mind. He heard her saying: "I would lie with you, I would lie with you." But soon enough, like the winds cooling his forehead, the words shifted. "I would lie with you" became "I would lie in you." The vacillation continued until her words achieved their final form: "I would lie to you, I would lie to you." He felt her warm breath, heard her singing whisper, and knew that "I would lie to you" was the only truthful statement he would hear from her all night.

GINA

This is all I know: one moment I was sitting cross-legged in meditation in my living room, staring into the orange candle flame.

And the next thing I knew I was sitting cross-legged beside a campfire. A thin trail of smoke rose up from the orange coals.

I saw two people wrapped in blankets on the ground. A third lay sleeping a few feet away.

I blinked. It was cold. I smelled the campfire. I looked straight above my head and a few stars sparkled in the dark sky. The moon was a crisp sliver.

"What am I doing here?" I whispered it, or at least I thought I did. The next moment, I saw one of the blankets shift. A head lifted.

I stood up, feeling my legs shaky as I did. Still in my blue bathrobe and L.L. Bean slippers, I walked softly across the dirt. There, sitting up in her blanket, was Señora's wide face, her long white hair rippling softly over her shoulders. She smiled.

"Ah, finally you come," she said. "I knew you would come."

I shook my head. "How could you possibly know that?" I asked. "And why? What am I doing here?"

"Shhhh!" She put a finger against her lips. "Please not to wake them, we have a long way to go in three days. All the way to San Francisco for the doctor."

Only then did I notice the wagon. Only then did I see the two horses tied to a large live oak tree. Señora rolled onto her knees and after a fashion, she pulled her buxom body upright. She led me toward a large rock quite a ways from the campsite.

"I so so happy to see you," she said. I realized that I am at least two heads taller than she is.

"OK, but how can I possibly help?"

She chuckled. "Surely, you remember what I ask. To write the true story of my precious Renata. You did promise me."

I inhaled. What a bitch this book was turning out to be. "Yes, yes, I know, I know I promised." I pulled the belt on my terrycloth bathrobe tighter. "But I can't possibly help you tonight, here, beside this campfire."

"Ah, you be completely wrong, my dear Gina." She smiled broadly. "You see here. I want for you to watch for yourself the true of the situation."

"The true? You mean the truth? What situation would that be exactly?"

She grasped my hand into the strong muscle of her hand, and holding a finger to her lips, she tiptoed me back to the campfire.

"Now you see, over there beside my blanket, yes?

"I guess." I strained to see who lay there.

"I swear that is the sweet child of my heart, dear Renata."

"OK, if you say so."

"NO!" Her face fell into deep wrinkles. "You see here for yourself. You must got to see that she sleeps beside me, far from Antonie."

I took a few steps toward the other sleeping figure. I couldn't see clearly. But in the weak glow of the fire I could make out his angular face, and long wavy black hair.

I walked back to the other blanket. Lying there was the wispy nun, her head still bound in her black and white veil. Her slender face looked pale.

"Yes, I can see clearly now."

"Ok, then you know how to say what is the truth. That Renata does not sleep with her cousin."

"Yes, I see that." I yawned. The sky was now glowing orange and pink above the towering trees.

"You must make the promise to write that!"

"I will do my best," I said. I looked her straight in her gray eyes. She frowned and her eyes bore holes into mine. "OK, I promise."

"I am glad you agree to the story the correct way." She picked up her blanket, shook it out and wrapped it around her shoulders. With the sunrise came a little breeze. She lifted two pieces of wood and crossed them over the coals. She added some thin pieces of kindling. The fire roared up.

"May I go back home now?"

"You could stay for breakfast, a bowl of some hot cereal I make." She gestured to a greasy black kettle. I can only imagine what was inside.

"No, I think I'd rather have breakfast at home. A bagel maybe."

"This bagel I don't know." She bent over and blew on the fire. Sparks flew.

"But as long as you make the story be right, you are free to go."

10

SISTER RENATA'S DIARY

July 25, 1883

Dr. Astorga swears by mercury. The silvery liquid has helped more of his patients in the late stages of syphilis than any other cure. Or so he claims. For medical reference he relies, oddly enough, almost exclusively on the writings of two 15th century Spanish physicians.

"Is there nothing more…modern?"

I posed that question to Dr. Astorga in the first hours after Señora and I arrived at his elegant Nob Hill office, struggling to hold Antonie upright. All three of us wore the same red crust, road dust fixed into our skin, our clothes, and even, our faces and teeth.

I asked my question politely. Or at least, I thought I did. But considering the physician's reaction, clearly he heard my query as a direct assault on his knowledge and competency.

"So you seem to know a thing or two about syphilis, then?" Immediately, I reddened. His lips thinned and then froze in a sneer.

"Oh no, sir, I do not," I mumbled, dropping my eyes to the polished surface of his desk. "I know nothing at all of this illness."

Astorga sat behind his grandiose oak desk. He tented his fingers together beneath his chin. In everything about him there was an affected air; even his softly drooping eyelids struck me as…dare I say…haughty, and even worse, deceitful. Forgive me Lord, I did not like this man, not from the very start. But as I sat there, wanting to disappear from the room, I thought to myself, what choice have we got but to stay, no matter what? This doctor was certainly Antonie's only hope.

I glanced at my cousin, resting against Señora's shoulder, the two of them sharing a bench off in a corner. Antonie was tightly wrapped in Señora's magnificent blue shawl, but it seemed to make no difference at all. He shook so badly that I could practically hear his teeth chatter.

Incredibly, Astorga took no notice of that. Instead, he proceeded to give us a long-winded story explaining how one Ruy Diaz de Isla happened to treat the syphilitic sailors of Christopher Columbus' famed crew in 1493.

"It all began you see, with a rather grimy mistake. Columbus' sailors, it is believed, chose very unwisely to wash their vermin-infested drawers in a pond of water at Palos, the port from which Columbus sailed, and that water later irrigated the vegetables. The cabbages, it is said, erupted in syphilitic lesions that were frightening to behold."

Astorga paused, his lips curled in his authoritative smile, a grin I already found hateful. It took all my internal force to ignore Antonie's groaning. The doctor's face at that moment was abhorrent to me: I still see his large square jaw, the neatly clipped mustache, and all those giant yellow teeth, one of which was capped in gold. The doctor's black hair was perfectly coifed, but so bizarre: he wore a fairly top heavy pompadour, and on the sides, each oiled wave was pressed close to his skull.

At that moment, Antonie fell into a coughing fit. I thought for sure that Astorga would begin his physical examination of my cousin. But the doctor was ignoring Antonie and me, choosing instead to continue with his lecture on syphilis. I caught Señora's eyes, which flared. Was this doctor going to help Antonie? But I knew I didn't dare challenge the physician with a question once again.

Leaning back in his grand armchair, fashioned out of rich burgundy leather, and hammered with silver studs, Astorga pointed to his wall. "That tract hanging there is the actual frontispiece taken from Ruy Diaz de Isla's famous book, *Tractado Contra el Mal Serpentino*."

I stared at the yellowing page, framed ornately, the paper decorated in slithering black serpentine figures. The lettering was impossible to read. But Astorga proceeded coolly to explain and all I could do was stare at Antonie and Señora as the doctor spoke.

"The tract was written in 1539, and still has not been translated into English. Of course I was able to read it in its original Castilian," Astorga boasted, punctuating his statement with a hatefully patrician gleam. "Without question, Diaz de Isla's scholarly work provides us proof that the scourge originated in the American equatorial island of Hispaniola."

I shifted in my chair and thought, Dear God, keep me from tearing this man's hair. Antonie had stopped shaking, but he was further collapsed into Señora, his head now resting in her lap, his legs extended well off the bench.

At that moment, Astorga rose, and so did my hopes, thinking yes, yes, he will attend to Antonie now. But instead, Astorga crossed to the other side of the office and reached for a large book on the top shelf of his bookcase. "There is of course a second and quite notable 15th century scholar, poet, philosopher and physician in this field. Francisco Lopez de Villalobos, and he was among the very first to recognize and treat the disease."

He carried the book around to the front of his desk and sat on one corner, where his leg was only inches from me. "As a young medical student, I traveled in 1862 from Barcelona to London, to the British Museum, where I sat in the stacks and read from cover to cover one of the four remaining copies of Villalobos' book, this very book you are looking at right now. Remarkably, Villalobos' work is still in use three centuries later. He was the first, we believe, to introduce the use of mercury and that treatment remains our best defense in the battle against this pernicious disease.

"Villalobos wrote his book shortly after the arrival of Columbus, and it contained a lovely poem that I have framed in ebony in the other room..."

While Astorga mused over poetry, Antonie's breathing was becoming more labored. I shifted uneasily in my chair. Was there nothing I could do to hasten this doctor to perform the business of curing? Did he know nothing but what was between the pages of his dusty old books? In one corner of my eye, I could see Señora struggling desperately to hold onto Antonie as he thrashed to the left and the right. But to Astorga, Antonie might have been invisible.

Astorga flipped through the flimsy pages of the book.

"You know, dear Sister, that both of these fine Spanish doctors of the fifteenth century were of strong religious faith?" He paused and I shook my head slightly.

"I had no idea," I replied.

"Yes, both doctors were most decidedly religious men," he continued, examining his well-manicured nails. I watched his lips, and thought for a moment, is that indeed a look of lechery forming there?

"Like all good religious men," he went on, "both of these fine doctors believed that las bubas, the Spanish name for syphilis, was a scourge delivered on men specifically because of their…" and here he paused, and his voice dropped, and his face came forward toward mine, so that I could see the very pores of his skin, "… because of their carnality, the vile nature of their sins."

My face colored again, and I was about to reprimand him, for how dare he speak so freely with me about the connection between Antonie's illness and sexual excess and sin?

My mouth opened, and I heard a scream, and for a fraction of a moment, I thought perhaps it might be my own.

But no. It was Señora. Antonie had rolled from her lap onto the floor. He landed with a loud thump. My cousin's hat had fallen aside and his long hair was splayed every which way. I jumped from my chair and was there at his side in an instant. Without any hesitation, I eyed the doctor, who was still sitting astride the desk.

"My God, will you please come here immediately, my cousin needs you, desperately," I screamed. And then, perhaps because it had been so many days since I had slept, I seemed to lose all touch with reality. I screamed louder.

"Can't you see that he needs immediate attention? Are you a doctor at all or are you some kind of a librarian? Have we come all this way just to listen to lectures from your stuffy old books?"

Señora took hold of my arm, and held me back. I sank, wilted, to the floor. The doctor rose and his eyes widened and froze as he crossed the room in two large strides. He reached toward me and

I thought for sure he would strike me, but I didn't care. I'd already decided, I was ready for whatever transpired there.

Instead, though, Astorga grabbed his black leather bag and kneeled on the floor beside Antonie, who was on his back, his face more grey and sweaty than I'd ever seen before.

"Move aside," Astorga commanded. I settled beside Señora, who was kneeling there, murmuring prayers in Spanish.

The doctor laid the stethoscope on Antonie's chest, and took my cousin's pulse. "He is indeed quite ill," Astorga muttered, and I had all I could do not to strike the doctor with a fist. At his direction, the three of us—Astorga, Señora and me—proceeded to lift my cousin and carry him to an adjacent room, where we hoisted him onto a clean bed.

"I will be ready to begin shortly," Astorga said, and then he left the room for a moment, evidently to prepare the mercury.

And so Señora and I sat on opposite sides of Antonie's bed. Señora lay one hand on his shoulder and tried to comfort him. I looked up noticed on the wall over my cousin's head, a large ebony frame. And in it, a poem, evidently the one that Astorga described.

As Señora prayed, I read the poem. Curiously, it brought me tender thoughts of the convent. And my heart was squeezed as I realized anew how far I was from home:

> *"Hatred, strife and combat*
> *make man forget his God.*
> *Passion clothed in filth*
> *lifts up its noisome head.*
> *Thus is man and*
> *mother church trodden in the sod.*
> *And honest men forget*
> *their nuptial word and*
> *seek in darkest night*
> *the harlot's golden bed."*

GINA

One morning I woke up shivering. The phone was ringing.

Thinking it was my alarm clock, I rolled over to my nightstand to slam the snooze button, but my arm felt nothing. No radio. No nightstand.

I sat up. Blinked. Where was I?

Oh of course. On the sofa. I had slept there all night. Joel was in Washington, D.C. on business, and Jonah was overnight at a friend's house.

I had spent most of the afternoon writing, sitting on the couch with the laptop. The last thing I remember is laying the laptop on the floor and lying down on the sofa with the afghan covering me.

The phone stopped ringing.

I yawned, lifting my hand to my mouth. I gasped: My arm was dripping in bright gold fringe. I was wrapped in the shawl. Señora's. I pulled it tighter. The golden fringe twinkled in the lamplight. I held the blue to my face. Rubbed the side of my thumb over the dazzling blaze of red and yellow and pink roses. Then I ran the silky knots of the gold fringe between my fingers.

I had fallen asleep in my ordinary clothes, and woken up cocooned in the magical shawl. Ah, there was no end to the power of Señora and her beautiful *rebozos*.

I looked around the living room, half expecting to see the dear old lady, holding the guitar. But no. I was alone.

The phone rang again. I lay there on the couch, trying to decide whether to ruin this wonderful moment by answering it.

I picked it up.

"Hey you," Joel said. "Where have you been?"

I stared at the shawl. "I....fell asleep on the couch."

We chatted a few more minutes. Joel had a meeting to go to.

It was nine o'clock in the morning. I sank back onto the sofa and hugged the shawl tighter around me.

Finally, I got up and ventured into the kitchen. I stood there drinking a gigantic glass of water. And then, a second glass. I toasted a poppy seed bagel and ate it with a heap of cottage cheese.

Suddenly, I was there with Señora peering down at Antonie in the bed.

His torso was bare.

I gasped. There were red pustules all over his chest, and splotches of wet silvery liquid coating them. He glistened.

"OH LORD!" I gasped. Grabbing Señora's hand, I turned my face away. I felt faint and leaned against her shoulder.

"OH mi'ja!" Señora was the only thing holding me up. She guided me to a chair in the corner. I settled into the seat, and realized I was wearing habit and veil.

But who was I?

At that moment it didn't matter because I was kneeling and throwing up rather violently. Señora had her arms around me and she held my forehead as I leaned over the floor.

I didn't realize it at the time, but Renata and I shared a tendency toward what my doctor calls "hyperemesis." Basically when you start throwing up, you can't stop.

At some point as I was upchucking, I was vaguely aware of Astorga at the door. But I vomited more and more. Finally I was on my hands and knees, and the only thing coming up when I heaved was sour green bile.

I looked up and I was face to face with the dishwasher in my kitchen. To my right was the oven.

Then I was back in Antonie's sickroom with Señora and Astorga looming overhead. I saw Astorga reaching into his bag. He took out an enormous needle.

I closed my eyes. Dear God, what was he going to do?

Before I could react he kneeled beside me. He slipped my sleeve up and the next thing I knew I was screeching. It felt like he had driven a burning hot poker just below my shoulder.

I cried louder. Señora was holding onto me and cradling my head against her fleshy chest. I began sobbing.

"Shhhhh," she said, rocking me back and forth. I felt her arms around me, and I could see the two of us in reflection in the glass door of the oven.

I cried and gagged and finally I began to sniffle. Whatever he had given me…

When I woke up I was curled in a fetal position, with my cheek on the kitchen tile. I blinked. I was staring into my own vomit. Oh my God, I thought, where is the shawl. I sat up and it was nowhere to be seen.

It wasn't until much later, after I had showered and drunk a cup of tea, and some ginger ale, that I went back to my laptop on the sofa.

That's when I eyed the shawl, the gold fringe, those amazing roses. The shawl was neatly folded, the golden fringe glowing like a goddess's hair, sitting neatly on one arm of the sofa.

11

SISTER RENATA'S DIARY

July 27, 1883

This evening, while our new wagon driver Tango watched over Antonie, Señora and I took our evening meal in one dark corner of the hotel bar. At first, Señora resisted the idea of leaving Antonie, but I convinced her this way: "If we are to care for Antonie, we will need our strength. We must feed ourselves a decent meal."

The two of us sat at a table separated from the boisterous drinking patrons, but the separation was nothing more than a maroon velvet rope. There was nothing to keep us apart from the cigar smoke or the raucously loud laughter that floated up everywhere around me.

I kept my head down throughout the meal, staring at my plate and cupping my hand over my nose when I felt smoking blowing right at me. Time and again, I thought to myself, oh how desperate I am to be back home.

Upstairs was poor Antonie, languishing in sweaty sheets. For the last three nights we have had to tie him to the bedframe so he wouldn't thrash himself right off his mattress and onto the floor. He has slept for only moments at a time, and otherwise, he twists and turns in his bed, and occasionally he calls out, pleading with us to untie him from the bed.

One moment he can seem almost normal. His temperature is steady, his face is cool, and he speaks more or less in a normal way. Some days he is coherent all day. But other days are rocky. He is coated in sweat, and sometimes, a ghastly rash, and when he speaks, his voice is hoarse, and often, he calls out nonsense and obscenities to people who aren't even there. The last thing he said to me, before Señora and I fled his room, and came downstairs to the bar for dinner, was that he wasn't certain I was ready to dance the farruca on the bar, because the footwork was so grueling, so intricate and demanding.

"Of course I know the music because I play it over and over at home," he said, his head flopping side to side. "But you, Renata, you must rehearse more. You have been sitting in the room here and you are not going to remember that intricacy of steps."

Señora gave me a desperate look, and I grabbed her hand and squeezed it. "My dear cousin, have no fears about me," I whispered, as we rose and Tango pulled a chair up to the bed.

I admonished Tango to watch him closely, and to make sure he kept rinsing washrags in cool water, and placing them on Antonie's forehead.

Señora and I headed downstairs to dinner.

We dined slowly and sumptuously on two thick, pan-fried steaks, mashed potatoes, cornbread and carrots. And we shared a pot of baked beans. The hotel waiter, a thin young fellow with a sallow face, and practically no hair, offered us seconds on potatoes and beans and cornbread and Señora and I, suddenly realizing how ravenous we were, decided to have whatever was offered.

Finally, the thin fellow cleared our plates, making a large stack of white dishes. He stood there with the unsteady pile in the crook of his arm and described the house dessert, a bittersweet chocolate bread pudding.

"Could I interest you ladies in a bowl?" he asked, focusing a languid gaze first at Señora, and then me. I shook my head no, but Señora enthusiastically raised her hand to accept the waiter's offer.

"Yes, then, one order coming up," the waiter said. He promised to be right out with the pudding, and said he would bring Señora and me some coffee "on the house," a special brew flavored with vanilla.

As we waited, the bar grew steadily more crowded and noisy, and darker and denser with the grey smoke of the cigars and cigarettes. So dim was the air that at one point when I looked up I could barely make out Señora's brown features across the table from me. The smoke puffed and swirled around the sconces on the wall, and curled in lazy spirals toward the ornate tin ceiling overhead. All around me was the unpleasant din that accompanies rowdy men, drinking.

A more sordid place than this hotel I have never been. If it weren't for the fact that Antonie may find a treatment here that could save his life, then I would push Señora to leave tomorrow morning. For how long are we committed to this place, I'm not sure. I am yearning to be back among those golden hills, and I'm sure Antonie would prefer to be there too. Oh how I miss that sweet air at night. How I miss staring into the ink of the night sky, seeing every star in the heavens. Here in the hotel, what we hear is that frightfully loud player piano running incessantly, hour after hour, night after night.

The waiter brought the coffee and dessert, and almost simultaneously, Señora leaned over to me and whispered something that I couldn't hear. She was gesturing too, but I had trouble understanding her over the noise. For a moment, I thought she was pointing to the garish red wallpaper behind my head, or to the glass lamp on the table above me, its pink flowered shade decorated in long strands of shimmering silver fringe, not all that dissimilar from Señora's shawl.

But no, as I turned, and followed her gaze, she was pointing well beyond the table, and the lamp, to a far corner of the room. There I could barely make out a tall, elegantly dressed man holding a guitar. He had one leg lifted to a stool in front of the player piano, and for once, thankfully, that monstrous instrument wasn't bombarding us with its frenzied tunes.

Señora was smiling, and pointing to the guitar, and I knew from that dreamy far away look in her eye that she was anxious to hear the music. I was thinking about Antonie all by himself, upstairs in his room. I was just about to volunteer to return to my cousin when the handsome gentleman unleashed a furious rasqueado from the guitar.

Squeezing my hand, Señora led me across the room to a table so we could watch the man make the guitar sing. His long fingers clamored nimbly across the strings, working so fast that it was impossible to keep track of what he played. I lost myself in the music; I closed my eyes and let it fill every corner of my mind, and carry into the deepest layers of my chest. Oh how I missed my guitar, how I wished desperately just to hold it now. The thought of its curved wooden body, its gentle pressure in my lap and against my chest, resting there, set a chill going up my arms.

The guitarist, who had one pointy black boot raised to the player piano stool, must have picked up something then, because at the very same moment that I opened my eyes, he nodded and winked at me. I blushed, and dropping my eyes, I turned to Señora, who was as enraptured by the music as I was. Closing my eyes, I had the instrument in my lap. I could almost feel those six taut strings against my fingers. How delightful it would be to hold my own guitar now, its sleek rosewood against my palms.

At that moment the guitarist—silver-haired, and of slight build, but meticulously groomed in grey velvet pants and a dark purple vest with a red satin cravat—began singing.

His voice was so unexpectedly full and low and altogether so beautiful that it made me catch my breath. Señora grabbed my arm. "Magnífico," she whispered, and I nodded, and I thanked God for this wonderful encounter. The first song was a slow melody that squeezed at my heart, and it was followed by a lively rhythm in which the guitarist kept teasing us all by stopping, and waiting for a few moments before he resumed his strum.

I sipped my coffee and drank up the flamboyant sound of the melody that he had chosen: a rumba, one I vaguely recalled. Out of the well of my memory, I remembered my uncle, or maybe one of his friends, opening a juerga, our flamenco party, with a similar passionate tune. I could see myself circling the fire, holding hands and dancing with the others.

As I sat there clapping, Antonie's face came to mind. Two days ago, as I sat mopping his brow, his delirium took over again, and he began speaking his crazy thoughts about me dancing.

"All that spinning you do, Renata, doesn't it make you dizzy?" he whispered, and instantly I tried to silence him.

"Antonie you have wild ideas in your head. Dr. Astorga says it is all because of the illness, but still, you must stop. It would be completely sinful for me to dance. When you are in your right mind, you know full well that I haven't danced since I took my first step into the convent now almost ten years ago."

The rumba ended and we clapped and some of the bar patrons whistled and stamped their feet. They pounded impossibly loud, so hard that it sounded like their shoes would come through the wooden floor. Bowing, the guitarist announced his name: "Yo soy Victor Cavella," he said. He told us that he had once played and sung with a flamenco troupe not far from Cádiz in Andalucía, and the song he was about to perform was his own tribute to his hometown so many miles away.

Without another word, he began a rhapsody that alternately thundered and lapsed into sweet refrain. The music caught me up so completely that I found myself singing along. When I heard laughter ring out, I had no idea that I was the object of the humor, until Señor Cavella strolled toward our table and smiled and tipped his head toward me. I blushed and felt ashamed and instantly regretted my behavior. But at the end of the performance, Señor Cavella gave me a rose, and the crowd clapped, and I glanced at Señora and her face - for the first time in weeks—looked light and giddy and carefree.

Who could blame us for remaining downstairs in the bar far longer than we had planned? Señora and I had been tending to my cousin night and day for weeks. When we weren't mopping his brow, or feeding him broth or tea, we were cleaning his putrid wastes, and praying as much as two people possibly could. Here, now, inside the bar, the guitarist was infusing our sore hearts with a much-needed dose of festive rhythm and lovely songs.

It wasn't long before we noticed Tango's dark curls, and his curious eyes at the bottom of the staircase. I stood, immediately concerned, but he reassured us. "Antonie is asleep and he will stay that way," Tango said, and so, there was no reason to return so soon to the sick room.

As the smoke thickened in the bar, so too did our enthusiasm for the music. Tango extended a hand to Señora and swept her onto the dance floor. She resisted at first, shaking her head and shyly trying to push him away. But he persisted, and with a little coaxing from me and little more from Tango, Señora was soon moving her feet to the beat of the alegría. The guitarist had chosen a lighthearted gypsy dance, and Tango moved with the romantic music, guiding a laughing Señora in a small circle around the floor.

As I watched her giggling, she reminded me suddenly of my dear Sister Teresa, if only in the way they both have ample faces and chins that jiggle when they are happy.

Patrons gathered around and clapped Tango and Señora on. The heels of countless heavy boots came pounding down against the wooden floor. Listening to that familiar sound of heels on wood, I could imagine the zapateado, the dancer's footwork, in my youth. I drank the music in, and as I did, I sank deeper and deeper into the memories of my childhood, a past so completely cut off from the present that it might have happened two centuries, rather than two decades ago.

When I closed my eyes, there I was, a girl again, hugging my knees in the dark, my hair billowing, me staring fearlessly into the moonless night. To think, there was a time in my life when nothing frightened me. Sitting by those campfires, I was huddled securely within the circle of singers and twirling dancers, protected by the guitar music flooding my back.

I felt a protection from the world that I haven't felt since. If only those enchanting nights by the campfire, dancing, singing, clapping, could have continued forever. If only my family and I had never ventured forth to America, where I would lose not only my parents, but the entire world, the whole way of life in which I had grown up.

My thoughts were interrupted by Señora, breathless, jolly, collapsing back into her chair. She was flushed, nervous with excitement. Tango kissed the back of her hand and the patrons cheered. Right then, the guitarist switched moods. He launched into a traditional melancholy tune, and his swooning voice filled our ears.

This piece was good and slow, a soulful number that allowed me to drift back into my reverie again.

My eyes closed once more, and I pictured my mother, Regina, her gorgeous hair the same jet black as my own. I saw her clapping and raising her arms overhead, snapping her fingers or playing the castanets. I pictured her lifting the lavish ruffles of her skirt, swirling in the tongues of light thrown off by the campfire. With my father watching, and playing guitar, and smiling and laughing at her from afar, I saw my mother's dazzling eyes, her teasing smile, her black dress rising high up her thighs.

Her skin glistened, and her face was blistered by a brooding look that centered most intensely in her eyes.

Sometimes my father would lay aside his guitar and pay my mother the highest compliment he could by joining her in dancing. The two of them were a ravishingly beautiful couple. My father dropped his arms, and my mother raised hers, and they circled each other in tight unison, their feet hammering the floor. Their heads faced opposite directions, and yet, mysteriously, their smiles, their gazes, were attached, riveted to one another.

Now and then their fingertips brushed, and in that touch, they passed back and forth to each other the soul of the music, even as they shared the rhythm one to another.

In my mother's hair, there was a beautiful peiñeta, the oyster shell comb that her mother, (my grandmother, Anabel, who was Antonie's grandmother too) had given her as a child. In my mother's hand, she is carrying her handsome Andalucían fan. I can see the pretty orange and yellow flowers that seem to be growing out of the lacy black of the fluttering fan. I can see too the delicate black lace shawl around her shoulders, and the fringe on its edge pulsating in time to the wild rhythm of her hands and feet.

The same rhythm comes out of my father's dense patter of footwork. It seems to crawl up through his hips, tipping his shoulders back, pulling his torso straighter, taller, and then, swinging into my mother's hips, staying there, swaying there, and ending finally in the dancing curve of her lips.

"Eso es un duende," Señora whispered to me then, cutting into my memories of my parents once again. I cringed. Duende is the word for the mysterious spirit that forged my parents' people, infused their way of life. Duende is the impulse that has defined their lives, their music, their food and wine, their very passion for living. When my parents died so suddenly, I lost their world in an instant; their music, their dancing, all the singing disappeared and I faced a life devoid, completely purged of animating force.

Sitting there in the bar, my eyes closed, I was dancing with my mother, or my father, or both, my mother who lifted and twirled me as high as her shoulders, my father who exalted me even higher. And faster, too. Finally, I recall dancing with Antonie after I moved to California.

Although completely clumsy (I used to tell him that he had not two but three left feet), and impossible to teach, he was nonetheless an enthusiastic partner in all my childhood dances. He was my one and only student, always devoted, always game to try another step. He would trip and stumble and he often fell. But just the same, he permitted me a luxury, to be endlessly rehearsing for a performance that never came.

Ah, how Antonie encouraged me lingering in my fantasy. For more times than I care to count, he replaced my mother or father when they had disappeared. When I danced with him, I was really holding onto a memory of one or the other of them, or both.

Occasionally as we danced, I would whisper to him, "Oh Antonie, I miss my mother and father so desperately." My cousin would nod and absorb my sad expression, but he would not reply. At other times I would say to him, "Oh my cousin how I miss my 'real' family," and an odd hurt look would shadow his eyes. "You know, Renata, if you would just let me, I could be the best family you ever had." I realize now how much I must have hurt him when I simply turned away, saying only, "No, Antonie, that can never be."

In the bar there, I saw, suddenly, the key to my troubled past with Antonie. Clearly, during childhood, I had used him. Time and again, I had willed him to be something that in the end, I refused to let him be. Through him, and the music we shared, I connected to a time when I had been completely innocent, enjoying happiness with my dear family all around me. Yes, I had needed a family, and willed him to be just that, but then, as soon he made the offer, I withdrew permission.

At that moment, an odd sound roped me back to the bar. Señora was grabbing my arm and screaming for me to open my eyes. I did and what confronted me at first I didn't quite believe. There, ever so slowly descending the staircase into the bar, was a skeleton. Antonie was scowling, and collapsing forward, and hanging on for dear life onto the railing. He was also howling something I could not hear. His steps wavered, keeping an awkward time with the slow and languorous tune progressing from the guitar. Wrapped partially in his disheveled satin bathrobe, and walking barefoot, Antonie's face was pale green and haggard. His body could not possibly have looked more frail, or limp. He was in every way, sagging, a cloth bag with all the contents removed.

Señora and I bolted from our chairs, and quickly met him halfway up the staircase. Antonie leaned into Señora's arm. My attempt to touch him met with a stiff rebuke.

"Don't come near me, you…you whore," he screamed. "I heard you, I heard it all. You've been dancing again, dancing, while I'm up there barely breathing." My mouth dropped open, but no sound poured forth. Pushing me away, he and Señora made it down the stairs and across the bar. She looked back at me, shaking her head, a crushing pity in her eyes.

"Antonie, please, let me help you," I cried. But as I went to his side again, he pushed me away with even more force than before.

"How dare you leave me up there to rot!" he yelled, his words slow and slurred, his lips blurred purple. The whites of his eyes were tinged crimson. "I'm dying and you…you are not the least bit concerned. You sneak downstairs to dance on the bar. I must be crazy to love you as I do." He stumbled and the next thing I knew he was lying in a crumpled heap beside the bar. Señora and I bent to help him, and Tango joined us. Antonie's head was bloodied, and he had smashed his nose.

"Tango, please, please get Dr. Astorga," I cried, cupping Antonie's bashed head in my lap. Someone handed me a bar towel and I mopped his brow. He was hot and his breath was so rotten and sour I had to turn away.

Señora, crying, fell to her knees beside me. She prayed aloud and I prayed too, in silence. I said over and over again, "Please, Mary, please God, please help us. Please we are desperate here, please help my cousin!"

GINA

No warning. Here I am in the hotel bar, cradling Antonie's bloody head.

I look up. I see the brass chandelier with its circle of white candles, the golden flames flickering.

But wait. How can this be? It is now 8:33 in the morning in North Egremont, Massachusetts, and I am sitting in meditation on my living room floor.

No matter. The chandelier overhead begins spinning, so slowly I can hardly see it move.

I close my eyes. I am trying to concentrate on my breathing, on observing my thoughts, on emptying my mind.

Instead, I am in the hotel bar and Antonie's forehead is bleeding into the white cotton skirt of my nun's habit.

"Please, Tango, get the doctor!" I scream. He goes, but so slowly.

After an eternity, Dr. Astorga is kneeling beside me, swabbing my cousin's head with warm soapy water. He wraps the wound with a fresh white bandage that he passes beneath my cousin's chin. I smell iodine and alcohol and sweat. I look up to see Señora with a basin and a rag; she is bathing Antonie's feet.

Señora and Tango and I carry him back upstairs. Astorga has given Antonie something that has put my cousin to sleep.

I tell Señora that I will keep Antonie company until I am absolutely certain he is out.

Señora leaves, and I settle in the chair beside his bed. I decide to pray the rosary. I reach to my waist for my beads. But then I realize my feet are sore, so I need to take off my shoes.

I bend down to unlace the ties. That's when I eye the pale blue pages beneath my cousin's bed.

I reach for the pages and begin to read.

"Bar Dancer."

How could my cousin, in his desperately ill state, still manage to write this filth about me?

I read and read, page after page, and my head spins like a dancer, going faster and faster. I don't want to read my despicable cousin's words. I want to wash myself clean of his endless lies.

"Please, God," I say, "let me go home."

I concentrate on the air passing in and out of the tip of my nose. I focus on the bed where my cousin is lying, inert. I observe the blue pages folded in my hands.

And then it happens. I am sitting on the floor in meditation.

Time passes. I decide to chant the vowels that correspond to each of the seven chakras in my body.

The sound starts in my tailbone and it snakes up my spine to my mouth. My teeth vibrate. My tongue wallows.

The chanting seems like it goes on forever. It is loud enough to carry over into eternity, and certainly, into another century.

12

ANTONIE

"Bar Dancer"

Antonie awakens with the cotton sheet of the bed making a tent over his head. His first sensation is that he is slippery, his back and buttocks pasted to the bed in his own sweat.

Each time he breathes, the sheet comes in and out with him, and with it comes that same metallic taste in his mouth. In his feverish state, he imagines that he is tasting the muzzle of one of his guns.

There is another taste too, the sour twinge of blood, and something else he cannot identify. He fears the taste and the accompanying odor, because there is death lurking in both, the scent is clear evidence, he believes, of his own rapid decay. Gathering his energy into one limp hand, he pulls the sheet from his face. He fills his lungs with fresh air, and he gags, and coughs, and there is immense pain in his chest when he tries to sit up.

Just then, it occurs to him that no one is sitting beside the bed, offering him a cup of water, a teaspoon of soup. There is no one praying or mopping his brow or smoothing his hair or saying soothing things to him in Spanish, as Señora does. No. He is lying in this sickbed very much alone.

Where have Señora and Renata and even Tango gone? He asks himself, how could the three of them have abandoned me when I am so very weak, so terribly hot, when I can barely reach for a glass?

He pushes himself up to both elbows. He knows what he must do. But who will help him? Who will walk the four steps across the room, bend down to the floor, reach for the chamber pot that he's got to use so desperately right *now*?

His lower lip shudders. Utterly exhausted, he falls back onto the bed. In that moment, a flurry of Spanish music fills his head. There is the sound of a guitar, someone playing a fluid arpeggio coming up from downstairs. There is hearty laughter and loud catcalls, too, a raucous of deep voices mixed with glasses slamming on wood, and occasionally, a female voice ringing high above the rest.

Eyes closed, he has a scene before him, and it has a clarity that he hasn't had for weeks. It is the music that calls him, reminds him of a long ago place and time when he and Renata danced as children.

There now is Renata dipping forward, careful even as she swivels and bends, stepping left, then right, making a series of tight turns with one arm curved so gracefully overhead. The whole while she is dancing she also smiling, laughing at his awkward attempts at dancing. Only too painfully, he is reminded that he wasn't the perfect partner.

"Please, go slower, slower," he would plead. Or, "show me again, Renata, just once more show me how to complete the turn." At that, her laughter would ring out.

"Oh Antonie you are hopeless I'm afraid. Will you never manage to learn these steps?" She would resist, but he made her show him again. The ruffles of her dress would twist this way and that, and she would lift her arms and flare her fingers and skirt and proceed. At the end, she would say one sentence that went straight to the core of her motion: "Just make it look like poetry," she declared.

Now, from downstairs, a peel of female laughter erupts. After all these years, Antonie surely knows that laugh. The sound of it creeps like cold water down his spine, and simultaneously, as if stiffening him, it pulls him up into a semi-upright position in his bed. He fumbles for the table, and is hardly able to take the cup of water in two trembling hands. He drinks, water dribbling down his chin. In the next moment, the cup drops, spilling its contents into his lap.

Recoiling, Antonie rolls to one side, and lies there, panting, his mouth wide open, his nightshirt soaked. Again the laughter rises from downstairs, and with it, the guitar gets louder. His eyes fall shut, and now, doesn't he hear the clatter of her metal cleats on wood?

"Dear God, could she...would she...has she actually agreed to dance down there...in the bar?"

His heart gallops as he forces himself to the edge of the bed.

Driven now by a vision of her in the black and red dress, he pushes himself to a sitting position again. He moves his legs off the side of the mattress, and rising unsteadily, he gropes for the mahogany headboard. But wait, this is not his bedroom at home. His hand meets only the wall. Ah but that wall is all he needs, it gives him a place to lean as he stands. Eyes shut, sweat glazing his face, he rises and moves inch by inch toward the door.

"I will...I will get...down there," he groans.

Taking hold of the handle in two hands, he pulls the door open and balances himself against the doorframe. A cheap gilded mirror greets him in the hall, and in the first horrible moment, he wonders who that pathetic creature is, and where he himself went?

His pallor is a deathly purple. His lips are grey and blue. But he pulls his attention away from the mirror. Now is not the time to worry about his appearance. The staircase looms.

Suddenly, a wind catches the door behind him and slams it shut. The sound is enough to push him forward to his knees. He crawls unsteadily toward the first step. When he reaches it, oddly enough, the step begins to blur; then it turns wavy, and actually disappears. He rubs his eyes and the step returns. And there he collapses into the grimy yellow wallpaper of the staircase, a wallpaper of ivy and rosy flowers, a faded pattern greased in years of stains and handprints.

By all rights, that should have been the last step for Antonie, because he is far too dizzy to go any further. But so motivated is he that he fights the lightheaded swinging feeling behind his eyes, and uses every bit of might to extend one skeletal foot further down the staircase. The whole leg trembles. But his foot is sure in purpose, and soon it meets a step exactly halfway down the staircase. Pulling up on the railing, he achieves an upright position. He stands, wavering, staring into the hotel lobby, his eyes fiery bright.

"You…you…" he cackles, and if he could, he would shout out the word he is trying to form: "whore." But nothing emerges. There is not an ounce of air to carry any sound. Instead, he simply glares, his eyes frozen wide. And points one bony finger.

There on a long table in the center of the bar stands Renata, poised, her arms raised, her head thrown back, her throat naked and alluring. Thankfully, he cannot see her face clearly, but he doesn't need to. What he sees in his mind's eye is sufficient to confirm his worst fears: she is wearing the dress.

And worse, she is wearing her most seductive smile. Below her shapely legs, the table is surrounded by leering men, all of them shouting, leaning their glasses and beer mugs inward, raising their fists, grabbing below her ruffles to fondle her thighs, throwing money at her feet.

The words he wants to utter—"I will kill…kill…you…her…and all of you," never come out; he sputters, and bloody yellow foam rises to his lips. Gracefully, as if he is a diver, he tips forward and then his legs give way, and his hand comes loose from the railing and he spills forward like a feather drifting into the wind.

In the next moment he knows only one thing, that he is collapsing, tumbling down the staircase, and that the pounding and slapping of his body failing on the wooden steps is no affirmation of anything but his complete weakness.

At least, though, it brings the sound of the guitar to a sudden halt. Renata, taking in the fact that her cousin is sprawled across the bottom of the stairs, drops to her knees and hauls her ruffled dress to the edge of the table. Hands grope her but with a few swift kicks of her steel-heeled shoes, she fights off her admirers.

She swings her legs to the floor. The shouting rings out: "Hey we want more," and "I paid for a full show, where are you going, sweetheart?" and "What happened, Señorita, the fun's just started."

Renata ignores them all and elbows her way to her cousin.

Crouching beside Antonie, she wipes blood from his lip. Cradling his bruised head, she strokes his tumble of wavy black hair.

"Oh Antonie, I told you to stay in your room," she murmurs.

His mouth is slack, and his coal black eyes fall shut. He wants to spit in her eye, because that's what his gut urges, but he is far too embarrassed. Because in all of the commotion of falling, he has soiled himself, his urine has soaked his cotton gown, and it is still leaking down his legs and the ruffles of Renata's satin dress.

All he can do is lie there, in intense humiliation, glued to the stairs. All he wants to say to her is, "you are no better than a whore!" But he has no breath to speak the words, and not an ounce more energy to move his lips or even to open his eyes and cry.

GINA

Here it is, probably the winter of 1997. I can't remember exactly. I know it was back in what I refer to as FV One, for my FIRST VERSION. I was still trying to come up with a convincing voice for the narrator, Malvina, who was overweight and cranky. (I ditched her after FV One.)

Señora hadn't been to visit me in almost a year. I had started to lose faith. Why exactly was I bothering with this tome?

That's when I decided to try hypnosis. My friend Kellie met me for coffee at Dottie's café in Pittsfield, where I have done a lot of writing.

Kellie is a writer and artist and photographer and an all around fabulous person. We sat down with our steaming cups of latte, and I confided that I was trying to find a hypnotist. Kellie is a friend I can count on, someone who will cheer me on and support all of my crazy ideas.

She smiled. "Great idea, I have a friend who might have a name!"

Long story short, I had a phone number within three days. I called and made an appointment.

The day I arrived in West Stockbridge was snowy and overcast. The staircase up to the hypnotist's Main Street office was creaky and narrow. There was a video store (remember those?) to the left and a funky vintage clothing store on the right. The first thing that hit me at the top of the stairs was the smell of smoky bacon. It was horrifying, and it made my stomach roll.

Then I smelled an equaling strong scent of burning patchouli.

The whole bacon thing may explain why I started out having a kind of uncertain feeling about Susan Coolidge. She was grossly overweight and had stringy brown hair. But she had a lovely smile and lively green blue eyes.

We shook hands and she directed me to a large tan lounge chair that stretched out. She went to the large windows and pulled a black curtain across to darken the room.

"Now Gina, I am going to start to count backward," she said. "And by the time I finish you will feel like you are in a deep state of mind. A soft place. But you will not be asleep. And you will probably not remember much of what you say. I do tape record the sessions so you will have something permanent."

She asked me in a lovely, melodic voice to close my eyes and breathe in deeply.

"Keep holding your breath for a count of five and then release the air out of your mouth, very slowly."

I did as instructed, three times, and then she began to count backward from 30. I know it sounds crazy, but I felt her voice billowing over my ears and settling into my chest. I don't remember when I lost track of the numbers.

All I know is that I was somewhere very very pleasant. I felt like I had been there before, perhaps many times.

"Now Gina, I am going to ask you just a few questions, and then I am going to talk about what you've said. Tell me, why are you here?"

I tried, in a few sentences, to tell her about Señora's visit five years before. I didn't tell her the plot of the novel, but I told her I had been having great difficulty coming up with a convincing voice for the narrator.

"Are you sure there is a narrator?" she asked.

My head started to whirl. I felt confused and disoriented but I knew what I wanted to say. "Of course there is a narrator. You can't write a novel without one."

She smiled. "There are no fixed rules when it comes to art and the mysteries of the subconscious. So tell me a little about the sister."

My heart sped up. I hadn't mentioned Sister Renata. Or Sister Teresa. Or the name of the novel. How could she possibly know about the nun?

"Uh, well, Sister Renata is on trial for murdering her cousin Antonie. She can't prove her innocence because he has been writing lascivious stories about her."

"I see." There was a long silence. "What about your own sisters?" The word sister sank in slowly.

"One of my sisters is ten years younger than me."

"Yes. When I close my eyes, I see her dark hair, there is a cloud of it. And she speaks with a bright star in her voice."

All of this was starting to seem…well, kind of absurd. But I was in a deep state, and it was hard to hold onto thoughts.

"Have you asked Heather to read what you're writing?"

Heather. How the hell did she know her name?

"She has read some of it, yes. She is very supportive, but she can't give me any direction."

"And what about your other sister…hmmm…Cathryn?"

"No," I said, swallowing hard. "Carolyn."

"Sure, yes." She paused. "What I would like to say is that I feel the past becoming more present all the time."

A long period of silence ensued. I was totally in a fog. What was she saying? How did she know so much? It made no sense. Whose past? Whose present?

That's when something completely astonishing and totally upsetting happened.

What came out of my mouth was an ear-piercing scream. A blood-chilling scream that seemed like it went on forever. A scream that sounded loud and desperate enough to carry over into another century.

The screech that erupted in me came with visions. Suddenly I was sitting beside my mother's bed, as I did years ago, when she couldn't breathe because of her asthma. And then I saw bars, like a jail, and I was five years old in the hospital with pneumonia, captive in a crib. I cried and cried and held onto the bars, screaming for my mother. But she never came.

In the next moment, I fell silent. I was standing in a pool of

Antonie's blood. That's when I heard Susan call out to me in her reassuring voice.

"Easy now Gina. Easy."

I felt one of her hands, as thick and strong as a bear paw, pressing down on my shoulder, and when I screamed and thrashed about, she took her other hand and laid it firmly on my forehead.

"Steady, now, Gina," she said. "I'm with you honey. Nothing will happen, I promise."

But it wasn't until she moved her sweaty hand to my mouth, and muffled my scream, that I finally fell silent.

At that moment, Susan started to whisper. "I am now going to count up to 30. And when I reach 30, you will have no more desire to scream. You will no longer hurt, or feel pain of any kind. Your ordinary state of mind will be restored.

I sat up, exhausted. My throat ached from the yelling. It felt like it had been raked with a metal brush. She brought my chair back to an upright position and I sat there, panting.

"Something really threw you for a loop there." Her smile was reassuring and so was her hand on my forearm.

I couldn't speak. I shook my head side to side. Up and down. "Yes," I croaked in a voice that was no more than a broken whisper. "Yes."

"Do you want to talk about this?"

I shook my head again. "No, I just want to go home." For a split second, though, I couldn't remember where home was. I only knew where home *wasn't*: here in this spooky darkened room.

Susan pulled her chair closer. She smelled like lemons. "I would be remiss to let you go just yet. I have a microwave here and I will fix you a cup of tea. With sugar. I hope you will agree to sit here for a few minutes and collect yourself."

So I did.

And as I sipped the tea, Susan sat beside me. She put on some quiet music. Occasionally, she would glance at me. And smile.

"Are you OK to drive?" she asked.

I stared at her but said nothing.

"I've been known to drive patients home," she said, smiling.

"I …I feel…I…I am…confident I can get home." For a split

second I thought I might start screaming again. Oh no, no God, no more. I wrote her a check and left.

Later that day, about five thirty, I was preparing to nap when I had a visit from Señora. She said absolutely nothing. She simply patted my leg. And nodded. She sat there in her splendid shawl, smiling. The next thing I knew I was spilling deep into a dream. Or was it? I was back in the dry golden hills of northern California. Sitting on a blanket under a live oak, sipping lemonade with Sister Teresa.

What was time after all? It kept rolling back and forth like a ball of light. I had absolutely no ability to catch it.

13

SISTER RENATA'S DIARY

August 7, 1883

I hold my face in this fine mist of water falling from the holes in the bottom of the pail, and let the water run over my lips and tongue. The water and the sunlight cleanse me and silently I mouth a prayer of thanks to Sister Teresa for this purifying gift and silently I thank the Lord for sending this good woman to us, but particularly, to me. Holding the washrag in my clasped hands, I bow my head, allow the water to soak my short ruff of hair while I stand there giving thanks and praying, thinking He knew, yes, He knew, how does He do that? How does the Good Lord always know exactly what we need?

Lifting my face, I gently pass the washrag across my brow. How good—how heavenly—this feels. That's the word Teresa used. How good it is to be back from San Francisco, too, every cell in my body is grateful. How hateful that was, how long and miserable the stay, and maybe because of that, I feel like I could stand here, water raining down, drowning out a host of thoughts that I would rather go away. Again I pray, I say a Hail Mary, two, most of all I ask Him how He knew to send Teresa here? How He knew that she would come and that she would be my only ally, she would give me some bit of advice to begin and end each day, and our friendship would grow and grow, and more than that, she would give me the clearest water to cleanse the heat and dust and dirt and sins away.

She brings this gift to me at the very moment I am most in need of cleansing—my body and no less my spirit. I arrived back here in such a dreadful condition, I hate to think what I looked like, my clothes crusted, my soul in the worst state it's ever been. I hid in my room that first morning after Señora pulled up to the convent with the wagon, Antonie lying in the back beneath a heap of blankets. She kissed me once on the forehead and I climbed off the wagon without even a word of goodbye.

Weary is not the word for what I was. Too tired to eat. To sleep.

And that very next day, dearest Teresa completed the project that has now come to my rescue.

For days and days, Teresa had toiled away in the workshed, foregoing lunch (which for Teresa is a major sacrifice) in order to bring to fruition her blueprint for the shower. Often in the past, when we weeded and watered the garden together, she would, as she always does, wonder her ideas aloud to me. One day not so long ago, as she thinned a new planting of carrots, and harvested early radishes, Teresa shared with me her hunch: that she could erect a showering device that would not only refresh us quickly and efficiently but also would save us many gallons of precious water.

I recall her chuckling and running the back of her hand over her sweaty face, as she said the plan had occurred to her that very morning in a vision: the washtub sitting in the crotch of a live oak tree. It was a Saturday, and the idea had come to her fully formed, more or less, during silent prayers.

"It came to you during prayers?" I whispered in horror over my hoe. I was preparing the earth for a row of perpetual spinach. "You were contemplating the construction of a shower in morning chapel?"

Sister Teresa smiled her slyest smile, and the flesh that always presses at the edges of the white fabric binding her face pressed further, and the delicate skin that is always a baby pink turned a bolder shade of rose.

Yes, she said happily, she had already prayed her apologies to Him as soon as the vision had come. And she was prepared to confess as well, to tell Father Ruby in the confessional, that it was the construction of a shower that had preoccupied her for days in chapel.

Sometimes, she argued, God has His reasons for sending His visions the way He does, quite out of the blue. And He had his own timing, too.

"Perhaps," she went on, staring at the tender carrot seedlings poking up from the sandy soil, "He did it today because summer is so broiling hot, and He knows full well what it's like during our worst season for water. In His wisdom, He knows our well almost always goes dry, and He knows water is always in short supply and He knows, or I think He does, that I might have come up with an idea to address the problem." She looked at me, and nodded, and smiled shyly.

Apparently, while I was away, Teresa had made considerable progress on her invention. The second day after I arrived home, we were sweeping and tidying Father Ruby's quarters. Teresa had taken the sheets from his bed, and we were together laying a clean set in its place.

"Would you tell Mother Yolla I plan to work again through lunch?" We had just billowed a white sheet above our heads and now it was floating into place on top of the priest's mattress.

"You are foregoing mid-day meal again?" Lunch was our major meal, and it was now getting to be Teresa's habit not to eat it. And as a result, the waistline of her habit was beginning to swing more loosely across her belly. "But what am I to tell her?"

Teresa's eyes twinkled. "That I am not hungry and quite busy with one of God's directives," she said flatly. Her smile revealed that familiar gap between her two top teeth.

At lunch, I informed Mother Yolla of Teresa's decision to go without food. Mother Yolla's eyebrows rose noticeably higher, and she set her soup spoon down beside her bowl.

"And what is it that occupies the good Teresa's time?" she asked.

"I believe, Mother, that she has some special work of the Lord's to complete, something having to do with hygiene," I said, bowing my head. I averted my eyes and lifted a spoonful of broth to my lips. Mother Yolla said no more. For the next few moments, I said a small prayer of gratitude that the Lord had smoothed the way for Teresa to complete her plan.

Not more than five minutes later, however, we heard a thunderous racket, a clatter of metal on metal coming from the shed. My first thought was that Teresa must be hurt. Several of us, including Mother Yolla, flew from the table to the shed out back. There in the dense heat of the shed, with sweat dripping from her overheated face, stood a smiling Sister Teresa, hammer in hand. She was bending protectively over a pail and getting ready to hit it again. She had already attacked the pail in earnest, apparently, because there were already a score of tiny holes in the bottom surface. Smiling broadly, Teresa bowed her head, and said to Mother that by the time lunch was over, her project would be complete.

"And what exactly would your project be here, my good Sister?" Mother Yolla wore her sternest countenance, and her arms were crossed in a kind of armor over her ample bodice. Her wrinkled hands disappeared into the sleeves of her habit.

"My project, good Mother Yolla, is a shower," Teresa replied triumphantly. By then a small crowd of nuns had gathered in the shed. I eyed Teresa's face intently, looking for signs that she would falter. Had it been me, and had I seen the fierce look on Mother Yolla's face, I would be on my knees, begging forgiveness for missing lunch and for insisting on doing something that had come so suspiciously from my imagination.

But not Teresa. She stood in silence, and then gestured to the holes in the pail. "The water will trickle down through these holes," she said, gesturing to the pail. And above it there will be a washtub with a hole, so all I need now is the washtub…"

"My good Sister," Mother Yolla interrupted, her thin lips thinner than ever. "Who told you that you were free to destroy a pail? Have you any idea how difficult each of these is to obtain? Or what the expense is for the convent to replace them? Have you? I ask you again, who told you that…"

"With all due respect, my good Mother," said Teresa, genuflecting as if she faced an altar. "But it was the Lord Himself who instructed me to find the pail, and now, the washtub."

Mother Yolla's mouth dropped into that settled O of hers, and her eyes shot saucer wide, and for a moment I thought perhaps her face had frozen that way. But as soon as Sister Teresa rose from her knees, her head bowed and her hands clasped in prayer, I saw the Reverend Mother's expression ease.

"Yes, Mother, I swear to you," Teresa whispered rapidly now, "this is exactly what the Lord instructed me to do. Who knows His ways better than you. Perhaps you would be so kind as to guide me further in this endeav…"

"Silence!" Mother Yolla spoke the word like a dagger. Her lips folded in on themselves, and in a moment, Mother Yolla began to look so much older, more wrinkled, than she was. Her wrath sent a shudder through both my arms, my legs, and my knees felt shaky. I wondered what effect the Reverend Mother's look must be having on dear Teresa.

Glancing at my friend, however, I had no way of knowing, as her face was directed toward the earth. I stood there, praying for my bold companion.

A long period of silence followed. Without being instructed, the rest of us began to disperse.

One by one, heads bowed, we filed out of the shed until only Teresa and Mother Yolla were left.

It wasn't clear how Mother Yolla would resolve this impasse. Her exasperation with Teresa was as clear as the blue sky. And it was nothing new to any of the rest of us, as Teresa was too brave, too inspired, to be sufficiently deferential and polite. Still, we also knew how fearful Mother Yolla was of displeasing the Lord, of interfering, as she put it, with "His most mysterious wishes and inexplicable ways."

What exactly transpired next will always remain a mystery. Suffice it to say that in the end, Sister Teresa was provided her washtub, and the two heavy chiseled beams she needed to suspend the tub and pail from the live oak. Looking back, it seems a miracle to me, but then, when one knows my dear Sister, one knows that Teresa indeed does surpass reality.

The very next day, there was suspended from the oak a makeshift shower. At first, not one of us modest nuns was willing to wash our faces or even our hands from the water dripping from the pail. That was before Teresa attached two sheets to the branches holding the washtub, to afford some privacy. Once she had the sheets in place, I volunteered to wash behind the shed. God knows I needed it!

Teresa, her habit pulled tight around her ample hips, mounted the ladder over and over, lifting pails, slowly spilling into the washtub water she took from the well. She made some twenty trips up and down the ladder to fill our shower. Even with all that toil and climbing, she remained gleeful. She went back and forth across the scrubby yard until she was out of breath, trampling sagebrush as she toted the water. Several of the nuns gathered around her, teasing her soundly.

"Don't slip," they cried. And, "All those water trips are bound to make you thin." I for one offered repeatedly to help her in the task of toting water, but she was determined to complete the gift of water by herself, at least, as she put it, in this early "testing" phase.

And so this is how I came just yesterday to be the first and principal beneficiary of Teresa's invention. When she was satisfied that there was enough water for a "proper spray," she instructed me to "hop to." That was my signal to disrobe. I hesitated, and a cry went up from the rest of the nuns gathered, but Teresa hushed us with her curt statement: "Oh blessed me, we see each other in the flesh every single day, but if you must, then just turn your foolish eyes away."

And so I put aside my clothes, letting the black habit slip into the dust. And she recovered it just as quickly and hung it on the nail that she had hammered into the side of the tree. The rest of my clothes disappeared and then, there, was me, bare of any cover.

I wrapped a towel tightly around my middle and stepped inside the circle of the sheet. Before I knew it, Teresa removed the plug in the washtub and I heard a little trickle of water pouring into the metal pail overhead, and then, before I was fully ready, I felt the cool water as it came sprinkling onto my forehead, then down my neck and chest. I screeched and jumped back, and then began enjoying the spray.

All around me, from the nuns ringing the shower, there rose up a cheer. As cool water rinsed my sweaty face and chest, there was a ragged clapping and yelling. When I looked up, I saw Teresa at the top of the ladder, peering down at me, her face flushed and plump and pinkly triumphant. I smiled up at her and gave a small wave and in that instant it came to me out of the clear blue, like an ethereal cloud appearing suddenly in a sunny sky, what plan the Lord had for me.

It was my duty to be available to my poor cousin Antonie until the end. I was destined to be his nurse and caretaker, to offer solace and all the comfort he needed during his impossibly difficult illness.

At the same time, I was also destined to come here behind the shed to the live oak tree, to Teresa's shower, where I would wash myself in cool water and free myself of all the ugliness and soiled thoughts that Antonie had released on and about me.

Realizing God's plan, I closed my eyes, and drank in that moment when I stood in the shower.

And now, every time I am standing there, I do the same. I let God's plans rain down on me. I accept them. I whisper, "Thy will be done." And as I write this now, I realize: Teresa's shower is some kind of glorious confessional for the body, one of Mother Nature's doing through Teresa.

GINA

Who knows what day it was? What year?

I step into the lovely Italian marble shower in my bathroom and suddenly I know in my body that I am the nun. I feel the water trickling over my shoulders.

In the same moment, I remember this: my Italian grandfather Gino, used to chase me around the house yelling "Sheester Gina, Sheester Gina," because he couldn't pronounce the word sister.

Why did he do this?

Because, at the age of four, I announced to my mother that I wanted to be a nun.

14

SISTER RENATA'S DIARY

August 25, 1883

I have the smell of blood and slaughter so thickly steeped in my lungs that I feel myself a beast. And when I close my eyes, my mind is reeling, dancing in blood.

Perhaps by writing I will expunge it. I must try.

Mother Yolla forced my hand to the ax today. She insisted I perform the dreaded task early this morning, because dear Teresa, the convent's chief poultry assassin, has been stricken with the same stomach virus that has beset at least eight others this week.

Each nun who falls ill gets so feverish and dizzy and has such intense head and stomach pain that she is forced to lie on her back, flat as a pancake. I make a point of saying a special prayer daily for all of the ill, and one too, to keep myself healthy.

The summer air hung thick and still over the golden hills when I awoke this morning.

I stepped outside the back door and uncovered the tin washbasin. The sun even at 7 a.m. was braising, and the air was quivering. Despite the heat, I found the morning something of a blessing, and began humming a bit of the alegría I had been trying to teach Teresa before she took ill.

I was just scrubbing the rings out of one of Father Ruby's collars and enjoying the cool splash of water on my arms, when I saw

Mother Yolla leave the rectory and cross to the convent courtyard where I was standing. As she approached, I could see that the intense heat had her breathing with difficulty.

"I must ask you to kill three chickens for me today," she announced. I squeezed the collar I was scrubbing.

"Oh Holy Mother," I wailed. "I'm not...oh please reconsider. There must be someone else at the convent who can do this chore. It's not that I don't want to help, but I have never killed a chicken before and more than that I...well, I hoped I would never have to, as I do so firmly believe that there is a universal life spirit inhabiting each and every being, all of God's creatures, even those so humble as the chickens and..."

"Oh Renata please stop this babbling at once!" Mother Yolla interrupted, swatting the air with impatience. Beneath her eyes were deep circles, the color of smudged ashes. "I am so weary with nursing the others. Half the convent can't stand up straight and the rest of us are on the verge of falling over. It will be a miracle if the entire lot of us doesn't end up ill. I know full well that you hate the idea of killing chickens, but there are, I assure you, much worse things. All of us, ill and healthy, need a good meal and I have no one else to ask. So I beg you not to challenge me or to question my motives in assigning you this task."

"But..."

"No BUTS." Her words sliced the air like a sharp blade. "I need the chickens prepared for a special meal tomorrow. We are expecting a guest of Father Ruby's, an itinerant priest passing through on his way back to New Mexico. Father is so anxious that we make a good impression. And so we will not disappoint him. Now please leave the collars to soak in the sun, and attend to the chickens immediately."

With that, Mother Yolla retreated into the convent. I followed her with my eyes, eyes that were filling quickly. "I can't," I cried, speaking softly. "Oh Mother Yolla, please don't make me because I just can't."

Try as I might, I could not hold back my tears. Nor could I block a vision arising in my mind: that of Teresa, chasing fowl. Slowed as she is by excess weight, Teresa sometimes pursues a chicken from one end of the yard to the other before she pounces on her victim. I marvel then, to see her wrestle the awkward squawking bird to the ground, wings writhing and askew.

Moments later, with the chicken's neck stretched and pinned to the chopping block, the head flies, courtesy of Teresa's swift ax. When the chicken's head is free of its body, the bird goes into what Teresa calls its death dance, a spirited strut around the yard spurting blood from its open neck like a small fountain.

Teresa tells me that she does the job of killing so quickly that the birds "never know the blade." Ah, but I am not convinced. It is my opinion that as soon as they eye the chopping block, the wood thoroughly caked in the liver-colored evidence of earlier murders, those chickens have some primitive understanding of the fate that awaits them. I said as much to Teresa, but she told me to save my worry. "I applaud your delicate concern for God's feathered creatures, but we all have to eat."

Once I appeared just as she was completing a particularly messy kill. She had slaughtered half a dozen fowl, enough to feed several extra guests. The blood dripped down the lower half of her skirt, and her shoes were feathered. "Oh how dreadful," I said, staring into the slick red pools. "How will you ever clean all this up?"

Teresa's large hands were bloody and red swaths zigzagged her face. She answered in a thick spray of brogue.

"Ah just be glad Renata that we are blessed enough to have chickens to kill. Had we not the chickens, you see, you and I both might be out chasing wild turkeys from morning to night."

I abandoned the tin basin and made my way to the chicken house at the slowest pace two feet might go. I had never held a pair of rubbery chicken legs in my hand, but somehow I knew the feeling now, I knew exactly how tough and wiry the fowl's limbs would be. I stood at the picket fence, staring at the pointed yellow beaks and the wild black eyes of the birds as they took their jolted steps around the yard. A chill shuddered me.

"Ever faithful I am to you Lord, but now, here, I say I cannot do what Mother Yolla commands. I need Your help to complete this awful task. I ask you to guide me through." I remained there praying in silence.

My hands wobbling, I stepped through the gate. The chickens scattered to four corners of the yard, pecking the dry ground, frantically poking and thrusting their heads in that jagged motion that leads them scurrying forward. Holding my breath, I hurried after one particularly fat white fowl, its wattle wobbling furiously beneath its beak.

Then, when that one danced off, I turned to chase a thinner but larger bird, brown as a walnut. That bird too evaded me. "Oh God please help me to do this," I whispered, bowing my head. "Please, I didn't ask for this and it is a complete mystery how and why it should be done."

If God was listening to me, His answer was only another loud chorus of raucous birds. "Bock, bock, bock," rang out through the busy yard. Sweat gathered on my brow and in my armpits. I covered my ears in despair and sank slowly to sit in the bare dirt.

I stayed that way long enough that the birds began to gather around me, and soon I was circled by a cackling thicket of brown and white feathers. I cringed, and opened my palms and before I knew exactly what was happening, a large white chicken with two eyelets of yellow on its wings approached and set its red spiky claws within inches of my hand. My eyes widened and my fingers followed and soon I held the chicken by one leg.

"Ayeeeya!" I cried, jumping to my knees, and dangling the bird in one outstretched arm. The bird was splayed in five directions, wings stretched, legs askew, beating and pulling, wildly determined to get free. I too felt pulled apart, half of me wanted desperately to set the animal down. But now that I had made my catch, something else, something new arose in me too. I tightened my grip around the rubbery twig that was the leg.

A fierce dance ensued, with the chicken leading me. Twisting and whipping this way and that, the flailing fowl shed feathers in a desperate effort to break my grasp. "Oh I am so so sorry," I cried, half to the bird, and half to me. But nothing could be heard above the ear squall pouring from the chicken's beak, and from all the rest of the birds.

It was time, I knew, to twist the bird's neck, the way Teresa would, either that, or set the creature free. Toward the chopping block I stuttered, eyeing the ax that would do its duty. An odd pain shot up the back of my neck, and quivered across my hips, as I contemplated the job ahead. It would take a good aim to catch the swinging bird by the neck. I couldn't see how I would manage to grab the chicken and at the same time, avoid being impaled by the nail-like points of the open beak.

As my mind scrabbled in confusion, I recalled telling Teresa that I believed an animal's fear in the face of death had to translate into the condition of the meat that graced the plates on the dinner table. I suggested that it might be a good idea to place a burlap bag over the chicken's head before approaching with the ax. Teresa was chasing a pair of Rhode Island reds as I said this. She didn't honor me with an answer.

"My dear Renata," she called out, "I am almost on these two, and so I hope you know to stay clear when the heads fly off. Because these chickens will keep dancing about the yard, headless, and the blood flooding out of the open neck is no pretty sight, certainly not for one with a weak stomach."

At that, Teresa grabbed one of the prancing reds, and with the swiftest and surest moves I've ever seen, she twisted the neck in her two capable hands, as if instead of a flesh and blood chicken she held a soft towel for drying dishes. Instantly, the bird limped into her bosom, and within moments, Teresa had it straddling the wooden block.

"Thwunk," went the ax under the nun's powerful arm, and with that, the fowl's head spun off, and so too did my eyes and stomach. I proceeded quickly into the convent, where I spent most of the day, praying. At dinner, facing the bird on the platter, I complained of stomach pain and had nothing to eat at all.

But now the situation here called me to duty. I cinched the neck, and twisted, but the fowl didn't go limp. This proved my undoing. I swung the bird to the block, and then struck wildly with the ax but as I did, the bird flip flopped across the stump. I had a firm lock on one of the chicken's legs, but that was all, and the situation unnerved me totally.

Every feather, every muscle, every ounce of bird was determined to escape my falling blade. Between the frenzy of feathers and the squalling jumping chicken flesh, I had all I could do to get the ax to land close to the bird.

After several tries, and with my right arm tiring, I finally caught the bird with the blade, but it wasn't the neck that I made contact with. The blade cut across the breast of the chicken, splitting the cavity partially open. Blood spit out and hit my face. A sickening sound came out of the fowl, awful to my ears. It seemed only to turn my horror worse.

The sight of the blood and the horrible noises coming from the bird set off some perverse chain of events. Sickened by what I'd done, by what I was about to do, I became that much more determined to finish the job, to end it as fast as I could. But the harder I tried to put the chicken out of its misery, the more misery I inflicted and the sicker I became. Each thwack, each slice into the chicken's body, turned my horror and the carnage worse.

There I stood, pummeling and slashing at the bird with the ax, hitting and missing, hitting and missing, something wholly evil coming over me. I struck until the bird was a bloody mutilated pulp, one however that was miraculously still making noise and still jumping and hopping around the chopping block.

Through most of this torture, I was numb, surely, to what I was doing. But suddenly, maybe because I was out of breath from wielding the ax, I paused momentarily, and something reached inside me. I saw the sorry state of the fowl, saw what desperate violence I was visiting on such an innocent creature, and I proceed to vomit.

When I was finished, I began howling for Mother Yolla. My screeching arose from a place far deeper than any I knew. It was hardly a human sound at all, and certainly not one the nuns knew. I continued, though, screaming to the heavens, begging her to come. Soon enough, she came as did one or two of the other nuns.

All of them I think feared the worst, that a bobcat or grizzly had made his way into the yard, and was hard in pursuit of me or the chickens. When they reached me, and saw the condition of the chicken, they simply stared, so stunned were they at what greeted their eyes. I had stopped axing, and now I was bawling and all covered in vomit and blood. The poor axed fowl, meanwhile, had been savagely chewed up by the ax, but was still alive, still twitching and squawking a sickly, dying squawk. I had such a thick taste of blood and feathers in my mouth I started to vomit again, but nothing was coming up.

"Hand me that ax!" Mother Yolla commanded, rushing to relieve me of the weapon. In my state of confusion, I suddenly feared for my life. Stricken by guilt, and utterly unhinged, I honestly thought that the older nun intended to strike me instead of the chicken. I started to back away.

"Give me that ax now!" she yelled, forcing the handle from my grasp. The next moments seemed to go in slow motion: Mother Yolla raising the ax, the blade catching the sly glint of the midday sun, the ax falling and slicing clean through the chicken's neck and then stopping dead, coming to rest in the wood of the block.

The mutilated chicken didn't do the strutting death dance that a headless fowl ordinarily would. True, a small fountain of blood bubbled up from the open neck. But the pitiful creature couldn't move because I had hacked away the leg that I hadn't been holding tight. Minus one limb, and its head, the bird was nothing more than a heap of bloody feathers on the stump.

The wings flapped and the bird pumped its final flood of life onto the ground. A hush fell, and all around me got dreamy. My eyes rolled and I started to fall. All I remember is slumping into Sister Peters, and reaching out to take Mother Yolla's free hand.

15

ANTONIE

"Roseblood"

Renata didn't expect Antonie to summon her to the hacienda that day. When Tango arrived at the convent late in the morning, a hot muggy day, she was pulling up beets and harvesting cauliflower and broccoli.

"Señora says please, you must come right now," he said. She stared at the slight man, his straight jet black hair tied in a ponytail. She considered ignoring the plea. But how could she deny Señora?

When the wagon pulled up before the hacienda, Señora was waiting at the front door, more anxious than Renata had ever seen her before. "He wants you upstairs," she whispered, her large eyes wide and her hands twisted around each other. "He is acting…not himself today."

"Has he eaten?" Renata asked as she followed Señora inside. The older woman, who looked smaller than usual, almost child-sized, shook her head.

Speaking in Spanish, Señora proceeded to describe Antonie's supper the night before. She had prepared him chicken broth and a slice of boiled tongue and the sweet red pepper paste that he loved so much to spread on tortillas and bread. She cooked the plump peppers to a pulp, then mashed them so smooth that he didn't have to chew at all. Still, he had eaten practically nothing off his plate, Señora said, sadly shaking her head. "He has eaten nothing this morning."

"Come como un pájarito," she whispered. "He eats like a bird."

Renata mounted the stairs and knocked on Antonie's door. She waited no more than a few seconds before proceeding inside. Thick white candles burned on either side of his majestic bed. He lay there, mouth wide, his head tipped back so far that candlelight played on the profile of his chin and throat.

"Antonie?" she whispered, leaning close to his face. "Antonie, do you hear me?" He slept on, and she settled in the leather chair there beside the bed. His chest rose and fell in an easy rhythm.

Eying the guitar that leaned, as always, against the wall to the left of his bed, she picked up the instrument and began to strum. A bulería first, and then a favorite sigiriya—the death march from Catalonia—the one she had written herself. She let each note ring out on the strings, but he slept through even the loudest playing. It was only after three folk songs, when she began the first long strokes of the malagueña, that he woke with a start.

"Buenos días," she said, putting aside the guitar. His eyes fluttered and when he was finally fully awake, he sat up on his elbows. His face was creased in anger.

"It's about time you come," he whispered. "I've been waiting for so many days."

"You must be confused," she said. "I was here the day before yesterday." He stared at her blankly.

"Please lay back down," she insisted. "And if you do, I'll play for you."

He shook his head. "No," he said in a commanding voice. "I want you to stay, to dance for me. In fact, I insist on it."

She got up from the chair, leaned over him, and pulled the covers up to his chin. "I don't think so," she said. "I am here for a couple of hours. Let me make you some tea and…"

"NO!" he screamed, pushing the covers—and the suggestion of tea—away with his hand. His voice came out high and thin, a reedy whisper, as if he was speaking through a very thin tube. "I am not interested in tea. You know very well what I want Renata. I want you to dance. And more than that. You know what I need and I am tired of begging for it. Now hurry. Go into the next room, and get dressed in the red satin, the outfit you know I prefer for you."

She sat back down. She was frowning. So many times before she had simply yielded to him, quietly submitting to his authority. He would command her to dance and she would retire to the next room, the one with the oak chest and the round mirror, and she would proceed to remove her black habit and don the ruffled red satin dress.

As she put the dress on, she would also don the identity he loved, that of the Spanish dancer. Today, though, she was in no mood for that.

"I'm sorry Antonie," she said, eyeing him with a dark look, "but I am not going to dance for you today. And if you keep this up, I will not be dancing anytime soon!"

Antonie's face crumpled. He fell back on his pillow. "But I was counting on you," he begged. "I was looking forward to this more than you know. It's been weeks and you promised that the next time you came that you would..."

"Hush!" Renata placed her fingertips over his purplish lips. "Things happen my cousin to change what we promise. Isn't it enough that I've come here today to visit?"

Slowly, Antonie gathered the strength to sit up. He spoke slowly and with intense anger. "I have no more patience with you," he began. "For too long you have played with my feelings. You have denied my love and affection. I won't tolerate that anymore."

She sighed a bored sigh. And smiled. "Well I'm afraid that you have no choice in the matter." She looked away. "So once again I will bring you a cup of tea and some..."

"STOP!" Antonie was breathing hard. "I ...I didn't want it to come to this...but now..." His voice trembled.

She shook her head. "Why are you making this fuss today?"

A strange leer came across his face. He sat in silence, contemplating her for a moment.

She turned to face the other direction.

"So if you must know," he said, "that I have decided to expose our relationship to those in the community who would be interested."

Renata pivoted and glared at Antonie. "You wouldn't do that, I know very well you are bluffing and…"

"Ha!" He extended one bony finger. "I have prepared a letter, to be delivered to the newspaper, that describes the way you visit me, with Father Ruby's permission. I have written about the ways in which you please me, how in addition to nursing me, you shave me, sing to me, play the guitar and dance in provocative dresses…"

Her eyes flew wide. "You wouldn't do any such thing. You have no intension of exposing your miserable life to all the world."

He laughed, and kept on laughing, until she leaned over and slapped his face. His hands flew to his cheek, and his eyes filled with fire.

"I will also be sending a similar letter to Mother Yolla," he said, "telling her how it is that you meet my every need. And how experienced you are in satisfying the sexual desires of a male animal like me."

"YOU WOULDN'T DARE!" She tried to slap him again, but he was ready with his arms crossed. He grabbed her shoulders and pulled her off balance, and she fell onto the bed.

"Oh, but my darling, I would indeed dare. And I will, unless…"

She yanked herself away from him. Her face was grim and tears had started spilling out of both eyes.

"Unless what? You wouldn't dare reveal a thing, because you know that they would stop me from ever coming here again."

"Yes, perhaps they would. But you my darling would be cast out of the convent. And who knows where you would go? Or how you might end up. Perhaps you would make a life for yourself as a dancer in a bar or a café?

"SILENCE ANTONIE!" Renata screeched as loud as she had ever yelled. "And what did I tell you about calling me YOUR DARLING!" Her eyes went wide. "I am NOT your darling!"

Antonie started laughing again. But this time he stopped himself. "There is of course a way to stop my letters from leaving this room." He smiled, revealing a tooth missing from the side of his mouth.

Renata saw the glee in his smile. She started shaking her head.

"You can't make me do a thing," she said, her lips in a vicious twist. "I would rather rot than give into your putrid desires. Your body, your face, disgust me!"

Antonie sat forward. She had never spoken to him like this before.

In the past, she toyed with him, she teased him, and on rare occasions she gave in to him. But she had never revealed her feelings like this.

"You slut! You have done it now. I have loved and adored you more than my own self, Renata. But you are cruel and hateful, and now you will see how cruel and hateful I can be!" He dropped back to the pillows.

Now it was her turn to laugh at him. Her laughter grew louder and louder and more raucous.

"STOP!" he yelled, covering his ears. "STOP!" Who was this woman he faced? Who had erased his darling cousin, Renata, and replaced her with this vicious demon?

She stopped. And then her face turned grave and serious. She turned, walked to the mirrored dresser and picked up his razor. Her eyes gleamed in a dark and eerie way. She carried it slowly back to his bed.

"Renata, please, my cousin, don't fool with me like this. Please!"

She lifted the razor, and the way she was holding it over the candle, the light of the flame glinted off the steel blade. "I will indeed stop fooling with you Antonie, that is, if you are willing to drop this nonsense and stop threatening me."

Antonie pulled the covers up to his chin. He had never observed Renata behaving like this. What had happened to her? Where had his sweet cousin disappeared?

"I want you to know something Antonie." Her eyes narrowed. "All this time you have "donated" money to the convent, in exchange for..." here she paused and her face darkened with hatred... "for my services," she nodded, and lifted the razor and set one of her delicate fingertips against the sharp blade, "all this time you have done this, you have made me feel so...low. So much like chattel, like chicken or cattle, something that has been purchased, sold, as though I am the meat you buy for the evening meal."

Her eyes were full of fury now. "For this, Antonie, I will never ever forgive you as long as I live." She had the razor in two hands—the razor she had so often used to shave his face. She brought it right up to the skin of his throat.

He was crying now, and he was frightened. "I...I am so so sorry Renata, my dear cousin," he said, his purple lips trembling. "You know it was simply because I loved you so much. I will...I will..but I must have you. I must. I am drowning in my desire, I cannot keep living this way... please!"

She grabbed him by the throat and squeezed his neck. She took the razor and nicked the skin at his throat. He screamed.

And then perhaps frightened of what she had done, she threw the razor on the floor and stood staring at him. They remained like that for a few moments. "Oh dear cousin," he whispered, holding his hand to his bleeding neck, "I hope...I hope that...you must not leave! You won't go running off now will you? All of this is so silly, unnecessary, we can repair our love. Perhaps tonight, tonight if you stay you can dance and..."

His face was small and childlike. His voice craven and trembling. His mood desperate.. He reached for her, but she moved away and he rolled half onto the floor.

"Have you heard anything I've said to you?" she screamed. "I am not dancing anymore. I am done dancing. And I am done with this filth that passes for your romance. Your ridiculous fantasies. Father Ruby be damned. I will no longer do your bidding, and his, as I am nothing but a...a.." The word wouldn't come. Finally, "sinner" emerged in a whisper. And then one more word.

Whore.

"No, no, not that, not that at all," he called out, and it took every last ounce of his energy to speak. "Please my dear cousin don't do this to yourself, or to me, please, it brings me such pain to hear you speak like this."

If he could have, at that moment, he would have taken her in his arms and covered her with kisses. He would have whispered, "My darling, my darling, please don't cry. Let's forget all that we have said in anger." He would have taken her into his bed, as he had from time to time before, and they would have stayed together for the day.

For her part, the words she had spoken were out of her mouth now, and it was as if they had finally reached her own ears. She listened to them and realized the folly of what she was saying. She was trapped in this sordid life with Antonie. There was no getting out of it…unless…"

She picked up the razor and stared at it for a long time. She wiped the blood away with her fingers, and then stared at the blood on her hand.

Then, moving slowly, she carried it back to the dresser and set it down. "I'm leaving now," she said.

"Oh please don't leave me! How can you be so cruel?" He reached out one thin hand.

Ignoring his pleas, she headed quickly toward the door. And that is how she left him, without even a glance backward, his hand hanging limp over the floor.

GINA

On some October morning (I'm not sure what day or what year it was!), I woke before six o'clock a.m. My eyes weren't even open when I knew that I had to go right to the guitar, just as I had so often in the old days.

After such a long time without music, here I was now desperate to do it. I sat up and gently kissed a sleeping Joel on the forehead.

I peed and put on the flowered shawl that Señora had given me the first time she appeared. I hurried downstairs.

Yawning, I tuned the guitar and suddenly I was yearning to see Señora.

I played an alegría, and soon I was singing, words began pouring out of me as if they were silvery water flowing down a snowy mountain quickly melting into spring.

She wears white, she wears white,

She wears her cotton dress

tightly bosomed in flowers.

I wait here, I wait here

And soon she appears, her eyes are live coals,

her skin the color of mud,

She is here as flesh and blood,

But she is here as spirit too,

Pure air, pure air, pure spirit,

Ah, she is here, the Señora I adore.

Maybe because I was so relaxed, or maybe because I was really half asleep, playing guitar felt more natural, more comfortable than it had ever felt before. It was as if I had never stopped. Oh I wish my teacher Maria could see me now!

The strings kept ringing out beneath my fingers, the words flooded from my throat. I felt the flamenco surging through me and I didn't concern myself with any wrong notes. I played the A major chord, and did the rasqueado strum, with just the right amount of pressure, the light-handed technique that Maria always used to impress on me. Then I slid my left hand down the strings, with my fingertips squeaking, playing the A with two flats on the first fret.

I let the chord ring out, and suddenly, I stopped.

I swear I heard something. Or someone. Speaking.

Could it be?

I looked around. Stared into the dark corners of the room.

Nothing.

I put the guitar down and went to the kitchen for matches and then I lit the white taper, the one that Señora brought with her that very first time she visited me.

And in the light of that single candle, I picked up the guitar and started into my chords again. In the glow of the taper, I played the alegría with all my heart and soul and prayed that Señora would appear.

Over and over I played the A chord, sliding my fingers down the fret, back and forth I went, because I love that progression so much. And then I switched to the D chord, and went back and forth between the D and its parallel chord on the first fret, two flats. Two flats. And maybe that was what did it, something about my playing this configuration of the D chord on the first fret. It got my heart thrumming. It got something pulsing, ringing from my fingertips right up through my forearms and elbows and shoulders.

I stopped. I looked up. I gasped.

There she was, filling the rocking chair, comfortably wrapped in another flowered shawl, this one black with red and white roses. She was smiling and nodding to me. Wide faced, gentle, she was a cracked image: broken teeth, chipped nails, her housekeeper skin so soft and mud-colored and smelling of soap and cream and corn tortillas roasting over an open flame.

"Oh Señora," I said, and laid the guitar aside.

"No, no, por favor, play your guitar!"

And so I played with even greater joy. I gave the sweet little rasqueados more articulation, each fingernail uncurling, springing, zinging across the strings. Those rasqueados ring out, so light, so airy, that I am carried, lifted up with the music, just the way Maria used to tell me should happen with flamenco, when the duende infuses the music and brings it deep into your soul, right into the center of your chest, where it pulses and makes the rest of your body come alive.

I sang the words to the alegría, too, but as I did, I realized that they were in English, and not Spanish. So, how was she to understand?

But no matter, she was Señora and she was there, adoring the music, her skin milky brown, her white cotton dress, bosomed in flowers. She rocked side to side and I played and sang to her, my silly words filling the air:

Here she is, now, the tree of joy,

Here is Señora, sprouted from the air,

See her heart, the soft pulp of hibiscus.

See her eyes, coins of darkness,

They arise, they come alive,

They are as black as the blackest eyed Susans.

I switched to a joyful bulerías, the one I love, and I played it through, improvising on the chord progressions, and singing whatever words came to me right on the spot. Señora got clapping in time with the beat and at the end, she applauded me.

"Magnifico, m'ija," she said, and I felt pride surge through me. I bowed slightly. I was in a minor state of euphoria.

"Muchas gracias, Señora. Ah, Señora, te gusta café?" She nodded, and we went together to the kitchen and I made a pot of my favorite Arabian mocha java, and we shared it together.

And as we sipped the hot liquid, I realized why I had summoned her.

"Tengo una pregunta muy importante, Señora," I said.

"Sí, m'ja."

"Will I ever finish this story?" I tell her how impossible it feels, so difficult that I am not sure I am capable. "No estoy seguro," I said.

"Ah, sí," she replied. And smiled. "No te preocupas." Not to worry.

"Pero es una problema muy grande," I say, waiting for her to agree.

But she just looked at me. She nodded very slowly. I watched those dark eyes of hers. They were depthless. And yet, light seemed to arise from those orbs. Light that shifted. Suddenly I felt like I was looking into two dark crystal balls.

All of a sudden I knew exactly what I had to do.

I stood up. Maybe it was the coffee. Or the idea. But I was suddenly buzzing. I was so excited that I felt like I could—dance. I stood up and grabbed the old woman's hands. She comes up only to my shoulder. She giggled and I laughed, and we began dancing around the kitchen.

"Sevillanas," she cried out, referring to the famous flamenco dance from the city of Sevilla.

I grabbed her hand, and we began, a bit clumsy to be sure, but laughing as we turned to one side and then another, moving in tight circles around the kitchen.

A day or two later, I felt a strong impulse to write. Perhaps Señora was right, I just had to stop worrying. And I had to start playing guitar every day!

16

SISTER RENATA'S DIARY

September 7, 1883

How did I end up in this miserable jail cell? How did my life turn upside down in one bloody afternoon?

I sit here trembling so much that I can barely hold the pen. When I tried yesterday, I couldn't hold it at all. But I know if I don't write it today, I will collapse onto this grimy jail floor.

This is what happened. I swear I am guilty of no crime. I'm still trying to absorb what happened to Antonie—and to me—some three excruciating days ago.

There we were, Señora and me, discovering him on the floor, we were so helpless, kneeling, screaming, crying, our knees sliding in gore, our aprons soaked scarlet red. We found him there, poor Antonie, he lay limp, lying on his side.

His face drained almost as white as this diary paper. *His head tilts back at the horrific gash, Dear Mother of God, my cousin's throat is ripped one side to the other!* His lips are bloody, his eyes wide and black. But still he breathes a faint breath. What has he done here? What has he done?

I know AS GOD IS MY WITNESS THAT I'M not to blame. I know THERE WAS NO CRIME. NO CRIME. None at all. I know how desperately we, Señora and me, tried to save him. I know too that I'm trapped here, inside this cell, chained at the ankle. Drained of energy. Staring out of that tiny barred window into the courtyard at the gallows where the toothless jailer says they will hang me.

There I was on Wednesday morning, three days ago, peacefully living at the convent. I was in the kitchen, speaking to Mother Yolla, telling her that I planned to weed the cabbage and broccoli garden. I wore my long white apron over my habit.

There wasn't a moment of warning.

Suddenly I heard a man's voice at the door. "Mother Yolla?" he asked, knocking sharply.

She opened the door.

"I'm sorry, Mother Yolla," he said, stepping inside. "I'm sorry ma'am, for giving you no warning, but we're here to arrest one of your novitiates. Sister Renata. We are charging her with first degree murder for killing her cousin."

I gasped. Mother Yolla looked stunned. How could this happen?

The next thing I knew, he put me in handcuffs and pulled me out of the door of the convent.

And so began my agony. They brought me here. This is only the third day in the cell but it feels like I have been here for three years!

Teresa visited me the second night—they refused her entry the first. She carried a basket of food and tucked underneath the flaxen towels, she buried my diary and a pen and ink.

"Please, Renata," she begged. "Write down exactly what happened. Señora told me to tell you, write what you know to be true."

So I did, and when she returned last night, she asked to read the entry. I refused.

"But it's your only hope. Just give it to me. She wants you to. Señora sent me here directly, she told me, she cannot stand by, and let you hang for a crime that you didn't commit."

I sat staring at Teresa. I felt the hard cold stone of this bench. I bit into my cracked lip. I tipped my head—no veil, no veil, no more nun's veil, I have just a brush of hair—hacked short, cut away by that whiskey-drenched old jailer the other day—I tipped my head back to the clammy wall.

"I'm sorry but I cannot let you read that diary entry."

"But why not? All you need to do is give it to me, my dear heart,"

Teresa whispered. She was standing now, now reaching her fingers through the bars. "I will go immediately to see your lawyer, DeLuria, I will bring him the diary. I KNOW that he will help you Renata. I know he will bring it to the court. I will stay until he does. But first you must give it to me. You must! Because if you don't Renata, you will…" Shaking her head slowly, she whispers.

"Just give it to me, *please.*"

I stared at Teresa through the bars.

I started sobbing again. "How did this tragedy come to be?" I whispered. I dried my eyes with my sleeve.

"Don't cry, Renata, please don't cry my dear friend." She whispered. And then she cried too. "Please share with me what happened?"

I nodded slowly. "If I do what you ask," I whispered, "I unlock a door to the crime which I'm not prepared to open!"

"But why?" Teresa stamped her food. I stared at her through the bars. I said nothing. I shook my head. "I am prepared to go immediately from here to see your appointed lawyer, DeLuria; he will help you Renata. But you've got to cooperate!"

I stared at her through the rusty bars. My heart pounded. I could not yield up the diary entry that might save me. If I did, I would have my freedom, but I would spend the rest of my days regretting my decision.

And now my hands shake. And now, I cannot make myself write a word more.

17

September 8, 1883

NUN MAY HANG FOR COUSIN'S MURDER!!

By John P. Tolder
Correspondent

VALLEJO, CALIF. A man murdered and a nun—his own cousin—charged with the bloody crime! A convent stunned and a prominent California family shattered! This only partially tells the tale of one of the most dreadful crimes of modern times. This quiet law-abiding town has been rocked by a grizzly killing, the kind of sensational crime that is not likely to disappear quickly from the headlines or the imaginations of the stunned local populace.

"This is not your everyday murder," observed District Attorney G. W. Wordsworck. "The grim and sordid details would satisfy even the most blood-thirsty criminal minds."

Wordsworck promised to seek the death penalty. "If the nun is convicted, I promise you, she will hang."

A mighty retinue of state and local law enforcement authorities have descended on this pleasant locale, known for its groves of huge live oak trees, to investigate the death of one Antonie Quiero de Lopez, a prominent (and the ladies agree, a handsome) landowner, discovered lying face up on September 3rd in a pool of blood in the bedroom of his magnificent hacienda-style home. According to authorities, his jugular vein had been severed with a straight razor.

Arrested and held without bail in the murder is a young novitiate of the Sisters of Saint Dominic. On September 4, exactly a day after the horrific crime, Sister Maria Rosa Renata (a first cousin of Senor Quiero de Lopez) was arrested and escorted from the convent, her head unveiled and hanging in shame.

The very same day she was arrested, a sheriff's deputy found the nun's discarded black habit, coated in blood. "It had been buried hastily behind the vegetable garden," Wordsworck said.

The devoted nuns who remained in the convent were said to be in a frightful state, mortified by the idea that one of their own was capable of such brutality. One nun, Sister Teresa, said it was "impossible to believe" that Renata had killed him. "She wasn't capable of killing a chicken. Certainly she will be cleared of this."

The accused remains behind bars in Gallejo in the county jail while authorities prepare their murder case.

The nun would say only that she had been the "victim of a complicated conspiracy orchestrated" by her cousin to frame her for his murder.

Central to the case, according to authorities, is the discovery of a set of highly incriminating (and blood-stained) hand-written pages found in the victim's rolltop desk. Sheriff's authorities say the light blue pages provide a titillating account that lays out, scene by scene, the shocking details of Sister Renata's lurid relationship with her cousin.

"These documents not only place Sister Renata at the crime scene but show us in perfect detail how and why she killed her cousin," D.A. Wordsworck said. "It is fair to say that these documents guided us right to the culprit's door. They laid our case right at her feet. From the writing we see that Sister Renata is not only a murderess but a lying seductress too. She managed to live a double life, and she kept her fellow nuns in the dark about her behavior. That double life has ended now."

Wordsworck called the letters "a godsend to find. But it is frightful for this evidence to come to light, since the letters reveal a cold-blooded, cold-hearted, premeditated crime."

Considering the circumstances and the public outcry, Wordswork said the death penalty is in order. "It is the only suitable punishment for this 'truly wicked' crime. I'm determined to see the nun hang!"

18

SISTER RENATA'S DIARY

September 11, 1883

My dear Teresa,

Can you see me here, trembling as I write? Can you see what I see? The newspaper in my hand that paints me as Antonie's killer? The newspaper that spells my doom? The newspaper that assumes all of my cousin's horrific stories are true?

All around me, Teresa, I stare at yellow slime that looks and smells like urine dripping from the walls. I am caged in a cell that is barely large enough to hold my bed.

This isn't any bed! I have a narrow metal cot—it has become my world! There is a tiny window that is shoulder high, but I dare not look outside. There is nothing more out there than the choking yellow dust of the courtyard and the gallows...and the dangling rope!

The jailor, cackling and jangling his keys, sang out to me my first day, "Hey, lookie see out there Sister, that's where you are going to die sweetie, so ya' better start sayin' yer prayers!"

Can you see me here my dear Teresa?

How is that I have landed in this hellish place? Sometimes I wish my cousin had sliced not his own throat, but mine!

Oh and here, here at my feet, how could I forget this foul foul pail. A swill that so disgusts me that it makes my head dizzy! Its odor fills my nose and gags me!

And what passes through the rusty bars for food?

That word food, it has no place here. And with the smell, is it any wonder that I haven't the least bit of appetite?

I pray night and day. I ask the Virgin Mary that there may be some miracle. Because I need one here. A few minutes ago, the jailer, smelling of whiskey, threw the newspaper story between the bars.

He was cackling again. "Read this, princess," he said. As my eyes saw the words "I promise you, she will hang"—a warm flood of fear spilled through me. I think my dizziness is going to sink me to the floor.

I may die here before they hang me. I may decide not to drink another sip of that water that tastes like the rust of these bars. I may stop eating and drinking altogether, and I may just pray for a quick demise. I apologize my dear Teresa. I realize that my giving up all hope like this is not what you want to hear, so I close my eyes now and say another prayer.

I so look forward to your coming, Teresa. And now, just thinking of you, I feel so much better.

I can see you in my mind, my dear Sister. I see your cheerful face and your eyes that match the blue of the sky and suddenly, now, here, I feel my spirits lifting.

Yes, Teresa, I feel that you are here beside me in this hellish cell. I am so so thankful that you brought me the diary and I thank God and Mary too that you argued on my behalf, and that they finally allowed me, after all your arguing, to keep it. Perhaps this is after all, the miracle, that I can sit here and still write my own words.

Words that are even stronger than the words of this hateful newspaper. (All lies, all based on the hateful stories my cousin Antonie told!)

But now, I see, I see you and me together, and I realize that I have the power to spin my own tales.

I have the power of words that can lift me out of this hellish cell, I can tell my own story that will take me up the hillside behind the convent, do you see us there on the golden hillside beneath the branches of the live oak?

I do Teresa, I see you and me, together again. I see it all, the blue sky, and the trees, and I smell the warm dry sage in the breeze that bathes my face. I feel the blanket on the dry grass, and now the two of us, we just sank down on the blanket there in the shade. And just like always, we are laughing and telling jokes again about Father Ruby. I sit up and taste the sweet and sour lemonade that you have made me.

There is bliss in these pictures I have in my mind. So yes, you know that I will keep writing here, have no fear about that, and I will keep the faith too, as you told me, because what else can I do except pray and pray and sob and write and write and hold onto some hope *for a miracle?*

What I will do now is what you have been pushing me to do for such a long, long while now. I will write more about my early life with Antonie. That way, when this diary emerges, the world will see what horrible things happened to me as a little girl!

19

SISTER RENATA'S DIARY

September 13, 1883

To this day, and to the end of all my days, I will carry the madrone tree deep inside me. But never did I expect to share my shame in words, at least not here on this page.

So many years ago, I confessed the sins committed beneath the madrone to Father Crucifer. In the months before I became a novitiate, the nightmares grew so terrifying that I woke up feeling like I was choking. I would lie there, a sweaty heap in my bed, and I would dread falling asleep again because they, the night terrors, would return. Finally I was so sleep deprived that I knew I had no choice but to bring the dreams to the confessional; I poured my heart out there in that cedar closet, with only the dark screen between me and Father Crucifer. After the confession, I knew for certain that I had been forgiven of any responsibility. Father Crucifer himself told me that I was not to blame myself for what happened. My cousin the brute, had abused me.

Alas then, why now must I relive the madrone again here? Why is it that as I rot away in this cell, I am plagued once again by what happened so long ago beneath that red-skinned tree? Why am I cursed to have to re-experience the nightmares? Why have I been waking up with Antonie's wild young face and strong sweaty hands still strangling my sleep?

Teresa insists that the dreams have started again for a very simple reason: I am enraged at Antonie for landing me here behind these rusty bars. My fury, she says, is beyond containing. There is so much hatred, so much anger, bottled up inside me that it is resurrecting the old pain. All of it is beginning to eat away at my heart. Worse, it's starting to drown my soul.

"You must write it all down," Teresa said in her last visit. "If you don't, I'm afraid, his victory will indeed be complete."

So I will confess it again, even though it seems so unfair, that he made me the victim once, and now again, I'm the one who's suffering.

I see the tree so clearly. The handsome red madrone grew at the far end of Uncle Rio's vast fruit orchard. Peaches and pears, plums, and a few apples filled the orchard. Antonie and I spent many happy days in the orchard the first summer I arrived. We would take the guitars, and a lunch basket prepared by Señora with lots more food than the two of us could possibly consume. And we would play guitars for hours. He was a good teacher, mostly because he didn't say much, nor did he correct me very often. He played and I copied, and he played, and I copied better the second time. The days melted away.

He took me to the madrone for the first time at the end of July. The madrone snaked into the sky about 30 feet high, towering over a thicket of live oak that lined a small ravine. We sat by the muddy bear creek on the bank of that ravine and Antonie explained to me that the creek ran high until about April every year. By this time of the season, though, the creek was bone dry.

"Which is sad," he said, "because we have no place to cool off in the summer."

He turned and looked at me and when I turned to look back at him, I saw a strange glint in his eye. I had started to see that glint more and more but I was young, and unfettered, and I chose to ignore it.

A moment later, he asked me if I wanted to see him climb the madrone.

I wrinkled my nose. "I'm not sure," I said. "I suppose if I were certain you knew how to, then, sure, I would say yes. But how do I know if you can do it?"

He shrugged. His eyes shone. "I guess you will just have to trust me." He unbuttoned his shirt and threw it aside. His chest was bare of any hair at all. But he was far more muscular than I expected he would be. I realized that his body was that not of a boy at all, but a sturdy young man.

He hoisted himself to the first branch, which was just above my head. Turning, he stood above me with his legs apart and he called down to me.

"You would love it up here, and I could help you climb up."

"Not a chance," I said. I was wearing a long skirt, and even the thought of my feet leaving the ground frightened me.

He took hold of a higher branch. He pulled himself up to the next height and threw himself forward, bending over the branch and hanging with his head below the bough. The branch swayed.

"Oh be careful," I gasped from below.

"I know exactly what I am doing Renata," he called back. The last I saw of his face was his smile, which I didn't often see. He was so very quiet most of the time, so solemn. Now all I remember is that awful smile. Not a smile of joy, but one of conquest.

I watched him pull himself to standing on that bough and then he was so high into the green blue greenery of the tree that he disappeared from view.

"Now it's time to come down," I cried nervously. "I cannot see you anymore."

"But I can see you," he said triumphantly. "And I can see everything else from here too. I can see clear to the house, and up to the ridge."

"Good, but it's dangerous. Please Antonie, please come down."

Frowning nervously, I found a rock on which to sit. I caught my skirt under my knees and tucked it close around my ankles. I sat there rocking back and forth, waiting.

I heard the leaves swiping against each other. I heard a branch crack. And a gasp. "Uh oh."

I stood. "What? What? What is happening up there?"

He grew silent.

"Antonie? Please, can't you at least answer me? Tell me what is happening?"

I could feel my pulse running. I could imagine having to race back through the orchard to the house to have to tell Uncle Rio that Antonie was stuck in the tree. Or worse, that he had fallen. I don't know how Uncle Rio could take another blow. Another loss would surely kill him.

"Oh drat," Antonie called. Another branch cracked.

"What are you doing?" I screamed.

"Oh, oh, it's OK I think… I think I've found a way down," he called. I raced outward from the trunk to try to see where he was, and how he was making progress, but to no avail. I couldn't see a thing.

"I guess…I guess I will try coming down this way, by sitting down," he said. I could almost imagine him up there. I could almost see him sitting on a branch and thinking.

"Please please please Antonie can't you come down right now?" I cried. I was practically sobbing.

"I'm trying Renata. I'm trying."

I kept picturing myself having to tell Uncle Rio that Antonie had fallen. All I could think was, Antonie will die, joining his mother, and then Uncle Rio will be destroyed. And all that will be left will be me. And Señora.

I came back to the trunk. I gazed upward, and just as I did, he slid right by me, yelling, dropping from the branch above me. He landed at my feet in a heap and fell to the side.

"DEAR GOD!" I cried, watching his collapse.

For a moment I stood, frozen in place. I saw his face. So so still. His eyes were closed. His mouth hung open.

Slowly, I dropped to my knees beside him. I was sobbing. "Oh my dear dear cousin, please please please wake up," I cried. "Oh why did you have to go up the tree? Why why why?" He lay there, as still as stone. I began crying harder.

"I don't know what I will do without you. Please please please, Antonie, can't you please wake up?" I knew I had to go for help, but first I bent forward and reached one hand toward his nose, to see if he was still breathing.

My fingers were just grazing his upper lip when his eyes flew open and smiling, he grabbed me. I gasped and pulled back but not in time. He had my hand vised in his and he pulled me forward making me fall right on top of him.

He cupped his other hand around my neck and he rolled over me as if I were a log beneath him. All the while I screamed and thrashed. "Oh let me go, let me go, oh you are so horrible, why are you doing this, let me go!!!"

By then, though, he was straddled on top of me, pressing his fleshy lips into mine. He caressed me over and over again, he covered my face with his wet lips, despite my yelling, despite my telling him to "get off me, let me go, get away, just get away from me, let me gooooooooooooooo!!!!!"

He wouldn't let up. He took both elbows and planted one on either side of my neck, to make it harder for me to move. Then he planted his face deep in my neck.

"Oh my dear dear cousin," he said. I could feel his lower body, dear God, I could feel him growing rock hard, as if he had grown one of the madrone's own branches there inside his trousers. He pulled up my skirt and he lay full on top of me. I tried to scream but he held a dirty sweaty hand over my mouth. He never removed his clothing, because he didn't have time. But he pressed himself against me, and he rubbed himself in a fury, while I lay there, helpless, yelling into the palm of his hand, over and over again he thrust against me, and finally, he shuddered, and fell heavily against me.

A moment after he had finished his dirty business, he rolled over to the side, and I rolled the other way, and bawling, I curled up into a little ball. And when I could find my strength, I picked myself up and ran all the way back to the house.

The world as I knew it, it just collapsed that day. I never said a word to anyone about it, until three years later, when I was about to become a novitiate. But no matter what Antonie said, or how many times he tried to apologize for his monstrous behavior, I never gave him even a moment to speak of it again. Quite simply, my relationship with him—and life itself—was never the same after that.

GINA

My sister Carolyn is worried about me. We got together for coffee a few weeks ago and I made the mistake of telling her that I'm rewriting the book, again. I could see her face cringe.

The next thing I know she wants me to go see a different shrink.

Being a nurse, she has connections. She finds a psychiatrist at Harvard Medical School. She makes the appointment. She tells me to be ready on a Tuesday. She is taking a day off from work so she can drive me to Boston.

It's January and while the highway is clear the snow is deep on the ground.

We don't chat much driving. She plays classical music. I know that's supposed to be relaxing but it makes me nervous.

We get there after getting lost a few times in Boston.

Sitting in the waiting room, I am really nervous. What will I say to her? What fancy treatments will she prescribe?

The doctor, a pleasant young woman with soft curly hair, opens the door and invites us in. We shake hands and exchange the necessary pleasantries.

Then my sister goes into high gear.

"We're here today because I think my sister is delusional."

"HUH?" I turn to face her. "You never told me that!"

She turns to face me. She smiles and puts a hand on my arm. "I know, honey. I was afraid you wouldn't come if I told you."

"Excuse me," Dr. Phillips says. "I need to get a little background here." She is holding a clipboard with a legal-sized yellow pad.

"Gina, why don't you begin."

I stare at the giant prayer plant in the corner of the room. I tell the doctor about my "situation." The novel. The writer's blocks. Me teetering on the brink of depression.

"But not delusional," I say, turning and frowning at my sister.

"Are you troubled by visions?" She asks, taking a break from writing.

"Well," I say, trying to figure out how much to reveal. "I have written two other novels, and this one is…different."

"How so?" She is tapping the point of her pen against the pad of paper.

"Uh, well, I kind of slip into the life of the novel now and then." I don't think I should tell her about all the times it's happened.

"Doctor," my sister interrupts, "this is exactly why we are here. My sister has indicated to me that she believes she has visited the past via this novel."

I cringe. The doctor will want me to take more medication. Have Cat scans and MRI's. I turn, focus my eyes on the grey carpet.

The doctor doesn't say anything. And then she speaks.

"Gina, do you know what past life regression therapy is?"

I almost fall off my chair. It was one thing to hear it from Michaela, the zero energy-balancing lady in Vermont. It's another to hear it from a shrink at Harvard Medical School.

I stare. "I know there is such a thing," I say. "Not sure I know what's…involved."

Dr. Phillips smiles. She has a very kind face.

"If you would like, I could recommend someone here in Boston."

"That's not really practical," my sister says. "It's too far for us to come in on a regular basis."

"OK, then I know a couple of practitioners in Northampton," she says.

I am speechless. This is the same advice I got from Michaela.

She goes to her Rolodex and flips through it. She comes back with a card. "Here you go," she says, "handing the card to my sister. I think if I had a choice I would see Nancy N."

A few more minutes go by. My sister and the doctor are in conversation, but I am not listening.

I've got so much anxiety just thinking about the idea of a past life.

I smile and thank the doctor. But when we get outside and back to the parking lot, I make my decision.

No matter what my sister says, I'm not going to go. But I don't have to worry. We get in the car.

"Well that was a damn waste of time," Carolyn says. "I'm going back to the person who recommended this shrink so highly. I'm gonna tell her that Dr. Phillips is a total kook!"

I look outside. It's snowing.

I am so relieved. I smile and press my nose to the cold window.

20

SISTER RENATA'S DIARY

September 17, 1883

Dear Teresa,

I am living again Teresa. I am breathing once more. If I ever doubted there was a God, or that Mary listened to me, that she responded to my pleas and prayers, I could not possibly doubt that anymore.

It is in part this journal, recording my head and heart.

But there was this miracle the other day: Señora delivered me my guitar!

Before, there was just me, lying here, withering up in this cell, but now? Now there is me and there is my beloved instrument and this wonderful song, a carcelero—my prison song—that frees me!

Are you listening as I play Teresa? Do you hear my carcelero, just listen to these words:

"In three days I've eaten

Only bread and tears:

That is the food

the jailers give."

I sit and I play and I sit and I sing, and I keep singing no matter how much the jailer screams at me to stop! I sing until my voice gives up to gravel, and my fingers have bloody tips.

But I am alive and free and remarkably happy!

It isn't just the guitar. It is this writing too. I keep focusing on what you said, "write it all down."

I must stop a moment and say a prayer of thanks, to God and to Mary and especially, to Señora. She is the one who saved me! She had the courage and she had the wisdom too, what I now call the wisdom of whiskey!

She came to the prison last week, my guitar bundled in a blanket in the back of the old grey wagon. She is so small—all of four or five feet—but she stood up to the horrible old jailer. She marched into the jail carrying a basket and the guitar in a blanket. In her broken English, she told the jailer she wanted to see me.

He laughed, but he stopped laughing after she pulled out of the basket a bottle of Antonie's most expensive bourbon!

When he saw that bottle, the cackling jailer (his name is Jimmy Bean, can you imagine a stranger name?!) whistled and clapped!

Bean broke open the bottle and drank the whiskey on the spot. But not before dear Señora had gotten the key and delivered the guitar to me. And the blanket. And a basket of the most sumptuous foods!

When she and I had finished snacking on apples and cheese, she picked up the guitar and tuned. Then she took me back to the music she used to play—including those sweet old tientos—when I first arrived at Antonie's hacienda as a child.

"What kind of bird is that

Singing in the olive tree?

Go tell it to be still,

Its song makes me so sad!"

And then she switched to one that is so much sadder, a siguirya:

"A la luna le pio

la del alto cielo

come le pio que saque a mi pare

de onde está preso."

I implore the moon

up there in the sky,

Implore it to help my father

Escape from his prison cell.

I began crying. I couldn't believe she had come. And now that she was here, I didn't want her to leave!"

Noticing my tears, Señora changed gears, singing a gay and witty sort of palo which has a never ending number of poetic verses, because you make them up as you go along.

Just imagine. What I. Did. Just imagine. Where I fled to.

Only the stars can tell you. Only the sky can guess.

So now sit down and I will try to tell you.

You will see it all come clear.

When the water goes still as a mirror,

And we peer inside.

Do you see now, why I appeared here?

Do you see now, why you must

Tell the world my story? Yes, tell the world

Just sing it, shout it out,

how we turned the past. Together,

We moved her story, Renata's,

and his false history, Antonie's,

Around.

At this point, we stopped. She set the guitar on the blanket and I placed my head against her shoulder. Señora gently rubbed my arm. She kept singing, and as I started to fall asleep, I was thinking, she will sing into eternity.

I woke when she got up to go. As she left, she had to step over

Bean, who was a pile of whiskers and whiskey-soaked flesh on the jail floor. Bean came to for a minute or two, during which time Señora assured him in her broken English that he would have "more weesky" every week if he let me play the guitar!

Are you listening to me, Mary, when I kneel now on this miserable mud-packed floor, when I say thank you for this miracle you have delivered me here?

Sitting here singing and playing, I can feel blood running through my arms and legs again. And I'm eating the empanadas that Señora made—such heavenly food!

Dear Teresa, will you visit me in this foul place, soon? I will swoon you with my music, just the way I used to play for you in the old happy days, when we laid on the blanket under the arms of the live oak!

Please bring whatever food you can carry. And one other thing Teresa, will you bring me a canteen of your perfect lemonade?

21

SISTER RENATA'S DIARY

September 23, 1883

Why is it that if a newspaper delivers up lies in print, people are so willing to believe them, no matter how wild they may sound?

Why is it that no one, Teresa, not even my own lawyer, Steven DeLuria, can allow for the possibility that I was framed by my delusional cousin Antonie, whose great gift was to tell a believable story?

DeLuria came to see me today, and honestly, he seems to be as twisted as his pencil-thin mustache that curls in elaborate waxed spirals on either side of his narrow face! I welcomed his visit, at least I did at the beginning, as this was the first time I had seen him since they threw me into this hellish cell more than two weeks ago! But it took only moments for me to see that he was miserably uninterested in my case.

He sat on the bench, close enough for me to smell his pomade, and he kept shuffling through papers in his satchel. What in God's name was he looking for? Ah, then his hand landed on that damnable newspaper, the *Examiner,* and he held it up, and then shook his head and said, "I am afraid that this isn't going to help you one bit." As if I didn't know it! What a laugh.

I was holding onto my guitar, thankfully, and I squeezed the neck of that beauty then, because I would have had a hard time holding myself back. I wanted to slap his face. My heart started racing and I felt a ring of sweat start up my neck.

"Of course it isn't going to help, sir," I said. "Do you think for a minute that it was my choice?" I blinked back tears, which felt hot on the rims of my eyes.

"Maybe you hadn't guessed this, Mr. DeLuria, but I would just as soon not be here." By then I was sniffling out loud.

He cleared his throat and straightening up, he handed me his embroidered hanky—lace on a man's hanky? Then he stood—he is so tall that his head grazes the slimy yellow ceiling of the cell. And he dresses well, at least he has more ruffles on the front of his shirt than a chicken has feathers on her back side.

"I am wondering how you plan to defend me?" I said, giving him a hard steady look.   He took hold of his narrow chin—in addition to the mustache twirled and waxed at both ends, he has one of those excessively pointy goatees.

"I think before I can possibly develop a defense, I will have to spend more time learning about your situation."

"My situation? You mean how it is that I am sitting in this foul place accused of murder?"

"Well, I want to know how it is that you have come to believe that you are a victim of what you call...this complicated conspiracy?"

" Believe?" I wrapped my arms around the body of my guitar and held tight. "Mr. DeLuria, let me be clear about one thing before we start." I felt my heart slamming against my chest. "I am innocent of all wrongdoing here. My cousin simply framed me by writing his ludicrous tales about me."

He kept rubbing his chin. "I see," he said.

I stood up. I held onto the guitar. "No, I'm not sure you do see!"

I picked up my diary. "So if you want to know my side of the story, here, it's all here, day by day, exactly the way things really happened."

At first he wouldn't take the journal. "My day is very full," he said, "and I'm afraid that I won't have a chance to get to this for at least a couple more days."

I shook my head. "A couple more days? My first court appearance is at the end of this week, on Friday morning, or at least that's what they said." I whispered. I was horrified by this...bad excuse for an attorney.

"I know full well what the court schedule is, my dear," he said. "But there are two other cases besides yours that I must attend to. So now, if you will excuse me," he took a magnificent gold watch out of his pocket. "I am scheduled for an important lunch engagement shortly."

The word lunch set me into a rage. I dropped back on the bench.

"Oh, please, please don't let me stop you from your lunch," I said, angry enough to spit. "And what is it that they are serving today? Leg of lamb? Consommé? Fricassee of chicken?" My eyes narrowed, my voice rose. "And what for dessert sir? Apple pie? Berry cobbler? Will there be a scoop of ice cream on the cobbler?"

He studied me curiously, as if I were slightly mad. "I will be back," he mumbled, "and when I return, I will consider your journal." He nodded his head in the direction of my diary.

"Never fear, I will be right here waiting," I said. He left the cell and I tell you if it weren't for the guitar...well... I see now how this will go, nobody but you and Señora know the truth. Nobody will believe my side of things.

GINA

For years I have had this recurring dream. I don't recall when it started.

My eyes would snap open, and the light in the bedroom would be greenish white, and Joel was there sleeping beside me, but he was turned facing the wall.

All of a sudden Señora was there, standing above me, and I would be overwhelmed by the smell of fresh roses. "M'ija," she whispered, and there in her arms was a giant bouquet of the most magnificent yellow roses. Each of them was tipped in red, as if they had lips!

"Sí, sí, m'ija, for you," she whispered. I sat up and she laid them in my lap. I was thrilled.

But then I would be in the cell and Señora was sitting beside me. It smelled like pee.

She would pull me close and smile and her brown eyes were so peaceful they put me at ease.

"Please sing," I would say, and she picked up the guitar and began to strum something I didn't recognize.

She opened her mouth to sing but there was commotion outside the cell. The jailer was screaming and all of a sudden the outside door to the jail flew open.

It was Antonie. And he looked just terrible. His normally long black wavy hair was chopped off. In spikes. Wet and matted. His eyes were dark and empty. And he had lost a lot of weight. His black pants were baggy.

But now, now how did I miss this: his throat was gashed, Dear God, he was holding his own head!

And then, blink, he was gone and Señora was there with the guitar, strumming, always singing the same carcelera:

"Ya van tres días que no como

má que lágrimas y pan:

estos son los alimentos

que mis carceleros me dan."

At that moment, I would wake up.

And there would always be a single rose—yellow with bloody red tips—on the floor beside the bed.

22

SISTER RENATA'S DIARY

October 5, 1883

My dearest Teresa,

Sometimes I sit in this cell and I am an animal in a cage. One thing saves me: my mind making these pictures. I see you and me walking through the fields near the convent. Do you see the sky?

How about the sunset that night last April when we walked together so many miles? The sky such a glorious orange and yellow and pink and purple and powder blue.

Your letters are my only comfort. In the moments when I am so frightened I cannot even whisper a prayer, I clutch my rosary beads and hold your words against my chest.

How could this happen? How could I be facing the gallows for a crime I didn't commit? How could my cousin do this to me?

At times when it gets to be too much for me, I pray to the Virgin Mary, or I read your words and I repeat them over and over like a soothing chant. Tears pour out when I hear your voice. My greatest terror is that there may come a day when I cannot hear you!

Oh Teresa. I could always count on you to make me laugh. Each morning before prayers there you would be, solemn, straight-faced, imitating our pie-eyed Mother Yolla. Her scowl. Her waddle, how like a cow she walks. And then I would dissolve into tears, all the while praying, "God, please forgive me for laughing."

Believe me, I am laughing no more. For I am certain now that I will die, as that hopeless lawyer DeLuria appeared with me in court a week ago and he was abominably bad. You could barely hear what he said. The judge asked him three or four times to speak up!

And when he did say something, he made a few dreadfully weak statements and that was that. I sat with my wrists handcuffed and my head bowed, ashamed that I even agreed to let the foolish lawyer—his impeccable ruffled shirt—speak for me!

After they led me back to the cell, I sat for hours staring through the bars out the window into the courtyard. As the afternoon wore on, the sun got hotter and hotter and brighter and I grew more and more weak and dizzy. Fearing that I might faint, I finally did the unthinkable, Teresa, I tore off my wimple and veil. My hair feels like dry matted straw.

Is this the end of me, Renata the nun? I have begun to think so! Even as I am playing my guitar, my heart is as heavy as an iron stove lid! Forgive me, Teresa, but I have more and more moments lately when I've begun to doubt that there is any Divine order at all, or any loving presence above or within me.

Occasionally as I sat staring out the window, a wagon would come into view, the wheels throwing up thick clouds of yellow dust. Finally, the jailer brought dinner—a cold, grey mass of greasy potatoes he called stew—and I couldn't bear to eat it. In a perverse mood, both he and I were, and maybe because it was so hot, he wasn't cackling for a change and I was desperate to talk, so I asked him if he thought the hanging would be good theater.

"Er, watcha say there sister?" he asked, as I suppose he didn't know the meaning of the word "theater."

"What I mean, Mr. Bean, is when I hang outside there in the courtyard, will it attract a large crowd?"

His eyes lit up. "Oh course it will, Lordy, to see a nun swingin' by a rope, hell, it'll be a real good un," he said, nodding his head. "Criminy sakes how often do ya get a chance to hang somebody from the church?"

His eyes widened and took on a gleam. He stood there jangling his ring of keys, smoothing his hand over that impossible stubble on his chin. Then, when I said nothing, he silently pushed back his soiled hat. I saw that stitched flap of skin where his eye is missing. This is the first time I ever really looked at it.

I ought not to have asked the next question. "Have you seen...many hangings?" I whispered, my dry throat knotting up over my words.

"Oh in my day I'd say I seen a dozen or so," he said, smiling. He has only three crooked teeth where there should be a top row. "But ma'am, this one beats all the rest. I mean, I never seen anybody hang who was wearin' a dress." He slapped his thigh and shook his head. And then he clanged the keys against the bars and left.

What a dreadful man. How could he possibly be so cold-hearted, telling me this? Making me see myself spinning by the neck at the end of a rope, my skirt open at the bottom for all to see?

I sat staring at the cold stew. In the last few days, I have been dry heaving even at the sight of food. I'd rather he just didn't leave it at all. I called out to the jailer and told him to take the bowl away.

The day seemed to last forever. The sun sank lower and lower, and with it went my spirits. In the perverse mood I was in, I kept riveted on that spot out in the courtyard where my body will dangle from a rope. I tried to pray, Teresa, but honestly, I have begun to wonder, why bother? Is there anyone listening? Would a merciful God permit all this pain?

At some point during the night, I must have fallen asleep. I dreamed I was swinging from a rope that hung from a crucifix. I had been hanged, but somehow because I was on the cross, I didn't die. I woke up with a start, collapsed into the slimy wall of my cell. Oh Teresa, this is hell on earth.

And did I tell you, I still have a chain around my ankle, as if it were needed? As if there would be any way I could move from this cell! The skin at the ankle grows raw, and it has begun bleeding and the blood mixes with the rust of the chain.

In your last letter you said the newspaper intends to publish the stories Antonie wrote, starting with his first, "Renata Dancing."

Dear God is there no justice? All that rubbish, the filth and lies Antonie wrote about me, now being released into the world.

If they do print his stories, dear Teresa, is there a way to bring my diary to light? Will my words carry any weight at all? I am desperate the world should know that I am innocent. I committed no crime.

The jailer comes now with a cup of tea. He leaves it. But dear God Teresa, it is lukewarm and has an oily film and there is a hair from that mangy dog floating on top. I cannot bring myself to eat a bite, or drink either. The jailer says I might die of starvation. And I say, that might be the best way. Whatever God wills!

Your loving sister, Renata

GINA

April 6, 2007 I remember the day exactly. Jonah's 17th birthday. We are having two of his friends over for dinner and I am baking his favorite carrot cake.

I haven't written for over a month. I write and write and then I rip it all up and crush it into a giant ball and throw it away. I am trying to make my peace with the fact that I will never finish the story I started more than a decade ago.

I know that Señora thinks differently but she would agree if she knew how I felt.

I am stirring the cream cheese icing when suddenly, the bowl disappears and I am back in that dark and putrid jail cell screaming for the f.p.

"PLEASE PLEASE BRING THE PAIL THIS INSTANT OR THERE WILL BE A MESS IN HERE!"

The jailer wobbles in. "Hold yer horses, lady."

He opens the cell and I can smell his breath. Whiskey.

Fortunately he has emptied the pail before bringing it in. He unlocks the chains on my ankles and wrists. He leaves.

After I use it, I call him to take the pail away. He takes his time.

When he comes, he locks my ankles and wrists.

"Isn't this silly?" I ask. "I don't need these chains. Explain to me how I could possibly escape this cell?"

"Ah, go to hell," he says as he wobbles out the door.

"Don't you dare swear at me!!"

I turn and there is Renata, chained beside me.

"Thank God you're here," I say.

She says nothing. Her black hair sticks up like ragged tooth-picks. Her cheeks are sunken pods. She coughs, and her breathing sounds like my asthmatic mother's used to sound.

But her dark eyes, how they sparkle. She lifts the chunky crucifix that dangles from the rosary at her waist. She touches it to her parched lips and then to mine.

She doesn't know that I am a Jew. After all these years together, I still haven't had the courage to tell her. But then, I never told her either that I as a young child I desperately wanted to be a nun. Why should I tell her these things? She is MY character, isn't she?

Suddenly I have this realization: I don't know if I am jailed in-side her. Or she inside me.

She says nothing.

When I speak, my voice is wavering. "Honestly, Renata, I'm sick to death of this story. I don't want to write any more. I want relief. I want to put an end to all of it."

She squeezes my hand. "I know how difficult this is. I know it will take a miracle to save me, but you will find your way. I am certain of that after what the Virgin told me. Remember. You must pray to Her and always come back to the present moment."

Maybe. But how do I tell the nun that the present moment sucks?

I turn to say something. She's gone.

Tears flood my face. "Dear God, HELP ME PLEASE!"

Without thinking, I start to chant. I learned how from a yoga teacher.

I close my eyes and begin:

Ohhhhh. MMMMMMMM… Over and over again. Ohhhhh. MM-MMMMMM….

The vibrations help to calm me.

The next thing I know I am doing what Renata told me to do.

Oh Mary, I'm so frightened. I've got to get out of this jail. I never bargained for this when I took on the nun's story. I am not sure what is happening but I feel like I am trapped by my own words and stuck inside my own story. Or her story! I am losing my mind here. PLEASE MARY PLEASE FREE ME FROM THIS CELL. FREE ME

FROM THIS STORY. Let me go back to my life and my family, help me, either to finish the novel (which I WOULD LOVE TO DO) or make Renata and Señora and Antonie stop haunting me!

I turn. Señora is at the door of the cell with a blanket in her arms. I am just about to speak, to reach out to her when, *poof!*

Mary must have heard me because once again I am staring into the bowl of icing. Jonah is in the kitchen saying something. "Is it OK to add one more for dinner Ma? You remember Artie, from basketball?"

I blink. "Oh….uh sure, honey. That's fine." I take a big breath in. I sit down at the kitchen table, cradle my head in my arms.

Thank you Mary.

23

SISTER RENATA'S DIARY

DEAR GOD, What day is it?

Teresa I'm losing track of time. Maybe it's because I cannot eat a bite of food, or because of this heat wave, driving up from hell itself. All I know is that the dust blows endlessly through the bars of the window and I'm coated and crusted in fine yellow powder!

I don't know what day it is anymore. I wake up in such confusion that I find myself wondering if I am even alive. I run my hands around my muddy face and up and down my arms to remind myself that I have skin and that I am in it!

My journal is such a treasure. Surely you spent a year's savings on this chiseled leather beauty—anyway, I keep the diary in my hands when I sleep. Lately, in the mornings, in a wash of confusion, I begin reading what I have written. Because rereading my diaries helps me feel alive.

Because without hearing the words I wrote, I am not me, I am not Sister Renata anymore.

I keep going back to the opening page.

Over and over, I read my own words—"And now, how to begin. And why, why am I about to pour myself onto paper? Pure and simply, I write now because I don't trust my cousin anymore. I need a record of events..."

My eyes pass over these words and I know for certain that I wrote them—I wrote them when I still had hope, when I still thought life made sense, when I used to wash my face and hands and arms before I went to chapel each day. When I cooked lunch in the convent on Fridays at noon, when I would stand at the sink, humming a little Spanish melody, the ones Señora would teach me.

I remember you and me together, standing by the laundry sink. We washed Father Ruby's sheets, side by side.

That's when I felt I was still *in* the world. That's it. I still was *in the world* and now I am not. Now I am not alive, not really, at least I've got to keep convincing myself by talking out loud or by singing when I can. By shouting out.

But then I tire of shouting and my voice gives way and sometimes the old jailer comes by and tells me to shut up because I am driving him crazy.

I sink back onto the moldy wall and I have all I can do to take another breath. I sit here in this cage with nothing but the gallows outside my window.

Last night, I grabbed the journal and started reading my own words right out loud, the jailer yelled at me telling me to shut up and I yelled back NO NO NO NO and then I yelled louder, I began screaming my words, I read the whole first entry in a screeching voice, at least that's how I started, and then by the end, it had become something of a chant.

The jailer took a crowbar and slammed and banged it across the bars. I dodged him at each poke, he threatened to unlock the cell and beat me but I just laughed, I laughed Teresa, I said to him "Go ahead sir beat me if you wish to, go ahead if you dare, but I am going to read, to shout until I have not a shred of voice left!"

I know full well that I am verging on madness tempting him to hit me. And when I'm shouting I am shouting to a world that for certain isn't listening.

I will die soon. DeLuria is hopeless. Why do I expect anything from him?

I am this thing that was once Sister Renata, face of crud and crusted yellow sweat, hair of chopped straw. Ha, the jailer brought an ancient fragment of mirror here the other day, and shoved it between the bars and cackling his vicious laugh, said, "have a look Sister."

I saw I saw. But all that doesn't matter.

I won't let anyone take my dignity away. My dignity, like my words, are what is here in my mind and soul. I cannot allow anyone to take that inner voice, my divine connection, away from me.

As you are wont to say, Teresa, I must have faith that my words, this diary, will somehow, in some miracle that I pray for, help to clear my name.

GINA

Joel has always my best and most generous reader, so I kept giving him chapters.

He would be sitting upright in bed, laughing at some points, and saying what a scoundrel Antonie was in others. He kept insisting that I had to try to sell the book by focusing on sexual abuse.

Every time he said that, I would feel my stomach tighten. I didn't want to think about selling the book. The last book I had tried to sell, *Seeing Red*, landed me in a tsunami of depression.

"I guess I will have to think about marketing but that's not what I want to think about now. Not at all."

One night, when he had read about 100 pages, I asked him which chapters he liked the best.

"That's hard to say," he said, yawning and setting the manuscript aside on his night table beside his glass of water. "I love the first chapter with Renata dancing. But after that, maybe the scenes in the bar. 'Bar Dancer' is so sexy."

Which may explain what happened next. It was an hour or so later, right after I switched off the Rachel Maddow show.

He rolled on top of me and we began kissing and I felt myself, and him, getting excited.

Things were proceeding quite nicely when suddenly I was overwhelmed with visions of Renata, her red ruffled skirt swiveling around her thighs. I didn't want to be there, I didn't want to see myself as the seductress. That wasn't Renata. That was Antonie being a sexist pig.

But then it got even more intense. I was inside her body, I felt sweaty, I saw her skirt from up above. And then it switched and I was the nun on the floor cradling Antonie's bloody head once more.

"What's the matter?" Joel asked.

"I...I am there. Right there in the bar. I'm inside her. It's scary Joel, I am right there."

Joel sighed. "We can try again in the morning," he said, sounding annoyed. He rolled over to face the wall.

"No, no, I don't want to wait, it's just...it's just so crazy and overwhelming to be back there. I can smell the cigar smoke, and see the gleam on the bar and the red velvet-textured wallpaper."

Joel said nothing. I heard him start breathing into sleep.

"NO, please honey, please don't fall asleep," I yelled.

"Wha...what?" he jerked awake.

"Please don't leave me alone back there. Please! I don't want to be in the bar, not at all. Please turn back to me. Hold me."

Which he did.

And after a while, I felt my body next to him. I felt my breath going in and out of my nose. I held him close, and we loved each other in a very tender way. Gradually, Renata slowly faded away into the night.

24

SISTER RENATA'S DIARY

October 20, 1883

Will you be surprised Teresa when I tell you that I am now my own lawyer? How you laugh, I can see so clearly that jolly face of yours so pink and flushed! Your head tips back, your eyes begin watering the way they do when you cannot hold yourself in.

But it's true Teresa, I am a lawyer, Teresa, in all but name.

DeLuria came by two days ago, in his crisp starched shirt. All the ruffles tipped in black satin thread. He dresses impeccably, as though he is going to the opera and not a fetid jail.

His head is empty. We sat in the cell here, and he began to tell me once again that when he examined the evidence against me— the stacks of blue pages with all the "sordid" stories, the evidence against me, he said, is "overwhelming."

I blinked. I laughed out loud and slapped one hand on my knee and when I looked up I saw him looking at me as though I was crazy.

I suppose I was being a bit rude, so I covered my mouth (but oh I've become someone altogether quite new here in this cell, Teresa, a woman with no restraints I tell you no restraints whatsoever!)

I cleared my throat and sat up straight and said, "My dear sir, have you in that fine leather satchel you are carrying, a report from the scene of the crime? There must be an official report of the crime, yes?"

He lifted his gaze, a bit disdainfully, curious I suppose that I was asking HIM a question. "Well, naturally I do. Somewhere here, there is a report by the Sheriff. Naturally I have reviewed all the necessary documents."

I left him to sift through the many papers he carries in his handsome leather briefcase (same color as this my chiseled diary Teresa!) I found myself humming something while he searched, and, quite unexpectedly, the next thing I knew I was WHISTLING! This is not the Renata who left the convent two months ago, Teresa, this is Renata ANEW!

I looked up and found him glaring at me. "Must you whistle?" he asked in a very steady voice.

"Oh, quite wrong of me, sir, so sorry," I said, smiling. He resumed his search and I resumed my humming, a tune that Señora and I have often played and sung together.

He found what he was looking for. A single page filled with the slanted handwriting of the Sheriff, describing the way they—the authorities—found Antonie on the day he died. DeLuria was about to start reading when I laid just two of my fingertips on his coat jacket, and he recoiled. Granted my fingers are filthy—his would be too if he was forced into this hellish cell!

Well, so he instinctively pulled his arm away, out of my grasp, as if I might give him some disease!

"There is no need to read it to me," I said. "I know exactly how my cousin died."

"Well so what is the point here?" he demanded.

"The point here Mr. DeLuria is this: my cousin died a bloody bloody death. But the only question to ask is how did he die? By whose hand? And I know full well it was not MY hand that took his life away."

"Ah but the authorities have the story that describes you scratching his neck and threatening him with a razor! The story is clear it is a damnable piece of ev...."

I stood up and stamped my foot and yelled. "It is a damnable batch of lies! All of Antonie's stories are lies!" My eyes flamed and he shrank back against that moldy cell wall.

All I could think was, his perfect wool waistcoat will be moldy green when he leaves here!

"I have seen that story, Mr. DeLuria, and I know very well what it says. It suggests that I sliced his throat, but I assure you, that interaction between the two of us never took place. That piece of writing was just one more of Antonie's fantasies, composed by him in an evil attempt to frame me for his death."

Looking impatient, DeLuria turned his head as if it was a swivel on top of a barber pole. He examined the Sheriff's statement. For a long moment, he remained silent. And then of all things, he lit up one of his slim cigars.

It occurred to me to say to him that there was insufficient air for him, me and a cigar as it is quite beastly in the cell. I thought better of telling him this; instead, I began a coughing fit as he inhaled and blew out rings of blue smoke. I coughed and coughed until he put the blasted cigar out beneath his boot.

"Thank you, very kind of you," I croaked. He picked up the tin cup of water to his right and holding it as if it were a dead crow, he handed the water over to me. I smiled and took a sip.

"So I suppose that we might question the last story and thus, the Sheriff's report," he said at last.

I smiled and nodded. "Exactly, as we should question all of those other foolish stories." I waited a respectable moment. "And thus, it would seem to me a reasonable defense, yes? To lay before the judge and jury the fact that these stories are all a farce!"

I let that sink in, dying to know what he was thinking but reluctant to ask. He twisted his neck this way and that and sat up straighter.

"I cannot promise the judge will be convinced," he said finally, in what I can only call a "small" voice. "I must report to you, unhappily, that there is a good deal of bad sentiment against you. The momentum of this sentiment is decidedly strong and it is growing, thanks to press reports."

Folding my lips in on themselves, I quietly laid my hands one on top of the other in my lap. I said nothing. And then I spoke.

"Mother of God, are you indeed the best lawyer available to me? Isn't it your job to prove to the judge that the stories are poppycock? What sort of lawyer are you?"

"I beg your pardon, that is... insulting."

"Yes, well, my dear DeLuria, you are incompetent." I stood up once more and would have paced the jail cell had I no chain, and had there been room. "I keep waiting for you to say something that convinces me that you have my best interests at heart. Or even my interests at all. But I am starting to think I might be better off on my own in the courtroom." I stood with my hands behind my back, imagining myself pacing the courtroom representing myself.

"The prosecution assumes that those foolish pages, those stories, tell some kind of truth. Their case against me rests entirely on stories composed by my cousin when he was suffering from syph..."

He interrupted. "No one has established that those pages are indeed the work of your cousin. This needs to be established in court. For all we know they may be anyone's writing. They may even be your own writing." He gave me a leering gaze, which only served to make my mouth drop open.

I laughed. "I hope you are joking," I said.

I bent closer to DeLuria and I whispered. "Is this possible you are as foolish and stupid a man as I think you are? Did you in fact just say what I think you said, that I may be the author of those pages? My dear dear DeLuria what would possess me to write a set of stories that incriminate me? Stories that portray me as a murderer and a whore?" I laughed louder, and sat back and laughed some more.

He ignored me, and began filling the satchel with all of his papers. I took a step nearer, bent even closer to him.

"Have you thought that there cannot possibly be anyone else who wrote those stories but my cousin? Have you thought it through DeLuria?"

My voice was hoarse, my face flushed, and I'm sure, my breath was a foul cloud.

He pulled away and finally squirmed out of range.

"Good day Sister," he said, and then he called to the jailer. "I am through here!"

"You most certainly are," I cried out. The jailer appeared and opened the cell and DeLuria disappeared.

So you see here, now, Teresa, how I've come to be my own counsel. Once DeLuria left, I sank onto the bench here, and the full impact of what I face in the courtroom next week hit me.

It is all but certain that I will be convicted. There is a pile of evidence that should by rights be dismissed without consideration. And yet this idea did not occur even to my lawyer.

Pray for me Teresa. Pray!

GINA

It was November 20, 2013 and after not seeing her for almost a year, I had lunch with my dear friend Nina. She and I have often marveled at the fact that we can go months—even years—without seeing each other, and when we reconnect, it's as if we have been chatting and emailing every single day.

The way we met: our sons, both October babies, attended the same pre-school. Over the years, Jonah and Julio had countless play dates and sleepovers, and the two of them have stayed close even as they have grown up.

What drew Nina and me into an even tighter bond, however, was Nina's horrible go-round with breast cancer in 1994.

She tells me I saved her life, and I think she may be right. I was the one who pushed her to have the lump in her breast removed, even when her lunatic of a doctor said he would take a "wait and see" approach.

I can't remember every detail. But suffice to say I remember that she ditched the son of a bitch who had been content to let her live with a lump in her breast. And I do remember calling Sloan Kettering, out of the blue, and finding a doctor to see her almost immediately. I remember taking the train to New York City with her, and us sitting together pouring over mammograms, as if we knew what we were looking at!

Within a month, she went through her surgery at Sloan, and I stayed with her throughout. At one point I remember so clearly a nurse who was tending to Nina in the recovery room saying to me, "Are you her sister?" (She has no siblings or close family at all)

I clearly remember thinking for a moment, and then saying, "Yes, we are sisters."

Back to my lunch with Nina in November; we splurged on a fancy Italian bistro, with a soaring ceiling, lots of windows and big potted plants and marble surfaces.

We sat there talking about life and family. During the course of the conversation, I said something to her about the fact I was thinking of consulting a medical intuitive for a problem I was having.

"You know," she said, very casually, "my good friend Teresa is working with a psychic."

I blinked.

"Nina, you have a good friend named TERESA?" I asked.

"Yeah, she and I were neighbors when I lived in Brooklyn. My father owned a brownstone and Teresa and her husband Brad lived next door. We were practically sisters."

Too many sisters. Too many coincidences.

"Nina," I said, "how does she spell her name?"

"T-E-R-E-S-A. Why?"

I laughed. "Because my character, you know Sister Renata, the one I'm writing about again, her best friend at the convent is a nun named Teresa. When I first started the book, I spelled it THE-RESA, but then just a few weeks ago, I changed it to TERESA."

"Wow, that really is strange," Nina said, "especially because..." Her eyes opened a little wider. She shook her head.

"Because why?"

"Because like I just said, Teresa told me the other day that she had just gotten in contact with a psychic in New Jersey and..."

By this point I had stopped eating.

"...and?'"

"The psychic is a former nun."

I felt my heart thumping. I felt energy sizzle up and down my arms. "You're kidding."

"No."

"What does this psychic do for Teresa?" I asked calmly, despite the fact that my head was swimming.

"She connects her psychically to people who have died. Like her husband, who died six months ago. Teresa in fact just mailed me this book called *What the Dead Can Teach Us About Life*, by James Van Praagh. It's amazing and apparently, this ex-nun in New Jersey is giving Teresa information about Brad and other loved ones and the information she has given her is very accurate."

I swallowed. The waitress appeared and I could barely speak.

Nina scribbled down Teresa's phone number on a napkin, and I called her the next day. She told me in detail how the psychic nun confirmed all kinds of personal details about her husband, information that only Teresa and Brad would know. Like the time they had a personal visit at the Vatican with the Pope himself.

So why didn't I phone the nun? Honestly, I was scared. I still am.

It's bad enough that I keep flip flopping back and forth in time. Talking to people who lived in 1883.

For now, I'm going to hold off. Until who knows when?

25

SISTER RENATA'S DIARY

October 29, 1883

Dear Teresa,

Maybe it was the ghastly heat. Or the unrelenting sunlight. The courtroom baked me like an oven.

And surely it didn't help that the judge, a hulking man without the least bit of patience, infuriated me. He refused to consider my argument that I be allowed to represent myself at the trial. He refused to listen to why I wanted to fire that foolish attorney of mine, DeLuria.

I started the day feeling achy and a bit queasy.

Bean had unchained me, and he and the Sheriff walked me over to the courtroom at 9 a.m. I know this because there was a giant clock on one wall. All I could think was, my life will be decided beneath the thin black hands of this big round clock.

My head was dizzy right from the start. My heart felt like it was pumping twice as fast as it normally does. I had placed my veil and wimple on my head. But the veil was crumpled and crooked, and my face was dirty, and I know—I could smell myself—my habit was a disgrace.

I sat beside DeLuria and we didn't speak.

We sat for ten or fifteen minutes before the judge arrived. He wore a dark robe. He had a head of white wavy hair. Thick waves.

As soon as the judge entered, my dizziness increased. I started to sweat. I stood and could feel myself sway. DeLuria glanced my way. And frowned.

I felt the blood drain from my face.

We sat. The two lawyers went to the bench. I set my face into my fingers. I saw you in my mind Teresa. And I saw Señora. I saw her wide brown face.

DeLuria returned to where I was seated and then it was time for me to stand and approach the bench. I looked to DeLuria, waiting for him to take my arm. He didn't. He simply looked at me as if I was a filthy dog. Too dirty to touch. I glared at him and my head felt giddy, my mind felt like it was coming loose.

I stood and with your face and Señora's in my mind, I walked forward.

Speaking politely, I asked the judge if I could represent myself.

The judge said, "absolutely not!" He went on. "No one in your position could possibly handle the task," he declared, wiping his spectacles and looking a little bored.

"But sir, I am certain that I could do a better job as I have an instinct for how to..."

"You have no knowledge of the law except as you have violated it!" He shouted at me.

"I beg to differ sir, I have a good sense of what needs to..." He interrupted.

"We will proceed and you my good woman, need to sit down immediately and stop the foolishness you are displaying here."

"May I just..."

"NO YOU MAY NOT!" He slammed the gavel on the bench and DeLuria, by now at the bench, grabbed my arm.

"You've got to sit down," he whispered. He dragged me back to the table and he and the Sheriff forced me to sit down. I could feel my face grow exceedingly warm and I had a strange pinching sensation in the back of my neck. I felt sick to my stomach.

It was at that moment that the judge told me to stand up once again. I inhaled and stood. He proceeded to begin reciting my crime. The next thing I knew, I was lying face down on the floor, my eyes closed, my mouth open, and I was tasting the filth of dust and dirt on the wood.

I could not move. I felt hands reach underneath my shoulders. I was scooped upright.

I remember being held. I remember wobbling. I remember De-Luria and the judge both swirling before my eyes, in dizzying figure eights. I remember a lurching sensation in my stomach and then everything coming up and out onto the floor. I was heaving up the slop of gruel I had eaten early in the morning in the cell.

At that moment, I heard someone yell, "Catch her," because I was falling again.

I was carried swiftly out of the courtroom, and they lay me down in a small cramped space, a kind of closet outside the courtroom.

I lay in the dark for who knows how long.

I dreamed. I went back to the stone grotto behind the hacienda. The one Antonie's father built for his mother. My cousin and I used to go there so long ago.

The grotto is low. It is tiny. It is surrounded in roses. There is a statue of the Virgin there and I swear I could smell the roses.

I kneel before the statue. I look up. The stones are so close I can practically kiss them. I touch the smooth surface of the stone.

I close my eyes and I hear...Señora praying. I hear her saying the Hail Mary in Spanish.

The whispering. The whispering grows louder. You are praying too Teresa. The two of you are kneeling with me in the grotto. We are beginning another Hail Mary.

We are saying the rosary together, the three of us.

Señora speaks. I know Teresa I know this isn't possible. I know. But I heard her so clearly, lying there in the dark.

"M'ija, m'ija," she whispered. She stroked my brow.

This isn't possible, I know.

The stones are smooth in the grotto. In places the stones are coated in dark scum and patches of bright green slime. Sometimes there is water dripping from the center stone. It passes right behind the Virgin's head. It falls into the dirt and forms a muddy spot on the ground.

I am seeing my cousin now. There he is. Antonie is a boy. And me, I have just arrived in California. We play guitar in the grotto. We make up this old story about the water dripping from the center stone. We used to say that in the very old days the water used to fall into a little pool where babies were baptized. Sick people and crippled kids would come to the pool. They would take silver cups and fill them with the holy water. They would drink the water and be healed. They would kneel in the pools and walk again.

I am talking out loud in the dark. And then the door opens. I raise my head expecting DeLuria. Or the jailer.

I blink. Because it is Señora. I swear she was there. The old woman wore a simple white shawl covered in red roses. She walked toward me and reached for my hand and placed something there.

And much later, when they finally moved me back to the cell, when I was well enough to walk very very slowly back to the jail, I knew I had not dreamed this.

Because you see, here, here is the rainbow rosary. Señora's own personal rosary beads are in my hand.

26

SISTER RENATA'S DIARY

November 13, 1883

The jailer slams his keys against the bars of the cell to wake me up the next morning. The sky is black outside the window and I can see only a crisp white curve of moon.

I sit up. "What..what time is it?" I ask, thinking it must be the middle of the night.

"It's time for you to get up," he says. "You got ten minutes before we go." He hobbles away before I can ask him where we are going.

Soon enough, I find out. He leads me in handcuffs out of the jail to the tiny blue house I've stared at for so many weeks. It sits low and tidy across the dusty courtyard and it has an inviting front porch.

When we get closer, I read a sign over the door: "Kitty's Corner Café." The door has a large window covered in a lace curtain and a brass bell beside it, and now the jailer rings the bell.

Even standing out here on the porch, I can smell breakfast cooking inside. Bacon. Toast.

The sky above my head is lightening up. Overhead it is turning a sugary blue.

A young woman—her hair pulled tightly away from her face—moves aside the lace curtain and peers out the window. She unlocks the door and without a word, Jimmy Bean leads me inside. The smell of food is so powerful that it makes me a little dizzy.

"Mornin' Kitty Pole," the jailer says.

"Mornin' Jimmy." She points to a table in the corner by the window.

"No, now we don't want to be attractin' no public attention," he says. He leads me to the back corner and we sit down at a table with a crisp white tablecloth.

He smells of tobacco and whiskey. I smell of so many things.

The young woman has large dark eyes and she wears a starched white apron. "What will it be Jimmy?"

"Bring the coffee right away and then fix up some eggs and bacon, some toast. Please be quick about it."

She nods and glances at me quickly and then leaves the room through a curtained door. She returns in a moment with two mugs of coffee. She sets one down in front of me. I stare into the cup. Suddenly I feel tears gathering behind my eyes. I realize that this is the first cup of coffee I've had—or even smelled—since September 13th, the day they whisked me out of the convent and into that hellish cell.

"Why are you doing this?" I whisper. Tears are falling onto the tablecloth but I am unable to wipe my eyes.

The jailer is stirring a teaspoon of sugar into his coffee. "Warn't my idea ma'am. The judge's instructions. Told me to get you a decent breakfast before the trial this mornin'. No more of your fancy fainting tricks." He snorts in derision.

I sniffle.

"Well, unless you plan to spoonfeed me, Jimmy, I cannot do a thing with these on," I say, nodding to the handcuffs on my wrists in my lap.

He fumbles for the key and unlocks the handcuffs. I sit with my hands limp on the table. I feel like I am unable to move. But then I sip the coffee. Heavenly!

Soon the woman is back with two plates, heaped with food. She sets one plate before me. Scrambled eggs. Crisp bacon. Potatoes. Toast.

"Anything else you need Jimmy?" she asks.

"Yep," He scratches his stubbly jaw. "I want some chili sauce if ya' don't mind. That kind you serve at lunch."

"Sure."

I stare at the plate. The food looks so good it doesn't seem real.

"Get eatin' while the gettin's good," he says. "We gotta be outta here before the breakfast crowd appears."

I lift my fork and take a small bite of the eggs. They are fluffy and light. I pick up the bacon. In the old days I would never have eaten with my fingers, especially being so dirty.

But now I am indifferent to the filth. I place a bit of the bacon on my tongue, and leave it there. I swear I'm dreaming.

The young woman brings the chili sauce back. It's green as pea soup. "You OK?" she asks me.

I am about to say that I can't suddenly eat a full breakfast after weeks of what I've been used to. Grey gruel. Slop. Greasy stew.

"You are a wonderful cook," I whisper. "It...it tastes...so good."

She looks at me with those dark eyes. Nods. "Glad," she says. And then she disappears through the curtain.

I eat most of the scrambled eggs and all of the bacon. But there isn't time for me to finish the toast. The young woman wraps it in a napkin for me. The potatoes stay behind.

"Thank you," I say. The jailer reaches over and snatches the toast away.

"I'll be takin' that if ya' don't mind," he says.

Kitty turns to me. "I am...happy you came," she says. And then she nods and stares at me with those large dark eyes. "And I hope the day... goes your way."

As the jailer replaces the handcuffs and leads me outside into the courtyard, a shaft of sunlight shines straight into the window of the restaurant. I glance back. Kitty is standing beside the window staring at me.

Jimmy leads me back to my cell and I am greeted by the smell of the foul pail. After the delightful breakfast odors at Kitty's, the pail's stench is almost unbearable. The pail is full and like always, I have to yell at Jimmy to take it away.

A few minutes before nine a.m., the Sheriff is there, and the two of them lead me to the courtroom. DeLuria greets me and we take our seats. At nine sharp the judge appears. We stand and the first thing he asks is if I'm "fit to stand trial today."

For a moment I think it's me he wants to hear from. But then DeLuria answers. "She is indeed, your honor," he replies.

"Well, good thing, because we need to get on with it," he says.

The jury traipses in and I stare at a motley group of twelve men—one of them exceedingly plump, and one exceedingly short—who file slowly into the courtroom. They do not look at me, at least not at first.

But I look at them, and then the worst fear comes over me. How can I possibly get a fair trial from this group? How is it that these men constitute a jury of my peers? And how is it that a jury of my peers has not a single woman?

After some preliminaries, the attorneys approach the bench and ask the judge some questions.

The judge keeps removing his spectacles and wiping them.

Finally, the attorneys leave the bench and the judge asks the prosecutor and DeLuria to make their opening statements.

As the prosecutor launches into his statement, his voice booms. He lays out the crime I am accused of committing. He apologizes that he has to shock the courtroom with the gory details of Antonie's murder.

I've heard it all before. Or should I say, I've read it all before. The newspaper has made the grizzly details of Antonie's death a front page story at least three times. Now that story comes spewing from the prosecutor's mouth.

And then he dabbles in my misdeeds and alleged scandals. My Spanish dancing. The visits to my cousin's hacienda, and the seductive way in which I would supposedly shave my cousin's face.

He dramatizes his silly speeches by lifting one arm and jabbing his long finger in my direction. I keep looking away.

I sit there, trying not to think about coffee and scrambled eggs and bacon. And praying that DeLuria will surprise me and find a way to present the truth of my case to the jury.

27

SISTER RENATA'S DIARY

November 20, 1883

My dear Teresa,

I am chilled and feverish and I have a thick congestion burning in my chest.

I write with the hope and prayer that you will come at once. And that you will bring with you the herbs that Señora Ramos uses so effectively for lung congestion. A doctor came to see me and he mumbled something about pleurisy.

All I know is that I am shivering and sweating and when I start to cough I cannot stop and when I breathe I wheeze and I cannot catch my breath.

When you come I will tell you about the trial—Teresa, let me just say that DeLuria has made such a profound mess of things—worse than I ever thought possible—that I have almost begun to pity him.

Almost.

DeLuria has turned out to be more of a fool than even I dreamed he could be. So astonishing is his incompetence that if I had the funds to hire a *real* attorney, I would probably have little difficulty getting this charade of a trial overturned on appeal.

His defense?

Teresa, he strode in front of the jury and delivered one of the most implausible opening statements imaginable. He made a statement that was so outrageous that I could see the jurors smirking and shifting uncomfortably in their chairs.

I could feel them staring at me. I saw one or two shaking their heads.

He began by standing and approaching the jury and with great flourish, directing the jury's attention my way. He was wearing what I have come to call his silly shirt, a powder blue affair with satin-edged ruffles at the chest. When he walked, his boots made a loud clatter on the wooden floor. His hair was pomaded and his mustache freshly waxed and twirled and all of that made him look even sillier.

He started with a question.

"When you gaze at the nun sitting over there in the sunlight, what do you see?"

Immediately he answered: "You see a young woman with a face that is the picture of innocence.

You see a slight woman with wispy hair, and a sweet, quiet expression. You see her hands folded so delicately and resting on the table."

He pivoted on the heel of one black boot and with his hands behind his back, he passed slowly in front of the men waiting to pass judgement on me.

Then he stopped and faced the judge. "But there is something you do not see!"

He paused and then directed their attention back to me by pointing a finger in my direction.

His voice dropped into practically a whisper. His eyes grew large and then, Teresa, I swear, he went...crazy.

"My friends, I want you to look again at this innocent young woman. Because what you see is not really what you see. The woman sitting before you is afflicted by a devilish disorder of the mind. You may never have heard of this disorder before, because it is only in recent years that it has been observed."

My heart started slamming against my chest. I was so frightened to hear the rest of what this imbecile was about to say that I couldn't look at him. I closed my eyes and held my breath and that's when I felt the first burning sensation in my chest!

"Members of the jury, it is my job to explain to you, to prove to you, that this young woman who sits before you may answer to the name Sister Renata, and she may indeed be a devoted nun of the Dominican order. But my friends, there is more to this woman than meets the eye."

Pause. Silence. Shock.

Me still holding my breath. All I could hear was the clock. Tick, tock. Tick, tock.

He went on.

"Even though it appears that you are seeing just one person sitting here, one innocent-looking nun, that is not the case. The nun sitting here suffers from a frightening disorder, a most troubling disorder."

He swirled around and pointed one hand—finger extended—at me, and the other hand—finger extended—across the room at the jury. For a moment it looked as if he was going to twirl across the courtroom floor, or worse, perform some kind of bizarre dance in front of the judge.

"It may be difficult to imagine," he said in his most theatrical voice, "but what we have here is a woman who has two separate identities, two separate selves, and these selves are pulling her apart." He looked up toward the ceiling and started shouting. "You must understand that through no fault of her own, and because of a deep malady from which she suffers, this poor nun is not just one person. Friends of the jury, Sister Renata has a double personality!"

He walked over now and stood before me. I shrunk back, moving as far away from him as I could. He raised his hands heavenward and brought them together and slowly down in front of him, as if symbolically, he was slicing me in two! Then he turned to the jury, his tone pleading, as if he was in desperate need for them to believe what he was saying.

"My dear friends, I hope I will be able to convince you that this poor woman has two individual selves living inside her body! And one of them is trying to destroy the God-fearing self you see here today."

Yes, Teresa, DeLuria's defense was that I suffer from some kind of malady that gives me a multiple personality—this notion is something he apparently read about in a magazine somewhere!

I covered my face in utter horror. I wanted to stand up and scream, "PLEASE STOP. Please, no more, you're only making matters worse!"

Fortunately, the Judge registered his surprise. "Mr. DeLuria, I very much look forward to your presentation of witnesses and expert testimony on this matter."

At which point, DeLuria smiled but remained silent.

The judge took a recess and said we would resume the trial in the afternoon.

And we did. What transpired this afternoon was just more distressing news. It turns out DeLura doesn't have any expert witness! It is almost too much to bear.

I must tell you Teresa, that by the end of the day, when DeLuria gathered up his papers and left the courtroom wearing those foolish ruffles, and that hair of his all slicked and pomaded, I felt sorry for him. Oh, yes, I felt fury to the depths of my being as well. But he was such a miserable fool that I actually found myself feeling a mite sorry for the man!

How could DeLuria deceive me like this? How could he fail me so miserably?

I am so weary. I sit here with a cup of tea. That woman from the café has started bringing me food. She is a good woman. How she convinced the jailer to let her in, I'm not sure. When I asked, she just nodded and smiled and said, "I'll take care of it."

I am here Teresa. Waiting for you. And praying you will come soon.

28

SISTER RENATA'S DIARY

November 26, 1883

Oh Teresa I am so so disappointed that you couldn't come. Sometimes I think that God has completely abandoned me! Why would Mother Yolla forbid you to leave and come to stand beside me? Is this some of Father Ruby's meddling? He is an evil man...

I feel dead inside. I feel my chest wide open and full of burning rocks! I will try to summarize. Close your eyes and imagine me being beaten up! That is how it felt, an agony of evil words. It lasted two and a half days total, and it would be laughable if I weren't crying so hard!

I will try to lay it out quickly as I have no desire to relive the pain. Instead of calling witnesses, the District Attorney used Antonie's preposterous stories to paint me as a conniving temptress and a heartless murderer. And something he revealed and I had not known: my cousin named me the sole inheritor of his estate! That of course was the perfect motive for my alleged murder.

His harangue lasted practically all of Thursday afternoon and Friday morning. He insisted on reading every single story of Antonie's! After each one I would repeat to myself: "THOSE WORDS ARE THE WORK OF MY COUSIN'S MIND. HE WAS SICK..." He would interrupt my thinking precisely at that point and then, start reading the next story.

I sat there dying inside, so humiliated hearing the filth that my cousin spread on one thin sheet of blue paper after another. At one point I stood up and turned to the judge and said, "I have my diary that tells the truth about what…"

The judge banged his wooden gavel "We will have no more outbursts in my courtroom!"

You once told me that I had to write it all down. I have done just that in my diary pages. I asked DeLuria if I would be able to introduce my diary pages as evidence to counter the lies that Antonie wrote. And here is what DeLuria said, and I quote him:

"I doubt the diary will make any difference. Who will listen to your rambling daily journal? Why would anyone accept the words of a woman over those of a man?"

Despite his doubts, DeLuria read my diary. His reaction: "Why are there no entries about Antonie's death?" He was talking of course about those three pages I ripped out of the journal.

Without those pages, DeLuria says the diary is useless. I tried to convince him otherwise but he wouldn't hear a word of it. And then I realized that he had his heart set on proving his ludicrous idea that I have a double personality.

His evidence to support that contention was pathetic! He stood up Friday afternoon and read from a short history of the condition:

"The first case of Dissociative Identity Disorder was described by physician Samuel Mitchel in 1816. Mitchel defined the condition in this way: 'At least two identities or personalities recurrently take full control of the person's behavior.'"

He paused. The judge asked him if he had any more to say.

"Yes, your honor," DeLuria said. "There are several cases that laid the foundation for Dissociative Identity Disorder. The first ever case was that of Mary Reynolds in 1811 and was documented by Dr. Mitchel. He also documented the case of Rachel Baker. Her main symptom was that she would preach in her sleep as well as write poetry and music."

The judge turned to face him. "And this constitutes the sum total of your evidence?"

DeLuria spoke. "Dr. Mitchel had a young assistant, Johnson King, and he agreed to appear in these proceedings."

"And," said the Judge, "what happened?

"I'm afraid that he broke his leg and couldn't travel."

"Mr. DeLuria, we need an expert to support your contention that Sister Renata suffers from this disorder."

DeLuria stood there, staring at the Judge. "Apologies," he said.

That was it. He returned to his chair, and the Judge gaveled the day's proceeding and pointed one finger at DeLuria. "I will see you, Mr. DeLuria, in my chambers!"

GINA

September 2007

Here it is, the big blank screen. I've been on such a roll. Chapter after chapter kept pouring out. I've written maybe 50,000 words.

And now, here I am with nada.

Nada word.

I am facing an empty plate. A zero mind.

I am going through chemotherapy.

Perhaps that is why I have a blank screen. I can't think straight.

I have been in treatment since July 16, 2007, at 11:43 a.m. I see the clear fat sausages hang from the IV pole. I sit in a pea green, fake leather chair.

My hair, my eyebrows—all gone.

Inside my chest is a tumor the size of a cantaloupe.

I won't bother telling you the details. It's hellish enough to go through it the first time. No point in reinscribing the pain.

OK here's one detail: in order to do the biopsy, the doctor used a device that looked like a gigantic hypodermic needle. He drew the sample into a tube that was an inch in diameter and a foot long.

Is it any wonder I can't write?

Before I discovered the cancer—at the end of June when I noticed that I had an egg-shaped lump on my breastbone—I was riding along on a torrent of words. Renata was in jail, on trial, accused of murder.

But suddenly, I was in the jail of chemotherapy for a crime I didn't commit.

I feel like I don't have energy to walk. To talk on the phone.

I eat intermittently, in between bouts of throwing up.

Apple sauce. A scrambled egg. Two pieces of toast. Chicken broth with pastina.

I AM WRITING RIGHT HERE SO WHY CAN'T I WRITE ABOUT RENATA?

The book is the book is the book. I am in the Sahara. There are no words in the bank. There are no crumbs in the bread drawer.

Is it any wonder that the book IS GOING BELLY UP? I have turned all my attention toward healing. Toward staying alive. My family is so wonderful.

Jonah, at BU, wants to quit school and move home. Absolutely not!

Joel drives me to Sloan Kettering in New York City every week and sits with me during every treatment.

All summer and now it's the fall. All I can do with *Sister Mysteries* is stack up the pages into a neater pile.

One night recently I couldn't sleep. I got up and fixed myself silver tea. My mother used to fix it all the time. Boil water, add milk and honey.

I had just begun to drink the tea when Señora appeared in the kitchen. She took a chair. Neither of us spoke. She laid both of her fleshy brown hands over my pale hand.

I am here with you, she whispered. She disappeared.

I finished the tea and went back to bed.

A white sheet is binding my bed. A white light is blinding me. I keep my eyes closed because the light is so bright. They keep the lights on all night here. I try to sleep but I can't stop crying.

What am I? Three years old? I am in the hospital with pneumonia. I am screeching for my mother but she went home a long time ago. She left me here behind bars.

Before she left, she whispered to me, honey, just be quiet and go to sleep now. I will come back tomorrow!

It's always the same thing. Over and over and over again I am in the prison. We are together, Renata and me. I can feel her breath on my shoulder, my neck. I can see the white wimple so tight, binding her forehead. Making a pink crease. I stare at her eyebrows beneath the wimple. I think of his eyebrows. Eerie how similar her eyebrows are to Antonie's. But then they are cousins.

I am sinking now. I am sinking into the swill of chemicals.

I am sinking into too many dreams.

I sink directly into Renata's dream. Her dream of a tree. That damn madrone tree, behind the hacienda, under which Antonie seduced her as a child.

Seduction? It isn't seduction when you are raped.

It is cold sitting here in the dank old prison cell. All by myself, I am sitting beside Renata. The two of us, prisoners.

I turn my face away when she squats over that dreadfully foul pail.

I sit here shaking the bars. Let me out, I shout. The nurse tries to settle me down. I scream over and over: I want my mother!

Iron. I smell rust on the bars. I smell rust on my fingers and hers.

I feel my mother's fingers through the bars of the crib.

The doctor at Sloan Kettering has me taking an antibiotic so that—with my chemotherapy-induced immune system—I won't get a serious case of pneumonia.

She and I sit here and suddenly my hands are free and I am strumming the guitar and Renata is singing something sweet.

Now I am dreaming about the chemicals in the IV. I am drinking the chemicals from a silver cup. I feel like a swill.

I am in the dark putrid swamp that is chemotherapy.

I will never see the world quite the same way.

I look up and see my mother in the dark, trying to sneak away from my hospital bed.

I see my mother in a robe and veil like the Virgin Mary.

My mother's hair is black and thick and wavy. She has not a single grey hair. Her hands are dry and rough from washing clothes in Clorox and Tide. I hold tight to her fingers.

My sister Carolyn is only a year old. In diapers.

My mother stands above the crib and holds my hand. She has the loveliest smile. When I fall asleep she gently lets go of my hand and tiptoes out of the room and that's when I start screeching again.

When I wake, I am throwing up. The anti-nausea drug (Zofran) doesn't work.

"Joel!" I scream. "I'm puking again!"

He does for me what my mother would do—she passed two years ago.

WE ARE ONE THE NUN AND ME. She is in jail for a crime she didn't commit, just like me. I am in the jail of chemotherapy. I am in the jail of Catholicism.

And now I can see you—whoever you are—laughing. How dare you laugh!

Now I make the sign of the cross with my eyes. Now I look up at the scummy green walls at Sloan. Now I think, I am asleep, thank GOD, because otherwise everyone who reads this will think, she needs a hospital of a select kind, the kind they select for you when you have lost your mind.

Now I think I must get out of here. Now I know I must escape and take the nun with me, as we are joined at the ankles by a rusty chain.

Now I must explain how this story unfolds because it is held together just with pins, the pins of my lips.

Now I am a fish out of water. Now I am swimming free. Now I realize how he tricked me, telling me to lie down with him beneath the madrone tree. Now I realize that I am caught. Now I realize that I am totally and utterly mad.

Now I remember what the doctor said—the chemo affects your head. It fills your brain with chemicals just like the rest of you. You will feel crazy. Your head will be a swill.

From time to time, Señora will appear. I tell her I cannot write. She hugs me, holds me to her pillowy bosom.

She whispers: you will write the book again, I promise.

29

SISTER RENATA'S DIARY

November 27, 1883

What finally woke me: the smell of eucalyptus. And peppermint. And Señora humming something deeply familiar as she pressed a warm wet compress against my bare chest.

I thought I heard Teresa's voice. I thought I heard her telling the jailer, Jimmy Bean, "just stand aside, Mister Bean, just stand aside. We have a mighty sick woman to attend to here, my dear sir." Her familiar brogue was a sweet boost to my spirits. I lay there in such a sweat and fever that I wasn't sure. I was deliriously happy to hear Teresa's voice, but was Teresa really here?

How could she be, when Mother Yolla had forbidden it?

I managed a whisper: "My dear Teresa, how did you manage this?"

She smiled. "I simply told Mother Yolla that I would expose the way Antonie had filled Father Ruby's coffers." She smiled wider.

She turned to Bean and assigned him a job: he was to keep the fire boiling under Señora's copper kettle outside the jail, while Kitty, from the café nearby, volunteered to stir hot towels into Señora's mixture of herbs: eucalyptus and mint, thyme and hyssop and cardamom.

Teresa, meanwhile, forked one towel after another up and out of the boiling kettle and let them hang briefly over the jail's porch railing until they could be wrung out and carried inside. Then she would slip the hot towel between the bars and take away the one that Señora had removed from my chest.

Hour after hour Señora sat with me, humming, humming, that familiar something, the old flower song, placing one after another warm towel on my chest. And finally when it grew dark, she lifted my head to her generous lap, and circled us both with a blanket, and I slept that way, parked on her soft lap, into a second day, while Kitty took Teresa home and gave her a meal and a place to sleep.

On the second day, Señora applied the mustard poultice, which, unlike the other herbs, is not such a pleasant affair. Teresa gave Kitty the bag of black mustard seeds, and had her grind them in a coffee grinder, then she mixed the mustard powder with enough flour and hot water to form a yellow paste.

Kitty carried the paste in a bowl back to the jail. Señora spread the paste with a wooden spoon on a large square of soft muslin soaked in hot water. She lay that on my chest—the skin between my breasts was by now pink and raw from all the wet plasters. She covered me with the mustard paste on the muslin and then covered that with a second piece of dry cloth.

At some point, I began coughing. The congestion was loosening a little, and Señora helped me sit upright and rubbed and patted my back and made circles and now I coughed and wheezed but I was awake. Teresa made me a parade of different teas and forced me to drink. Mint tea, then thyme tea, and even, Señora produced a lemon from her basket. Kitty supplied a teapot and Teresa filled the pot with hot water and lemon slices. Soon Señora was supervising me drinking cup after cup, each rich and fragrant in lemon and each with a dollop of honey and a sprinkle of cayenne pepper.

The second night, Señora went home with Kitty to sleep, and Teresa sat with me, holding my head in her lap. I sank deep and was dreaming of wagon wheels all night. Wheels turning and turning, wheels larger and larger. I was wheezing when I woke.

But I knew right away the fever had eased. My mind had cleared. I yawned. And coughed. And couldn't stop coughing and kept spitting up phlegm into the foul pail. When I sank back to the bench in exhaustion, Teresa mopped my brow.

"My dear Renata, how you have suffered. But my dear, I believe that you've got a wee bit of color in your cheeks this morning."

Soon Kitty appeared with Señora. They had fresh rolls and hard boiled eggs and a pot of steaming chamomile tea. After we ate and drank, Teresa said she had something "quite urgent" she needed to attend to. Little did I know she was about to work a small miracle.

She disappeared from the jail, and was gone for not more than half an hour.

And yes, I am accustomed to miracles with Teresa, like the shower she hammered together at the convent, but this miracle was truly a wonder considering that I am here, a prisoner in this godforsaken cell.

Teresa returned with Jimmy Bean and he unlocked the cell, and cuffed my wrists. Teresa helped me to my feet and held me by the shoulders. "Come along now, Renata," she said, as if it was perfectly normal that I would leave the cell in her company.

"But where...what...where are we going?"

Teresa said nothing to me. Without a word, Bean led us out of the jail into the sunlight. I was weak and tired, but Teresa and Señora were on either side, supporting me.

And if I tell you what happened, I wonder if you will believe it! We crossed the dusty courtyard to the tiny blue house, which has on the first floor, Kitty's café—the place I had breakfast a couple of days before. But our destination was not the café, but the back staircase. We climbed the creaking wooden stairs, and at the top, was Kitty's place.

We entered, the three of us, and there was Kitty, and behind her, I faced, for the first time in more than two months, a clawfoot tub filled with warm bathwater. Kitty smiled, and stood in an apron, holding up a large towel. Bean stood outside the door, as Teresa promised she would be "guard" inside.

Teresa helped me remove my habit. I had worn it for so long, it had taken on a stiff and crusted look. I was so dirty and yet, I had stopped smelling my own odor.

But now, I was sinking into the most delicious bathwater. I was shoulder deep. I was up to my chin. I was in heaven. I smiled. Teresa smiled back and Señora clapped her fat brown hands together.

My body has never felt such complete and utter warmth. I kept thinking, I cannot ever leave this bathtub.

Kitty had some fresh lavender she dropped into the bath, and I lay there, and I said a prayer of thanks, and let the water and the smell of it restore my spirit.

GINA

I am writing. But more: I feel like I am lying in a basket covered by a cool blue towel and electrical wires. Sparks are flying backward and backward taking me to that crib in the hospital where my feverish brain keeps catching fire.

The shadows in this cell have long teeth. The teeth are turning into bars. Now I have to use that foul pail, for my puking.

Now Joel takes me to the ER because I can't stop throwing up.

Now the incompetent nurse can't find a vein. I explain to her that I am in treatment for cancer. She jabs and pokes and makes me bruised and blue.

Who can help me?

Señora visits. The chemo, she reminds me, is curing my cancer. I hug her.

Renata reminds me of the same thing.

I love Renata. I wouldn't want to be any other nun.

I tell her that my name, Gina, is short for Regina.

She looks at me in disbelief. HER MOTHER'S NAME IS REGINA!

Excuse me, I have to puke. I sit here a minute. I could do it here in the ER. Or in the toilet in the bathroom at home.

Or I can do it. With Renata.

I puke into Renata's foul pail. But now, it's my own.

30

SISTER RENATA'S DIARY

November 29, 1883

Had I known that Teresa was going to take away my black habit after the bath—burning it in Kitty's barrel behind the blue house—I would have refused the bath. No matter I hadn't bathed in weeks.

And no matter that it was a delicious and refreshing bath. Yes—the warm water was perfect and the suds so gentle and soothing. Kitty brought one after another fresh teakettle of steaming water, until Mr. Bean knocked on the steamed up glass window of the outside door where he was standing guard.

He was getting impatient, as my bath was taking a rather long time, and it was up to him to make sure that I got back to the jail.

The curtain kept him from peering inside where I lay in the tub.

"You ladies had better be gettin' done in there pretty quick."

"Ten minutes more," Teresa yelled.

"Five not a second extra!" he shouted back.

"Mercy, Mr. Bean, I've got to wash her hair!"

"Make it fast!"

She chuckled. And under her breath, "OK, then, rub a dub dub, Renata." She kneeled, groaning as she rearranged her plump self beside the tub. With Kitty pouring lukewarm water over her hands and my head, Teresa shampooed my shorn scalp. I smelled the lavender soap. I felt the brisk work of Teresa's strong fingertips scratching my scalp to come alive. Oddly, the clean odor of the shampoo filled me with some kind of hopefulness.

My head rinsed, I was helped by the two of them out of the bathtub, dripping, and into a set of towels. A wonderful sensation. I smiled and pulled the towels tight around my shoulders.

I looked around the room. "What happened to Señora? And what did you do with my habit?"

"Ah not a chance you will ever be seeing that item of clothing again my dear," Teresa said, scowling. She stepped behind me and used the second towel to shuffle dry my hair.

"But...what...I *must* have it back, you know I must," I said. "Otherwise, I go back to the courtroom in two days and...and what... what exactly do I wear?"

Teresa stopped toweling, and turned me around. She took my face in her two thick hands and stared hard into my eyes. Her cheeks were pink in steam from the bath. I could smell coffee on her breath.

"Renata, my dear, there is not a thing we can do, not today anyway. I gave it to Señora while you were soaking and she tried to wash it out back there where Kitty does laundry. My dear, the both of your sleeves were so rotten in dirt that they came apart in her hands— and there was a giant tear at the bodice. I'm going to bring you another habit on my next trip."

Her voice, lilted in Irish brogue, was usually music to me. But not now. "Where is Señora, please?" I asked.

"She's taken over the café for Kitty, she is fixing us a good evening meal, a tortilla soup, with one of Kitty's chickens, even, and we will be bringing a bowl to you as soon as it's cooked!"

Meanwhile, Kitty emerged from the bedroom at that moment with a neat stack of clean white underclothing. "Here you go," she said, offering it up to me. "And I have a powder blue muslin dress in the closet, I think it will fit you. It's a bit snug on me."

I felt warm tears rising out of my eyes, covering my face like the bathwater had a few minutes before. I began to shake my head. The smell of lavender now was overpowering, and it almost made me dizzy.

It occurred to me now that I was still weak with the illness that had practically killed me only days before.

"If...I had known, I would have refused the bath," I whispered.

"Renata this is just silly, you will be perfectly presentable in court wearing the blue muslin. And in a week or so I will have another habit here for you." Teresa tried to lift my chin but I wasn't having any of it.

Bean was banging on the door. "I give you two more minutes or I'm coming in," he yelled.

My teeth came together. "Let him in then," I seethed, feeling a deep exhaustion set in. I needed sleep. Desperately. It had been a long few days. "Let him see me naked for all I care. What does it matter, as I have nothing proper to wear!"

I was sobbing now, into the towel that Teresa had used on my hair. Kitty put her arm around my shoulders, and squeezed, Teresa had my hands. I cried harder.

"Oh Renata, I am so terribly sorry. I know this isn't easy for you," Teresa said. "And you are still so weak. Come sit down, we don't want you to get chilled."

I let her lead me to a chair. Kitty brought an afghan and covered my head as if it was a veil.

"Can you for a moment imagine how it feels?" I shuddered. "I've been caged there in that ... animal pen they call a jail for so many many weeks. And yet the whole while, I had my...I kept myself going knowing who I was. Feeling that I am, that I was, the same nun who had been dragged from the convent on September 13th."

"But now my habit is gone. Gone! My veil, long since lost to me. Without them, I am... what am I Teresa? *Who am I?*"

She hesitated a moment. Her eyes widened, her face grew a darker pink. "It is not your habit or your veil that made you a nun," she said, her tone soft and solemn. "It was never those things that made you who you are! You are the same Renata you were before you left the convent."

I shook my head sadly. "No, no I am not," I said, quietly. "I have no idea who I am but I am definitely not the novitiate I was eight weeks ago. I have fallen too low for that."

Mr. Bean was trying the door handle. It was locked. He shook the handle and it rattled the glass loudly. "I tell ya I'm going to bust down this door if you're not out here forthwith," he yelled, "and I don't care if I do see her nekked."

Something in the way he said that word "nekked"—the foolish old man—ignited me. I stood up, letting the afghan slip off my hair, and I marched to the door, wearing just the towel. I pushed the curtain aside. I stuck my tongue out at him. "Go away," I frowned.

He must have seen that I was just in the towel because he took a quick step back. "Git yourself dressed immediately," he demanded.

I closed the curtain. I scooped up the stack of underclothes Kitty had given me. "Please if you would, show me the dress," I said, marching into Kitty's bedroom.

Teresa wanted to help but I refused. I closed the bedroom door and dressed myself. When I emerged, with the pale blue belted muslin in place of my scratchy wool habit, Teresa smiled. "God made you a beautiful woman, my dear," she said. "And it is no matter what you wear. You look lovely." She handed me my old shoes, newly polished. "You are standing in nun's shoes."

"And Kitty's socks," Kitty smiled.

I walked toward the door. As I reached for the lock, I turned.

"Kitty, I want to thank you for everything," I said.

"Of course," she smiled. "I am happy to be able to help you. I believe in you Renata and I believe in my heart that somehow, it is in God's plan that you will be set free. I have been saying extra prayers for you for weeks now, every time I attend mass."

I smiled. "Thank you." I let Bean handcuff me and lead me back to the cell. The smell of the foul pail as I stepped inside was worse than I remembered it.

"Get this out of here," I demanded, and perhaps because of my tone, he did it right away.

GINA

Now I see the truth: that I caused my mother's asthma, because she had to visit me so often in that damn hospital. Every night, it was cold, she caught cold, and she told me

"I got sick visiting you."

Like Renata, I am being punished for something I did not do.

I see too that my mother and me both suffered horrible illnesses of the chest.

Now I see the IV. Now I see my mother in bed, hunched over pillows gasping for breath.

Now I feel the delicate chemistry of the STANFORD FIVE. Consider what that monster at Sloan Kettering did, pumping me full of five innovative chemicals each week for 13 weeks. The doctor tells me I am a "poster child" for chemo.

The doctor lists for me the chemicals: one is vincristine what a name vincristine.

Here I am writing again. Señora is here in the chair beside my bed. She plays guitar and we sing to the music.

Señora smiles.

She whispers to me or is it Renata? "You tried so hard to protect me, m'ija. You tried too hard. You carried far too heavy a load." It is time, she says, it is time to explain who killed Antonie.

Señora rises from the chair and stands beside me; she squeezes my shoulder and covers my forehead with one hand.

She covers me like a baby with the blue shawl. She comforts me.

Oh, that shawl. Dazzling blossoms. She hands me a single yellow rose. A rose with red tips.

Suddenly she disappears and the VIRGIN MARY takes her place. Now I am lying in bed praying every single day to Mother Mary.

I hide there in the folds of her blue veil. And breathe.

31

SISTER RENATA'S DIARY

December 2, 1883

How quiet the jail is tonight.

How bright the moon is outside the window. A perfect white button glowing in the dark cloak that is the sky.

Will she come back again?

Will she bring the other?

I stare between the bars into the courtyard and close my eyes and I realize that I must have been dreaming.

Of course I was dreaming.

Or was I? THAT WAS SEÑORA! She was here. She was here in her flowered shawl. I see her wide face the color of coffee with milk. I see her...and all the bright flowers on the satin shawl.

And I see the other too! She brought the Mother. She brought Her to me.

Or did she? Do I see what I think I see? Am I thinking clearly? I have eaten nothing. I have slept fitfully. I blink and my eyes play endless tricks on me.

What takes the place of Señora's face is horrifying:

The rope. Those five wooden steps.

And if it weren't for her coming, appearing here in the cell. If it weren't for that, for the Mother Herself saying, "Bless you my child, keep steady, have faith!"

If it weren't for that, for the explosion of light that surrounded me, that flooded me, I would say there is no hope.

With my eyes open, with my pen writing words precise and clear here in black ink on this white paper, there is only this to say:

Yesterday is the day that the trial finally ended. Yesterday is the day that the last days of my life were numbered. All that remains for me is the five steps up to the gallows.

At the judge's insistence, DeLuria dropped the preposterous defense about me having a double personality. Instead, after consulting with the Judge, DeLuria decided to subpoena a dozen of the nuns from the convent to testify on my behalf at the trial.

All twelve of them sat behind me, a phalanx of faith and devotion. DeLuria brought each nun in turn to the witness stand to testify on behalf of my "outstanding moral character."

It took most of the afternoon in that stifling courtroom to hear from each of the 13 nuns (Teresa included.) One after the other they sat for the ordeal, listening to the insults of the prosecutor.

To all of you who came on my behalf—to Sister Baptiste, Sister Philomena, Sister Hermione, Sister Marietta, Sister Felicity, Sister Annabelle, Sister Celina, Sister Genevieve, Sister Pauline, Sister Rafaela, Sister Margot and Sister Lucia—I am forever indebted to you. I am forever grateful. I salute your courage, and your endurance. Traveling by carriage all those miles from the convent on those dusty roads. And then sitting on backless benches in that stifling courtroom all those many long hours. Enduring all the questions, the snide remarks, the stern looks from the jurors, all of it.

No matter. At the end of the day, the jury took exactly one hour and 34 minutes to return to the courtroom. I was in the cell only a few minutes when the jailer returned to "fetch me" for the verdict.

I sat at the defense table, hands folded, holding the well-worn family Bible that Teresa had brought me. I watched the 12 men shuffle back into the room, carefully avoiding my eyes.

The judge spoke. "Gentlemen of the jury, have you reached a verdict?"

The foreman, a portly man with a bright red nose and wearing a leather vest, stood. "Yes, your honor, we have."

The judge nodded. Turned to glare at me. "Please stand and face the jury."

I stood, and DeLuria stood beside me. And behind me, I heard all of the nuns who had come to support my case. I felt them all rise with me!

Suddenly there wasn't nearly enough air in the courtroom to breathe. So I held my breath. My hands trembled so I held them to my chest as if in prayer.

"How do you find the defendant?" I heard the judge's question, but it sounded so far away to me, as if I had been wholly delivered up to another world.

"We find the defendant guilty, your honor."

Without knowing why, I smiled. I will never understand that beatific smile. Perhaps it was a release. Finally, I was hearing the words that I had dreaded to hear for so many many weeks.

A tender hush rose up behind me. I felt a hand at my back, one on my elbow, I know not whether it was DeLuria or Teresa or one of the many other nuns. My legs turned so soft that I felt they would no longer support me.

I collapsed into the chair. There were words being said, I suppose the judge was pronouncing the date that I would be sentenced, but now I felt again that I was not present in the room. Or I was immersed deep under water. Or he was speaking Russian or French. DeLuria tried to pull me by the arm, hoping I would stand again, but it was too late. I had turned into dead weight.

I sat there hands folded staring into the oak table. I studied the grain of the wood, and I felt that I could continue sitting there staring at that beautiful grain—the whorls so intricate—for as long as they would permit me.

But it wasn't long before I was lifted at both elbows and my wrists were shackled again.

DeLuria was telling me he would file an appeal and I was about to say,

"Mr. DeLuria I feel that is a mistake, and not necessary, you see you have done enough already."

But my lips were forming words I couldn't say. I was already being shepherded out of the room. And as I headed out, I glanced once at the bank of eyes and tears and black veils. Sister Pauline was making the sign of the cross and Teresa was holding Señora in her arms and rocking her.

I was all too soon back here, locked in, where I sat in silence until Teresa and Señora came and the three of us held hands through the bars and cried together and said nothing.

What could we possibly say when all is lost?

Finally, the jailer came and told them visiting hours were over. Teresa protested, but I begged her to go. And so they did, but not before Señora left a basket covered in a gingham cloth—jars of canned vegetables and one of apricots. Ah, but nothing appealed to me, not even the cup of chamomile tea that Kitty later brought me (I took it, however, because as long as I was sipping the tea, Mr. Bean allowed her to sit with me.)

The sun dropped behind the courtyard and that moon I am still staring at rose in the clear dark sky. I must have fallen asleep. When I awoke, I saw that Mr. Bean had left me a bowl of soup which had grown cold, and a crust of bread. I dumped both into the foul pail.

I have a stone dead feeling in my stomach, as if someone had come in and stolen the core of me away and left a gaping cold trench. An open grave.

I have no idea when it happened.

When she came.

I know only that at some point she came.

Or did she?

During the night, when the moon was close to the roof of Kitty's café, I stood looking out the barred window. I stared into the courtyard where the gallows will stand and I finally said it out loud:

I am convicted of premeditated murder. I have been found guilty of killing my cousin Antonie in cold blood.

And I would have written that there is no more to say.

That all is lost. That there is no more hope for me. That nothing more remains but the sentence and the sentence we know already is me hanging by a rope.

But then she came. She has come before to me, Señora. She came clear as a ringing bell, she came shortly after I was arrested, she arrived here in this very cell, singing in the key of eternity. She came another time, after I collapsed in the courtroom, and then she brought me the rainbow rosary.

And perhaps because I was saying that very rosary tonight, praying with all my might for a miracle again, she came again, just as the moon settled like a bright bubble on the horizon, just before the bubble burst, and flooded the sky with white light.

She sat here with me, my dear old Señora, playing her guitar, and singing her lovely carcelero.

I am quite convinced of it now but how to explain this PRESENCE?

And how to explain the other, the glimpse I had of the Virgin Mother?

She is real. She too was here tonight, as clear as I see these bars she stood above me, as bright as the moon glowed, she showed herself to me in a fabulous light.

She the Mother filled me with love, I glowed too I glowed too. And I am afraid to write it down here, perhaps I fear that the miracle will disappear.

And I've grown nervous that the jailer when I sleep takes the journal, for what purpose I am not sure, he doesn't read a word. But just in case, I will slip the journal inside the powder blue shirt-waist dress.

And I sit here, and with me is the guitar that Señora played and now I sing and play and I sing and I pray.

And she is back, and

Now she sees my tears and changes gear. Now she is singing a gay and witty sort of palo which has a never ending number of poetic verses.

She sings:

Just imagine. What I. Did. Just imagine. Where I fled to.

Only the stars can tell you. Only the sky can guess.

So now sit down and I will try to tell you.

You will see it all come clear.

When the water goes still as a mirror,

And we peer inside.

Do you see now, why I appeared here?

Do you see now, why you must
Tell the world my story? Yes, tell the world
Just sing it, shout it out,
how we turned the past.
Together
We will move her story, Renata's
and Antonie's,
and his false history,
and hers,
around.

GINA

I can withstand the chemo hiding beneath her veil. I can disappear from the doctors and all the misery they have inflicted on me.

Now Señora is back, standing with the Virgin Mary.

Now Señora appears and Mary is gone.

Now Señora is whispering to me, REGINA. Now she is whispering to RENATA.

This is what she says: "I am taking the diary entry. The one that reveals what happened the day that Antonie died. You can't hide it anymore. You can't keep the truth inside. I am bringing it to the lawyer. I am bringing it to the court. It will set you free, mi'ja. It will free you at last."

I open my mouth to protest. I am resting in bed, my head a swill. I am resting in prison, my head against the slimy wall.

No, I say, I refuse.

She shakes her head and raises one hand:

"¡Silencio!" she commands. "Ahora, niña, es necesario decir la verdad. Es muy importante." *It is necessary to tell the truth. It is very important.*

My heart beats faster. I stare at her. "But what will happen to you?" I wail. "What will happen to you?"

She smiles. And in perfect equanimity, and in perfect Spanish, she says, "I have prayed to HER. I have placed my heart in HER. I am not afraid because I pray each moment of each day to the Virgin Mary."

She convinces me to do the very same thing. While I am suffering in chemo, I know she is there. All I have to do is pray to her and something wonderful happens. A friend emails or calls. A package arrives. I stop puking.

Now Señora makes the sign of the cross, and then she places a single kiss on my forehead, and A YELLOW ROSE WITH RED LIPS ON MY BED.

And before I can say another word, she is on her way.

And the rest, the rest is all a dream.

32

SISTER RENATA'S DIARY

December 7, 1883

I am dreaming about my cousin Antonie—blood spurts from the ragged gash in his throat, and both my hands are coated, warm and slick, the way they were that abominable day he died.

Antonie is grabbing at my neck and his eyes are two fierce black coals burning into me. I'm gagging because he's choking me and my arms are thrashing back and forth as I desperately try to free myself, when suddenly, a glass explodes and shatters. I scream and shoot straight upright.

When I open my eyes I realize that it is Kitty sitting beside me, her fingers circling my throat! It is barely sunrise, the windows glow pink in early light. With all my thrashing, I've accidentally sent the glass of water sitting by my bed flying and it's shattered on the floor.

"Why...whatever are you *doing*?" I say to her, my heart slamming.

Tears spring to my eyes as I feel the dream and the image of Antonie's eyes, and my bloody hands, pressing in on me.

"I am so sorry," she says. "But...your breathing was so...so shallow Renata...I wanted to make sure that you were still...here."

"Of course I'm still here," I say, irritated, feeling a single warm tear leaking out of each eye. I pull the covers, drenched in water, up to my neck while she collects the broken pieces of glass off the floor, piling them into her white apron.

There are moments lately when I wish the three of them—Kitty, Teresa, even Señora—would just go away. I'd just as soon they let me be, let them lead me to the gallows and be done with it.

But they refuse. The three of them have teamed up, making me their project, the central object of their daily activity.

My lungs degenerated terribly while living all those weeks in the moldy jail, and after I was sentenced, my wheezing became continual and I developed a deep raspy cough.

One morning Teresa found me unconscious on the floor of the cell. Full of rage, she lit into DeLuria, and convinced him to petition the judge.

Somehow, Teresa prevailed. So now, now that I am scheduled to die by hanging in a matter of weeks—just by chance, the date is set for January 6th, the Feast of the Epiphany—now that I have only days to live, the court has seen the wisdom of transferring me to an "external facility," that is, Kitty's place. The blue house, which has as its first floor, the tiny café, and upstairs, Kitty's residence.

The jailer, Jimmy Bean, ostensibly stands guard outside the front door. But more often than not, he's got that bottle of whiskey in his hands. And he falls asleep. And we hear him collapse off his chair onto the porch. Once he tumbled down Kitty's staircase.

What irony, that the court would want to make certain that I stay healthy long enough so that they can hang me.

Teresa insists that Kitty has a plan, a promise of "new hope."

Teresa delivered this bit of news to me a few days ago, after bringing me a cup of dandelion tea. I refused to drink it, but she lifted a teaspoon of the steaming brown liquid right up to my lips.

"My dear, I intend to remain here in this position until you give in and drink this damn tea, so please be quick about it."

I blinked. In all the years I'd known her, Teresa had never once let profanity slip from her lips. "Ah so now you swear, do you?"

"Oh yes indeed, I do when I need to make my point. Now just drink the tea would you please?" So I did, I took the rose petal tea cup—part of Kitty's best set of dishes—from Teresa's hands, at which point she settled back into her chair. "Kitty says it helps cleanse the liver."

"And why exactly does my liver need cleansing?" At which moment Kitty emerged from the kitchen.

"The liver stores anger, and in your case, there is plenty of reason for it." Kitty has a ready store of healing herbs, and tinctures she brews in her café kitchen.

Perhaps that is why there is something about this house. A certain nurturing way it feels. I'm not sure, but Teresa calls it a "blessed spirit that circulates between the walls," and she claims that even the convent "never felt this way."

She may be right. All I know is that by treating me with gingko and feverfew, Kitty has managed to make my cough virtually disappear, and my wheezing is improved.

It helps too that I now sleep like a lamb (despite this morning's episode) and that I eat like a queen, thanks to the fact that Señora has taken over cooking all the evening meals at Kitty's café. (In this way, Señora is earning her board here, while Teresa does laundry and keeps house for her share.)

So there are four of us living here in the tiny three-bedroom blue house. Why exactly Kitty has decided to open her home and heart to us, why she is so attentive to me, I cannot say. Teresa has alluded to the fact that Kitty has a long sad story, one she will not share. "There is enough you have to carry in your heart right now, no need for more sorrow."

I suspect that Kitty lost a child. At least I know this much: there is a portrait, a sketch in pastels, of a young girl, fawn-colored eyes, and soft strawberry curls gracing her delicate shoulders.

The portrait sits in Kitty's room above her bed, and once, I happened to pass by Kitty's open door and there she was, touching the portrait as if she meant to graze the child's face.

There is no evidence of a man having lived in this place, and again, I questioned Teresa, and again, Teresa set her lips together and wouldn't say.

Whatever it is that motivates her, Kitty regards me as her pet project. Her own cause celebre. As she put it to me one evening, when she'd set a fire going in the fireplace, wrapped me in a red and yellow quilt, and fixed me still another cup of strong dandelion tea. "You have suffered more than anyone ever should, Renata, and I'm not going to rest until we set you free."

So now, today, it seems as though there is news. After collecting the shards of glass from the floor, I fell back to sleep, and when I awoke, the sun was pouring into the front windows. Teresa had fixed me what has come to be my favorite morning meal: buttery biscuits and raspberry jam. She left three of them, and a cup of tea, now cool, on a tray.

Soon I heard murmuring, and then, a squeal of excitement.

Kitty came flying up the outside stairs and opened the front door. Teresa followed.

"No, it's not a promise, but it's reason for hope," Kitty said, waving the official-looking letter.

Over the next few minutes I was able to get the full story. Working single-handedly, Kitty has written a letter on my behalf to the Governor of California. George Stoneman.

And so now I can understand why a few weeks ago, I woke up to Teresa and Kitty murmuring to each other. I had heard the words. Stone. Man. And then, "Maybe he can help." But I had no idea what they were discussing.

It turns out that this Governor of ours, a war hero, believes strongly in prison reform. He has granted dozens and dozens of pardons—247 to be exact—and commuted almost as many sentences.

Kitty went to the trouble of writing a long and passionate letter to the Governor, explaining my situation, and asking for help.

The letter in her hands was not a pardon by any means, but a request for more official information. "In other words," said Teresa, "It is up to DeLuria to present the request."

"Yes, indeed, we will need his help," Kitty said, "but isn't it wonderful, he answered!"

She handed me the letter and I must say it was a thrill to see the Governor's scrawl across the page. To think that he would consider looking into my case.

I felt my face get warm, and tears spring to my eyes. "Thank you Kitty," I said, and it was difficult to speak.

She kneeled in front of me. I realized in that moment that she had the same fawn-colored eyes as the little girl in the bedroom portrait.

And while her hair was graying, there were strands of the strawberry color. "I promise you Renata," she said, taking my hand, "that we won't stand by and watch you die. You have my word, we will have your case heard by the Governor himself!"

Teresa squeezed my shoulders. And I must say, for the first time in months, I felt a surge of hope. At the same time, I recalled all those horrible hours in what amounted to a cage.

Perhaps that's why I started to cry.

Teresa and Kitty wouldn't tolerate my tears for long, however.

They made me get up and take a bath, and we spent the day planning a celebration. Señora made my favorite evening meal, tortilla soup, and Teresa baked me a spice cake.

33

SISTER RENATA'S DIARY

December 13, 1883

Kitty is busy writing letters and what's more, she is getting friends and neighbors, and fellow nuns back at the convent to write letters too. What began as Kitty's pet project—convincing Governor Stoneman to spare my life—has now taken on a life of its own.

She has even placed a sign in the café window offering a free meal to anyone who will write a letter! And now she says that the newspaper is set to run a story on the letter campaign.

As soon as I heard the word "newspaper" I cringed, thinking back to that first horrifying story after I was arrested—I felt crucified in words. And all subsequent reports about my trial were in the same vein. But Kitty assures me that this is going to be a different story, one that explains why an ordinary citizen has come forward to advocate for a woman in need.

Apparently, there are others she has convinced. All I know is that I woke from a nap four afternoons ago, lying there in the parlor on her sofa, with sunlight bathing the quilt that covered me. As soon as I woke up, I realized that Kitty had visitors.

I had been dreaming that I was, of all things, a centaur, half horse, half woman, and that I was galloping off to war! I woke up with tears in my eyes, because I realized that I was almost certainly going to be killed in battle!

That thought had me sniffling and teary when I came to, but there across the parlor, sitting at Kitty's oak table, were three strangers, two rather portly ladies, and one very tall thin woman. All of them are neighbors of Kitty's. Two were sipping lemonade Teresa had fixed, and the third had a glass of port. A plate of cookies sat on the table, and from what I was able to see, the two heavyset ladies were doing justice to the sweets.

It occurred to me that perhaps Kitty was soliciting letter writers by promising the writers free food and drink.

In any case, I lay there, wrapped in the quilt, remaining quiet, just observing, listening to Kitty explain her mission. "Sister Renata is no more guilty of a crime than you or me!" Kitty began. "I can tell you that she has a journal and I've read parts of it, and the way she cared for her cousin, Antonie, she is worthy of a medal. And this is the same man she is accused of killing."

The ladies remained quiet. The two cookie eaters continued to nibble.

"Her cousin, I'm afraid, was very ill, and..." Kitty paused. "Lord help me, but he wasn't right in the head. He wrote some bizarre tales about her. Plain and simply, he lied, but because of his position around here, everyone believed him, and Renata paid the price." Kitty sat forward. "And so I see it as our moral duty to help set her free!"

She brought her fist down hard on the oak table, hard enough so that the plate with the cookies rattled. The three neighbors shifted in their seats. The two heavy women stopped eating.

"Sister Renata's lawyer believes that there is a good chance that the Governor would spare the nun's life if a significant portion of the community is sympathetic to her situation," Kitty continued, now folding her hands and looking from one woman to the next. "And so I'm asking you, can you write a little letter asking Governor Stoneman for mercy?"

This particular meeting with the neighbors was just one of many that Kitty has held, either here in the parlor, or downstairs in the café. She has called a public meeting for next week to lay out her case. She asked DeLuria if I would be permitted to attend but as I am technically in jail, and this is not a courtroom proceeding, he said I would not be allowed to go.

After Kitty delivered her pitch the other afternoon, the tall woman asked a question. "I guess I am wondering this, Miss Kitty. Why didn't you try to keep her from gettin' convicted in the first place?"

"Well that would have been ideal, I agree, Alice. But you know the court works the way the court works. And her lawyer, the truth be told, was barely able to hold his own." Kitty took a sip of lemonade herself.

"What else you should know is that it took me some time to grow firm in my conviction that Renata is innocent. I went to every day of the trial, and as you know, I've had her in my house here." She gestured in my direction and the next thing I knew I had all four of them staring at me, still snuggled quietly under the quilt on the sofa.

"Oh, Renata, you are awake, I would make you a cup of tea and I will as soon as I am finished here."

"Thank you Kitty, I think you're doing plenty as it is. Not to worry about my tea!"

The three neighbors gazed at me as though I was a panther or a mountain lion in captivity. I suspect that never had any of them seen a convicted murderer up close. I pulled the quilt up over my chin.

And in a matter of minutes, the three of them were on their way, with the tall woman saying she would "give some thought" to a letter. The other two cookie-eaters refused to commit to doing anything on my behalf.

After they left, Kitty reassured me that she had met with several other neighbors in the café earlier in the day and "had at least seven promised letters." Of course promises are cheap, I keep reminding myself of that fact.

But now, today, Kitty has shown me a small stack of actual letters—eight to be exact. Some are just a few paragraphs long, scrawled in the sloppiest penmanship I've ever seen.

But there is one letter that I must admit, I've already read it a dozen times, it too is short, but it presents my case in such a highly favorable light. And what's more, the handwriting is some of the prettiest I've ever seen!

34

SISTER RENATA'S DIARY

December 17, 1883

When I have those moments of despair, when all else fails to cheer me, well, then there are the flies and I tend to them religiously. I laugh thinking about myself doing that. Tending to flies. I realize someone might think that I enjoy killing flies.

Absurd. That is never my intention. Well. Perhaps occasionally it is...

The café downstairs—Kitty's place, is a breeding ground. Kitty and Señora are always frying. Endlessly. Bread dough. Donuts. Chicken. Home fries.

Or if they're not frying, they are baking rolls or stirring tortilla soup or grilling steaks in flat pans, and the odors bring the godawful flies up to the windows and I know I shouldn't kill them but I do, I am determined to keep the windows clean, I mean I see that as part of my job.

So I try to catch them in the dishtowels. I try not to squash them, as it bothers Sister Teresa so, she values all life, every morsel, so I try not to let Teresa see me do it, if she happens to enter the room and I am about to swat the fly, I just scoop it into the towel or...

Sometimes if I've just killed a fly, I will sit on the towel.

But that's not what I want to tell you. What I want to tell you about is the visit to the newspaper office two days ago with Kitty and toothless Bean, the old jailer who put me in cuffs behind my back. I was allowed to go only because of Kitty's letter campaign; she is determined to convince Governor Stoneman to free me. She is a saint that woman.

Kitty is becoming a dear friend to me. I know now the name of the child in the portrait. Her name was Lynda.

Why and how she died, I do not know. I have tried to ask Kitty but she will say nothing. I have begged Teresa to tell me the story but she simply shakes her head.

Oh. There now. There is another one, excuse me, I am determined to keep the damn windows clean and fly-free, I mean, I am sorry for swearing, there is more of that these days, Teresa heard me take the Lord's name in vain, she complained to me, but that's what has happened, I am changing, I am...something is coming loose inside me, my tongue feels unhinged, my mind, pressed, I think perhaps it is the flies buzzing, and me waiting for the worst possible end, the buzzing, the waiting, they will drive a person crazy.

I've got the dishtowel but now the fly is gone.

That being said, what I am meaning to tell you about is our visit to the newspaper, the reporter sitting there when we arrived, tapping on an elegant old machine, I've never seen one th...

It's back. Excuse me. I will get the fly and that will be the end of it.

I'm back.

Frankly, when Kitty told me that we would "drop by" the newspaper, I was horrified. The idea that they were going to do a story, I was at first so very concerned. Not surprising, considering what the San Francisco newspaper wrote about me, hanging me before I had even been tried!

I told Kitty that I was quite upset. I told her that I wouldn't go to the paper I call it *The Gaze-Ette*—because they were sure to write a piece that, my God, there, there is another fly.

I got that fly. I ...

And another, landing here beside my journal.

And another. UGH. A bloody mass here, a cloud of a dozen or more swirling around me.

Later.

I apologize for the interruption but I had to get them all. I must get them. They buzz and circle, surround my head and they land in the windows and bounce against the glass. Rather disturbing to me.

I know all this about the flies might not seem important but I dreamed about flies last night. I am not certain why. Perhaps because they are trapped. Perhaps because they are trying so desperately to flee.

The flies and I stand at Kitty's window and we desperately want to be free, and so I let them go if I can but when there is a cloud of them I fumble with the dishtowel.

Too much. Too many. So many that I must kill them, I kill them and the truth be told there is some kind of unhealthy satisfaction in that.

Back to the visit. This is a newspaper that prints lies. Or at least, opinions.

We arrived at the newspaper office—a single room with a kind of closet attached where they keep and operate a telegraph—we got there just after noon. The room was intensely warm.

A gaunt young man sat at the typewriter. I was introduced but as my hands were cuffed behind me, I could only drop my head.

He gazed at me over his spectacles. Which by the way were dirty. Streaked!

His name: John Dimson. Dark and wavy blonde hair, rather oily. And a wiry blonde mustache. Black topcoat. So formal. So funereal. And in that heat. What possesses him? In my case, I have no choice but to dress in black. Sister Teresa brought me a brand new habit, after my last disintegrated in the prison.

After we sat down, he removed the topcoat. White shirt, yellowed collar and beneath his armpits, great wet stains. He pressed the nose of his round spectacles to his face. He has a most unpleasant laugh. And he refused to look at me. He has a way of swaying slightly right and left as he speaks.

He banged on the typewriter, snapping the keys into submission while Kitty explained to him her letter-writing campaign. He stopped when she removed from her purse and presented to him the letter from Stoneman. He sat back and read it and then pulled at his mustache. He laid the letter down on the oak desk.

"I don't see the Governor here making anything that begins to sound like a promise, Miss Kitty," he announced rather somberly.

"Well of course not," Kitty snapped back. She took the letter and folded it carefully and tucked it back into its onionskin envelope.

"The point, Mr. Dimson, sir, is that we have to convince him, the whole town must be on her side writing letters, all on her behalf, all sympathetic, and then we send them to him, and then perhaps he can be convinced."

Another. Another fly. Three. Easily caught however in one dish-towel swipe. Oh, sorry, just two. One injured. Not sure. Ah. Here, now, a fleck of a wing right here, in my hand.

Then I wipe the window clean.

"So, Miss Kitty, this letter-campaign. How many have you collected? And how is it that you are approaching individuals, to ask folks to write them?"

Kitty pulled herself upright. Nodded and smiled. Explained her pitch. Told Dimson how she gives one free café meal to each letter writer.

Announced our up-to-date total: 27 letters.

Dimson took a handkerchief from his hip pocket. Wiped his forehead. I sat, thinking about my own face. I had to be, pink flushed damp. But with my hands at my back, there was nothing to be done.

It was at that moment, I saw the fly.

Land on Dimson's typewriter. There.

It sat. Dimson was asking Kitty how many letters she thought she would be able to collect.

I watched the fly. I stared as it dropped into the pit where the keys pound the paper. I didn't see it.

Kitty was saying there was—obviously—a "time constraint." I am scheduled to walk those five steps to the gallows on the 6th.

"I am hoping for 200 letters," she said, lifting her chin in defiance.

"Miss Kitty, for heaven's sake, that would be remarkable. We have only 642 citizens. You are saying that approximately one in three people will be willing to wr..."

"It is entirely possible," she interrupted. "And there is no loss in trying, now is there Mr. Dimson?"

He gazed at her with a narrow-eyed look, and gave a quick shove to his spectacles, pressing them to the bridge of his nose. Wrinkling his mouth, and looking a little bored, he turned to the typewriter. He placed his fingers on the keys. I thought about the fly there in the pit. I gasped.

Dimson and Kitty looked over at me. My eyes widened. I kept staring. I felt like…a fly!

"I…" I nodded. "A fly. There. Just now landed in your typewriter." I nodded again. Kept pointing with my chin. Dimson frowned. Looked rather annoyed by this whole business. Our visit.

Just then the fly lifted out of the typewriter and circled once, then headed for the window. Dimson continued typing.

We left. No sign of fly as we left.

The article, Dimson says, will be in the newspaper by week's end.

35

SISTER RENATA'S DIARY

December 20, 1883

Three days after visiting the newspaper, we woke up to old Bean the jailer knocking on Kitty's door. He can't read, the poor man, but he'd learned that the *Gazette* had printed our story and he'd been promised a quarter by Kitty if he bought the newspaper and brought it to the house for us to see.

As she closed the door, my head was spinning in memories. I've seen what newspapers can do when they want to skewer you. It happened to me when the San Francisco paper wrote about me just after I was arrested for Antonie's murder.

But here now was still another newspaper, the local *Gazette*, and judging by the look on Kitty's face as she placed the paper on the table, it wasn't good.

Kitty muttered something and I asked her to read the headline out loud. She inhaled. And read each word at a painfully slow tempo.

Local Woman Needs Anyone
With a Pen and A Bleeding Heart!!

I winced and sank deeper into the sofa.

Kitty cleared her throat and carefully unfolded the paper and spread it on the oak table. She and Teresa pulled up their chairs. I just stayed put there on the couch staring at Kitty's remarkable tin ceiling, my eyes tracing the curlicue patterns.

"Aren't you going to look with us?" Kitty asked quietly.

I shook my head back and forth, very slowly, feeling the tears gathering. A tight panic began squeezing at my insides. "No, you two can read it first, and if it's as bad as I think it will be, I'm...I'll just pass. I am not sure I have the stomach for it."

And so Teresa and Kitty read John Dimson's article in silence. I put my hands over my face and only once glanced up when I thought I heard Kitty sucking on her teeth. At that moment I noticed Teresa shake her head ever so slightly. They finished. They sat there.

My heart hammered. I wasn't able to speak. I wanted desperately to know. I wanted desperately not to know. I wanted most of all to go to sleep. But how could I possibly forget the fact that I was going to the gallows in a matter of days?

Finally Kitty spoke.

"Well that young man deserves a good sharp boot right smack in his backside."

"I'd agree completely," Teresa said. She sounded rather weary, even though it was still early in the morning.

"But then," Kitty went on," I could tell right away. The moment I laid eyes on him last week. His whole demeanor. That reporter is well-named. Dimson. DIM-witted Son of a..."

"Oh KITTY!" Teresa covered her ears and shook her head vigorously as if to rid herself of the vulgar outburst.

"Well, sorry for that, Sister, I do apologize, but that man wrote the least sympathetic piece of dirty laundry I've ever read, and hung it out for all to see. And not only does it hurt our cause, but the story isn't even accurate. I am sure that I told him we'd collected 27 letters, not 17. I know for a fact because I had the stack in my hand for Pete's sake."

Teresa inhaled. "It makes no difference really. If he'd written 27, or 207, in that awful story, it would matter not one bit!"

By now, I felt that I might wet my pants. My mouth was so parched and dry that my tongue felt withered. I couldn't speak but I started to cry. Teresa and Kitty rushed from the table to the sofa, where I lay.

"Heavens, don't take it so hard," Kitty said, sitting beside me and squeezing me in a tight embrace. "It doesn't matter what the silly paper writes. I will go door to door, starting this afternoon!"

"And I will go with you," Teresa said, placing a hand on my arm.

I sat there sniffling. I wanted to say, "I'd just as soon you don't. I would just as soon you accepted the inevitable and gave up. I would just as soon you had never tried." But none of that came out of my mouth. I had so little energy to speak. What did it matter, what I said? What did anything matter now?

I knew that I had to read the article for myself. But how to find the courage? The strength?

"Teresa, dear, if you wouldn't mind, would you be kind enough to bring the paper here to me? I don't know that I have it in me to sit there at the table with it."

"Of course I will," Teresa said.

Kitty stood. "But wait. Before you read a word of that foul stuff, you need a good strong cup of tea," she declared. She stopped. "Or would you rather my famous chestnut coffee?"

I considered saying that I wanted a shot of old Bean's whiskey.

"A cup of tea would be delightful," I said and forced a smile. And so Kitty made me tea, and brought it to me in one of her grandmother's fine china cups, a pretty green. And she also buttered me a fresh biscuit with raspberry jam.

And only when I'd finished both of these did Teresa bring me the dreaded newspaper article by Mr. John Dimson. Once more I had in front of me the writing of a man who, like Antonie, was using his clever words to destroy me, turning my life inside out!

36

December 19, 1883

Local Woman Needs Anyone With a Pen and a Bleeding Heart!!

By John Dimson
Crime Reporter

We all know Kitty Pole. She's our one and only café lady. At one time or another, Kitty's made her famous chestnut-flavored coffee for each and every one of us here in town.

And yes, she fixes a mighty tasty breakfast at that tiny café tucked beneath her sky blue house.

Her sweet potato homefries are famous. Her ham and pepper omelets are divine.

Oh, and she whips up a fierce plum cobbler too. (Ask anybody who's tried it!)

But what's got into Kitty now? She's trying to cook up a stew that is altogether new for her. She's meddling in the court system, and it's not clear what she's up to or what she expects to get out of doing it.

For the last few weeks, Kitty's been going door to door—even promising free café meals—to anybody who pens a letter to our good Governor Stoneman. Kitty's turned organizer, asking that all of her neighbors team up to request a pardon for our no-torious Sister Renata, the nun convicted of slicing her cousin Antonie's throat!

Dear Kitty, with all due respect, what goes on here? Maybe the café business is too slow?

According to the *Examiner* story, published right after the mur-der last fall, Señor Quiero de Lopez' jugular vein was sliced with a straight razor.

The very same day that Sister Renata was arrested, a sheriff's deputy found the nun's discarded black habit, coated in blood, bur-ied in the vegetable garden behind the convent!

During the trial, a dozen of Sister Renata's fellow nuns trav-eled to Gallejo to testify on her behalf. Each of the Dominican nuns went into great detail about Renata's character. Not a blem-ish, they claimed.

I wish I could believe them!

After all was said and done, Renata was convicted last month of first-degree murder.

She is scheduled to die by hanging on January 6th, a mere three weeks from now.

But now, along comes our own Kitty Pole—who by the way is housing the convicted nun right there in her blue house (by ar-rangement of the court, I should point out!) Something's come over Kitty, because now the good café lady is trying to stop the whole criminal justice system in its tracks!

What qualifies Kitty—a splendid cook to be sure—to think she can stir up sympathy for a convicted killer? And how does she expect to gather enough letters here in our small village? So far she's collected a total of only 17 letters, so it looks like she has her work cut out for her!

When she came by my office recently to chat, this is what she said: "We will be making a bad mistake if we send that poor nun to the gallows. I've read the nun's journal, and if you would do the same thing Mr. Dimson, then you'd see she can't possibly be guilty of her cousin's murder!"

Just for the record, I read the court transcripts, and I've seen the nun's diary.

But what makes Kitty so convinced that it exonerates the nun?

Kitty claims that the nun was framed by her clever cousin. Perhaps.

But what about that bloody corpse that the authorities found? And the nun's habit, coated in blood, buried in the garden? That's the kind of evidence that's hard to ignore.

Kitty flushes to her roots, and her cheeks turn cherry pink, when she discusses the trial. She turns even more passionate when she asks folks to write letters.

"Well of course I am passionate," she said. "It is a human life at stake here. Think about that! The point, Mr. Dimson, sir, is that we have to convince him, the Governor. We must! The whole town must take her side, writing letters, calling for her pardon. If we show him that we are sympathetic, perhaps then he will be convinced!"

Perhaps, Miss Kitty.

But perhaps not. The question is, will Governor Stoneman listen?

And by the way, Kitty Pole, you might take a few moments to think about that other human life—the one that was cut short by his own straight razor!

Poor man, that Antonie!

Miss Kitty, you've got some serious cooking ahead of you! And the whole town's watching too, to see if you really do succeed in setting a convicted killer free!

Why should our good Governor swallow this story?

37

SISTER RENATA'S DIARY

December 22, 1883

We sit side by side on the sofa, Kitty and me, and she has the bundle of letters piled neatly in her lap. Kitty's face is a study in happiness and her eyes shine with excitement.

Tomorrow morning she is scheduled to package up the letters and deliver them to my lawyer's office. DeLuria will carry the letters directly to Governor Stoneman's office in Sacramento and in a few short days we will know whether he will pardon me.

Kitty is patiently waiting for me to answer her question.

She has just asked if she can read a few of the letters to me before she places them in a box and ties the box with twine. Teresa is sitting across from us in the rocking chair. The two of them are just sitting there, trying not to stare.

Meanwhile, I am gazing into the cup of chamomile tea that Kitty has fixed me. I inhale.

"So," I say. "I do know how much this means to you. I know how excited you both are, but..." I take a sip of tea and then shake my head slowly. "No, I would prefer not to know what they say."

Kitty shoots a quick glance at Teresa and back at me. She sets one hand very gently on top of the letters. Her hand stays there. After a moment, she leans forward a bit on the sofa and speaks very quietly. "I completely understand that you're very nervous about all of this," she says. "There is so much at stake. But if you knew how much passion is contained here, Renata, if you knew how much concern, even love, if you would just let me share a bit of it wi..."

"Please Kitty, NO!" I set my teacup down in the saucer with a rattle. I am frightened suddenly that she is pressuring me. I feel blood rushing into my face. I shudder just glancing at the stack of pages sitting there on Kitty's knees.

It is indeed a rather sizable batch of letters she has assembled.

After an extraordinary effort on Kitty's part, she managed to convince 145 people to put pen to page on my behalf! It is a particularly impressive outpouring of support, especially as the local newspaper had tried so hard to deride my case with their damnable article.

And now here I am, not wanting to read a single one of them. Indeed, I want to forget that they even exist. I want to forget that it is these thin pieces of paper—some covered with impeccable handwriting—that might help to decide whether I live or die.

"I know that I should be pleased about the letter campaign. I should be feeling encouraged, and hopeful." I nod and turn to face Kitty. "I am terribly grateful to you Kitty, I really am, but...I cannot bear it." The last few words are hard to hear.

I clasp my hands together and hold them tight.

Kitty stares into her lap.

The last few weeks have been such a blizzard of activity for her and for Teresa. The two of them have been tireless, knocking on doors day and night, gathering letters, convincing patrons of the café to sit down and write to the Governor demanding my freedom. In some cases, they fixed free meals for letter writers. In some cases, they had Señora baking bread or pie or cookies, which were passed out freely to those who picked up pens to write.

After all of that exhausting effort, it is hard now for them to hear me say I don't want to know what the letters say.

"I do understand that all this makes you nervous, Renata," Kitty says. "But I don't think you can possibly understand how many people have stepped forward." She pats the bundle of letters.

"You cannot imagine how many fine, fine letters have been written on your behalf."

I sniffle. "I am sure you're right Kitty. And perhaps if...if we are successful, then, perhaps afterward, after it's all over, but now, now I feel that I cannot possibly listen." I am starting to feel lightheaded, and a sense of dread. Lately that feeling of dread has started to come over me more and more, often in clouds that billow around me like a grey fog.

Teresa bends forward. Her voice is reassuring. "I wonder Renata." She pauses. Bites into her lip. "I've got to ask you this one thing my dear. Is this decision not to hear the letters, it is perhaps...because you feel superstitious? Are you thinking that if you read the letters out loud, then perhaps it might jinx your chances of succeeding with the Governor?"

I study Teresa's sky blue eyes. What she is saying had not occurred to me. But maybe I *am* feeling superstitious. I shrug. Clasp my hands together more tightly. I remain silent. Teresa clears her throat and continues.

"I have been told that the Governor is deeply compassionate toward prisoners, Renata, as the General himself was a Union soldier taken prisoner during the war. It is said that every time he signs a death warrant he is sick for a day or two!"

I glanced at Teresa and her blue eyes felt like they were boring into me. "Perhaps I am superstitious," I say, shaking my head. "But most of all, I am just so so exhausted by...by everything. Much too tired to listen. This whole business, the trial, the letter writing, the newspaper story, while I certainly do appreciate everything you've done, Kitty, I...I'm sorry, but I am just too tired."

I sit there staring into the letters. I have other thoughts I could share: *In the end I am afraid that all of this letter writing is a waste of time and paper and ink. I think it's hopeless to send letters to Governor Stoneman. My case is closed. Over and done with. I am going to die and I might as well let them get on with it.*

My heart is pounding. I am holding my sweaty hands together so tightly that the joints of my fingers ache.

I don't dare say any of it. I look up. My hand trembles as I reach for the teacup again and take a small sip. I haven't had any appetite, and no matter what Señora makes for me, I don't eat.

That might be one reason I feel so weak. So light-headed. So full of dread and despair.

I hear the wind whistle outside Kitty's house. There at the door is old Bean the jailer, probably slumped against the wall, asleep on his watch. The three of us sit there a little longer and finally, I announce to them how tired I am. I ask if they mind if I go to bed. Neither of them say a word.

Kitty gets up from the sofa and sets the letters neatly on the table. And then she and Teresa wrap themselves in their wool shawls and leave the house.

I am left all alone, lying here on the sofa.

I watch a single candle burning. The white wax melts and dribbles in bits and globs as it slides down the side of the candle toward the table.

And now I realize that Christmas Day is only three days away. How will I go to mass? Dear Mary, is it wrong for me to pray that the Governor responds positively to our pleas?

The stack of letters sits on the opposite side of the table. As I sink into dreams, it occurs to me how easy it would be for all of those letters to go up in flames.

GINA

Dear Mary,

Renata is here with me. And we are frightened. We've got no hope, so we are praying, each in turn. We are afraid to face each other because when we do, we reach out and collapse in tears. I sit here now and I watch the dark cups of murky chocolate that are her eyes. She nods at me.

My own eyes grow wide. I am sitting in meditation now before my old mahogany table. That is what I cannot comprehend. That I can shoot between centuries back and forth. That I can be her being me. That I am holding Renata's hand, and her journal and pen, and then, in the next instant, I am sitting cross-legged in front of the blue candle that burns every morning with a yellow flame.

It's not always the same. Sometimes I am her with no memory of me. Sometimes I am me simply creating her inside my mind.

In the glow that the flame throws, I see a shadow flicker and all of a sudden, I swear I see Señora. Can it be? Is she here in Kitty's parlor? Is she wrapped in her long flowered shawl?

My eyes are watering. I blink. Have I fallen asleep? I rub my eyes. No. This is no dream. I seem to be in all places at once. Like you Mary. I am flying in gauzy blue skies in robes of the same hue. I sit beside Renata and then, we sit before my table.

I have long since stopped trying to figure this out. I am not sure anyone can. Who knows whose history belongs to whom?

I breathe in. And out. And so I still myself at the meditation table in front of the candle and I wear the same robe as Renata and I pray. To Mary. To hear me. To encourage me to write after all these years!

I am up on my knees now, in front of the meditation table. I am watching the shadow that is Señora and I have my hands pressed and crossed over my chest. Mary I am ready. My heart. My heart, Señora Cuoracura, is ready to pour forth, to do whatever is necessary to do to go free. My heart is ready to whisper. To shout. Hear me. Hear me. After all these years, I know why you are here. To hear me. To cure my heart by listening. To lead me to freedom.

I am finally ready to start. Señora lifts her flowered shawl and cloaks me inside.

I turn to Renata. Awestruck. Renata winks at me. I don't think I can say anything. I am astonished. They knew this. The two of them, with Mary's help, have been planning this for. How long? For more than a century for sure.

38

SISTER RENATA'S DIARY

December 29, 1883

The dark sky is navy blue, and split by the thin golden crescent that is the moon. I stare at the crisp curve, shining eye to eye with me.

Soon it will be sunrise, and I will have been sitting here, awake, staring out the window, all night. I am dressed head to toe in white, as Sister Teresa brought me a brand new habit, pristine.

It occurred to me that maybe she was thinking, I need to be clean when I go to my death next week.

There is no more hope now. The reply from Stoneman has come. In one sentence, the Governor dropped me, sent me tumbling into oblivion. This man, known to have pardoned so many, gave not a word of explanation in rejecting my plea. In just one stiff and official sentence, he has done me in, turned me into Stonewoman and sent me rolling. There is no escaping the gallows now.

If I were in a normal state, I suppose I would have cried yesterday when Kitty carried the thin white envelope into the house. It was shortly after noon. The mail always arrives by stage before 1 p.m.

As soon as I laid eyes on Kitty, I knew instantly that the news was not good. Her pasty white face. Her wide eyes, locked onto my own.

She blinked, and without untying her black bonnet, or taking off her cotton gloves, she dropped into the straight back chair. She sat there, all in black, holding the envelope in one hand, and the letter in the other. She kept blinking, and I was thinking the worst. After all, she looked as though she might just dissolve in tears. Finally she got one short breathless sentence out.

"My dear Renata," she said in a hush, "Governor's decision has come and I…"

She stopped again. I was sitting there on the sofa, the guitar in my lap. I had been, oddly enough, strumming an alegría, a happy melody to which Señora used to sing some wonderfully silly lyrics about a goat who kept appearing, day after day, in a young woman's garden. The goat turned out to be a suitor.

But watching Kitty's face, I stopped strumming.

She raised one gloved hand to her face. "I have some very bad news," she whispered.

I felt a kind of numb veil descend over me. I could say that I was surprised, but I wasn't. But I also couldn't quite believe that what was happening was real. Everyone else—or should I say Kitty and Teresa—were feeling so hopeful when they sent off the petition, and the supporting letters, to Stoneman's office last week. Being the Christmas season, my dear friends thought that the Governor might be persuaded to be more lenient toward me.

I had, in spite of myself, allowed my hopes to rest in the arms and faith of my two friends. Now, that hope was gone. My life was as much as ended.

"Read it to me Kitty," I said. My voice had a shredded quality, as if it had been scraped with a knife.

She sat there, staring.

"Please," I said. "You must read it to me."

She cleared her throat. "The petition for clemency in the sentence against Sister Maria Rosa Renata, convicted for the murder of Señor Quiero de Lopez, has hereby been…"

Her voice trembled. It took a full minute before she finally spoke the word. "… denied." Her chin dropped to her jacket, and I could see the tears falling. I turned away, set my attention on a large yellow cloud passing by the window. I allowed my mind to be carried up there, to rest in the cloud.

I had not been outdoors for weeks. At least, I will be hanged in the sun. At least in my last breath, I will be inhaling fresh air. There is, at least, that. I tried to think something beyond that thought.

Kitty was crying and trying to take a seat next to me on the sofa. She was trying to take me into her arms. I ought to have let her, but I wanted my space. I pushed her away.

"Please, leave me be," I whispered. "I wish to be alone, so that I might pray."

Finally, she rose. Sniffling, wiping her nose with her hanky, she asked me if I wanted tea. I shook my head slowly. "No. I only ask that you to leave me in peace. Please. You owe me that."

And so she did.

After, when she was gone, I didn't pray. I just lay on the sofa and stared at the clouds passing by the window. I could have done that all day.

39

SISTER RENATA'S DIARY

January 3, 1884

Now the sun comes to the lip of the window. Now I see the gallows. Now I see the noose. Now there is a date for my hanging. An hour ago I kneeled down in prayer, in total darkness. I asked Mary for a miracle—a way out. I said the rosary with my eyes closed. I felt those smooth beads slipping between my fingertips, and whispered to Her, PLEASE PLEASE HELP ME!!

Some time passed—who knows how long. I'm not altogether sure that I didn't fall asleep. The next thing I knew I was rocking there on my knees. I was saying PLEASE PLEASE. I felt a slight puff of air, as if someone was there, right next to me, breathing against my face. I felt a wind—ever so slight—brushing right past my cheek like a feather.

I opened my eyes, clutching the rosary. At first I wasn't sure whether I was awake. To my wonder and surprise there She was, beside me in her powder blue veil! Her face was porcelain and her cheeks, blushed pink. She glowed with a kind of light I've never seen. The light was alive. It vibrated and made me tremble.

She smiled and nodded and pointed out the window.

"Go my child. While there is still time, go."

My eyes widened. Her voice was so very kind and so deep and intimate. It was as if she was speaking right inside my head.

And her smile. It filled me, and now the window, with that bright, bright light. A light splashing every which way. A light alive. I've got to find more words for how light can be so full of energy that it feels alive.

She was pointing still, gesturing to the sky gathering the same powder blue color as her veil. My eyes sailed into the distance, toward the navy blue rim of the low Santa Cruz mountains.

I blinked. For a moment it occurred to me, I must be losing my mind.

But no. No. Mary herself was there, I swear it. Glowing, nodding, pointing, offering me my freedom—it was that clear and simple.

The road—dusted pink in salmon light—calls now. No one need know. No one at all is awake. The jailer, old Bean, drank a small tub of tequila at dinner. He's slumped under the staircase there in front of Kitty's café. The others—Kitty, Teresa, Señora—I hear one of them snoring.

I turn to the door. Do I dare? There is the way out. There now is a way to spare my neck from the loop of rope swinging at the gallows in the town square. If I don't go now, I will be heading tomorrow for the gallow stairs.

Do I go? My heart is slamming but I am moving—quietly, silently—toward the door.

40

SISTER RENATA'S DIARY

January 6, 1884

Stopping now out of breath...

I walked out the door.

I walked out that door hands...fingers...body trembling... ankle so sore where the chain cut in before never healed...

sun lowering...a couple of hours to go before it sets...

what happens after dark...

look up, madrone, deep red... trying to take in what happened... What happened?

How did She appear? How did I WALK FREE?

I will be sleeping under trees, stars tonight. Air warm and sweet, dry grass, golden hillsides. Sky bright bright blue. I AM SO FRIGHTENED... thrilled and excited too. Trembling now, feeling tears...because I am finally finally...

free.

Nothing it was nothing. Escape? All I had to do was get up off of Kitty's sofa and take the cloth satchel I packed—canteen, journal, biscuits, cheese and apples.

Heart slamming, I walked up to the door turned the lock and then, opened... the door. Morning air cool misty so fragrant and there I was at the top of the stairs with the world waiting.

Tears now. Tears...

so careful going down the stairs one by one see inside Kitty's café. Nobody. No sound. Bean lying there, a liquored heap at the bottom. Just lying there snoring. Arm with the bottle and then...I saw his jacket thrown to the side. I took it. I stole Bean's jacket. And kept walking. Fast.

With my heart practically dancing in my throat, sweat sprouting, I just kept walking forward. Thinking for sure, someone bound to come running behind me. Someone sure to come running up guns blazing yelling STOP!!!! STOP!!!!

But no.

I was free.

I am free.

Who knows for how long. But for now, I am free.

A nun, running. My face will be plastered on posters everywhere before the day is out. Must disguise. Bean's jacket falls below my knees.

Must keep walking now, hurrying through golden hills, trees. Redwood and madrone. Oak.

Thinking of Teresa now, how worried she will be, but she should not fret...I had help, the Mother Mary was there, she freed me, she will I pray continue to see me now. So glad Teresa was sound asleep, now she can be honest saying she had no idea where I was and what happened. Where am I? What I am doing?

No idea. I am going...beyond here. Beyond the old life.

To whatever awaits me. Must not think now. Must go forward, now. God help me. Now, move now. Go!

GINA

Before silence. Something in the grass. Swaying. And then, a sloppy light. And now, it might go this way: the squeak of guitar strings, before the black squirrel of handwriting separated itself onto this white page, there was quite suddenly one innocent nun.

A character named Renata was staring into my soul, and eying herself in a tiny oak mirror. Almost immediately she began to sin, dropping her black habit and soon, I was transfixed, following her in a dream as she went spinning across my mind in red satin circles of light.

Now, I think, I might just finish this story after all, the one I started in a flush of excitement after Señora first visited me so many Januaries ago.

All I need do is continue to speak. All I need do is escape the past.

All I need do is leave all my doubts about writing at the cell door as I help the two of us escape from prison. All I need have is enough clarity of mind to save the nun Sister Renata and me.

Just continue. Just keep writing. Just keep up this narrative, because eventually it will unchain her. And me. Like me, she was feeling ever more desperate. The gallows was ready. The noose was tightening. The ticking was getting louder. The date for her hanging was locked in place.

I have no choice. Nor does she. We proceed together through the door into a brand new world, one of our own making.

41

SISTER RENATA

The nun steps slowly, swaying as she approaches a thicket of low-lying grass. She holds the back of one hand up against her eyes to ward off the bright California sunlight. Her gaze drops into the golden grass and her eyes pop open and she jumps back, screaming and pointing at a thick coiled snake. Her face is bright pink and she is breathing hard, clutching both hands over her racing heart.

Soon, though, her face registers a different expression. She blinks and rubs her eyes. It takes her a moment to realize that the snake is nothing but a branch, one long bough of the giant live oak nearby.

She sinks onto her knees and drops into the grass. She has begun to see all kinds of creatures that aren't there. This morning, she saw a bear coming towards her. Except the bear never moved. It proved to be a shadow playing on a dark rock.

She reaches out gingerly and runs her fingers along the snaking bough. Feels the rough surface of the wood.

Her stomach caves and growls. She pulls a handful of thin blades of grass and chews the tiny white bulbs at the base. She has eaten so much grass that her stomach cramps. She dares not eat any other plants as she isn't sure what might poison her. It was always Teresa who used to delight in pointing out edible native plants. Too bad Renata never paid a bit of attention to Teresa's little botany lessons. Renata recalls only the handfuls of strawberries they would find after hours of walking.

Now, she is hallucinating green olive trees. Twin green olives hanging from a branch, ripe for the plucking, make her dry mouth water.

It's been at least three days since she's eaten. Or is it four? Every crumb of the biscuits she squirreled away is gone. There are no more nuts or seeds. The very last morsel of food she set on her tongue was a shred of damp apple; she left it there to dissolve, as if it were a communion host placed in her mouth by Father Ruby.

She has rationed herself the water. She has one or two more warm mouthfuls before the canteen is empty. Lying in the golden grass, arms and legs askew, she is tempted to drink, but fights the temptation.

That's when the sound comes. A soft music begins to circulate inside her head. A tune that Señora used to sing.

What she is hearing now rising somehow up the hillside is impossibly, the Ave Maria. A clear voice is ringing through the blue sky. She looks up. Her eyes ache and she isn't sure what is happening but she doesn't care.

There isn't a cloud in the azure and the music is the most beautiful she's ever heard. Whoever is making this music is an angel.

If this is now her time to die, well, then, she is prepared.

She looks left and right, and the sound of the music just grows louder and louder. She settles back into the grass. She loves this music. This voice.

She smiles and says a Hail Mary, a second. If she is to die right now, so be it. With the music filling her head, and a light inside her heart.

Her eyes close and then open. She is fully awake, warm and burning up with fever, drenched in sweat, realizing that all this time, she has been asleep. All the music. All of that. So real, but it must have been a dream.

Trembling, she reaches for the canteen. She takes the last gulp of the warm water and then sits up coughing and gagging and spits it out. A beetle had crawled into the canteen and into the last mouthful of water.

The beetle skitters away. She wipes her faces and drops back into the grass. As she does, she hears crackling in the brush. Footsteps.

A branch snaps. More crackling, now just a few feet away. Fear floods her stomach.

Grizzly? Moose? Mountain lion? Some other beast? Whatever it is it's coming closer and she is far too weak to move.

Mouth dry, she closes her eyes and clasps her hands together and prays. Tears spring to her eyes as she murmurs in silence: *If I am to die today, may it please Mary be quick and painless. Please I pray that you grant me just this one th...*

"Ma'am?"

She stops praying.

She would love to think that someone has just spoken a human word to her. But how could that be?

"Ma'am, excuse me, but are you alright?"

Slowly she drops her head to the right. She is gazing directly into the bright sun. What she sees is a man with a large cloud of curls circling his head coming up the hillside. The sun shines through the curls and turns them a burnished gold. He has a kind of halo.

He is holding something in each hand. She lies there, mouth hanging open. Unable to speak. Tears start to leak out of both eyes. She licks her cracked lips. "I...Oh...I..." She cannot speak further.

"Hold on there ma'am." He turns, sets a rifle against the live oak. In his other hand, he is holding a jackrabbit by both ears. He sets the animal into the golden grass.

He returns to her side. Kneels. Takes a canteen from a leather satchel. "Here, you're burning up." He cradles the back of her neck while she drinks, then slurps, the cool water. "Slow, now, not too much too quick." His hand is rough but his voice is gentle. He smells like leather and sweat and tobacco.

Her head falls back.

"Are you up to moving?" he asks. "You ought not be lying here in the sun."

She shakes her head. She feels like dead weight. He lifts her up to a sitting position. Her head dances. Her eyes burn. She turns her head to the side and throws up the water she's just downed.

"Ma'am, I want you to swing one arm around my neck, and I'll lift you up."

Soon he is carrying her like an oversized child, and they are moving toward the live oak. There he settles her in the shade beside the rifle and the rabbit.

"How long you've been here?"

She shrugs, shakes her head. "Not sure," she says. She feels as limp as the dead rabbit. Her eyes ache so badly it makes her nauseous.

"So, if you will let me, I'd like to get you into the wagon. It's up a piece."

He helps her up, and they take one step with him supporting her arms. Then her head reels and her legs feel like they are made of cotton. Or clouds. She wobbles. Spins. She sees the grass begin to spiral toward her. She wants to scream out, but words never leave her mouth. She slumps and he catches her just before she hits the ground.

GINA

Señora bends over me. Kisses the top of my head.

"No tienes miedo," she whispers. Do not be afraid.

I look down in my hand. The diary. And from Renata, the slender pen.

My eyes are watering. "But after all this time, I'm not…how could you, I mean, where would you find…" In my mind is the thick layer of fear; how can I trust this dream any more than the others that have come before? How can I possibly have faith? How do I know that this one will come true? Do I dare? Begin to believe?

But before I can whisper my doubts, Renata sets the crucifix to my lips and squeezes my hand.

"It's time," she whistles.

Pressing my lips together. I open the chiseled leather diary. To a white page, as fresh as snow that falls at the top of the highest mountains.

The white page screams to be bloodied. And so. I will, spill it out, once and for all. I will ink in fever. I will be the praying demon. I will sin in entirety. I will dream all of it and all of it will come true. And in so doing, I will come up, free, and Renata. And I. Will Be Saved.

I could start anywhere, because it will all trickle back to the same place, but I may as well start this way: I will tell you about the sky the day that I first learned that I was steering toward the past. Naturally, I didn't know that was where I was headed. But looking back, the clues were all in place, if only I had paid attention. If only I had known, in those days, about the diaphanous strings linking me and everybody else to the stars. If only I had listened more closely to that woman Michaela, the one with the hands of light.

42

SISTER RENATA

She is dreaming that she is back in the convent, feeling the pinch of straw in the mattress clawing at her skin. In the dream, she smells corn posole cooking, her mouth waters at the fragrance, but just then, Teresa comes running to her room, she pushes open the door without knocking and stands there panting, holding up a spoon.

"You can't stay here," she says, frantically waving her head back and forth. The spoon dances. "Please, take the back door, hurry, don't wait even one minute more, the posse's half way to the far gate, riding with a fury." Teresa's face is flushed, her cheeks as pink and moist as a ham. "My dear Renata, if they find you, God in heaven, you're done for. They'll have you swinging from a tree in no time."

Renata keeps trying to get up from the bed, but she just keeps sinking further into the mattress with each move. The straw claws her. She doesn't understand why Teresa won't put the spoon down and help her up. But then she realizes, Teresa has disappeared. Renata is all alone. Terrified, she bolts upright, and now she is awake, sitting in the makeshift bed that he fashioned for her after carrying her, half dead, to his tiny cabin in what he keeps referring to as The Woodland. At the end of the bed is an aging, floppy- eared dog, staring at her open-jawed. His coat is smooth and shiny and chocolate in color. The dog's mouth hangs open, and he is drooling over his fierce-looking teeth and eying her curiously.

"Nice fella," Renata whispers, reaching her hand out tentatively toward the dog's head.

"Better just to ignore Pete, then he'll be your best friend." Renata pulls her hand back and turns, and the man with the head of curls—the person who saved her and brought her here—is leaning into the doorframe. From this perspective, he doesn't look tall. Not at all. In fact, Renata is pretty certain that she is a head taller than this man who carried her to safety.

When he first brought her to The Woodland, she was limp to the world, unconscious in the back of the cart. He carried her in and put her to sleep in his own bed for at least three days, while he occupied the small barn where the horses were stalled. Soon enough, though, she awoke. Her arms and legs ached and her backside felt bruised and stiff as stone. Her chest was heavy but thankfully, she had no fever. But scratches? Yes. And lots more: bruises, cuts and welts and gigantic bug bites. And several ticks she needed his help to remove, one or two from the back of her neck and one from the tender skin directly below her armpit—how mortifying to have one there, a precious few inches from her breast.

"It makes me fiercely embarrassed you doing this," she whispered as she lifted her arm, holding a towel to cover her breasts. He lit a match and proceeded to remove the tick.

Now she has the blanket tight around her shoulders.

"It is morning, yes?" she asks.

"It is indeed." He stands above her. He smiles and nods. "So are you hungry enough to eat a grizzly, like you were your first two days here?"

"No, but I am mighty thirsty," she says, holding both hands against her throat. He leaves and Pete follows and soon, the man returns with a tray. On the tray is a larger pitcher of water and a glass jar. He also brings her a plate with dark bread and a hunk of yellow cheese, and a cup of steaming broth. He placed an apple on a plate, too, and she is impressed because he has cut it paper-thin.

Mostly, though, she is thirsty. She is more than thirsty; she is a desert. Before she touches a bite of food, she finishes the pitcher and holds it out for a refill. Once again he returns with it, and once again she finishes the pitcher and once again she asks for more. After the third pitcher, she blushes and asks where she can relieve herself.

Without hesitating, he helps her out of the bed and supports her walking through the back door into the sunlight. A small outhouse stands a few feet away. He stays within earshot while she pees, and helps her back to the cabin and into bed.

It is only then, when she wants to thank him, that she realizes she doesn't even know his name.

As she finishes the broth—it tastes of something meaty, maybe the rabbit he shot—she decides she is not going to disclose anything about herself. But that means she needs a plausible story. And she has to decide how long she will rest there before taking off again... and then of course, she has to know where exactly she is going.

"I don't feel right taking your bed, Mr...?" She sets a slice of apple on her tongue.

"Arthur."

"Mr. Arthur."

"No, not Mr. Arthur. Just Arthur. Or just plain Art if you prefer."

"Well, like I said...Arthur, I will get myself up and out of this bed of yours just as soon as I'm a little more steady on my feet, don't feel right displacing you in this way."

He smiles. "It's a privilege to have you here, ma'am." He nods and looks down.

Her eyes narrow. "A...privilege?"

He reaches into his rear pocket and takes out a wrinkled piece of paper. He unfolds it and smoothes it with the side of one hand. Renata gasps. There—square in the middle of the paper—is her likeness—her face wan and pale, her hair stubbly and spare, and a scared look in her eyes. Her face is under the headline: **WANTED: CONVICTED NUN-MURDERER ON THE RUN!!**

She looks away, covers her eyes with one hand. Tears spring up. "My dear Lord. And here I thought you wouldn't have any idea who I was."

He looks at her sadly. "Ma'am, I did not have the privilege of attending the courtroom proceedings. But I followed your friend Kitty's campaign to get you freed. With all those letters she begged and pleaded. I for one composed a simple letter on your behalf. I dare say ma'am that your case has interested me from the start. I saw your image in the newspaper and said to myself, "that woman don't have the heart to razor a man's throat in half, not except if it were in self-defense."

Renata turns to face him. She wipes both eyes. She bites hard into her lower lip, as she doesn't want to start crying again.

"Let me just say that if there is any way I can help you, by having you stay here, or helping you escape clear out of the county, or the country, I'm ready and volunteering to help."

Now the tears come, and she wipes them on a towel he brought with the kitchen tray. Her voice trembles. "You are very very kind, Mr., I mean, Arthur." The full name sounds better to her. More dignified. "I have had every man aligned against me in this matter, starting with my cousin and then every other sheriff, jailer, juror, and judge. So to find a person, a man, who simply wants to help see me go free, it sure does a lot for me."

He nods. Smiles. "I'll do whatever you want me to."

A moment goes by. She speaks slowly. "I believe you would," she says, "But only God knows how you can help."

43

SISTER RENATA

Every morning, he made his way onto the porch while she was still asleep and while it was still dark and the moon was but a silver curl of a sliver within the dark pines. He would creep quietly into the porch and remain there until she woke up. He had shown her every kindness, every form of polite and respectful behavior, and he gave her every reason to believe that he was concerned and considerate. Still, she had her doubts. She still had not really begun to trust him.

She slept each night, buried deep in the blankets on the porch, her arms squeezing what would have been a pillow if it had been more than a second small blanket stuffed with straw and tied, just like the mattress was, with twine.

She never saw him come in. She would fall asleep watching the starlight, and wake up to the creaking of the rocking chair across the porch, the chair he had chiseled and shaped out of fir and aspen and blood red manzanita. He said nothing at all, but the chair began squeaking and it mixed with the sounds of the throaty birds coming to life in the marshy area behind the woodland.

The early morning air was cool and fresh and misty and when it moved across her face it tempted her awake. But then she heard his rocking and squeaking and immediately she resented the fact that he was there in the porch rocking in the chair. Why did he insist on intruding this way on her morning routine? It had been a week that she'd been there, and she had not worked up the courage to tell him that it had to stop.

It wouldn't be easy to tell him. He did everything imaginable to please her, including placing a glass of red poppies at her breakfast table each morning. He refused to let her cook a thing. He made her pancakes or scrambled eggs for breakfast. He fixed hot soups for lunch, and he skewered a rabbit or a chicken for dinner.

He had offered to hide her indefinitely in his woodland cabin. How he would possibly manage to keep her there, when the authorities were looking for her everywhere, she wasn't sure, but he had ideas. "We could shave off the rest of your hair and dress you up as a farmhand," he said at one point. She frowned at the thought, and said in a quiet voice that it suited her to remain a woman.

"Well then, maybe we could move you out of here." He offered that he would risk taking her by wagon to San Francisco, "where you could catch a train east all the way to New York."

Renata's stomach tightened at the thought of leaving her beloved golden hills, her blue California skies. And running from the authorities? That squeezed her stomach even worse.

"How would I elude them? You yourself said they have my photo pasted in every building that stands."

"And so, maybe you would have to become part of my baggage, maybe I could cover you up with a blanket and claim you as a chair." There were other silly ideas, but all of them were evidence that he seriously cared to try to help her.

Meanwhile, her own thoughts focused on how she could move on from the woodland cabin on her own power. With each hour she remained at the cabin, she knew she put herself in danger of being found.

GINA

I am having nightmares. AGAIN! I am circling around the same words I have been writing for more than two decades!

I lie awake every night with visions of a man dying in a pool of his own blood.

And she is telling me to let my body. Write?

Dear God, I think. Why did I come? I cannot possibly let my body do that, can I?

Slowly, I get off the table. I thank Michaela. And I write her a check for fifty-five dollars.

I am heading toward the door when she says, "Oh. Just one more thing."

I turn.

"Yes?"

Michaela cocks her head slightly and says.

"You must be careful that you do not let your negative thoughts take over. You will be up and down writing this project for..." and here she blinks, and smiles "for a long time. I'm afraid it could be," and here she eyes me warily, "a number of years I think. But you must continue to believe in what you are writing, or..."

I wait for her to say more.

"Or what?" I say, my voice small and shaky.

She knows something, I can tell. It crosses her eyes in a dark shadow. But she doesn't say it. And I am just as glad not to hear it. "Just go home and write again. It is very clear to me that you just have to write it. Put aside all doubts. Or at least, you have to try. And you must keep faith in the power of words to make reality."

I nod. Slowly. Staring. Wide-eyed.

"And in the power of your body and spirit to heal by writing those words."

"Right," I say. "Sure. I know that. I do."

I walk out the door. I get into the car but I just sit there. I drive down the long rutted dirt road and make my way home.

The very next day. I start writing. Again. The nightmares. And the visions.

Cease.

I write every day for months. I write every minute I am not at the office.

And then. One night. I dream. That I have taken a vacation. On the sun. When I wake up. I am. Burning with fever. My heart is racing. My face is so hot I run to the bathroom and splash it with cold water. It doesn't help. I take my temperature. 104 degrees.

I take two Tylenol and get back into bed. When I wake up the next morning, the fever is gone. But I am not feeling. Quite. Myself. I have a bright red rash covering my chest and throat. It looks like. Dragon skin. And inside I ache. My chest feels like someone has scratched at my throat. Like someone has planted rose bushes beside my heart, and the thorns are turning me bloody. And beside the roses is. A heavy heavy stone.

I stay home that day. I stay in bed and read. I need the rest.

And so I take it easy for a while.

Gradually the chest pain. The rash. All of it. Goes away. Over the next few weeks,

I start to write again. I am so busy writing that I don't give any of it. A second thought.

Every once in a while when I take a break from the writing, I look up from my computer. I think about what Michaela said. Months back.

"Your body wants to write this book."

At those moments, I get up from my desk and go to the mirror in the bathroom or my bedroom and stare at myself and wonder.

What does that mean? How can a body write a book? How can a body write

Anything?

I don't have any idea. So I just sit back down and keep writing the way I always have. With my mind. Pushing my fingers.

My writing swells into piles of pages and the pages spill over my desk and onto my shelves and floor, and I have three four five six piles, each a foot tall and still. I write, and write, some more.

Until one afternoon, several months later. A bump. Exactly. The size of a hard-boiled egg. Cut in half.

Appears near my collar bone. It looks like it has been bitten by gnats.

I count the gnat bites. Seven. How odd, I think. I call a friend who is into medical things.

"That's weird," she says. "I am betting that it's Lyme Disease. You should see the doctor right away."

I do. I have. A cat scan. And four. Hours. Later. The doctor phones. Me. And says the test. Shows.

"What?"

"You have..."

"No," I say. "I can't possibly have. *That*."

But. I. Do.

That day, I have to

Stop writing.

Because. My body has begun.

Speaking. A whole new language.

And I have no choice. But to listen. And slowly, I begin to understand.

44

SISTER RENATA

It seems much too real to be a dream. She is lying there in her bed at the convent, right where she's supposed to be, under a heap of quilts. She knows for certain that she fell asleep there, after an especially quiet dinner with Sister Teresa and the other nuns. Mother Yolla complimented Renata on the beet and apple and onion salad she had fixed. Teresa, looking a little pale, joked after dishes were cleared that "the salad was too too red," and it had given her a stomach ache and could she be excused from chores.

Later Renata brought Teresa a cup of tea, chamomile with honey, just the way she liked it. But Teresa was fast asleep when she pushed open the nun's door.

So why is Renata awake now, tossing and turning in her convent bed, feeling the familiar pinch of the straw on her back and across her shoulders. She is holding her rosary beads, which some nights she will say in order to fall asleep.

She keeps thinking of Señora. The old woman is pouring water into an old ceramic vase, the colorful dark blue vase that once sat on Antonie's kitchen table. It had come with Señora from Mexico so many years before. It was hand painted in white calla lilies and Señora would fill it every morning with roses or whatever flower was growing in abundance. Antonie ignored the flowers and the vase; what Señora did in the kitchen was Señora's business. "The kitchen is hers," he would often say.

Now for some reason Señora's got the vase in both hands and she has filled the vase with white lilies. Fragrant lilies—Renata has got the scent of them in her nose as she sleeps.

And then she sees Señora carrying the vase with a towel wrapped beneath it. Somehow, Señora is there in the convent, and she is setting the vase on a night table, right next to Sister Teresa's bed. Señora is speaking soothing words to Teresa. Señora sets a cool cloth over the nun's brow and takes Teresa's hand in both of hers. At just that moment, Teresa arches her back and pulls her hand out of Señora's. She thrashes side to side, and collapses into a fetal position. Her mouth falls open and she cries out. Her face is as white as goat's milk.

Mother Yolla is beside the bed and two or three other nuns have gathered too. They are kneeling around the bed and praying. No one is saying what's wrong with Teresa because apparently no one knows. The doctor is on the other side of the bed, and he has a stethoscope dangling from his neck. Mother Yolla and Señora each take one of Teresa's shoulders, preparing to hold her down while the doctor listens to the nun's chest.

"What? What? Teresa, my dear Teresa, what is wrong?" Renata is trying to wake herself up from the dream, and for a moment she seems to succeed. All she needs to do is wake up and walk down the narrow convent hall and she will be there with Teresa. So simple, so simple.

"She needs me, she needs me," Renata says, but for some reason she is having trouble waking up. She keeps trying to make herself sit up but the quilts are heavy and even when she pushes then aside, she can't get out of the convent bed, she is stuck there in the dark shivering, her head swimming.

But when she is finally sitting up, and she is finally awake, she is not at the convent at all; she sees the thick trees outside Arthur's porch, lit by the sliver of a moon. The night is perfectly still.

Renata pulls the blanket tightly around her shoulders. She is cold but sweating at the same time. Her heart is hammering and a ring of pain is circling her head just above her eyes.

She has only one thought: she will find her way back to the convent. She must. This dream has to be a sign that Teresa is in trouble.

She hasn't any idea what time it is, but she gets off the mattress and walks into the cabin still wrapped in the blanket. She stands outside Arthur's door for a moment trying to decide if she should knock. Wake him up. Ask his help. She's going to need a wagon to make the trip.

Biting into her lip, she decides to wait. She goes back to the porch and lays awake until the sky takes its first rosy color from the rising sun.

45

SISTER RENATA

Renata prays the rosary the whole way. The prayers relax her as she keeps Teresa front and center in her mind. What will she find when they arrive at the convent? Will Teresa still be alive?

Arthur pushes the horse as fast as the old road will allow. But the going is slow, the surface of the road rutted and pocked by holes and sharp rock.

They stop once to water the horse, and a second time, to eat some of the lunch that Renata packed. But soon they are back to the road, and the endless red dust, rising up in clouds. It's a long and jolting ride.

As the sun starts to approach the horizon, the road starts to descend into the golden valley. Arthur stops and massages the back of his neck with one hand. "I'm feeling a might weary ma'am, so I propose we stop here, take a little rest before we push down into the valley."

"Oh must we?" Renata cries. "We're so close now. And I have such a terrible premonition, I keep fearing that I am going to walk into the convent just after Teresa has...has ...." she shakes her head, sets her forehead against the rosary beads wrapped around her fingers.

"I won't linger, ma'am, I just feel like I need a little nap. It won't be a long sleep I promise."

Renata's eyes brighten. "I know. I can drive the wagon while you rest in back, I've handled a rig this big before." As Renata glances forward to the horse, she tells herself that this is more or less true, she once drove a smallish cart pulled by a donkey.

"I wish you wouldn't," Arthur replies. "I'd be worrying about you the whole time. The road gets even more narrow from here on descending into this valley."

"Yes, yes, I know very well this road, and this valley, I've walked it so many times. We aren't more than five or six miles from the convent now, I will be fine, I promise you." Her voice is calm and strong as she slips the rosary beads into her side pocket and reaches for the reins.

"I won't sleep for long," Arthur says, climbing over the seat into the back and pulling the blanket over him.

Renata squares herself on the wagon seat and pulls up the reins. Then she snaps them sharply, just as she had seen Arthur do so many times. The horse doesn't move. She snaps the reins again, and a third time.

"He can sense the new driver," Arthur says from the back. "And he can tell we're starting to descend."

Renata gets out of the wagon and approaches the horse. She strokes his ears and whispers lovingly. "We will take good care of you, and feed you carrots and apples when we get to the convent." She rubs his nose and spends a few moments with her arms around his neck. "We've got to get there," she whispers. "It's ever so important."

She climbs up to the wagon seat and this time when she snaps the reins the horse stalls for a moment but then moves forward, picking his way through ruts and rock. The light is still good, so Renata relaxes. Her mood rises the further they descend toward the convent. At one bend, she realizes that in the far distance is the line of live oaks where she and Teresa would always bring their lemonade and blankets after chores were finished. Her heart begins to race and her face tightens as she wonders what she will find when they get there.

Arthur is snoring from the back of the wagon. Renata pulls herself up on the seat as the road begins a particularly steep decline. The horse slows. She snaps the reins but with little effect. The horse is going his pace and that is as fast as they will go.

The sky is now a steely grey blue, the sun melting into the hills across the valley. There are pink and orange remnants of sunset in the clouds overhead. Renata has always loved the convent setting, and now she gets a rush of nostalgia for this place that she has missed so deeply these last months while confined to jail. Her heart beats faster, and she is filled almost to tears thinking of the love she has for all of the sisters, and even for Mother Yolla, despite her often ornery temper.

Arthur is sound asleep as the wagon passes through the final steep portion of the road. By now, Renata is so excited to get there, and so close, that she is tempted to stop the wagon and run the rest of the way, as no matter how much she snaps the reins the horse goes his own slow pace.

The sky overhead is redder than before, the sunset throwing a wondrous show as she sees the adobe steeple of the chapel. She cannot make out the bell, but she can see the dark cross at the top of the steeple. She can't keep herself contained.

She pulls the reins to a halt and jumps down from the wagon before the horse comes to a full halt. She shakes Arthur awake. "We're here, we're here, I'm going in," she cries, but doesn't wait for a reply. She is racing toward the convent picking her way around the gardens, and the apple trees, and soon she is standing on the back tiled patio where the fountain, absent of water, stands.

And in a moment, she is inside the convent, breathing hard. What she hears first is the clatter of forks and knives against plates. It hadn't occurred to her that she was arriving just in time for dinner.

Trembling, sweaty, out of breath, and still wearing the hat that Arthur loaned her for the trip, she walks slowly into the dining room. Her legs wobble as she raises one hand in greeting.

Eighteen faces, including Teresa's, stare back at her, in varying states of shock.

Teresa rises from her place, her hands on either side of her face. She paces unsteadily around the table to greet Renata. The two embrace and simultaneously descend to their knees, their hands clasped in prayer. The rest of the nuns gather around the two, questions shooting from all directions.

"Where have you been? How did you get back? Why are you here? Don't you fear they'll find you…"

Mother Yolla sets her hand on Renata's hat and lifts it off her head. Her hair is a short bristly cut, matted and dirty. But that doesn't stop Mother Yolla from planting a kiss on Renata's crown. "God Bless you my child, God will protect you now that you are here."

Renata, with Teresa's help, stands and lets herself be hugged and kissed by the excited nuns. Soon she's seated at the table, in her old spot, and a plate and utensils are before her. She holds up her hands.

"I'm in no condition to eat," she says, "not yet." And then she pauses and turns to Mother Yolla. "And I have a friend to get from outside. The man, Arthur, who found me half dead in the high chaparral and let me stay at his cabin. A perfect gentleman who rode me on his wagon to get here."

At that moment, Arthur appears at the door, hat held in two hands. "Good evening, sisters," he says, a tentative smile on his face. Mother Yolla approaches him and extends a hand.

"God bless you sir, God bless you."

"We'll set another place," Teresa says, disappearing into the kitchen. Renata rises from her seat and follows her. "My dear dear Teresa you are well, you are alive, you are well." Teresa looks confused.

"Yes, of course, why wouldn't I be?" Teresa is puzzled but lets Renata embrace her again.

"I had a dream, a terrible terrible dream, but it seems like it wasn't the sign I thought it was. I was convinced that you were so ill, so ill, that the doctors feared you were dying, I saw all the nuns gathered around you kneeling, and you in the bed, thrashing. I was convinced I would never see you again."

Teresa releases Renata. "My poor sister, I'm so so sorry for your dream. But I am so glad you are here." Teresa's face looks ashen. She looks down to the floor and then engages Renata's gaze once more.

She squeezes Renata's hand and pulls her closer. "It's Señora I'm afraid."

"What?"

"Your dream had me being ill. But it is Señora who suffers. I will take you to her first thing in the morning."

"She is sick, Señora is ill?"

Teresa nods her head gravely. "I been with her for the past seven days. She suffered a terrible fever the week before and yes, she was thrashing, and in seizure. Then she fell unconscious. The doctor says it's a coma and she..." Teresa pauses. Inhales. "I'm afraid he's convinced that she may never emerge."

Renata's insides drop. Suddenly she is so tired, so overwhelmed by fatigue that she feels she might collapse right there in the kitchen. She swings around and aims unsteadily for the rocking chair in the corner. But she only makes it halfway before she dissolves into the floor.

46

SISTER RENATA

Assisted by two of the other nuns, Bernice and Laura Lee, Teresa pulls Renata into the rocking chair. There she sits, slumped against one arm. Teresa runs for smelling salts, and Bernice boils water for chamomile tea. Laura Lee—a delicate girl with dimples and splotches of brown freckles—holds Renata in a sitting position.

Kneeling in front of the chair, Teresa passes the salts under Renata's nose, until the smell of the ammonia starts Renata's head moving side to side. "Enough," she whispers. "Please no more."

Teresa pulls the salts away. "We have tea for you Renata, tea with gobs of honey. You must be so thirsty. "She lifts a spoonful to Renata's open mouth. But after a few sips, Renata pushes Teresa's hand away.

"I must see Señora now," she whispers, wriggling out of Laura Lee's grip. "Please Teresa, please take me up to her."

"At least finish the tea, and put something solid in your stomach." Teresa bends closer and steadies a gaze at Renata. "I promise if you have a little of the rabbit stew we ate for dinner, and finish the tea, I will bring you to her."

Renata's face wrinkles up in disgust. "I've been eating rabbit stew for the last week. Just spoon me a few carrots and onions and some parsley and that will do."

Teresa hands the mug to Renata. "You drink this up. And if you're still thirsty, Bernice will fix you a second cup."

After eating half the vegetables that Teresa scooped into a bowl, and after finishing most of a second cup of tea, Renata rises from the rocking chair. Teresa takes her arm and they pass through the convent's dining room into the parlor and up the stairs.

Soon they are at Señora's side. Her face is small and almond-colored. Renata sits on one side of the bed, Teresa on the other.

Leaning forward, Renata whispers. "I'm here, my dear Señora. I am here beside you and I won't leave you."

Señora is lying in such perfect stillness that it isn't clear she is breathing. Teresa holds a finger below Señora's nose. After a few moments she takes her hand away.

"I have an idea," Renata says, getting up. "I'll be right back." She hurries downstairs to her old room, and drops onto her knees in front of the bed. The straw mattress is stiff and minus any sheets. Renata drags from beneath the bed the guitar she keeps wrapped in an old Indian blanket. She sinks to the floor and hums a low E, and quickly tunes the strings.

Soon she is hurrying back to the bedroom to Señora and Teresa, who smiles when she sees the guitar.

"It's worth a try, don't you agree?" Teresa nods.

Guitar cradled in her lap, Renata plays the carcelero that Señora loves:

"In three days I've eaten

Only bread and tears:

That is the food

That my jailers give.

How do they expect me to live?"

She follows the carcelero with a soleares and a farrucca and finally, a rousing bulerías.

Señora is motionless, the music passing over her like a soft breeze. Renata puts the guitar down and takes Señora's hand and kisses it. "I know you can hear me," she says. "I just know you feel me here."

She takes out her beads and together with Teresa, they say the rosary.

"It's late, Renata," Teresa says at the end of the prayers. "Tomorrow is another day. Please, I'll make your bed up for you. And I'll find a place for Arthur downstairs. Come now. Let her be."

Renata wraps her rosary beads around Señora's hand, and places a kiss on the old woman's cool forehead. Teresa is out the door and Renata is just about to blow out the candle on the night table when she hears a soft groan.

Whipping around, she sees the rosary beads trembling in Señora's hand. "Teresa, Teresa, look!"

By now, Renata has Señora's hand in hers. "You're awake, you're awake!" It takes a few minutes before Señora's eyes open. She blinks. Her lips tremble, and Renata sees a smile on her face.

"Oh my dear Señora you're back," Renata says in a hush. Señora opens her mouth but nothing comes out. "Don't try to speak. Don't."

Teresa and Renata stand there staring at Señora. The old woman opens her mouth. "Siéntate," she whispers in a hoarse tone. The nuns sit down. Renata takes both of Señora's hands in hers.

"M'ija," Señora begins. And then she whispers in Spanish. "It's my time. It's my time. I'm not long on God's good earth now."

"How do you know that Señora, you can't possibly know God's will."

Señora continues to speak to Renata in Spanish, in a hushed whisper. "There is no time for discussing this now. You must do for me what you have steadfastly refused to do all these months. You must find those missing pages of your journal and present them to the authorities. Please. Please, for me do this."

"No," Renata says, pulling back. "I won't. You know you can ask and you can beg, but I am not turning in those pages. Justice will be served and I remain in God's hands, with Mary to protect me too."

Teresa pipes up. "Señora is right. You've come back here now, Renata, and clearly there is no way we can protect you. Not for long can we hide you here. The gallows is ready and waiting. The authorities will hang you as soon as word gets out. Please, abide by Señora's dying wish."

Renata rises, and turns toward the darkened window, her arms crossed. "I vowed I would never turn Señora in. I made myself a solemn promise. I can't turn back on that now."

Señora struggles to one elbow. And out of her mouth comes a voice that I know so well. The voice in which she has spoken to me for so long. The voice that has pulled me back to Renata's world, time and again.

"Por favor Gina," Señora cries out. "Ahora es muy importante que vengas aquí. Por favor!"

And as I sit here, typing furiously, my laptop disappears and I let go of this world and move to the sound of Señora's voice. Suddenly I am in the room with the three characters whose lives I have entwined so tightly with my own.

Teresa and Renata stare at me. I'm wearing my blue bathrobe and white sox, and my hair must look like an awful fright. I haven't showered and I've got the sour breath one has after a night's sleep and a cup of coffee.

"Hola, Señora," I say and she reaches a hand out to me. Slowly I approach the bed. Renata's eyes are wide and forbidding and Teresa looks like she's seen a lizard crawl across the bed covers. I clear my throat and don't come any closer. "Hello Renata. We have met before," I say, my voice shaking. "I am Gina Rinaldi, a writer, and I love Señora at least as much as both of you."

"How could you possibly?" Renata asks, her voice sharp but shaking. "Where do you come from?" Renata scans me head to toe while Teresa stands with hands on her broad hips.

I clear my throat. "I've been working with Señora from afar. You would not believe me if I told you how far," I say. "It's much too hard to explain."

Señora sits up. She asks for her shawl and Teresa brings it and wraps it around her shoulders. Teresa and Renata stand beside her like protective soldiers. And then she begins to speak. Thankfully, she speaks in a slow Spanish that I can understand.

"This woman is writing your story, Renata. She's been writing it for 20 years."

I pipe up. "Actually it's 23 years. It was January of 1995 when I started this book."

"What? What are you saying?" Renata takes a step toward me.

Funny that I never thought her to be the least bit threatening. Before. "What book are you referring to? And what is this about 1995?"

Señora smiles. "I'll ask you to be patient Renata. What you are witnessing here my dear is the work of the Virgin Mary. Her miracles, as you know, we can never explain. This is one of those miracles."

"What do you mean?"

"The virgin, m'ija, she appeared in a vision one night, right after you were hung."

"HUNG?"

Señora nods. Her face is solemn. She lapses into Spanish. "You see Renata, time has come unhinged. After you died, I so regretted letting you sacrifice yourself on my behalf that I prayed continually to Mary for forgiveness. She came to me one night and said that together, we could rewrite history."

"My dear Señora, this makes absolutely no sense to me. Are you telling me you erased events that already took place?"

Señora nods her head again, more slowly this time.

I decide to take a step forward. Renata tenses and turns her back to me. "I am not here to hurt you," I say. "Please understand that's the last thing you have to fear."

Señora continues. "So why is Gina here? Because I called for her. With Mary's help, I found Gina, a woman who was willing to write the true story of Antonie's death. This woman you see here lives far into the future on the other side of the continent."

Renata collapses into the chair. She turns to face Teresa who looks just as dumbfounded.

"What Señora says is absolutely true," I say. "I come from a moment in history when we have such things as cars with engines and computers that write and think and mobile telephones and electricity and airplanes that fly."

"I don't understand any of what you are saying and I don't want to," Renata says. "I don't buy any of this silliness."

"You must listen," Señora commands. "Please Renata. If you fail to listen, you will most certainly hang, as you did the first time. The gallows is waiting and they will string you up in the hot sun in the courtyard without the slightest hesitation."

"I don't understand," Renata says. "How can this woman possibly help me escape?"

"Please, Renata," I say. "I just write the story. It's up to me to make you see the wisdom of releasing those pages from your journal. Those pages cannot hurt Señora anymore. You were right when you at first decided to hold them back, because the authorities would have hung Señora, a Mexican woman, without even a trial. A Mexican woman killing a white American man. But now Señora's time is up. And so it doesn't matter."

"How do *you* know that? How could you possibly know anyth..."

"¡Silencio!" Señora shouts. She lifts her head from the pillow and takes out a piece of newspaper. She unfolds it. The headline reads in big block letters, "NUN HUNG FOR MURDERING HER COUSIN." Two columns of writing appear and in the center of the page is a very clear drawing of the nun swinging from a rope.

Renata gasps. Teresa cries out. "My God!"

"I hope you see now that the danger is very real," Señora says. "I hope you understand why the Virgin has interceded here. This is what happened the first time around. You did hang for Antonie's murder. You refused to produce those pages of the journal that tell the true story."

"Let me see that newspaper," Renata says snatching it away from Señora with a shaking hand. Sweat sprouts on her brow. "I don't know how this is possible. This is not ....this is...out of this world. This is impossible. This is ..."

"Un milagro," Señora says, whispering the words. "Yes, Renata, this is a miracle. That we are here, today, the three of us, with this woman writer from the future. This woman who in fact can save you. Give you the freedom you have so long deserved. Let her do her work. Give her those journal pages. Let her write them down. Let the authorities see the truth. Nothing can hurt me. They won't touch me now. Not when I am this close to my hour of death."

Teresa speaks. "I am not sure I can possibly comprehend what I am hearing and seeing, Renata, but by God, this is indeed a miracle of some kind. I think this is your lifeboat Renata. You must cooperate. You've always told me that I would be the one to tell the true story after your death. It would be me who reveals at the proper time—after Señora's death—what actually happened to Antonie. But now I see there is no reason to wait. And every reason for you to go free. You must do as Señora and the writer say, Renata. You must trust this woman in the blue robe, because it is exactly the same color as the Virgin's veil."

Renata turns slowly to face me. I see her finely chiseled features, made sharper by the fact that she is so thin. Her hair is standing in a wispy black brush. She is as pale as cotton and has some premature white hairs. There has been so much happening to her since that chapter I wrote so long ago, when Antonie turned her into a flamenco dancer and she danced on the table.

She reaches out one hand and I don't hesitate to take it. Renata's fingers are cool and slim and delicate. She tips her face upward (she only comes as high as my shoulder.) "I am still not sure I understand how it is that you are from the future, but I must say, Señora is rather persuasive with this newspaper clipping."

I smile. "My dear Renata, I am seeing this newspaper for the very first time, right along with you. Suffice to say it's quite a blessing that the all-loving Virgin Mary somehow made it possible for Señora to get that clipping—without me having to do a thing—and that it has helped to convince you of my good intentions in writing your story. More than anything in the world, Renata, I want you to live. I never ever wanted to write the story of your hanging."

Teresa is sitting down now. And shaking her head. She sets one hand on each knee and whispers. "Amazing. Somehow the Virgin is helping to change history."

Señora turns. "Renata, find the missing journal pages please. Let Gina have them for her story."

"No, Señora," I interrupt. "It's not *my* story. It's *your* story. And most especially it's Renata's."

"In any case, bring the journal pages to me," Señora says, slipping down under the covers. "And then, if you wouldn't mind, I would love a cup of tea. Or better yet, the tiniest glass of sherry."

I chuckle and Renata leaves the room to retrieve the missing journal pages. Teresa heads downstairs to get the liquor.

And me? I pick up Renata's guitar and play for Señora one of my favorite flamenco tunes, a bulerías that my teacher Maria Z. taught me many years ago.

GINA

An hour passes. Señora Ramos is deep asleep—snoring soundly—after finishing her drink. I play the three or four songs I know by heart and then start working on scales.

Soon enough, though, it occurs to me that Renata has still not returned with the journal pages. I set the guitar against the wall and go out into the hallway. In my imagination, Renata's room was on the first floor, tiny, dark, spare and it faced the tiled courtyard. As I recall, it was three doors down the hall from Teresa's room. I close Señora's door now and descend the staircase, keeping perfectly quiet in my white socks. I make my way through the dining room and the small parlor and into the wing where the nuns' rooms sit, one after another. By this time, evening prayers are over, and most of the nuns have retired for the night.

I stand in the narrow hallway, where a single candle burns inside a glass dish. The low adobe ceiling is only a few inches above my head. If I am correct, the door on my right is Renata's. But what if I have remembered it wrong? I would disturb one of the other nuns.

I decide that I have to take the chance. I set two knuckles to the wooden door and tap three times.

No answer.

I knock again, a little louder this time. Then I position my lips into the crack where the door meets the frame. I whisper.

"Renata? Please, are you in there?"

Nothing. I am beginning to think I do indeed have the wrong room. I turn around and lean back on the door and look up to the ceiling. I am beginning to feel like a very unwelcome visitor. It occurs to me that I can simply stop all of this, and return to my laptop, where I belong.

At just that moment, the door swings open and I feel myself falling backwards into the room. Renata is stronger than she looks, because the next thing I know, I am looking into dark eyes. She's caught me and together we've fallen back against her bed!

"I'm so sorry," I stammer. I struggle up to my feet. "I really am not trying to harass you, Renata, I just want to do what Señora wishes."

"Come in," she says. I enter the tiny convent room, which is even smaller than I had pictured it when I described it in the book. The crucifix looms large over the narrow bed of straw.

"Please, Renata, I must have those journal pages. I'll be off as soon as I have them."

"I'm sorry. I am very reluctant to part with those pages. I've heard all that Señora explained, about the supposed miracle and the Virgin rewriting history. I hope you will excuse my skepticism, but I am still not convinced."

My stomach tightens and my face flushes hot. I feel a flood of anxiety rush up and down my arms. Did I really create this character who is so impossibly stubborn? I clear my throat.

"I understand your skepticism," I begin, speakly slowly. "For the record, I used to be a skeptic. I refused to believe Señora when she said I could free myself—and you—by writing this book."

She stares at me. "I never asked for your help."

"Of course not. It was Señora's job to do that."

"So please what is your point here?"

"I respect you for holding back the truth, Renata. I do. But the trouble is, it's just a matter of time before the authorities find out that you're back here at the convent. When they do, they will, as Señora says, lose no time taking you to the gallows. So please, I will get down on my knees and beg you if I have to, just give those pages to me so that the true story can be told and you will go free."

Renata sighs and sits down on the bed. "Maybe I go free. But maybe I won't. From what I've seen in the courtroom so far, it's going be very difficult to use a few handwritten pages from my journal to convince anyone that my case should be reopened. God knows how hard it would be to overturn my conviction."

"What you say is true of course Renata, but my God, we've got to try, haven't we?" My voice gets louder, prompting Renata to set one finger over her lips, cautioning me to speak more quietly.

At that moment, an idea hits me. I have a lawyer friend back in Massachusetts who works as a public defender. He will be able to fill me in on how new evidence can be introduced after a conviction. But the one sticking point remains: I can't do anything without that new evidence in hand.

"I will give your proposal some thought," Renata announces, rising from the bed. She is wearing a simple white gown. "It's been a long and tiring day, and I refuse to make this decision tonight." She pauses. "So if you don't mind, I would like to go to back to bed now."

I stand there, amazed. Here Renata is being offered a gift—a painless way out of her desperate situation—and yet, she seems so nonchalant, as if it doesn't matter that the death penalty awaits her. Didn't she see the newspaper clipping? Can she possibly be so indifferent to the danger she faces?

She holds the door open for me. I say a soft good night and return to Señora's room. The old woman is sleeping quietly, so I pull up her extra blanket and I leave. Little do I know what will greet me in the morning!

47

SISTER RENATA'S DIARY

February 13, 1884

My dearest Señora,

I shouldn't have waited so long to call Mother Yolla and the other nuns to your bedside.

I should have run at top speed to find someone who would get the doctor.

But I was afraid. That's a sorry thing to admit, Señora, but it's the truth. And by now, you know that's true of me. You know me so well. You know how fearful I am.

I finally ran downstairs and found Mother Yolla, who immediately asked Arthur to get the doctor. It took more than two hours for him and the doctor to return. And in the end, it took Dr. Thacker only a few minutes to examine you.

We all waited outside the closed door. Soon the doctor opened the door and stepped into the dim hallway of the convent.

"I'm afraid that she has suffered a stroke," Dr. Thacker declared, taking off his wire-rimmed glasses and rubbing his eyes. "It looks to me as though she has slipped back into a coma."

A collective groan rose up from the group of us at the door.

"Can you do something?" I begged.

He shook his head. "I'm afraid there is nothing possible," he said. "She may wake up, or she may not. It's out of my hands. For now, I suggest that you keep her company around the clock. Sit with her, make her comfortable, sing to her, and pray that she may get better."

He turned to Mother Yolla, and set one hand on the older nun's elbow. "I know very little about prayer," he said, his face pale and sad. "But I would highly recommend it in this case. And I will be happy to return tomorrow to check in on her again."

He turned to face Arthur. "Would you be so kind as to drive me back to town?"

As the two of them went downstairs, Mother Yolla gathered us in the hallway. "We will take turns sitting by her side," she announced simply. "Who will be first?"

Five hands went up including my own. Mother Yolla chose two of the other nuns, who promptly opened the bedroom door and disappeared inside.

"Oh but please let me stay too," I begged, pressing my hands together over my chest. "I might as well be with Señora since I won't be able to stop thinking about her for even a moment."

"No, my child," Mother Yolla replied. "You'll have your turn. But first, I need to speak to you in private." She eyed me carefully, and there was something so direct and piercing about her facial expression that it triggered a flush of anxiety in my stomach. I felt my mouth go cotton dry.

"Of course," I mumbled.

She motioned for me to follow her downstairs. We passed through the dining room and out the door to the backyard. I thought we'd sit beside the hummingbird feeder, but she kept walking. We ended up in the tiny chapel where the nuns seek a quiet place for private prayer and meditation. I so love this precious chapel, as it was built entirely of stone. Like the other nuns, I helped to lay the floor, which was no more than California palm fronds covered over by heavy blankets. There is room for two small benches.

I followed Mother Yolla inside. We sat down side by side.

"Please my dear, face me if you will," she said quietly. I moved to the other bench so I faced her. I felt my heart hammering in my chest. Our knees were almost touching. The air in the chapel was fragrant with a mixture of mint and sage, as we regularly bring those plants into the chapel.

Mother Yolla looked into her lap where she had one hand resting on another. She cleared her throat and looked up at me.

"My dear Renata, you know that I couldn't be more pleased to see you. We were all so terribly worried when you disappeared." I nodded, nervously squeezing my hands together. What was she about to say?

"I...I am so sorry I caused you and the others so much distress," I said, my voice thin. "I didn't mean to make my escape, it just kind of happened. And then there was no way to reach out to you or ..."

"Please," Mother Yolla said. She held up one hand to quiet me. "I understand that you did what you had to do."

"Yes, that's true," I mumbled.

"Sometimes we are forced to do things that we would rather not do," she said, gazing at me steadily.

I blinked. What was she coming to? What was she trying to say?

Again she cleared her throat. "This isn't easy for me. But I am going to have to turn you into the authorities. I cannot jeopardize the rest of us here at the convent. If they were to find you here, we would stand guilty of harboring a known criminal."

I blinked again. My chin dropped to my chest. Tears welled up in the corners of my eyes. I sniffled.

"I am so sorry Renata. You know how I feel about each and every one of my novitiates. It kills me to do this but Father Ruby insists."

I lifted my head. My face flushed. "So that's it, he's the one insisting." Mother Yolla remained quiet and stared into her hands.

"I should have known. He's the one who let Antonie take advantage of me all these years. He's the one who insisted that Antonie was family, that I owed it to my cousin to do whatev..."

"PLEASE, no more!" Mother Yolla's voice was sharp and unforgiving. "I insist that you show respect for Father Ruby."

I so desperately wanted to say more. But Mother Yolla was already standing. I stared at the large rosary beads—each bead the size of a large black bean—hanging from her waist. "As you well know, Renata, I am not the final arbiter here. Father Ruby is in charge. And we must do what we must do, even if we are desperately unhappy doing it. So please, please, please forgive me." She lifted one hand and cupped it over her eyes. Her head fell forward and the edge of her veil brushed against my hand. It had been almost a year since I'd felt the veil.

The next thing I knew Mother Yolla turned and rushed out of the chapel. I thought I heard her muffled cries as she fled.

48

SISTER RENATA'S DIARY

February 17, 1884

Dear Mary, You heard what Mother Yolla she said she is going to yield me up to the authorities she said she will turn me in, no matter that I will be hanged Mother Yolla said she cannot protect me she has to think about the convent Mother Yolla doesn't love me enough to save me!

Mother Yolla says she cannot risk the reputation of the convent Mother she said she is giving in to Father Ruby in so few words she said that she would rather see me dead hanged hanged hanged hanged than take the chance take the chance so now

What the

What

WHAT AM I TO DO?

If I run if I run I can't run away from myself and my duty anymore I cannot—where would I go San Francisco? Arthur says he will take me but what would I do marry Arthur marry him oh Mary

HELP ME MARY! Shall I run away or marry Arthur

Dear God I want to be a nun, I have always been a nun, Dear Mary

No, I wouldn't consider marrying Arthur he is a dear man a good soul but not a person not a husband for me

I WON'T LEAVE SEÑORA

I am sitting here in the dark alone with her in the middle of the night holding her limp hand with one of my own and writing here in my journal with the other, weeping because I cannot leave I cannot run away anymore I must face the facts that I actually will die, I actually will hang I will die so maybe that is what Mary wants? Why Why DEAR GOD I did not kill my cousin Dear Mary, I want to know what you want me to do WHERE DO I GO?

Señora squeezes my hand.

"What?" Is that what I think it is, is it?

"What?" I WHISPER.

"Señora…are you…are you awake" I drop the journal and bend over holding her hand it is dark there is nothing I cannot see the old woman's coal black eyes but I hear her speak, she whispers something can this be a dream did I fall asleep did I? did I? Am I hearing really hearing

Señora speaks:

"Tome las páginas de la revista. Enséñeselas a las autoridades por favor, Renata, que todo el mundo y sus seres iluminados sepan que yo fui quien mató a Antonie. Yo agarre el cuchillo, le dí la última puñalada el murió en un charco de sangre sobre mi regazo."

"Take the journal pages take them show them to the authorities please Renata let them LET ALL THE WORLD AND ITS ILLUMINATED BEINGS let all know it was me who finished Antonie, I held the blade I made the final cut and he expired in a pool of blood in my lap."

I am weeping now, so delighted that Señora is back, she is out of the coma, she is awake "YOU ARE AWAKE!" I hug her and my tears pour out onto her coffee-colored face, wrinkled and soft as a pillow.

"I will go get Mother Yolla and the others, I will get you some water, some tea, you must be so so thirsty," she doesn't answer but she squeezes my hand and when I turn I swear I see Mary the Virgen de Guadalupe, her sky a baby blue veil.

I WILL BE RIGHT BACK I squeeze her hand and she squeezes mine and I race out of the room and down the hall to Mother Yolla's room and knock once on the door and barge in because Señora is awake

SEÑORA SHE IS AWAKE! I SCREAM I PULL ON MOTHER YOLLA'S SHOULDER

"What..what??" Suddenly Mother Yolla is sitting up and out of the bed she and I race down the hall screaming SHE'S AWAKE SHE'S AWAKE SO ALL THE NUNS CAN HEAR and in seconds there are a dozen of us in her room and it smells sour and fouled as if Señora has peed her bed but no matter she is awake

Mother Yolla screams and Teresa screams

LIGHT A CANDLE,

Mother Yolla has Señora's limp hand in hers and she must be feeling the squeeze

"She squeezed my hand, Mother Yolla, she squeezed my hand and then she spoke to me, she told me what to do she told me to take...."

Mother Yolla interrupts me. "Renata, her hand is limp."

"That can't be, she was just holding and squeezing and talking to me."

"Come here my dear," Mother Yolla is not angry, just extremely tired, bone weary tired. "Feel her hand my dear."

I do. I feel Señora's hand and it is warm and as limp as a dead fish.

"But she was awake, I swear it. I felt her squeeze my hand. I know I did I did I did," and then I am caving in, I am sobbing uncontrollably now everything is caving in on me I am going to hang and my dear dear Señora is not awake now

I don't know how long we sit there. Teresa holds me.

Finally she helps me up and walks me back to my room. I lay down on my bed. Soon Teresa arrives with a mug of chamomile tea. I sit up and take the cup of tea.

"Teresa," I whisper after a few moments.

"Yes Renata?"

"This is the time."

"Time? For what sweet sister?"

I stand up. She does too.

I kneel beside the bed. Reaching deep into the straw of my mattress I pull out the folded journal pages. I stand and face her.

"Oh my dear Renata, please may I read them?"

"Of course you may. I would say that it's about time these pages see the light of day."

49

SISTER RENATA'S DIARY

September 17, 1883

If I write it all down, will it feel more real? Will I begin to accept the fact that it happened? I sit here staring into the darkness, my fingers trembling as I push the pen. If I keep my eyes on the page, I can almost pretend that I am back in my room at the convent. I can almost ignore the dank walls of the cell, and the chill, and the atrocious smell. And the swill of that dreadfully foul pail. When the sun rises, I will have to look up and see. Daylight reveals the walls, and all I can think is that they will close in and crush me.

Thanks be to God for Señora's visit yesterday. Thanks be to God that she brought the sky blue shawl.

All those roses, all those beautiful red flowers. It isn't altogether warm, but it is some comfort during these sleepless nights. And thanks too that she brought this white candle, and the pewter candleholder, for otherwise, I would have no light by which to write. And God knows, I must write. As frightened as I am, as desperate as I feel, I must write. I must fight the temptation to give up.

I will go back four days. Will I ever forget the date? It was September 13, 1883. It will always be, because time stopped that day. Life for me will never be the way it was before that day.

We had been back from San Francisco for exactly one month. It had taken me weeks to recuperate. I slept for the first few days and showered in Teresa's shower as often as I could. But still I felt my soul sinking. I would open my eyes each the morning and before I was fully awake I would think about my cousin wasting away, and poor Señora caring for him. I would cringe at the thought that I had abandoned her, that I no longer would consider even visiting my cousin. But I could not begin to think about him, or his illness. Or Señora. I could barely raise my head from the pillow.

September 13th came. It was a Sunday, and I was up early. I finally had gained enough strength back to attend Mass at sunrise. When I emerged from the chapel, there was Señora waiting for me in the wagon, her brow knit in torment and worry. I hurried to her side. Her eyes begged me. She patted the seat beside her. No words passed between us. I knew what was happening. I knew what I had to do. As I hoisted myself onto the wagon, Mother Yolla emerged from chapel. She called out to me.

"Where are you off to, Sister Renata?"

"I'm sorry, Mother Superior," I said, bowing my head. "My cousin is dying. I have no choice but to go."

Señora whipped the horse smartly, and we were on our way. The roads were a terribly bumpy surface at her speed. But we needed to get there. When we turned, finally, down the long dusty drive leading to the hacienda, I heard Señora whisper, "Gracias a Dios." I too said a prayer, that whatever awaited me would not be more than I could endure. I wasn't sure if Antonie would still be alive.

It was just before noon. A brilliantly beautiful day. I will never forget the sky: it looked as though it had been washed clean. I lowered myself down from the wagon and turned to give Señora a hand.

I followed Señora into the hacienda. She led me straight to his room. He looked so shriveled it was difficult to believe that he was still living!

When I approached his bed, he raised his face to me. He looked ghastly, a purple glaze clung to his skin, and when he spoke, his breath was as foul as the chicken coop back at the convent.

"Dear Renata, finally, you've come." His gravelly tone made me shudder. "Do you know…how happy I am to see you?" He raised his bony hand and I gasped. His skin had begun to rot right before my eyes.

At that moment, I recalled the day a month before when we had arrived back from San Francisco. It had taken the three of us, Señora and Tango and me, to carry Antonie inside the house. I remember how we moved him, knotting the sheet on which he lay at all four corners.

Tango took two corners, Señora and I each had a corner, and in that way we carried him—a remarkably light load in the sagging sheet—through the monstrous front door and up the polished staircase and into the bedroom. We laid him out on the bed—a shriveled bag of bones and skin—and a long orange shaft of light illuminated his body. I turned to open the window and the breeze swept inside and immediately his eyes went wide and he stared into nothingness as if he were entranced. He lifted his arms as if he might take flight, and then he cried out.

"I am home, dear God, I must be, I must be home, there is only one place in the world with this exceptional fragrance."

About that he was right. Everywhere at Antonie's, there is a remarkable scent of eucalyptus, owing to two giant trees that tower over the hacienda, planted ever so long ago as tiny saplings, a gift to Antonie's father presented by the first Australian family to set foot on Californian soil.

Now, a month later, Antonie was clearly on the verge of death. I watched Señora leave the room to fill a washbasin. When she returned, I stood beside Antonie's bed and swabbed his face with a cloth. Antonie appeared to fall asleep, and so Señora and I prayed for a short while in silence.

And then Señora made her mistake. She told me, within Antonie's earshot, that I was welcome to stay the night. Or that I was free to go, that she would be happy to take me back to the convent herself, or if I preferred, she would have Tango bring me back in the morning.

All of a sudden, Antonie's eyes snapped open. He had heard those words of Señora's, and they sent him into a tailspin. He sat up straight in bed. His eyes bulged, glazed black and bulbous, in those gaping grey bowls. Without the benefit of flesh in his cheeks, his nose stood out in an oddly prominent hook. And the whole of his face was locked in by his gaunt cheekbones, giving him a distinctly skeletal look.

"No, no, you cannot leave me again," he cried, grabbing my veil in two hands and twisting it between his fingers. Thus followed a pathetic scene in which I tried to disengage my veil from his grasp.

"But my dear cousin," I replied, "I must go. I cannot linger a moment longer. As it is, I was away from the convent for almost four weeks."

I yanked the veil away, and Antonie sank to the bed, but still he kept reaching for me. He took hold of my little finger and tenderly he brought it to his chin and his lips and it was pathetic. He was an infant again the way he suckled at my hand. "You know full well that Father Ruby will tell Mother Yolla what to do, he will explain that you have been with me, helping me to get well."

At that moment, his breathing became more labored, and he launched into a cough that sounded as though it came from the bottom of a deep, congested chasm.

When the awful sound finally stopped, he spoke, but ever so slowly, and with a heavy wheeze separating each word. "There… is…no…no…reason to leave. No…reason at …all."

I studied his horrifying face, his pale purple pallor, and I thought, oh but there is every reason to go, I must leave this house right away because if I spend one more day here, attached to you, a dying man, it will be my end as well as yours.

He began whimpering then, and again he grabbed my veil. Señora helped me wrench it from his grasp. I told him that I would wait until he fell asleep for the night before I left, hoping that he would drop off well before the sunlight disappeared.

Señora proceeded downstairs to fix some soup for his dinner. I remained in the chair beside Antonie's bed. His eyes remained open, and he stared at me with a curious mix of sadness, as well as resentment and anger. His eyes bore into me, as if they were drills. Finally I had to look away.

"Renata, bring me my blue journal," he commanded, gesturing to his desk. "Bring my journal and the pen as well."

I did, I brought the journal, and as I passed the book and pen to him, and helped to prop his bony back against two pillows, it never occurred to me that I was enabling him to make his last grand written attack. As he set to work writing on those thin blue pages, it never occurred to me to ask him what he intended to write. Why would I think to ask? Here, after all, was a man hovering on the very edge of the canyon of death. What did it matter what he wrote? What did it matter whether he wrote at all?

He scrawled slowly and in a lopsided hand, his head hanging low over his journal, stopping frequently because his fingers shook so that he could barely grasp the pen. At times, too, he would stop just to glare at me, and that look, while it scared me, still did not alert me to his intentions. How could I possibly know that he was weaving the last bit of his elaborate web, setting me up to appear to be his murderer?

After nearly an hour of scribbling, he sank into the pillows, spent.

"Enough of this," he said. But when I went to take the journal away, he clutched the book tighter to his chest. "I am not finished," he moaned, his lids closing. "I've got more to say and it is not something you may read."

"Well, then, just keep writing," I said.

"But I have to know something," he murmured. "You say you will stay until I fall asleep for the night. But then, when will you return?"

I bowed my head, and felt dizziness overwhelm me. I realized that I had to get out of this sickroom, now, because otherwise, I too would be sick.

"I...I will be helping Señora in the kitchen," I said, and I turned and was about to hurry out the door, when I stopped once more and said to him in an even tone, "God bless you, Antonie," I whispered. And to myself, I continued, "God bless you and may your soul rest in peace for all eternity."

"Oh please, please don't go away," he muttered. By then I had hurried out the door and down the hall.

"God forgive me," I whispered.

Señora was in the kitchen warming broth on the woodstove. She turned to me, and I sank to the chair, and began to sob. Señora placed a hand on my shoulder. It was at that moment we heard the ghastly sound.

It reached into my chest and squeezed my heart and roped it tight. And then an agonizing howl followed, a howl and a kind of unearthly gurgle. It seemed to drown even as it found its mark piercing straight toward my stomach.

Señora and I were upstairs and back in the bedroom in seconds, and there he lay on the floor. He had the razor in his hand, and he was still jabbing and clawing at his throat. Already there was so much more blood than I had ever thought possible from one human being. How could one man bleed so much? I split the air with my own screams, over and over again I yelled, pleading alternately between Spanish and English, between God and Señora, in my desperation and panic. The next few minutes seemed to go on for all eternity.

I raced to his side, and fighting all instincts, I dropped to the floor, into the gore where he lay. "I've got to, I've got to..." that's what I kept thinking, and telling myself, but I had no idea what I had to do, all my body wanted to do was run away, run so far that I could never possibly come back. Instead, though, I forced myself to stay, my stomach threatening to disgorge. The puddle, the blood, was so red, so thick, there was such a flooding of it from the ragged gash at his neck that I grew dizzy.

"Please God," I screamed, "Please God, help us!" and by then, Señora was screaming in Spanish. She laid one hand on my shoulder and I looked up and grabbed her fingers in mine. Then she kneeled too, and the two of us were a statue together, weeping and whimpering, staring into the worst nightmare there ever was, a man with a razor still in his hand, a man still intent on killing himself despite the fact he was barely alive. His lips were bubbling bloody words that could not be heard, his throat gurgled and rapidly disgorged the last drops of his dwindling pool of life.

I bent forward, and holding my breath, I touched his forehead, which was by now about the only part of his face that wasn't smeared in blood.

Feeling his cold skin I began bawling anew and howling, too, wailing for help, wailing at Señora, or who knows who, "Oh do something oh God please do something do something please do something end this ghastly mess!"

Soon the slide of blood creamed both my hands and pooled in my apron, and I turned to Señora and cried out, "What can we do?" With his last bit of energy, Antonie answered the question. He opened his mouth and guzzling his own blood, cried out, "Finish, Renata, oh please, finish me now."

I glanced at the razor still locked within his curled hand. But how could I do what he asked?

"No, no, I cannot," I screamed, and shaking my head, I lifted my hands in the air, and there, there was blood now everywhere, up and down my arms, all over my face and veil. I froze there, staring, shrieking, unable to speak, to think.

As I crumpled to one side, I saw Señora move. She had found some kind of power to act. I was hardly aware of what she was doing until she was there, doing it. She came forward on her knees, sliding in the bloody sleaze. Without a word, and with an otherworldly look on her face, she took the razor from Antonie's hand and lifted and pressed and she put her entire body into the action. She set the razor between her body and his wound and she went full forward, grunting as she did. And I heard a sound like bone breaking, or cartilage cracking.

I grew more dizzy and must have blacked out.

When I came to, and sat up, Antonie was a few feet away from me. He lay with his eyes gaping upward, his head wrenched to one side, his face practically white. There was blood so far and wide that it was indeed a new Red Sea around me. I was drenched through and through. I could do nothing but sob, my head just bobbing side to side.

I wondered where Señora was. But then I knew, because I heard her in the hallway, bawling, and speaking in low tones to Tango, and he too was crying, and trying to comfort her.

"Ven acá, ven acá," I cried, and when the two of them came into the room, I stood and cried out, "Señor Antonie es muerto, es muerto," and she and Tango joined in my howling and the three of us clung to each other. Finally, I told them that I had to pray over his body.

"Sí, sí, Señorita," Tango said.

Drawing on my last shred of inner strength, I kneeled and clasped my hands over his face and trembling, I said some kind of a prayer, all I know is that there were words, and I spoke them from my heart, and I started and ended with God and what happened in between I cannot say. At least I did something, said something, because I knew if there had been a priest present, he would do the last rites, and so this might not be the rites, but it was something come from God just the same.

That's when Señora came to my side, and she helped me up and whispered to me that it was important that I return to the convent immediately. She was most concerned, she said, that I needed to protect my reputation. And I agreed to go, I didn't know what I was saying or doing, but the minute I tried to sit up, I realized that it was all too much for me, this vision I faced was so overwhelming that I didn't know if I could move. There before me lay Antonie, now a grotesquely flayed slab of flesh, a cousin to me no more.

I set to crying anew, my head swimming: Oh Señora, I cried, how could he do something this horrible to himself? And how could he impose this horror on you and me, when we gave him every last shred, every single thing of ourselves we devoted, when we have worked so almighty hard the last weeks and months to see to his every need?

Señora sobbed along with me, but soon she took hold of my hands—both of us still bloody—and said that I must wash myself and Tango must take me home immediately. She promised that she would tend to Antonie's body, with the utmost care, and that she would alert the authorities.

"But there may be questions," I said. Señora waved my concerns away, certain that she would convince the Sheriff that Antonie had taken his own life. I was reluctant to leave, but finally I did, because Señora insisted, and promised that she would call on me if she needed anything at all.

Tango helped me up, and we set off. At the horizon, where I set my eyes, the sky had the most ethereal silvery blue color. A full moon was rising as we drove, and I kept my eyes glued to the giant golden plate as it made its way above the dark rim of trees.

When we reached the convent, I went inside the chicken coop and cried and cried. And finally, I went outside and found a spot where I could dig a hole. I shed my bloody habit there, and wearing the clothes Señora had given me, I hurried into the convent and found Teresa. When darkness finally came, Teresa helped me up the hillside to the shower, and I stayed in there, praying and praying, until the moonlight was full upon me.

When I finally stepped outside the sheet, I was bathed in the full moon's bluish light. I said a silent prayer, dressed, and returned to my room. I fell into a listless sleep, bouncing awake every few minutes, my mind endlessly remaking the horrifying images of him, there on the floor.

The next morning, as I was kneading a batch of bread, and about to weed the garden with Teresa, two tall men in pale blue shirts and black jackets and tall hats arrived at the convent door with a warrant. One had an oversized German Shepherd on a leash, and in the arms of the other man there lay my bloody habit.

Without giving details, they informed Mother Yolla that I was under arrest for the murder of my cousin. Yes, they said, they had every reason to believe I was the murderer as they found a stack of blue pages in Antonie's room—and the last entry described exactly the way the murder happened—the nun had slit his throat.

And no, they said in answer to her question, as they put handcuffs on me, I would not be returning to the convent any time soon.

50

SISTER RENATA'S DIARY

February 23, 1884

When I open my eyes, Teresa is standing beside my bed in the convent. My mouth is as dry as the sheet that covers my straw mattress, the mattress that prickles the skin of my back.

Teresa is crying, her face as wet and pink as a ham.

Sniffling, she turns away so that I won't see her cry but of course I know full well because she is using the bottom half of her white apron to wipe her eyes.

"Will you come with me today?" I whisper out of my cottony mouth. My heart drums inside my chest.

Teresa nods. "Of course." She sets one hand against my cheek. Her own cheeks are glistening in tears. "It's all his fault," Teresa says, sniffling, wiping her eyes again with the apron. "If it weren't for Father Ruby, Mother Yolla would let you stay here, and she would protect you I just know sh..."

"Shhhhh," I lift one finger to my lips to stop her speaking. "It's too late for that, much too late." I push the covers back, and sit on the bed for a moment. "My dear Teresa, I have no choice but to go back."

I get up from the bed, my stomach quaking. Señora told me to take the missing pages of my journal to the authorities so I will.

"What can I fix you for breakfast," Teresa asks. "I baked corn muffins but I'll make you..."

"No food, I couldn't possibly eat." I shudder. My eyes meet Teresa's. "I am so..." I am about to say frightened but if I say the word, then it will just hang there in the air scaring me further.

"You have to eat something! Otherwise you will go faint later today. Please let me make you something."

"Fix me a cup of oatmeal please?"

She nods and leaves the room. I sit back down on the bed. Somehow I have to dress and get in the wagon and go back to jail.

I slip the dress that Arthur bought me over my head. Soft calico with little blue flowers, red hearts. Soft cotton sleeves cover my elbows.

Soon I am in the kitchen where Teresa is stirring oatmeal on the wood stove. The corn muffins she baked earlier smell so pleasing that I lift one to my mouth and take a small bite. Teresa fills a bowl with oatmeal, and adds a tablespoon of honey. I sit down at the table and stare into oatmeal. "This is far more than a cup, this is a whole bowl, I feel I may throw up if..."

"Just hush and eat," Teresa says setting a cup of coffee in front of me.

Arthur enters the kitchen, clutching the brim of his hat. "Good morning ma'am," he says, his dark eyes opened wide. "I was hoping I'd find you here in the kitchen."

I nod. "Yes," I say, trying for a smile, but not succeeding.

Clearing his throat, Arthur drops his gaze to the floor. "You know that..." he starts, and stops and starts again... "Please if you would, let me take you in my wagon, I beg you just to let me do this one thing."

I study his weathered face, his frown. This is a good face, he is a good decent man, one that might be a good marriage partner for some good woman. But I can never marry. I am devoted to doing holy work no matter if the nun's life is over for me forever.

"Alright," I say, inhaling and pushing the bowl of oatmeal across the table. "Alright. But let's just go."

Teresa unties her apron. "I'm ready, I'll be outside."

Arthur fingers his hat, the brim stained. "The horses and the wagon are ready."

Teresa turns to me at the sink. "I think we should stop by the lawyer's office first, he should be there to escort you."

"I'm not sure that is necessary." I take another small bite of the corn muffin.

"Please Renata, you've got to listen to me on this." Teresa's expression is fierce.

I inhale. "It won't make any difference, he is so ineffectual I don't see..."

"PLEASE RENATA." Teresa steadies her gaze on me. "We've got to. We will need all the help we can get."

I stand and leave the kitchen without another word. I head for Señora's room down the hall. When I push the door open, Sister Camille is reading to Señora from the Gospels. Señora lies there, perfectly still.

"Please, Sister Camille, may I have a moment with her? I will be leaving shortly."

"Of course." Camille closes the book and leaves the room.

I lean over Señora's coffee brown face and then I kneel. "I don't know if you can hear me now," I whisper. "But I know you came awake last night. Please know that I am doing exactly what you said I should do. I am bringing the journal pages back to the courtroom." I take Señora's limp hand and expect her to squeeze mine. But no, her hand remains soft and damp.

I stand. "You will be with me in my heart," I say and kiss her cool forehead. At the door, I take one last look at this woman I adore. I leave the room and grab my traveling bag. Inside are the journal pages. I exit from the kitchen door, where I see Mother Yolla standing in the courtyard. She seems frozen, a dozen feet away. As Arthur helps me up into the wagon, she is as still as a statue. She looks so tired, so sad, her face is pale, she looks so much older than she is.

She just stands there watching, doesn't wave and we don't wave back. I can see now how difficult it was for her. She would have protected me had Father Ruby not forbid her from letting me hide in the convent.

Arthur snaps the reins and the horse bolts forward. The three of us, me sitting in between Arthur and Teresa, bounce down the rutted path leading to the dusty road.

We are headed back to the jail, to the courthouse to deliver me, to deliver the missing pages of the journal to try to convince them some

HOW? SOME WAY BUT
HOW I AM NOT SURE HOW CAN WE POSSIBLY?
WHAT CAN ANYONE SAY TO CONVINCE THEM
that I
don't
deserve
to hang!

51

SISTER RENATA

It is mid-day, beastly hot, the sky a warm resilient blue. Arthur has not been able to push the horse faster than a walk. The wagon's slow pace is making Renata impatient. Her face is flushed and warm and the thermos of lemonade that Teresa made for her is almost empty. There are three canteens of water, which ought to last the trip.

At one point Renata reaches over and takes Teresa's hand. That's when Renata finds the black rosary beads clutched in Teresa's grip. "May I pray with you?" Renata whispers and Teresa nods her head and smiles. She takes Renata's fingers and closes them around the beads. The two nuns pray silently for the next hour.

Teresa is praying that the lawyer, DeLuria, will have some idea how to introduce the missing journal pages to the court so that Renata's new evidence will convince the judge that the case should be reopened and the verdict overturned. Unfortunately, Renata is right about DeLuria, he's never had a bit of imagination or inspiration before, so it's hard to imagine that given one more chance to prove himself, he's likely to rise to the occasion.

Arthur pulls up the reins, stopping the horse. "We are almost at the crest of the hill where it dips down into town," he says. "Are we headed straight to the courthouse and jail or..."

"Before we go there we want to visit with Renata's lawyer, a fellow named DeLuria," Teresa explains. Renata clucks her tongue. "His office is half-way down the hill, before the store and the church."

CLAUDIA RICCI

He snaps up the reins and pushes the horse forward, at the same slow pace that he's followed all morning. "I see a creek running down the hill there," Arthur says gesturing with his chin. "I ought to stop there, give the horse some water, and a good rest."

He unhitches the horse from the wagon while Renata and Teresa descend to the stream next to a grassy knoll. Renata drops to her knees by the creek, bends over and splashes cold water on her flushed face. Then she cups her two hands together to drink. When she stands she has muddied her calico dress with two large spots at the knees.

"Please tell me you brought something else to wear in court," Teresa says, eyeing the mud. "You could lose your appeal if they feel you are disrespecting the judge or the legal system."

"I'm not trying to win a fashion contest," Renata says. "I have only this one dress."

"If only I could have loaned you a habit," Teresa said, her face sad.

"Don't trouble yourself about things you cannot fix, my dear girl. We will have to make do with a muddy dress."

Soon the three of them are back on the wagon and the horse is leading them slowly into town. Teresa points to the General store and tells Arthur to pull up there. Teresa drops down from the wagon first.

"Assuming he's even there," she says, "I will explain the situation to him, and see what he has to offer." She inhales and drops the rosary beads into her pocket. "We won't get our hopes up yet."

Renata smirks. "We won't get our hopes up that's for sure."

Teresa ignores the comment and enters the wooden building, where DeLuria occupies an office on the second floor. The building was once a small two-story house, so she climbs a winding staircase to reach his door. She knocks.

"Come in."

Teresa's heart bumps inside her chest. She opens the door. "Hello, I am sorry to barge in on you without any warning, but something extraordinary has happened with Sister Renata's case."

DeLuria's face is lacking the least bit of emotion, while Teresa's face and voice are flooded with urgency and passion. Tenting his long bony fingers together over his white, frocked shirt, De Luria looks bored. "To what do we own this extraordinary development?"

Teresa moves into the office and without asking, takes a seat beside DeLuria's mahogany desk. It is absent of any papers, or file folders, or books, which Teresa finds surprising.

"Do you remember Señora Ramos, Antonie's Mexican house-keeper?"

Still holding his fingers tented and resting against his closed lips, De Luria nods. "Yes, of course I remember seeing her in court. I know that she made regular trips to the jail, once to bring Renata her guitar, and at other times, foods in baskets and other such things."

"Yes, well, if you recall we have always made a big point of saying that Renata's journal was missing some crucial pages, pages that described the way in which Antonie died. Until now, Renata has refused to produce those pages and wouldn't even explain why."

"Yes, naturally I remember that there were missing pages." DeLuria now looks impatient, and even a little disgusted. "I told Renata time and again that she had to produce those pages if she wanted a prayer of a chance to go free. I told her that and she consistently and completely ignored me. Now what's she up to? It's a little late for whatever it is she's got up her nun's sleeve." DeLuria has a know-it-all sneer on his face. Suddenly Teresa wants to be done with him and this place. It gives her the creeps.

"Well, Mr. DeLuria, it seems as though Señora Ramos has fallen into a coma, or some kind of deep sleep, but before she did, she begged Sister Renata to produce those missing pages and to turn them in to prove her innocence. And so, Renata was finally convinced to do it. We have them with us in the wagon."

DeLuria drops his hands to his desk. "We? What do you mean 'we'? She's back? She actually had the audacity to come strutting back to town, to the court that ordered her hanged? Is she crazy? She must be, to walk back into the jail where she will go straight to the gallows."

He stands, and so does Teresa. "I know you are surprised. Just as we were in the convent when she turned up. But she is so certain that she can prove her innocence that she insisted on coming back today." Before Teresa can say anymore, DeLuria is out of the office and heading downstairs.

Outside, he breaks into a shrewd grin. "Well if it isn't the nun on the run," he says, his eyes glued to Renata. "You've got gumption my girl, that's for sure. That someone in your situation, facing certain hanging, would walk right back into jail, where the rope is swinging, that is downright astonishing."

Renata dismisses his tone. "I wish you would keep all of your comments to yourself," she says dryly. "It wasn't my idea to stop here. But Teresa insisted that if I was turning myself in, I would do better to have you at my side."

"Glad you decided to heed Teresa's advice," DeLuria says, slipping a thumb under each of his suspenders. His hair has grown longer, and curlier and it rests on the back of his collar.

"Well then are you ready to help?" Renata crosses her arms in defiance.

"I will indeed accompany you to the court. But if you think for a moment that we can just waltz in, you are a fool. That's not how things are done. No one is sitting there waiting. I will send word to the Judge immediately that you are prepared to turn yourself in. Knowing Judge Perkins, and the urgency of this case, he will see you this afternoon. I would recommend you come in and freshen up before you go to court."

Renata finds her heart beating beneath her crossed arms. She uncrosses her arms and takes a drink of water from one of the canteens. Teresa is standing by the wagon to help Renata step down. Which she does, not because she wants to talk to DeLuria, but because she really has no other practical way of turning herself in.

"Will she be able to ask for leniency?" Teresa asks.

"Of course not," De Luria practically spits out the words. "She's been on the lamb for months. She'll be lucky if they don't hang her on the spot."

"Look," Renata says, stopping in her tracks, "I'm only going back because Señora Ramos told me that I must, she insisted that I..."

"How nice of her, Renata. Now a question: since when have you been taking legal advice from an old housekeeper?" DeLuria laughed and his words came out sounding like a snarl.

Renata bites down hard into her lower lip, to keep from responding. She locks eyes with Teresa. "I am going it alone," she announces. "I don't need his help. Come on Teresa, Arthur, we have a job to do and we aren't going to get it done here."

Teresa turns to Renata and takes hold of her by both shoulders. "Don't do this Renata. You've got to let DeLuria help, he can introduce the new evidence, he can do it the right way and maybe make them see that you are..."

"NO!" Renata is trembling and her mouth is dry as sand. She pushes Teresa's arms away. "I'm not putting myself at the mercy of this man ever again. I can present the evidence myself and when I do I will have the Virgin Mary there to support me. That's what Señora told me would happen and that's exactly what I am going to do."

DeLuria gestures a hand in disgust and returns to his office. "Good luck," he says as he climbs the stairs to the second floor. "You'll need all the luck you can get that's for sure!"

Nothing Teresa says persuades Renata to reconsider. Finally, a reluctant Teresa climbs back to her seat beside Renata on the wagon. Arthur quietly takes up the reins and pushes the horse into a walk down the long hill to the courtroom and jail. As they grow near they can see the gallows still in place, the rope shaped like a single teardrop falling from the crosspole, waiting to hang Renata.

52

SISTER RENATA

The wagon pulls up in front of the small wooden building that houses the jail and the tiny courtroom. Arthur helps Renata down from the wagon.

She pulls herself up straighter. Taking in one long breath, she climbs the three wooden steps. Teresa follows.

Renata pauses at the door and turns to Teresa. "No matter what happens, I am ready now to accept my fate. I surrender to God's will. I will be sheltered beneath Mary's veil."

A strong gust of wind blows up against the two women, lifting their skirts and sending dust and grit into their eyes. Renata cups her eyes and turns to open the door.

"Renata, wait!" It's Arthur coming up from behind. "Can I please go in with you?"

She studies him. She shrugs. "I guess there will be no harm in that."

He's up the stairs before she opens the door. He guides her gently by the elbow.

As they step inside, Renata's stomach squeezes and a shiver goes up her back. The pitiful cell where she spent so many many weeks is now occupied by a man with dark skin and long black straight hair. He has a vicious scar on his cheek, and a single braid hanging beside his face.

Renata stares at the jailer, who is asleep, his feet propped on the wooden table.

"Hello," she says. He doesn't respond. She approaches the table and sets her hand on his leg and shakes him awake. He's disoriented, rubbing his eyes. Bean's first instinct is to reach for his keys dangling from his belt. The sound of the keys jangling sparks another horrible memory in Renata's mind.

In a moment he is on his feet and leaning forward over the desk. "What....what the hell, it's you, YOU! You came back!"

His breath is sour with liquor. She turns away, then faces him in silence. Her eyes are wide. Arthur is at one side, Teresa on the other.

"I hope you know that we're gonna throw you right back in the cell," he says. "And then you're cooked." He cackles. He jangles his keys. "Hurry up now, I gotta go tell the judge and the sheriff."

Renata stands her ground. "You don't have to put me in the cell," she says. "After all, I came here of my own free will. I am not going anywhere. I am here to prove to all of you once and for all that I am innocent."

The jailer cackles again and shakes his head. "You're dreaming, lady," he says, "But whatever. Take a seat on the bench there, and I'll be right back."

Renata remains standing, as do Arthur and Teresa. All of them are staring at the man in the cell. Renata notices now that he wears a turquoise nugget on a leather strip hanging around his neck.

The jailer returns in a few minutes, followed by the sheriff, who stands face to face with Renata.

"You do realize that we have every intention of carrying out the hanging," the sheriff says. Renata sees what looks to be a gleam in the man's eye, and a smile on his bearded face.

"I am fully aware of that," Renata says. "I am prepared to hang." She pauses. "But I would ask one thing beforehand: the chance to present new evidence, evidence that if accepted, is certain to exonerate me."

The sheriff is shaking his head no. "I'm afraid we can't go back into trial," he said, "there is no precedent for..."

Suddenly the judge, wearing a black suit, appears at the door. He places one hand on the sheriff's arm, and the sheriff repeats Renata's request.

"Jed," says the judge, "let me handle this."

The judge studies Renata, and glances at Teresa and Arthur. "I am willing to allow you one more hour in the courtroom," he says. The sheriff begins to protest, but the judge raises his hand, signaling silence, and then continues, "Be at the courthouse at 9 a.m. sharp tomorrow and we will let you have one more chance to speak." He turns to the sheriff, whose face is pinched with anger. "Jed, really, what difference does one hour make after all this time?"

The judge turns back to Renata. "I am assuming," he says, "that you have another witness?"

Renata nods. "No, but we have a set of journal pages, pages that weren't available in the trial."

The judge shakes his head. "It's unlikely to help. But whatever you've got, bring it with you tomorrow. As I said, I will give you an hour, tops. Do you understand?"

"Yes sir," she says. "Thank you for doing this."

The judge turns and he and the sheriff walk out the door.

"You sure you don't want even one more night here in this nice cell?" The jailer leers. He takes a step closer toward Renata; he smells even stronger of whiskey.

"Let's get going ladies," Arthur says, taking Renata and Teresa by the hands. The three of them head out the door into the late afternoon sunshine.

"We've got to find rooms," Art says.

"No, that won't be necessary," Teresa replies. "We have a dear friend here, a woman named Kitty Pole, who has put us up before. She runs a terrific little café and has a couple of extra rooms. I know she will be glad to open her door to us again."

And with that they climb onto the wagon and head for the sky blue house where Kitty lives.

53

SISTER RENATA

The sky is a milky blue when Renata and the others wake up. Kitty has already fed the chickens and gathered eggs and now, she is baking muffins for the breakfast meal she will serve downstairs in the café, promptly at eight.

Renata is first into the kitchen. Kitty is spooning corn meal dough into a cast iron muffin tin. She puts the spoon down and wipes her hands on her apron. Then she takes hold of both of Renata's hands. "I can't believe you're back," Kitty says.

"Nor can I. Sometimes I think that we may very well be making a giant mistake." Kitty turns back to her stove. Renata yawns, covering her mouth with the back of her hand. "But I can't live on the run. And I shouldn't have to, because I didn't kill my cousin."

Teresa appears in the kitchen. "Kitty, is coffee ready? I need a big lift this morning."

"It's yours to make my friend." Kitty reaches into the pantry for the pot. "Coffee is in the decanter beside the sink."

She finishes filling the muffin tins and takes her bowl and spoon to the sink. "So you have to be there at nine."

"Yes," Renata says. She is settled in the rocking chair that Kitty keeps in the corner beside the stove. "I get an hour to present the new evidence."

Kitty slides the muffins into the oven. "I don't know much about the law, but I have my doubts that..."

"I know, Kitty. I know." Renata pauses and then she whispers. "We can't be too hopeful but I have no choice."

At exactly ten minutes to nine, Renata opens the door to the small courtroom. Teresa and Arthur follow her into the stuffy room. No judge. No sheriff.

"So where shall we sit?" Teresa asks.

Renata shrugs. "It makes no difference, does it?" Her face is pale and pinched. Teresa wraps an arm around Renata's shoulders.

"My dear Sister, this is not the face we need today. You must stand up to them, find your voice, convince them that you deserve your freedom." Renata bites her lower lip. And nods.

Teresa whispers. "All you have to do is believe in your heart and soul what you know to be true. You didn't kill Antonie and you have proof now. Trust in yourself and in God. He will take care of the rest."

At that moment the judge and sheriff stride into the courtroom. The judge in his black robe takes a seat at a table that stands higher than the rest of the tables in the room.

"So I said we'd give you an hour," the judge says, folding his hands on the table. "Please stand and show me what magic tricks you have up your sleeve today."

Renata stands. She is holding the pages, which are neatly wrapped in brown paper, and tied with a thin piece of twine.

Renata takes two steps closer to the judge. "Before I let you see what's in here, I think it's only fair that we reconstruct the evidence used against me in the trial."

The judge clears his throat. "We are not going to retry this case, if that's what you had in mind."

"No, of course not," Renata says, her voice strong and commanding. "I'm not looking to do that. I simply want to remind you that virtually every piece of evidence presented at the trial was in the form of writing: my journal entries, which you ignored, and my cousin's wild stories, which cast me as a dancer and worse, a seductress."

The judge slaps his hands on the table. "I said it before and I will say it again, we are not going to retry this case. So get to the point."

"My point is that you never produced a single witness to the so-called murder."

"And again, you are trying to reopen the case. I am quickly losing my patience!"

"All I am trying to do is establish that in fact there was a witness."

He stands and yells. "If you knew there was a witness why the hell didn't you bring him forward?" His face suddenly looks like it's sunburned.

"I wrote about her in my journal, but..."

"Oh for God's sake, are you trying to make a fool of me?"

Renata lowers her gaze and hands the judge the brown package. "No, not at all, your honor, I would encourage you to read my journal pages, pages that I vowed I would never make public. Then I think you will understand. That writing carefully lays out my cousin's last hour."

"So who is this witness?"

"Please just read."

"I am not going to read any damn new pages. Tell me what is contained here."

Renata clears her throat. "These pages directly implicate...." Here, Renata's head drops forward. Teresa, standing to her right, puts an arm around Renata's waist and squeezes her arm.

"Get on with it," the judge says.

Renata continues. "These pages reveal the truth about how Antonie died and they make clear that the person who..." She is trembling now and Teresa squeezes her tighter. "...the person who completed the act, finished the suicide that Antonie had set in motion with his own razor...was..."

The sheriff stands. "Your honor, we've already established that her cousin was murdered. Where does she get the right to call it a suicide. It's just her overactive imagination...."

"Let me see these damn pages," the judge says, tearing the paper and twine off the package.

The judge sits down, takes his eyeglasses out of his breast pocket and begins to read. Renata interrupts right away. "I guess I don't have to point out to you that the paper, the ink, the slant of the handwriting, perfectly match that of my journal."

Leaning back in his chair, the judge pauses. "No, ma'am, you don't need to point this out to me." He continues reading. When he comes to the seventh page, he pauses and looks up. Then he continues reading. Finally, he throws the paper onto the desk and places his hands together, resting them on his sizable stomach."

"And pray tell, how is it that we never saw these curious pages during the trial?"

Renata closes her eyes, inhales and then slowly releases her breath. When she speaks, it's in a whisper. "I refused to implicate Señora. I wanted to... protect her."

"Well, what we have here is a most interesting turn of events." The judge stands and gathers the journal pages and hands them over to the sheriff. The pages are lost on him because he doesn't know how to read.

"Please give me the full name of this woman you call Señora."

"Must I? Isn't it clear from what you read here that my cousin was hellbent on killing himself?"

"The name please..."

"Señora Maria Cuorocora de los Ramos."

"And where can this woman be found?"

Renata closes her eyes. "She is in her final moments of life, weak as a newborn lamb, residing at the convent where she can get the care she...."

Suddenly Teresa gasps and lets go of Renata's shoulders.

Renata looks up and there at the back of the courtroom stands Señora, wrapped in a black shawl and leaning on a cane.

The two nuns are aghast. Renata stutters. "Judge, this is...this is... this is Señora, but...but just a day ago I saw her so close to dying that she could not possibly appear here."

Sister Teresa flies to the back of the room and helps support the old woman. Soon Señora is standing beside Renata. They embrace. Señora's face is looking so thin and pale it has a purple cast. She reaches into a pocket and brings out a sheet of paper. "Una oración," She whispers. She hands it to Renata and raises her hand to tell Renata to read it aloud.

Renata looks at the judge. "Part of it is a prayer she has written. Shall I go ahead?

"Don't ask *my* permission," the judge replies, "this is your dog and pony show."

She begins, translating as she proceeds: Dios mío, dios dios dios and madre mio, my God my holy mother Mary holy father and son and holy spirit to whom do I ask forgiveness? To whom do I confess? The priest, Father Ruby? The last time I slid the little door in the confessional I saw the black screen between me and the priest and I lost heart. I wanted so desperately to unload myself, I wanted to scream 'I have sinned in the worst possible way, I have sinned by taking the last bit of life from a man I knew and raised from childhood.' But I lost heart. I left the confessional and I visited Renata at the jail; I begged her to tell the world the truth, but once again she refused."

Renata raises her head.

"Please continue," the judge says.

"Dear God help me. Help me help my dear Renata to go free. No one but me can help her. I kneel here and beg you to hear me, from my humble position on this cold floor in the kitchen. I ask not for me not on my behalf but for her, she who faces hanging. I am determined to find a way to tell the world the truth, that I was the one responsible, I pressed the blade and severed his throat. I only continued with what Antonie started but of course I could have tried to get help for him rather than hasten his death. What I did was unforgivable. I dared to take the place of God, deciding whether a man was going to live or die. Please God please forgive me for what I did!"

There is perfect silence in the courtroom. The judge gazes long and hard at Señora—she seems to shrink in his gaze. "I am afraid that you leave me no alternative but to place the old woman under arrest."

Renata protests. "She is close to 85 years old. She rose from her deathbed to speak her truth. She only finished what Antonie set out to do. He wanted to die. She raised him from the time his mother—my aunt Eliza—died from smallpox—he wasn't even walking. Can't you see that arresting this woman makes no sense?"

Before the judge can answer, the sheriff steps forward and puts Señora into handcuffs. She offers no resistance. "Are we through here Judge? Can I take her away?"

"I would like to ask the nun one more question." He turns to

Renata. "Why for God's sake didn't you make it clear what happened? Why this long drawn out affair when you knew there was a killer and that killer wasn't you?"

"I wanted to protect the woman who raised me. She is my mother, my grandmother, my savior. And now, see what you've done, arresting her."

The judge shakes his head. "Let's go, Frank, there is no point in sitting here any longer."

All of a sudden the sheriff screams. He lifts the handcuffs into the air. Señora is no longer in the cuffs. Nor is she anywhere to be seen in the courtroom.

The judge roars. "What the blazing hell is going on here?"

Renata looks at Teresa. Arthur stands back and shakes his head.

"I expect an explanation," the judge says, slamming the table, but even as he says it, the command sounds foolish.

"We have seen the hand of God at work here," Renata says, kneeling, and speaking in a whisper. "The work of God and the work of the Virgin Mary, to whom we pray every day."

"Well I don't give a damn about your foolish religion or your prayers," the sheriff says. "Some kind of stupid magic."

Renata smiles at the sheriff. "Well then I invite you to find the old woman using whatever magic you happen to muster." She smiles at the judge. "May we leave now?"

"Don't leave town until we have gotten to the bottom of this foolishness," the judge says.

Arthur and Teresa and Renata are soon on the wagon heading back to Kitty's. Renata and Teresa hold hands and pray the whole way.

54

SISTER RENATA

Picture it: a bright hot day.

The three of them—Renata and Teresa and Arthur—are sitting in the wagon pulling up to the convent in a cloud of red dust.

Grit and grime coat the faces of the three of them.

Teresa dismounts first and turns to help Renata down. Renata wears a simple sky blue dress that hangs just above her ankles.

Sister Gabriella, the nun thinning carrots in the convent's front garden, cries out.

"Renata—Teresa—they're here! They're here!" She jumps to her feet and soon all the nuns are outside. They crowd Renata and Teresa like a flock of black crows. Everyone is asking, everyone wants to know what happened.

Teresa raises one arm into the air. She wolf whistles as only Teresa can. "If you all will quiet down," she says and the nuns fall silent.

She clears her throat. "Renata has been freed," Teresa announces. Cheers rise up. Goosebumps shiver up Renata's arms and legs.

"Tell us," says Mother Yolla, "how did this miracle come to pass?"

Teresa turns to Renata: "You explain." So Renata recalls the miracle in the courtroom. Señora materializing to confound the judge and the Sheriff. Renata finally showing the judge the pages so long missing from her journal. The pages that made it very clear that she was not the one who ended Antonie's life.

So now, both Teresa and Renata ask at precisely the same time: "Where is Señora?"

The crowd of nuns falls silent.

Mother Yolla speaks up. "She passed from this earth two days ago."

Teresa and Renata turn to each other. Then Renata calls out loud. "So this is truly a great miracle, because two days ago, she appeared in the courtroom. Señora is the reason I was allowed to go free."

No one speaks. Renata asks in a whisper. "Please, take us to her grave."

Mother Yolla leads the way. Behind the convent is the small cemetery, surrounded by a picket fence.

She points to the corner beneath a live oak tree. "She is over there, at least that is where we buried her remains. But her spirit lives on, who knows where else she will appear?"

Renata crosses the cemetery, and kneels before Señora's grave. Her hands come up to her chest in prayer. "I have so much to thank you for." She drops her forehead to her fingertips and tears flood her eyes. "May you rest in peace. And please know that you will be sorely sorely missed." She remains there, praying in silence. The other nuns remain outside the fence.

No one makes a sound.

And in time, Renata rises from the ground. She sighs and turns to join the other nuns.

"Mother Yolla, may I return to wearing the habit?"

"Of course you can my child. We have a set of clothing waiting just for you."

Renata inhales slowly. "Just so you know," she says, "it is so so good to be back here, where I belong."

That night Mother Yolla gives permission for the nuns to stay up late into the night. Renata plays the guitar and the nuns are delighted to sing song after song. Renata hopes that Señora will make an appearance but no, the revered old woman is nowhere to be seen.

And so Renata is free and clear and she remains here at the convent for four decades. After Mother Yolla passes, Renata takes on her role. Mother Renata. And she never forgets Señora—indeed she visits the woman's grave for a few minutes every day for the rest of her life.

GINA

A few months ago, I took Amtrak to Manhattan for the day. I had made an appointment with a past life regression therapist.

Mary—yes, that really is her name—came highly recommended. Still, I was twitching. Nervous to the point that my hands were shaking. I didn't know what to expect.

She greeted me at the door with a warm smile. Her blonde hair is curly, and she is tall and slender. She has lively eyes. Kind eyes.

"Please sit down Gina," she said, gesturing to the sofa.

After a few preliminaries, I explained the novel to her, as best I could. I told her it wasn't like any novel I had read.

I told her that I had finished the book, but still I didn't feel complete.

"I just want to keep writing it," I said. "There is something drawing me to the characters." I kept thinking about what my dear friend Meg has always said: "You never want to stop writing and rewriting this book!"

She's right. This book is alive. Slippery. It keeps changing.

What Albert Einstein said about electrons: they only take a fixed position when you pin your eyes on them.

So too with this book. It will only appear real when I stop writing and "see" it into print.

Back to Mary. She told me that she would count down from 100. "You will gradually drop lower and lower into a deep state of relaxation. Then we will be able to talk to Renata."

I closed my eyes and she started counting. I don't remember anything after 70.

* * * *

I am right there in California, as I have been so often, sitting on a blanket next to Teresa. I am surrounded by dry golden hills dotted with live oaks. The smell of sage. But at the same time, I know I am not there. I am in New York City, sitting on a couch in Mary's office.

I am watching my mind. And my body.

"So, what are you feeling?"

"Numb…and something…something else." The feeling rises up from my gut.

"I…I feel… guilty."

"Let Renata speak. Let her be in her time and place. Let her tell you why this guilt hasn't resolved."

I wait. I wait for Renata to speak. I hear nothing.

At least, at first. And then the words come pouring out.

"I ….I see blood…There is blood."

"Is this the murder scene again?"

I stare into myself. I shake my head.

"No. I don't think so."

I keep listening.

"The blood is pooled at my feet. I see my feet, bloody, blood dripping down my…"

Oh God, I whisper. Oh God. Please help me. I have lost my…

"What?" Mary speaks softly. "What have you lost Renata?"

"My…baby." My mouth is cotton. My face is hot. I am sweating all over.

"When did you have this baby?"

My voice squeaks as it comes out.

"I never…the baby just…it…it just slipped out of me…Before… before I went to…why…oh God Mary why did he do this to me?"

I am crying. I can't stop. Mary hands me a box of tissues and I sob into my hands and keep wiping my nose.

"What happened Renata?"

"He was…my cousin. I was so grateful we had each other growing up. But then…that one day, beneath the madrone tree. He wanted me to take off my shirt. I refused."

I start to cry again. I scream. "'HELP ME!! HELP ME!!'" I pause. "But…nobody came."

I cry until I'm gasping for air. There are more tears, but I want to tell her more, I want to share every detail. "About the red dirt. The dirt. He held me in the dirt." I can feel the dirt in my hair. My mouth. He is on top of me.

I am heaving. "And then. He….he…raped me! He hurt me so … oh it was horrible horrible, so vicious, oh God Mary he hurt me! He split me in half. He murdered my soul."

Mary is silent. I keep talking.

"The day I came home covered in red dirt, my Uncle Rio was on the porch drinking a glass of tequila. He told me I had to learn to be a lady."

"I could barely walk. But my uncle didn't seem to notice that anything was wrong."

I stop crying. "Now I am angry, I want to rip his face off!"

"Rio's face?"

"No. Antonie's! I would strangle him if I could. I would dig my nails in and gouge his face. I would take a knife and…"

Suddenly I see what is happening.

I stop. Catch my breath. "Señora knew. I told her I had to I had to…I was bloody and I hurt and I was dirty. Oh Señora come back to me. I miss you so badly."

I feel a warmth descend over me like a feather. A shawl of blue light. I stop talking.

Mary lets me be silent. "You don't have to carry this pain any longer," she says quietly.

"I was fortunate, I suppose. I lost the baby within a couple of months. It was…just blood, but so much…"

Mary waits.

"I was 14. I told Señora she had to help…protect me."

"And did she?"

"She did the best she could. She would yell at him when he tried to get too close to me."

Silence.

"I wanted to go to the convent immediately," I say. "Uncle Rio said I should wait until I was 16. But Señora persuaded him to let me go at 15. That year was holy hell for me."

I am not here. I am not hear. I hear the voice come out of me but it isn't my voice. It isn't my mind having these thoughts."

"And then when I got there. I was called into Father Ruby's office. He seemed like a nice man, a priest. But then…"

I am silent for a long time.

Mary says: "Remember, Gina, if her story is told, she and you will be absolved."

"It all happened after Uncle Rio died, I had been in the convent for almost ten years. I was 24. Antonie was starting to fall ill. He convinced Ruby that he needed me to help care for him. He paid Ruby a lot of money."

I remember.

"Ruby was an obese man, with greasy skin. And a red nose. He told me this was my duty, to take care of Antonie."

Mary speaks: "I think you have had enough today." She counts slowly again and when she is finished, I am thoroughly spent. I can't speak anymore. I lie down on the couch. Mary covers me with an afghan."

"Have a good rest," she says. "And remember this: everything we endure is something that brings us closer to God! Call in the Divine, ask the angels and the archangels and all the ascended masters for help, ask for love and peace."

I feel a warm hand on my shoulder. I look up and I see Señora's face. That wide brown face I have loved forever.

I sleep for half an hour. When I wake up, Mary has a cup of tea for me.

"You will be tired for a day or so. Make sure you drink plenty of water. And you ought to come back for at least one more session."

Over the next six months, I see Mary a total of eight times. I'm still processing these difficult emotions but I have made great progress.

And when I falter, I always pray to the Virgin Mary.

8/10/97

Señora's final prayer

Dio mio Dio Dio Dio, Madre mio, holy mother of holy mary mother of
holy God holy mary mother of Joseph forgive me please forgive the
thing I did. Who do I tell, to whom do I confess? The Priest? The
sheriff? The last time I slid the little door, I saw the screen, I
thought, I could unload myself today, I could say forgive me father
for I have sinned in the worst possible way, I have sinned in taking
the last bit of life of a man I loved starting the day he was born.
But every time I think, do it. Do it. Slide the door and then say it
and then it will not trouble you anymore and then the poor girl will
go free. She deserves this, only then when I think that, dear me, I
think I cannot say that there, I cannot begin to say what I have
done. And the girl, the nun, she doesn't want me to. I kneel hear me
God from my humble position on this cold floor. I ask not for me not
on my behalf but for her, the dead one I adored. I am on my knees, I
have not long so long to go, I know you know my every word is yours.
Take me, take me, take me now for what I've done, if that is the only
way to free me of this burden. I am here, I am the one with the bare
tile floor the floor I sweep and sweep, the floor I scrub on the same
knees, I would ask you now, forgive me for what I did.

"Prayer-ative"

(there is energy here but it refuses to be filtered into words.)

so just describe what you see:

tile, highly scrubbed, the surface smooth but not perfectly flat the
white walls, the beams,

the screams, I stir the soup, I hear the screams. It seems to me she
does it for effect.

where will I get her voice....I pray, I pray, I pray.

I had the chance to stop them...that day I saw them holding hands.
Oh, I said, that stands to reason. They go back so far, they played
the games they played.

(I feel it in the muscles holding my shoulders...Senora Cuorcora,
come out of me you are to be a housekeeper's voice who speaks in
silent prayer, she has the oiled black hair, she is short or tall,
timid, or all-knowing. fearful of what she hears in the quiet
silence, doesn't make a peep as she sweeps the tile she makes the
beds, she folds every corner, she takes the potato scraps, the corn
husks, to the neighbor's pigs, she has secrets she can hardly bear,
she wears that brown flaxen dress, a white apron, barefoot or soft
cotten slippers.

I want to scream because this seems so stupid, irrational or
whatever, that I'm sitting here trying to hear some non-existant
person's prayer...is that a curse...this feels like the worse thing I

---

*I wrote Señora's prayer in 1997, long before I knew
how the story would unfold. Our mysteries are
inside us waiting to be discovered.*

dreaming maples

CLAUDIA RICCI

Dreaming Maples

ISBN 978-0-971718-01-2

What daughter hasn't vowed never to make the same mistakes her mother made? In this mesmerizing novel, Candace Burdett, a young artist who was abandoned at birth, decides to prove a point: that she can do a better job loving a child than her own mother, Eileen, did. But adolescent Candace quickly learns a lesson: she has more of her mother inside her than she cares to admit. By weaving Candace's harrowing story around the painfully honest diaries kept by Eileen during her pregnancy, this exhilarating and often cinematic novel suggests what every daughter - and son - soon discovers: that heartbreaking family dramas make circles around each other, wreaking havoc in successive generations. Ultimately, the powerfully drawn characters of *Dreaming Maples* plunge through to a redemptive ending that will keep readers spellbound.

*"Ricci is a moving storyteller and
writes a lush and insightful novel."*

Lisa Stevens, Albany *Times Union*

*"Ricci has spun a well-developed tale of mother-
daughter relationships delving into the depths
of the human psyche...beautifully written..."*

Jennifer Smith, North Adams Transcript

*"Dreaming Maples is a book I will read
again and again, like visiting an old friend.
I didn't want this book to end!"*

Michelle Maglione, Brooklyn, N.Y.

Available at:
https://www.amazon.com/-/e/B0787DD3HN

seeing red

CLAUDIA RICCI

Seeing Red

ISBN 978-0-971718-02-9

At 19, Ronda Cari gave up a promising career in ballet when she became pregnant by her college professor. Now, 18 years later and the mother of two boys, Ronda gives up her marriage to follow her flamenco-guitarist lover Jesus to Spain, where he disappears. Her journey of discovery leads her to unveil the secret behind her lover's departure and reawakens her love of dance, this time through the magic of flamenco.

> "When I read a book I want it to take me out of my world
> for a while and make me a part of another world. From the
> beginning, Seeing Red had me. I was feeling Ronda's feelings
> with her, living through each situation, fighting her internal
> battles with her. I love this book and I loved Dreaming
> Maples, because both novels carried me on wonderful
> adventures in my mind. These books are why I read!"

Tyler Malek, Great Barrington, MA

Available at:

https://www.amazon.com/-/e/B0787DD3HN